The Bishop and the Witch

by

A.A. Prideaux

A CIP catalogue record for this title is
available from the British Library.

ISBN 978-0-9930676-1-7

www.paganuspublishing.co.uk
First published in 2015
Paganus Publishing
Ruthin
Wales

Printed and Bound in Great Britain

Cover Designed by
Richard Fulke Paganus Prideaux
© 2015

I am dedicating this book to Richard Fulke Paganus Prideaux for accompanying me on this adventure.

Sex, drugs and witchcraft unite John Prideaux, the future Bishop of Worcester and Anne Gunter during the Jacobean years of the early 17th century. The scene is Oxfordshire and the cast consists of King James I, many of the church elite of the time and a witches' coven.

This horror story is based on true events and real people. Following the famous Abingdon Witch Trial in 1604 and the acquittal of the accused witches, Anne Gunter later confessed that her symptoms were faked on the instruction of her father.

Brian Gunter was subsequently imprisoned in 1605 and appeared at the Star Chamber from February 1606 to answer the charges brought against him. Anne was finally free of her father and his debauchery.

When John Prideaux gave evidence about Anne Gunter at the Star Chamber in 1606, he did so as the well-known and respected Oxford academic of Exeter College. John was later able to rapidly climb the social and career ladder at Exeter College and through his friendship and collaboration with King Charles I, became the Bishop of Worcester during the difficult Civil War years.

This book is the story of meetings between John and Anne at a much earlier time and how those meetings could have had a bearing on the outcome of the trial and the hearing.

Demons, drugs and witches weave their way through this story of early 17th century revenge.

The Bishop and the Witch, is an alternative tale based on historical facts and written with a great deal of artistic licence.

Contents

CHAPTER ONE... 10

CHAPTER TWO.. 23

CHAPTER THREE 33

CHAPTER FOUR 44

CHAPTER FIVE... 55

CHAPTER SIX... 64

CHAPTER SEVEN 72

CHAPTER EIGHT.. 83

CHAPTER NINE.. 96

CHAPTER TEN 123

CHAPTER ELEVEN 141

CHAPTER TWELVE 157

CHAPTER THIRTEEN... 172

CHAPTER FOURTEEN. 187

CHAPTER FIFTEEN.. 202

CHAPTER SIXTEEN 217

CHAPTER SEVENTEEN.. 229

CHAPTER EIGHTEEN 241

CHAPTER NINETEEN 253

CHAPTER TWENTY.. 264

CHAPTER TWENTY ONE.. 280

CHAPTER TWENTY TWO 294

CHAPTER TWENTY THREE... 316

CHAPTER TWENTY FOUR 328

CHAPTER TWENTY FIVE 348

CHAPTER TWENTY SIX. 370

CHAPTER TWENTY SEVEN.. 390

CHAPTER TWENTY EIGHT 412

CHAPTER TWENTY NINE 428

AUTHOR'S EPILOGUE... 432

JOHN PRIDEAUX – BIOGRAPHICAL INFORMATION . 443

BIBLIOGRAPHY.. 447

I began this project merely to find out what Bishop John Prideaux had done in his life. I ended up knowing him very well and liking him a lot...

A A Prideaux

CHAPTER ONE

O God, That knowest us to bee set in the midst of so many and great dangers, that for Mans frailenesse we cannot always stand uprightly, guard to us the health of Body and Soul, that all those things which we suffer for sinne, by thy holy wee may well passé and overcome, through Jesus Christ our Lord.

John methodically repeated the prayer which his father had taught the family during a plague in their village. He had started counting the repetitions on his rosary when he set out on his journey well over a week ago. And once he realised that he could repeat the prayer one hundred times in only a couple of miles, the counting stopped. One wakeful night on the road, he had worked out that he prayed 50 times every mile and as there were 170 miles to walk, it meant that he would pray 8500 times. That was enough to know.

John was the fifth of ten children born to Dartmoor landowners. Although the family were comfortably off, it had not been possible to sponsor a university education for John. He wanted to be a clergyman and so had applied for the post of parish clerk in Ugborough. His audition failed during an embarrassing public audition, but led to his aunt, a member of the gentry, sponsoring him at Ashburton Grammar School and now on to Exeter College. Sadly, the sponsorship did not involve providing a horse to Oxford and so he must walk. It would be another useful way to learn humility.

His mother Agnes said that he needed to show more humility if he wanted to get on at Oxford.

"There will be people there who will run the country, the law and the Church. You must get to know them all."

Agnes Prideaux was happy with her life, but not content. When she married John, she had expected to be a lot richer and go to a lot more events than she had done. Of ten children, her boy John had shown the most potential and after seeking assistance from Sarah on the moor, John was going to Oxford.

John didn't know about the spell sown into his clothes, which promised to take him to the top of the social scale.

And ruin his life.

#

John was finding it necessary to say his family prayer more often than usual today, it being a particularly hard day. The heavy rain, falling relentlessly since dawn had soaked John through and filled the stream he walked alongside for navigation. He was cold and tired and knew that he should have something to eat. The bread and cheese in his pack had fed him since yesterday morning when he bought it from a woman at a roadside cottage. It would probably have to last until tomorrow when he arrived at Abingdon.

John did not enjoy the negative reception he often received when knocking at doors. Food was scarce everywhere.

Everybody was hungry.

Everybody was reluctant to help strangers, even strangers with money.

At home in Stowford, people tried to help each other out where they could. It was rare to see a neighbour starving. But the nearer he got to Oxford, the more problems he witnessed. He was finding it harder to buy food and had on one or two occasions met with some serious aggression.

Sometimes on this journey, John had been frightened for his own safety and he didn't like this new sensation. But he continued to talk calmly and pleasantly to aggressive strangers in the same he did to his fighting brothers and sisters. So far he had managed to stay out of trouble.

"I am on my way to Oxford," he told the old woman at the last cottage he called at. "I am going to be a priest."

"You are a man of God?" she asked scornfully.

"Yes, well no, not yet. But I shall be one day," he told her with some optimism.

"I suppose I can spare something. You are lucky that my family brought me extra food yesterday. They are very generous to me in these hard times."

"Oh, I don't want to take your food from you!"

"You won't be taking it, sonny. You will be paying me for it. I get food from my family, but I don't get money. Give me some money and I will give you food." She showed John a toothless grin and grabbed the money from his outstretched hand before putting it somewhere in her clothing. It happened so fast that John wasn't sure where the money had gone and he looked at his empty hand. The old woman, dressed in what appeared to John to be old sacking, went back into the house and slammed the door. John, left standing on the little step facing the closed door, took a look at the shabby front of the cottage and thought about the tidy cottages at home. He couldn't think of anyone who would tolerate this sort of filthy housekeeping.

Glancing around the back of the place as he walked away, he saw a pig grubbing about in the back yard amongst the rubbish and with his spirits low, he walked on. He still missed Devon and hoped that the feeling would pass as soon as he arrived in Oxford.

That was why he was trying to make the food last, knowing that there would be a market in Abingdon and he could buy food there. Then he would be in Oxford that same night, arriving at Exeter College to start work in the kitchens as arranged and wait for the chance to matriculate.

One more sleep on the road.

He would stop soon, earlier than usual today, because he needed to light a fire and try and get dry and warm. Looking around him, he could see some people still working in the fields, struggling to bring in the last of yet another poor harvest. With heads bowed from months of hard work, little notice was taken of the young man striding along the muddy track in the direction of Oxford.

How could this rain come down so heavily for so long? John, his mind wandering from his chanting, began a conversation in his head. "There has been rain before on the journey and the good Lord knows how rain can fall on Dartmoor, but this is so wearing. Perhaps it's because I am so near to Oxford that it all seems so hard. I have to find somewhere to stop now, I'm too tired."

The good Lord heard and answered his prayer. As he passed a track on his left, John could see a small stone building shrouded by trees and he knew in his heart that this was where he must stay tonight.

Within half an hour John had made himself comfortable inside the pen, which was usually used for the collection of sheep during the winter. He suspected that it hadn't been used for a long time because of the weeds growing around the sides and amongst the rubble. Stones lay fallen down in many places and any farmer worth his salt would have put them back in their correct position had he intended to keep sheep there.

John passed many of these pens on his journey and had slept in more than one. Only once had he been allowed to sleep at a cottage and that was days ago, where he arrived by appointment at the house of a sister of a neighbour of his in Ivybridge. The young daughter there had been most pleased to see John and had paid particular attention to him.

John smiled at the memory. He was not used to female attention, that being reserved for his outgoing brothers. John preferred to study and set up a spectacular life for himself and there was no time for girls and their silliness.

The Prideaux family still had good connections, but a generation or two past the connections were better. This branch had slipped a little down the social slope, second son and all that. John intended to lift the family up again.

He didn't want to let his mother down.

Pulling the cloak around tightly, he settled down to sleep. He dreamt of his family and felt the familiar sensations of homesickness which had swept over him every night since he left home.

He shivered.

"Why didn't you light a fire?"

"Too wet."

"I will light one for you."

"Alright. Thanks."

John woke with a start. There was a fire crackling away amongst some stones to one side of the pen.

He jumped up, dizzy from the deep sleep and stared disbelievingly at the scene in front of him.

A young girl or perhaps a young woman was bent over the fire, poking it with a stick. There was a small wooden tripod from which hung a metal pot with steam rising from it.

The girl had long golden hair tucked behind her ears and a dress of light, fine material. She turned to face John and smiled.

He smiled back.

"How did you manage to light the fire? And where did all this stuff come from? Pots and tripods and all that? " he asked.

"It's easy when you know how. I can do anything I want."

"Really?"

The girl smiled again and turned back to the fire. She checked the contents of the pot and then beckoned John over.

He obeyed and sat down next to her on a large stone which had once had its home in the walls of the pen. He pulled his cloak together, feeling chilled next to the girl even though the fire was throwing out a lot of heat.

"Who are you?" he asked her.

"Mistress Gunter. Who are you?"

"My name is John, John Prideaux."

"Do you want some food?"

John took the offered bowl and began to eat.

"This is good. What is it?"

"Dragon soup," she smiled.

"Well it's nice dragon," he answered.

Looking at her carefully in the firelight, he noticed that she was very young and he wondered why she was out in the dark making food for a strange man.

"Why are you here?"

"That's a big question." She laughed and John thought how well she spoke and dressed. This was no village girl.

"Why are you out here in the woods, when you should be at home with your family?"

"I don't want to be at home, but they think I am."

"They think you are?"

"They think I'm in my room, but I'm not."

"Clearly you're not."

"No, I'm not."

They continued in silence, John eating and Anne playing with the fire.

"So why did you come out here instead of being in your room?"

"Because I would rather be out here, not waiting in my bedroom."

"Why waiting?"

Anne stopped smiling for a moment.

"I always wait."

"Is it worth it? The wait I mean?"

"Never."

John sensed that this conversation could take a peculiar turn if he pushed it any further. But she was out here making him supper, so perhaps God had some sort of plan and meant them to be together at this time.

"Are you alright?"

"I will be alright if I stay out here tonight. He will expect me to be there and when I'm not he will go mad and start on the maid. I would rather he hurt her than me. I hate him."

"Who is he?"

Anne smiled at him, but said nothing.

"You don't have to tell me if you don't want to."

"I will tell you your future if you like."

"My mother does that. She tells me that I will be a great priest someday."

"Does she tell you that you will go down in history?"

"The Prideauxs are already in history. We've done loads of stuff."

"So have the Gunters. We shall be in history too."

"Why, what have you done?"

She chose to ignore the question.

"You know, whenever I need to escape at night I always come here, to this place. It's never used by anyone else, so I know that I will be safe until morning."

"You need to be safe? What are you frightened of, Mistress Gunter?"

She laughed quietly.

"It's something you don't need to be worried about. Perhaps I shall tell you about it one day when I'm older."

John said nothing. If truthful he was glad that she wasn't telling him anything. It all sounded not quite right and he didn't think he wanted to know about it. After all, he had things to do and places to go. He didn't want to sort out someone else's problems when he was having enough trouble sorting out all the things he needed to do and achieve.

He didn't mind listening to his sisters, but they would generally speak to their mother and the boys of the family would never hear about anything that was femininely personal. He was hoping that Anne did not decide to open up to him. He could nothing for her. This young woman was a stranger to him.

"How old are you, Mistress Gunter?" he asked.

Why did he just ask her that? What a stupid thing to say to a young woman, his mother would be furious if she heard him.

"I am twelve years old, John Prideaux. You are eighteen I know. You have recently celebrated a birthday."

"How did you know that?"

"I know a lot of things."

"I don't understand you, Mistress Gunter."

"You probably never will."

Mistress Gunter certainly made some odd comments.

"You look tired John, are you going to rest now?"

"I would like to because I'm really, really tired"

"Lie down and rest then."

"What about you? Are you going home? Do you want me to make sure that you get there safely?"

"No, I'm not going home yet. Not until the morning. He will look for me for a while longer. In the morning, my mother will be back from her women's meeting. Then I shall be safer. He will leave me alone then."

"Who are you talking about?"

Again Anne did not answer.

"Is there not someone in authority who can help you?"

John was feeling as though he should be doing something for the girl. Oh dear! It's all very well being neighbourly, but that brings problems. Like when a friend says, please take this kitten because my father is going to drown it if I don't find it a home by tonight. Then you have to take the kitten and feed and look after it for the rest of its life. Or not take it and feel guilty when you notice a tiny brown carcass floating in a bucket.

"He doesn't have a bucket does he?"

"A bucket?" she asked.

Feeling foolish he said, "I think I should take you home, if there is someone causing you trouble, then your father must help you. Being on your own out in the woods is not suitable for someone like you, Mistress Gunter."

"I'm not on my own, you are with me. I should think that I am far safer with you than waiting in my room."

"I don't understand what you are talking about." He should add that she ought to explain herself, but that could be uncomfortable listening.

"Just go to sleep John Prideaux."

Mistress Anne Gunter turned her attention back to the fire. No, she did not want to go back home. Father had been drinking because her mother was away and soon he would burst into Anne's bedroom and demand that she be nice to him. She hated being nice to him, but what could she do?

Tentative remarks to her mother had resulted in quick retorts along the lines of,

"Hush, Anne, don't talk about your father this way. He only has your best interests at heart. He loves you as he loves all of us."

And again she must put up with the drunken kissing and the touching which hurt so much. But she didn't cry anymore, he used to get furious with her when she cried, years ago. She lay there until he had finished. During the hot huffing and puffing he did on top of her, Anne learnt to leave her body. She watched impassively from the ceiling of the bedroom as her father jumped about on her inert corpse. What a funny thing to do, she thought to herself. So undignified.

Then she learnt that focusing her attention anywhere, while away from her body meant she could go wherever she wanted. Sometimes she sent her mind down the street and watched her neighbours and listened to what they said.

Through the past nine years, she had developed these skills and now Anne was able to leave her body at will, day or night.

"Anne sleeps so solidly," said her mother to her friends. "It's almost as though she's bewitched!"

Anne would go upstairs, lie on the bed and leave her body behind as she wandered about the village. No one knew she was there and were surprised when she could repeat things which had been said when neighbours had not seen her anywhere about. It amused some and unnerved others.

John didn't fall asleep, but he did close his eyes and try and relax, knowing that soon he would have to start walking again.

Complete the schedule, stick with the plan.

It was difficult to settle when he could hear the twelve year old girl crying on the other side of the pen. He thought about comforting her but deciding against it, he closed his eyes and slept.

CHAPTER TWO

As dawn broke, the two young people stirred. Light fell on them quickly, dispelling the dark which had made this unreal meeting normal. Dawn had also brought a mist which put out the fire and soaked the grass and stones. There was no incentive to stay where they were.

"Would you like to come back to the village?" the girl asked.

"I haven't really got the time to be honest with you," he answered. "I have to buy food and then get to Oxford."

"Come with me please John. I'm afraid of going home on my own. He will be cross with me." Anne looked up at her companion with the sad persuasive eyes and a pouting expression that would generally have belonged to an older woman. Anne had seen her sister use this look on men who came to the house. As a rule, their visitors were their father's friends and either held positions of sway in the locality, or had lots of money. Susan was keen on either sort and used to perfect her technique in front of the mirror, unaware that her younger sister was watching her and learning.

Anne was beginning to realise that her female strength came not from the physical, but from a more subtle level. The suffering inflicted on her by her father must also mean that she was desirable, for how else could he be persuaded to act in so debauched a manner against his own daughter? There must be something which she did to tempt him, unconsciously or consciously. But she knew nor cared which.

Men wanted women to be vulnerable. This gave them an increased instinct of protection and to such an extent that they believed the woman wanted and needed them absolutely. Anne knew at twelve years of age what pleased a man, even if it didn't please her.

She had not yet learnt that not all men were like her father.

Her practiced, yet not perfected look appeared to work for John said,

"I shall come for a short while and take you back to your door, though the Lord knows what I shall say when we get there."

This thought slowed his journey to North Moreton village. How was he going to take her back to her family and explain that they had spent the night together in a sheep pen? No, it should be fine, for the girl was only twelve after all. He had been looking after her. But twelve, perhaps that made it worse, in the eyes of others at least?

"Look here Anne. I will take you to the edge of your village and then I must carry on to Abingdon and continue my journey."

"Please!"

"I am not so sure that it's a good idea to tell your parents that I was in the pen with you. What would you usually tell them when you return like this?"

He surmised that if Anne had been away from home on other nights, they must have been prepared for some sort of a story from her. He knew that his own parents wouldn't be pleased if some strange man brought his sister home early in the morning.

Oh, this was too difficult.

They walked in the early sunshine Anne taking the lead, looking behind her every few seconds to make sure her new friend followed.

He did.

Back in Stowford the family rose early. There was much work to do on the farm and everyone must do their bit. John enjoyed working with the horses the best and whenever he got the chance, he would ride them and work them. When he got free time he would visit them in their stalls and brush and sponge them, shining their coats. The horses loved him and whinnied when they heard him coming.

Once, when John was riding Harry the large bay, a stallion owned by the Williams at Stowford House escaped from his field and attacked them. It had been terrifying. Harry turned this way and that, trying to avoid the attack which was vicious and prolonged. The only witness was a dairy maid, who upon seeing the accident progress, ran screaming back into the house.

Before help arrived, Harry bolted across the fields with the enraged stallion in hot pursuit. As they galloped, John suddenly switched consciousness and experienced everything in slow motion. He knew he and Harry were travelling at great speed, but it was as though he were sitting alongside himself watching. He could think clearly but had no connection to the feelings of fear he experienced before the shift. The scene continued in slow motion in front of him and he knew exactly how to solve the problem. It was the most bizarre feeling. One he hadn't had before nor since and although almost magical, he had not told anyone else about it. He was sure that no one would understand. He jumped off Harry who was heading for a narrow opening in the woods. Harry was still desperately trying to lose his crazed attacker and then, with little knowledge of how, John was rolling on the ground safe and sound watching the horses crash into the woods and vanish.

John had since actively sought out the sensation, but had no luck.

Shaking the old memory from his mind John looked up at the trees, whose overhead branches quietly dripped dewdrops on to the heads of the two young people below. He was reminded of the woods near his home and decided to sort out this conundrum once and for all.

"Do you live in the village itself?" he asked her.

"No, not right in the village. We live in a big house and have lots of land. It's the Rectory. My father is a very rich man and believes that he is very important."

"You don't think he's important?"

"Not particularly," was her answer.

Anne walked along the familiar road, having no fear of the reaction her father would have to her being away all night. It would be a bad reaction there was no question of that. But Anne was playing a long game of revenge. She didn't care about his reaction. Her hand trailed through the long grass at the side of the road. She grabbed hold of a bunch of grass and carefully twisted and plaited it as she hummed a tune unfamiliar to John.

John liked music and singing and tried to practice whenever he could. The Rector Andrew Helyer allowed him to play the organ for some of the services at Harford and he sang with enthusiasm during most of them. His playing was better than his singing and this had been proved during his audition failure at Ugborough. The congregation was given the job of judging the two candidates, another in the morning and John in the afternoon. John lost on his singing ability and had to accept the public's decision. As it turned out, his aunt, the Lady Fowell who was witness to his expulsion from the competition, felt sorry for him and now he was on his way to Oxford.

Although technically he was on his way to the house of some sort of important, rich father who had not seen his little girl all night. He was not looking forward to it.

"I've made a decision about this Anne."

"Oh yes? Well I have made a decision of my own. You leave me at the end of the drive and I shall go home alone. You go off into the village and buy your food there."

John, having had the wind taken out of his sails pursed his lips. "That's a good idea," he said.

"You are alright with this?" she asked him.

"Yes." Why should he not be? He had only just met her and whatever she decided to do was of no real concern of his, at least it shouldn't be. The fact was that he felt some strange connection to the young girl. A kind of soul connection as a person has with a member of their own family. A secret, subtle feeling that you knew each other from somewhere else. He wondered if she felt it too.

Anne not only felt it, she knew it. Another side effect of her ether travelling was an ability to see the future and read another's thoughts in certain circumstances. Sometimes, it happened all at once making her head spin and panic and at other times, she could concentrate as much as she liked and get nothing. It was very strange.

They arrived at a set of iron gates which led to a large house. Anne stopped.

"This is me," she informed John.

"Right you are. Good bye then Mistress Anne, it has been interesting meeting with you. I hope you will be alright now." This was odd. He noticed as he shook her hand, that he was missing her already.

"This is not goodbye John Prideaux, we shall meet again. One day I shall require your support and guidance. It will be a bad time for me and I will need all the help I can get."

"Well that all sounds very dramatic Anne, I shall look forward to it." He let her hand drop and as he did she leapt to him, arms encircling him and gave him a huge hug. He hugged her back, thinking of his little sisters and the unconditional love they gave him. It had been a long time since he had such a hug and he doubted that he would be getting any hugs in Oxford.

"See you John Prideaux."

"See you Mistress Gunter," he answered.

He watched her run up her drive, never looking back. This girl had presence and strong personality and as she moved away from him, John was put in mind of a boat going out to sea, wind caught in its sails and all eyes upon her.

He raised his hand and waved at the departing girl, a wave she did not see and so he returned the hand against his side.

As he turned towards the village, he was almost knocked over by a carriage being driven at full pelt towards the Rectory. The driver pulled up the horses with much stamping and snorting and this was quickly followed by an ominous crashing noise inside the carriage.

John placed his hands on the neck of the lead horse, a beautiful grey with frightened eyes. He guessed correctly that these horses had been driven hard for a long period of time. Sweat poured from the poor beast's neck and its flanks were lathered and quivering. A quick glance over to the partner horse showed that it was in a similar state.

"You are working these horses too hard, driver," he called up to the old man at the front of the carriage. The man wrestled with the reins and glanced back nervously to the door of the carriage. It wasn't long before John discovered the reason for the nervous glances. A large man, with a swollen nose had thrust his head out of the window of the carriage.

"Kirfoote, what the hell is going on here? Why have we stopped?"

"This man was blocking the drive entrance, sir. The horses had to pull up."

"Nonsense man, drive on."

"I can't sir, not until he has got out of my way."

The large man turned his attention to John, looking at him as though he were disgusting.

"What is the meaning of this? Why are you in my way?" Then, as if he realised that there was something else he should say he shouted again, "Do you know where my daughter is?"

"Your daughter? No! I don't know who you are sir!"

"Kirfoote said, "You are addressing Master Brian Gunter, gentleman of this parish. Get out of his way."

"Happy to," answered John, stepping smartly aside.

"Have you seen my daughter anywhere?"

"No sir," he lied in answer. He would begin the keeping of his vows later.

"When I catch the person responsible for keeping her away from the house, I shall have the law on him," he growled.

"Would it not be better to keep silent about your daughter's absence sir? It is not good for her reputation or yours to have everyone know that she is missing surely?"

"Damn cheek! Get away or I shall have the law on you. I've told you that once and if you knew me you would know that I always do what I promise. Now get out of my way!"

Master Gunter then did a most surprising thing. He took a rock from his pocket and threw it at John. It hit him squarely in the chest and John crumpled to the floor, shocked by the violence of the attack. Under orders from his master, Kirfoote forced the horses on and the hooves and the wheels narrowly missed John as he lay at the side of the road, woozy and dizzy.

He heard the carriage clattering up the drive and then suddenly, here it was again. That feeling, that sensation.

John knew he was where he was, lying on the muddy grass outside the Rectory of North Moreton. He knew it but felt as though he were slightly separate from the knowledge. The gates seemed to stare back at him, aware of his pain and confusion. Every curve on the ironwork reflected the sunlight and appeared perfect in definition against the shrubs behind, the curves spinning in front of his eyes. Honeysuckle and late roses scented around John, swirling in smoky formation in the air and then straight to his senses. The air which he breathed in fitfully was smooth and cool and flowed like water into his body. John was part of the whole experience. There above his head, he saw the young girl Anne floating, her eyes staring and her legs trailing behind her.

"Get up John don't stay here, he will come back and hit you again. Move away. Go to the village and on your journey." Had she opened her mouth to speak?

John got up and realised how much he was hurting. No more sensations of peace, no more floating Anne Gunter. He must have imagined it, knocked a little senseless from the assault. There on the ground next to him was a plaited grass dolly, wearing a cloak and carrying a bag over its shoulder.

"Like me," he thought.

He looked at his chest under his coat and tunic and saw the beginnings of a bruise, but luckily only a slight graze. He took in a few very deep breaths and although these made him giddy again, at least he knew that his ribs must be alright. He had seen that test done back at home, when his brother had fallen heavily from the plough. Pulling his Bible from the inside pocket of the cloak, he noted that one of the covers was scuffed and rumpled. So God had chosen to save him for another day.

John wiped the forming tears from his eyes and headed along the street.

CHAPTER THREE

He hadn't gone very far when he noticed a woman making her way towards him. She was old, well she looked old, but she might not have actually been old. She was bent over and appeared to be carrying bundled up sticks on her back. They were long sticks of wood, the kind you would generally find in woods and hedgerows. John didn't like seeing an old woman suffer so and wished that people did not have to do that anymore. At home wood was collected by the children, who chopped and stacked it in stores at the back of their cottages. The old women weren't sent out, because when the household needed wood, the wood collector had to travel further than their home area. So, it was quite a hard job and involved thinking a lot about wood.

But here, on the main street in North Moreton, an old lady was struggling on her own, no doubt trying to scratch a living in these unfortunate times. Sorrow for her and Christian charity persuaded him to cross the narrow lane and stand in front of the woman.

She was much smaller than him, even allowing for her back being bent double, she was barely higher than his waist. Her clothes were dark grey and black and smelled dreadful. She wore a short cloak of similar material, with a hood which covered her head. In this bent position all he could see was a hood, until she raised her head as she listened to this stranger speak.

"How are you, old woman? Is the load too heavy for you to carry?"

She looked out from her dirty hood and John became aware of a large nose and greasy hair hidden in its depths. It was not a pretty sight.

He said again. "Are you well, old woman?"

She stood up straighter, swung her load from her back and placed it on the ground.

"What is my load to you, boy? Why are you interested in what I have to do?"

The reaction wasn't quite what he had expected. He thought that she may have been grateful for his interest and perhaps he would have helped her carry her wood to her cottage. He had been thinking of his grandmother when he first saw the woman. Now he was not sure what he should do. The woman obviously thought him a young idiot, and he probably was.

"I just thought that you may need a little help with your burden. I feel sorry that you must work so hard at your time of life."

She moved the hood back a little further from her face using a filthy hand half covered by grubby cloth, worn so she did not burn her hand on the ropes which tied the wood. The revealed face was not a nice picture. She was dirt engrained and toothless, had sunken cheeks and a dirty nose. It made John wretch, but he carried on because of the good manners instilled into him by his parents.

"I see that you are having a bad experience in your life, I hope that one day soon, things get better for you."

"How old do you think I am, you cheeky bastard? I am still in my prime. Many men find me irresistible and for a small consideration I will make your day. What do you think of that, boy?"

He didn't think a great deal of it and his nostalgic thoughts of granny went smartly out of his head.

"No thanks, not interested in anything like that at all. No, not ever." He tried to keep the disgust out of his voice, not wanting to give any more offence than he had already.

"Your loss I'm sure." She looked directly at him and rubbing her face with the bandaged hand said, "Of course if I were to scream out that you had stopped me and were insisting on having me, then you could be in serious trouble, you being a stranger and all. Unless of course you would like to let me have a few coins?"

Thinking he was on to a pretty safe bet he answered. "Look my old dear. I don't think that there is much chance that anyone is going to believe that I tried it on with you. I'm 18 and you are about a hundred."

The old woman's face set in a scowl and she blinked. She moved her lips round and round, made a guttural noise and spat firmly on the ground next to John.

"Shove it up your arse, boy. I've felled better men than you. Don't cross me, you don't know who you are messing with."

This wasn't going how he planned. He noticed that the old woman was staring at the plaited dolly he still held in his hand.

"Where did you get that?" she asked sharply.

Looking down at his hand, he answered, "Someone gave it to me."

"Who?" The question came very quickly and she looked at John keenly. "Who gave you the effigy?"

"Effigy? It's a dolly, a little girl made it for me."

"Aaaah. A little girl is it?"

John thought that perhaps he shouldn't have said that.

"And do I know this little girl?"

"Err, I don't know, I shouldn't think so. W - What difference does it make?"

John's discomfort meant nothing to the old crone, for he was starting to think of her terms of being an old crone. She poked him hard in the stomach with her bony finger.

"Tell me where this little girl is. I want to meet her."

John felt weird when she looked at him in this way and he wanted to leave.

"I don't know where she is, old woman and if I did I wouldn't tell you. Look, I only stopped to see if you wanted some help and it's all getting a bit out of hand. I'm off to Oxford. North Moreton is a very strange place. I need to get out of it."

John pushed his way past her and walked on, all the time looking back. The old woman had turned to watch him go, her bundle still on the ground and her eyes burning into him. She pulled the hood back over her head and swinging the sticks onto her back made her way up the street and away from John.

As he turned away in order to continue his journey, he walked straight into someone else. A teenage girl dressed in plain, but clean clothes and looking frightened.

"Hello," he said.

"Hello," was the answer.

"I am sorry for bashing into you like that. I wasn't paying attention to what I was doing. I hope I didn't hurt you."

"No not at all. Were you just talking to my mother?"

"If that old woman was your mother, then yes I was."

"She didn't say anything horrible to you did she?" said the young girl, her eyes staring at John keenly. Her mother must be capable of insulting people on a regular basis. John felt sorry for the girl. She looked exhausted and upset.

"Don't worry. She didn't say anything that properly upset me." He knelt down next to her. "What's the matter?"

She rubbed her eyes and then sniffed, "I'm just looking out for my mother, she's off on one of her wanderings again and I don't want her to get into trouble."

"Why, what is she going to do?"

"Make a neighbour's horse sick." The girl wrinkled her nose and pulled at her hair in a nervous fashion. It was clear that she wasn't comfortable with what she believed her mother capable of.

"How could she do that Mistress, err?" John was conscious that he was getting to know a lot of people in North Moreton in a very short time. For some odd reason he thought of a statement a visitor to Stowford had made.

"A friend in need is a bloody nuisance." And this lot weren't even his friends.

"It's Mary, Mary Pepwell. That's my mother Agnes."

Mary remained silent for a moment, as she thought about whether she should confide in this young man. She thought that a stranger was probably the right person to confide in, as he wouldn't care one way or the other.

"My mother is a witch," she announced.

"Oh I see." John couldn't think of much else to say in answer. Mary Pepwell was sitting on the ground leaning against the hedge which hid the view to a cottage beyond. He couldn't see anyone else on the road now and so he sat down next to the girl, confident that he wasn't going to be setting off anywhere just yet. And how would it be if he just ignored her and continued on his way? He would be wondering for the rest of the journey or perhaps the rest of his life, what the end of this story was.

Another kitten.

He knew who the witches were at home or at least, who were supposed to be witches. There was a rumour that his parents had visited a witch who lived up on the moor before they married and she had forecast ten children. His mother wasn't too pleased about that, but the forecast turned out to be correct.

Mary was fiddling with the edge of her skirt, placing it around her fingers and folding it over one finger, under the next and so on and then pulling it tight. The fiddling appeared to be releasing the stress she was under. The action put John in mind of his little sister Elizabeth, who regularly did a similar thing with piece of material she carried around in her pocket. John had asked her why she did it and the answer was inconclusive.

"I have done it for as long as I can remember John, but I don't know why I started doing it. When I feel very tense I suddenly pick up the cotton and wrap it round and round."

"Does it make you feel better?"

"It stops me wanting to cry or scream," she said and then skipped away. John hadn't known why she should feel tense or worried and want to cry and scream, and he hadn't asked her why. Perhaps he should have done.

Perhaps he should ask Mary Pepwell why she was doing it.

"How do you know she is a witch?"

Mary looked at him in surprise. "Everyone knows that she is, she knows that she is. She told me and I've seen the things she can do."

"What kind of things does she do?"

"She can make babies ill and she can kill horses. I don't like it when she kills horses because I like horses a lot." Mary fiddled with her dress again and it looked as though she was going to cry. John started to put his hand on her shoulder, but she shrugged it away and he brought the offending arm back to his side.

"How does she make babies ill and the other stuff?" Did he really want to know the answer?

"She does things at home with herbs, but she mainly casts spells at night. People in the village complain about her and then come to her when they want someone to fall in love with them. They are such liars."

"What about your father? What does he say?"

The girl looked at John with renewed agitation.

"I don't have a father."

"You must have a father, it's obvious. Everyone has to have a father." Surely she should know that? Then realising that she could only be about 13 years old he added. "It's just that we all have a father."

"Well I don't have a father." She began to sob. "I will not catch mother now and she won't come back home for days." The grubby fingers had come up to her grubby face and she rubbed her eyes.

"Does she stay away from you a lot? Who looks after you when she goes? Do you have family?" John was genuinely worried now in spite of his desire to continue his journey to Oxford.

"Will you take me home please? I want to go home now. Soon, people will start walking down this road and if they see me, they will laugh at me and pick on me. Some boys throw stones at me until I bleed. Please take me home now. Please sir." Mary had fallen onto the road and was sobbing, her shoulders shaking. It was terrible to watch.

"Alright. I will take you home and get someone to look after you." He moved over to her and helped her up as well as he could. It was a difficult job, Mary was quite a well-built young girl and he had to lift her in instalments in order to get her on her feet.

The sobbing girl took hold of his hand and turned away from the Rectory, pulling John behind her. Mary Pepwell for all her thirteen years was forcing the direction in which they now travelled.

He wasn't comfortable with it. Again. What were the chances of this happening twice in one day with two girls in one village? He knew that they were probably opposite ends of the social scale, but still.

What sort of place was North Moreton?

"Is your home far from here Mary?" He hoped it wasn't, for now he was worried that someone would see them.

"Not far John, it will only take a couple of minutes." And then as an afterthought. "I am glad that you are coming back with me. I'm afraid that he will hurt me again if he finds out that I'm on my own."

John stopped in his tracks. This was going badly.

"He? Who? What do you mean Mary?"

He let go of her hand, remembering suddenly the way her mother had behaved. He knew enough of human nature to assume it was highly likely that Mary would copy the way her mother acted.

"No. I can't tell you who it is because you won't believe me. No one will believe me."

"What about your mother?"

"I told her years ago and she said that she would go to his house and see him about it. But she can't have done, because it keeps on happening." Mary was snivelling again.

"Has she not seen him upsetting you or does it only happen when you are away from home?"

"No, it only happens at our cottage when mother has gone out."

"That seems a bit of a coincidence." Realising that he had said that out loud, he continued. "I expect he watches to see when your mother has gone out." But he wasn't thinking that, he was thinking that her mother probably knew.

"I expect she tells him. She gets money and stuff from somewhere and I haven't found out where yet. You are still going to take me home aren't you?"

"Yes, I suppose I will. But only home and then I have to go. I must go."

John was beginning to imagine that he was in the middle of one of his granny's stories. The ghosts of a

Dartmoor village not allowing a man to leave and keeping him there by trickery was one he remembered. Yes, this situation was a bit like that story.

So they walked down the lane and came upon a narrow track on the right, hung over with brambles. There they were met by a young girl who had apparently been waiting for them.

It was Anne Gunter.

CHAPTER FOUR

"What are you doing here Anne?" asked John.

"How do you know her?" asked Mary.

"We met earlier," answered John.

"How do you know the witch's daughter?" asked Anne.

"We just met on the street outside your house and I'm bringing her home."

Anne raised her eyebrows at her new friend.

" I thought you had to rush off to Oxford," she said, hands on her hips.

Looking sheepish, John explained, "I'm going as soon as I get Mary home."

"Do you want me to help you?" Anne asked in a tone reminiscent of his schoolteacher, questioning and a little sarcastic.

"Please come, Mistress Anne. I would like it if you came to see our cottage." Mary looked pleadingly at the girl from the superior class.

Anne appeared to be making up her mind, because she said nothing for almost 10 seconds, which is a long time to wait if you have ever tried it.

"Ok I will, I don't want to stop out for too long because father will start to look for me."

Anne looked worried, but was put at ease when informed that Agnes was not at home and unlikely to be back for a day or so.

The three young people walked together towards the cottage. The way was through a small wooden gate which leant in a rickety fashion amongst the brambles and briars that formed the hedge surrounding the property. Mary pushed it firmly and John noticed that there was nothing holding the gate to the posts on either side. It was more like a piece of panelling blocking a hole in the hedge. The cottage itself was very primitive and not very substantial, completely different to Anne's large family home, of which Brian Gunter was so proud.

Brian Gunter, Anne's father was used to getting his own way. A self-satisfying, ignorant way it was too. His siblings were all influential around Berkshire. Where this influence did not come automatically because of the Gunter name, it often came as a result of pressure brought about by litigation or brute force.

Anne was born in Hungerford in May 1584 and moved with the family to the Rectory at North Moreton three years later. When her father took on the Rectory and began enjoying the tithe as a right, he was adding the North Moreton parish to others he already had in his portfolio. The contributions he enjoyed were now mainly financial and not in the form of stock as had been at one time. It had to be acknowledged that it did not make him popular with the locals from each parish where he collected the tithes.

The beautiful North Moreton Rectory was now the home of Brian and his family and although their position in the village, indeed the county was accepted, it could not be said that they were respected. However, many were fearful of him and his family, who would use any means to better their prospects.

Local yeoman farmers and peasants had experience of his bullying tactics, which could take the form of physical aggression, financial withdrawal, or litigation. He was a rich man, but not a popular one. Anne was right to be scared of him, but her fear was for a different reason.

As they took the few steps from gate to door, Mary became agitated.

"I'm sorry about the state of the place," she said apologetically. "We don't seem to be able to find time to clean up."

"Oh don't worry. Sometimes our servants don't clean up properly, but I don't get cross about that." Anne informed her unnecessarily.

John looked away in embarrassment. The difference between the girls was obvious. He focussed his attention on the Pepwell cottage they were standing in front of. It put him in mind of the cottage on the road a few days ago. Was it a few days ago? He couldn't remember. After so many days of monotonous trudging along the road to Oxford, the last twelve hours had been relatively adventurous.

The thatched roof reached almost to the ground, except for a few feet which was for the storage of wood.

He recognised a small stack of sticks, similar to the ones he had seen Agnes carrying earlier this morning. A large stone in front of the door formed a step which had been swept recently. A brush broom leaning against the low roof with a pile of dirt in front of it, pointed to the fact. The back door must have been made by the same person who constructed the gate. It was of such a poor standard that it could no more have kept draughts out than the gate kept out intruders.

"I'm sorry about the mess," said Mary.

"I was just thinking how neat it looked out here," said John kindly. He knew how much women fussed and bothered about cleanliness and how much they cared if someone noticed. It was the same with clothes.

"If your father goes out in dirty clothes, it's me that will get the blame not him," his mother would say.

"I thought it would be Alice who would get the blame, not you?" his sister Elizabeth had said. Alice was the maid responsible for the laundry.

She had been rewarded with a clip around the ear and a, "Don't be so cheeky Elizabeth. When and if," she put emphasis on the last word. "You manage to get yourself a husband and a family of your own. You will know what I mean."

Glad that John had said something nice to her, Mary said, "Oh thank you, mother doesn't do much cleaning, so I try my best."

"Well, you do a very good job," said John.

"I have never done any cleaning in my life," said Anne unhelpfully.

The group went into the little cottage one after the other, all ducking their heads as they did so. It took several seconds to get used to the space inside. Both Anne and John put their hands to their faces automatically because of the terrible smell which met them as soon as they crossed the threshold.

"Sorry about the herbs hanging up everywhere. My mother uses them in her potions and spells and such," explained Mary.

"What's the smell? It's terrible!" asked Anne.

"I'm afraid it's the animals. The dead animals. She uses those too."

"That's really horrible." John said, even though he had to admit to himself that he was fascinated by this revelation. He hated the thought of animal cruelty, but wanted to know how dead animals would help a witch. He had heard that witches needed animals to cast spells, but he didn't know why.

"Can we see please Mary? I would like to know how spells work. Can you teach me some things? Some simple things?"

"Why would you want to know how to do spells, Mistress Gunter? They can be dangerous," asked Mary.

"I suppose that one day it might be useful to be able to do some spells on people," she answered.

"What about getting hanged for a witch?" asked John reasonably. "I've heard of people who have been hanged."

Mary shook and looked startled. "Oh please don't talk about that sort of thing. It frightens me when you say that."

Once they got used to the smell in the kitchen they proceeded to have a good look round. Row upon row of herbs, grasses and flowers hung from the ceiling. Tied up in bunches and strung from nails on the beams, the young people moved them from one side to the other in order to reach the opposite end of the small kitchen area. The kitchen table was covered with the apparent paraphernalia of a witch. There were two dead chickens, one with its throat cut and blood still dripping onto the floor and the other with no head or feet attached. These appendages were lying in a dirty earthenware bowl to one side of the table. Flies busied themselves around the poor birds. Several knives of varying sizes and sharpness lay next to the bowl.

John counted six, no seven jars also on the table, some open and some closed. The three open jars contained successively, some rocks, then powder and oh no, eyeballs! All the jars were dirty and cracked and John doubted whether there would be free from any sort of contamination. John seemed to think that in order to perform a spell properly, it had to performed purely.

The fireplace held the remains of a fire in the grate and the metal pot which hung over it held only a concoction of grubby liquid and noted by John when he leaned over it, that it smelled disgusting.

"Would you two like something to eat?" asked Mary as she came over to the pot.

"No!" They said in unison, with rather too much enthusiasm.

"I understand, I don't suppose that it looks too appetising in that old pot. But I wasn't going to give you any of that. It's something mother has made and no one who wants to see tonight would try and eat any of it," explained Mary.

"Oh we didn't mean anything by it. It's just that we ate not so long ago, we had a large breakfast at the sheep pen." John said.

If looks could kill, then the look that Anne gave John would have finished his day right there and then. John for his part had only just realised what he had said. Mary was either too young or too slow; because she hadn't comprehended the information she had just been given. She pushed the pot to the back of the fireplace and threw some more wood on the fire and was rewarded with flames and heat. They all stood in front of it automatically holding out their hands and were silent for a time.

Mary tried again, "There are some sweet cakes which I made yesterday. I made them myself and nothing horrid or dirty has gone into them. I wouldn't eat them if mother had touched them. Mother doesn't cook or bake for me at all and so everything I eat I have made myself. She only makes things to harm other people."

She reached up to the mantelpiece on the wall over the fireplace and brought a box down which upon opening revealed some rather grubby cakes lying at the bottom. John and Anne, feeling under pressure reached inside and pulled out a cake each. Mary kept tight hold of the tin, but managed a little smile as her new found friends took some of her baking. It had been the first time that it had happened in her short life. The first time anyone had accepted her hospitality as though she were a real householder. It gave her a satisfied tingly feeling and this could explain why she was oblivious to the expressions pulled by John and Anne as they held the cakes in their hand.

John for his part was wondering how he could eat the offending article and not throws it back up. He didn't want to hurt the feelings of the young girl, knowing how his sisters would get upset if the Prideaux brothers ever made fun of their cooking. He saw Mary's eyes burning into his face and knew that it was highly unlikely that he could get away with throwing the cake out of the window. He still had a long way to walk and he didn't want sickness to hold him up. However, many people were without food at this difficult time and they ate worse things than a witch's cake. But, did they survive? He only had the young girl's word for the fact that she hadn't put some sort of poison in her baking. So, he stood quietly holding the cake which was beginning to go squishy under the tension in his hands.

Anne's mind had a different approach to the problem. Although under the control of her father, Anne was used to getting her own way in many matters and she had no intention of eating a dirty scrap of food, feelings or no feelings.

"How lovely of you to let us taste some of your baking Mary, but I'm afraid that my diet is taken care of very strictly by my parents and I'm only allowed to eat what they say. I get sick if I change my diet in any way and so must sadly offer mine to John too. I know he would be pleased to have the two."

Mary transferred her gaze from Anne back to John. Anne was from a better family than her and would often reject Mary. The pressure was now completely on John Prideaux. He knew it and thought that the best plan would be to get the moment over as soon as possible. He put out of his mind the smell and the sights of the kitchen and placed first one grubby cake in his mouth and taking Anne's cake from her proffered hand, put that in his mouth too. Surprisingly, the experience was not as bad as he had imagined. The taste was pleasant and the texture, if a little stale was palatable. He chewed, all the time refusing to catch the eye of Anne Gunter who had not taken her eyes from him.

The moment over, Mary beckoned them to the room at the back.

"This is where I sleep and spend lots of my time." she informed them proudly. The room was less than half the size of the kitchen and had space for a small bed and a tiny table upon which were a pamphlet, some ink and a quill. It seemed that Mary could read and write. On the bed was some sacking material which served as a bed cover. A dress very similar to the one which Mary wore today, was hanging by a hook on the wall above the bed. A tiny opening in the wall above the table had a view to the back yard.

"What's the pamphlet?" asked Anne.

"It's about a witch trial," answered Mary. "I've been reading about it and it's very interesting."

Anne picked the pamphlet up and scanned through it briefly. "May I borrow this Mary?"

"I haven't quite finished it yet." Mary wasn't pleased. She owned nothing and this pamphlet had only come her way when she had stolen it from her mother's friend a few weeks ago. She suspected that as soon as it was handed over to Anne, she would not see it again.

"I want it Mary. I will give it back to you. It won't take me long to read through, so I shall borrow it today and let you have it back." Anne was still feeling resentful for having been put in an awkward position over the grubby cakes.

John felt for the young girl and as he wasn't feeling sick yet from the cakes he automatically backed her up. "Leave her to lend it to you Anne. She can read it in her own time then."

Mary looked relieved, but Anne had a sulky expression developing on her face. She was making a conscious effort not to withdraw into herself. That was when she started to feel floaty and this wasn't the place to do it. She thought was there something familiar about the atmosphere in this little room.

"Where does your mother sleep, Mary?" asked John as he realised that there were only two rooms in the cottage.

"She doesn't sleep very much and when she does it's in front of the fire or outside," said Mary.

"Are you alright Anne?" asked John.

Anne Gunter was staring at the bed and her face was a picture of complete shock. She was looking at a rag doll which leant drunkardly against the wall. The doll was made from many different kinds of material and her face had been stitched, giving her a scary image which could never give comfort to a child. Anne recognised it, because it had once belonged to her.

"Where did you get my dolly from?" she demanded of Mary.

Mary was frightened but answered, "Someone gave it to me, as a reward." She grabbed the dolly and hugged it to her heart, kissing its ugly face and wrapping her arms tightly round it. She didn't want to talk about it anymore.

Anne looked at the witch's daughter and instantly knew that they had something in common.

CHAPTER FIVE

Brian Gunter had expected more of a welcome when he got home. Generally at least one of the maids met him at the door, but not this morning. Since it would appear that Anne had been missing since last night, he hoped that they were all out looking for her. It wasn't the first time she had gone off on her own.

Brian stood in the panelled hallway for a moment, gathering his thoughts. Anne could not be too far away from the house because he had asked everyone in the village and no one had seen her. Everyone knew that Gunter would ruin anyone who crossed him and people rarely tried. His daughter Anne loved and respected him as any daughter would, so Brian was convinced that a third party was influencing the girl. This third party was also persuading her to run away so many times. That could be the only explanation, for it was inconceivable that his daughter would rebel against him.

Suddenly a young girl ran into the hall, arms full and smashed right into Brian Gunter.

"Sir, oh sir! I'm very sorry sir." The maid was very apologetic, her experience of her master being largely negative. Banging into him in the hallway, even by accident was not to be recommended in this house.

She was rewarded with a hard slap to her head which knocked her almost to the ground. It wasn't the first time Sarah had been hit by her master, but this slap felt harder than the other slaps had done. She was startled at first and then very dizzy as she crouched on the ground with her hand outstretched for balance, grateful that she had managed to keep hold of the linen intended for the chest in the chambers upstairs.

"Get up girl, stop lazing about down there. Go and fetch me some food, I shall be leaving to go out again soon to find that wayward daughter of mine. Move your backside into that kitchen before I hit you again. And this time I will mean it."

Sarah stood up, dropped some of her linen, picked it up again and ran in a stagger fashion in the direction of the kitchen. By the time she arrived in the huge kitchen, her legs had given way and she fell helplessly into the flour sack which lay against the table.

"Now what are you doing girl? Isn't there enough going on here today without you causing us any more dramas? Get yourself up, now." The cook, Mistress Gregory, had no sympathy for the girl. She was already under considerable strain because of the turmoil going on in the house. She worked better when everything was calm and relaxed and since joining the servants at the Rectory she had rarely indulged in that pleasure.

"Oh Auntie, the master is very cross just now. He hit me hard around the head and I feel dizzy and sick." The sad sack of a girl slumped down on a wooden bench and cried into her hands.

"For goodness sake, stop that complaining and get some work done. He won't hit you again today if you keep out of his way. And stop calling me Auntie when we are here."

The girl Sarah sobbed even louder. But after being given a bang on the head with a floury spoon, she stood up shakily and made her way to the huge hot ovens and began to prepare food for the master.

Elizabeth Gregory had only recently started working for the Gunters. She considered the job to be totally below her station, her family being of yeoman stock. But needs must when the devil drives. When she married Master Gregory, she had expected to have plenty of comfort in her life and only do light work about the farm. Then her husband got himself in a bit of a pickle as far as his finances were concerned and that meant she had to work for Gunter. Gunter had encouraged her husband to invest in a business deal buying the leases at a rectory in Berkshire, but somehow it had all gone wrong and Elizabeth wasn't sure how. Had she been given the chance to comment on the deal, then the answer would have been a big no. But she wasn't given a chance at all. It was peculiar, she had said to her husband when he confessed the problems to her, that Gunter never lost money himself doing exactly the same things, so how come he had lost their money? Gregory appeared not to know the answer to this conundrum. But there it was.

There was the great possibility that they would lose the farm which brought the little security the Gregorys had. Then a solution was offered by Gunter to his erstwhile business partner and when Gregory told his wife about it, she almost killed him.

"Work the debt off as his cook?" she had screamed at him. "I am not a skivvy! Why should I work for him to pay off your debts?"

"Because we will lose everything if you don't," he answered simply.

The screaming and shouting matches which took place over the next few days at the Gregory farm were heard by everyone in North Moreton. Elizabeth Gregory had always been known for speaking her mind, whether invited or not and was not always a popular woman. It had become common knowledge that Walter Gregory had set his wife up as cook to Brian Gunter in order to clear his debts.

Naturally some thought that Walter was an idiot and a cruel idiot at that, forcing Elizabeth to pay off his debts. While others were glad that she was getting her comeuppance. These were usually those who had suffered from her sharp tongue and nasty mouth. In spite of days of arguing and complaining, it seemed that there was no way out of it. Brian Gunter even called at the farm and explained his suggestion.

"If you think about it Lizzie, it's for the best. I need a cook and your husband owes me a lot of money. This is the best way for all." The pompous man could see little problem with the situation. He could tell how angry Elizabeth was. The two of them had a little history together that the others didn't know about, but even with that experience, Gunter failed to realise what he was laying in store for himself.

She knew that to refuse Brian Gunter would cause the loss of their farm and that would mean no home for the children. So accompanied by her niece Sarah, she joined the Gunter household. The period of service was to be one year. 365 days and the debt would be cleared.

Elizabeth Gregory couldn't wait. And in the meantime, if she had a little fun and revenge at their expense, why should that be a problem?

Brian Gunter walked into the kitchen, his face bright red and his breathing quick.

"Cook!" he shouted. "Have you seen Anne anywhere? We have searched the whole village and there is no sign of her. I need to know where she has gone."

Brian Gunter was troubled, Elizabeth could tell, but she didn't care in the slightest. She considered Brian Gunter to be a thief and his children to be spoilt brats.

"Mistress Holland is getting upset about the whole thing, she has said that all this trouble and shouting will bring on the baby and it's not due for another month. She is the best daughter a man could want and I don't want her getting upset. I will brain Anne, horrible lying girl."

He put his hand on the table and began to draw circles in the flour. Then he picked up a spoon and slammed it down hard. Elizabeth Gregory carried on turning the dough she had been kneading round and round on the floury table and stared at Gunter with ill-disguised contempt. Mistress Holland was Gunter's daughter and she had made a very smart match with Thomas Holland of Oxford. Susan Gunter had been introduced to him when accompanying her father on one of his many business trips there. Not one to waste time,

Susan Holland was upstairs awaiting the birth of her fourth child. All three had been born here at the Rectory because Susan did not trust the Oxford doctors. The fact that most doctors were trained in Oxford had escaped her logic.

"No, we haven't seen her in here since last night. She came in the kitchen about six, just when I was getting ready to go home."

"Oh she came here did she? What did she want?"

"She didn't seem to want anything. She just hung around for a while, watching us clear up and then she went out the door. I have no idea where she went," Elizabeth informed him.

"Sir," said Brian Gunter.

"Sir?" asked Elizabeth.

"You should call me sir when you speak to me. At this house you are the cook, my cook and you will call me sir."

Elizabeth looked at him, mouth slightly open, all the while cursing him roundly.

"Sir," she said with ironic emphasis.

He smiled because he liked winning. Even very small victories were important to him. His mother would tell his friends about the necessity of allowing Brian to win at play. Any child, who did not allow him to win, suffered a severe beating at the hands of Brian and his brothers. The Gunters always had been and indeed still were a force to be reckoned with.

Suddenly there was a loud commotion coming from the direction of the hall, shouting and smashing about.

"What's going on out there?" he asked. "My house is going to the dogs, no order left anymore. Where's that stupid wife of mine? I'm tired of sorting everything out." He threw a ladle against the wall of the kitchen, narrowly missing the head of the maid Sarah who promptly burst into tears again.

"Clear that up girl," he said and he left the kitchen. As he left, the atmosphere was markedly less charged and Elizabeth and Sarah looked at each other.

"Oh Auntie, I can't stand working here any longer. He frightens me and he's always trying to get me alone. I don't like him." Sarah rubbed her eyes on her apron leaving them bloodshot and covered in flour. She picked up the ladle from the floor next to her and took it to the sink.

"What are you going to do with that ladle?" asked Elizabeth sharply.

"Wash it Auntie, it will be dirty." Sarah held the item in mid-air.

"Well don't bother. If these stuck up Gunters can't treat us with respect, then I don't see why we should look after them. I'm proud of my cooking and housekeeping, but I have a brain and a mind and I don't want to be here. So if some muck gets into their food or worse..." she said ominously. "Then its bad luck I should say."

"What do you mean Auntie?" asked Sarah.

"I mean Sarah, that if sometimes they get ill or have to spend too much time sitting down straining, then it's not my fault. If there are some days when they are confined to their bed, then it's not my fault and if ......"

"But Auntie you can't mean that you are going to poison them?" Sarah was aghast. She knew that Elizabeth came from a family who understood herbs and potions. The other Gregory women often called her a witch out of her earshot, just in case she was a real witch and could affect them somehow.

"Don't be a daft cow Sarah. I just said that if all of that happened, then it wouldn't be my fault." Elizabeth kneaded the dough with a renewed vigour, because she now had a plan and a purpose.

Sarah put the ladle back on the dresser side, making a mental note to wash it when her Auntie took one of her rests. She didn't want to catch any sickness, because wasn't it true that they ate the same food as the Gunters? Even if it wasn't at the same table? Perhaps she would ask her mother on her market visit later that week.

Sarah was not allowed any time off from her job, Auntie Elizabeth went home at night and arrived back in the morning, always cross, while Sarah slept in a tiny room at the back of the kitchen along with two other maids. She didn't want to lose this job and so decided that she would only back her Auntie when out of the hearing of her master and mistress.

She looked back at Elizabeth, who had split the dough and put it on a tray. Elizabeth took a bowl and began mixing some items together. She would be spreading them on the top of the bread. Elizabeth was smiling and humming. Sarah thought that she wouldn't eat any bread today. Perhaps, only bread with the crusts ripped off. That was a shame she thought, because her Aunties bread crusts were the best she had ever tasted.

CHAPTER SIX

When Brian Gunter arrived back in the hallway, he was met by his wife Anne. She was watching Leaver put her boxes down on the floor with a crash. Anne looked on with disappointment because her belongings were being treated with such little respect. She wished not for the first time that she were stronger.

Or single.

She wasn't happy about coming home. She never felt happy about coming home. Brian was a swine of a husband, who thought nothing of offending her in every possible way. She hated him even more now than she had done on her wedding day. Anne only married him because her father needed money for the farm and Gunter had agreed to take one of her father's properties with Anne and promised to ensure that her father was bailed out of his current problems. It had upset her greatly when she overheard the arrangements being made behind closed doors at her home between her father and her potential suitor. Between them the two men had broken her heart twice. Once because she believed that Brian had loved her and second, because she now saw that her father did not love her either. It made her meetings all the more important.

"Oh you are back home, wife. Much has happened while you have been away. I think from now on you must stay at home and not go gallivanting about the county." Brian spoke with the finality of a man who did not expect to be questioned.

"Why?" she said. "What has happened?" Anne was horrified to think that she may not be allowed out again.

"That ridiculous daughter of yours has gone missing and we have the village looking out for her."

"Which daughter?" asked Anne.

"The only daughter who has ever caused us trouble woman. Susan has never done anything wrong. She has made a good match and is doing her wifely duty of producing a child every year for her husband. Something that you never managed to do."

Anne hung her head, the years of abuse and insults had taken so much of a toll that she didn't have much fight left these days.

"I think that my father is referring to me, mother," came a voice from the top of the stairs. Everyone looked up in surprise at the sight of young Anne Gunter.

Before anyone could ask where she had been until this point, Brian Gunter ran up the stairs and pulling his arm back in order to get a better aim, struck Anne hard around her head. She fell to the floor unmoving. Mistress Gunter drew in her breath sharply and froze to the spot. Leaver began to run up the stairs, but his progress was arrested by a glare from his master.

"Is – is everything alright sir?" he asked, now unsure what to do for the best. He was appalled at the way Gunter treated his young daughter, but knew from experience that there was little he could do to help her.

"Of course it is Leaver, don't be an idiot!"

The girl lay still on the floor and Gunter moved towards her and kicked her tentatively with his boot. Even he seemed thankful when she rolled over and moaned. Her mother could take no more and finding some strength in her spirit she pushed Leaver out of her way. She picked up her skirts and quickly ran up the stairs. Her husband held her back as she reached the inert form of her daughter.

"Get out of my way you stupid man," she said to him.

"You just watch how you speak to me, woman," he answered. "I don't mind hitting you too."

"Shut up," she said. "Anne, Anne can you hear me? Oh darling child. Answer me. Its mother, Can you hear me?"

She was rewarded with another moan from her daughter as she opened her eyes.

"Mother, oh mother! I'm so glad you are home. He hit me, mother."

"There my lovely, let's get you up and take you to your room. Leaver, come here and help me!"

Brian pushed Leaver to one side.

"Come on you two. Let's get you into your room." Brian said as he moved towards the women. He was looking relieved that his daughter was at least speaking. He had realised as soon as he had struck her that it was probably a bit too hard.

"Go away Brian," said his wife. "You have done enough damage for one day. You are upsetting her." She pushed him away and this time he kept his distance...

Anne managed to get her daughter to her feet and with Leaver lending an arm they struggled to make their way to the bedroom.

"Call for Sarah would you Leaver, tell her to come up here and help me."

"Yes madam, I will fetch her now." He left the bedroom and went down into the hall. There he grabbed the arm of Sarah and half pushed and half carried her up the stairs.

"Oh Mistress," was Sarah's reaction when she saw Mistress Gunter tending Anne at her bedside. "What has happened? Was it the master again? Has he hurt her?"

The question was innocent enough. Sarah was so overcome with the emotions of the peculiar day she had experienced so far, that she let the words out of her mouth before she could think properly.

"What do you mean, again, child?" Mistress Gunter stopped her bathing of Anne and looked at Sarah quizzically.

Sarah held her lips in a firm thin line, not trusting herself.

"I demand that you tell me what you mean Sarah." Mistress Gunter stood up and looked her maid directly in the eye. "Has the master done this before?"

"Well no, yes. He's done different things Mistress, things that…" They were conscious of a shuffling movement in the doorway and Brian Gunter walked into the room.

"All of you get out," he demanded.

"No Brian, we are staying here," said his wife, using her bravest voice.

Anne stirred and sat up in her bed.

"What's happening? How did I get here?" She pulled her arms around her body seeking comfort. Something deep inside her woozy head was letting her know that she wasn't completely safe and she felt a need to keep herself very small.

"You had a nasty fall." Brian told her firmly.

"Oh," answered Anne quietly.

A feeling of familiar collective amnesia was descending upon the room.

"Get out everyone," repeated Brian and all left the room, leaving young Anne and Brian alone together.

"I didn't fall father, you hit me." Anne looked at him firmly, although she had her knees drawn up to her chest and her arms clutching them tightly.

"You are mistaken Anne, you know I love you. Come hug me and let me show you how much I love you."

"I don't want to father, please don't make me."

Brian put his hand to his daughters head and gently stroked her hair. Anne tensed visibly and a sick feeling overwhelmed her.

She moved away from the touch and was rewarded by her father grabbing hold of her hair tightly and pulling her back towards him. Anne screwed her face shutting her eyes firmly and pursing her lips. His face was so close to her's, that she could smell what he had eaten recently.

He said, "You will always do what I say and what I want, child. You have no alternative. No one will help you. I am your father and you belong to me."

She waited for the inevitable. Staring fixedly at her dolly she reached out to touch it with her fingers, the only part of her body currently able to move and pulled it towards her. Closing her eyes, she began the focusing she knew so well, necessary in order to escape the situation she often found herself in.

Then she was gone.

Anne ascended to the ceiling of the room and watched her father.

"Disgusting, disgusting man," she thought briefly as she went over to the window overlooking the street in front of the house. From there she saw her new friend John Prideaux talking to the witch's daughter Mary Pepwell. She could imagine what was being said, or perhaps she heard it? It was hard to work out which was which and so she stopped doing it. Any alteration of focus put her smartly back on the bed with her father and she would have to refocus. The older she became, the better she got at this focussing.

Tracing her finger along the edge of the window, she saw Agnes Pepwell walking up the street and wondered idly where she was going. No doubt to cause mischief of some kind. Then Anne returned her attention to John and Mary Pepwell. Their conversation seemed to be quite involved. They stopped talking and began walking towards the track which Anne knew led to the Pepwell hovel.

"They will be going to cottage, safe in the knowledge that the witch is going out of the village." Anne said to herself. This witch was a crazy witch. There were others not so crazy and Anne had determined that one day, she would be the best witch of all. Being a good Christian girl had so far got her nowhere.

"I will go to the cottage too."

Anne loved the way that she could just appear seemingly out of the blue and present herself in front of the young John and Mary. They looked shocked and a little guilty to see her.

"Who gave you the dolly?" demanded Anne of Mary.

Mary put her hands in front of her face and then over her ears. Her eyes were closed tightly.

"I can't tell you who – he made me promise I would never tell." Mary sobbed pitifully.

"Who did?" persisted Anne.

"Oh, Mistress! It was Master Gunter!" Mary cried as though her heart was breaking.

Anne Gunter sat down on the bed with a thump.

John Prideaux felt like an intruder on this scene, but did not feel as though he should leave. What a day.

"Has he given you many presents Mary?" Anne asked quietly.

"Yes Mistress. But most aren't as nice as the dolly. Sometimes sweets and once he gave me a penny!" Mary answered excitedly.

"What do you have to do for the presents Mary?" asked John, fearful of the answer.

"Don't ask her that!" said Anne sharply. She looked at Mary as an equal now, not as a dirty village girl.

"Don't ask her anything else. We don't need to know."

Anne couldn't explain the pain which rose within her and she felt an urge to leave the claustrophobic little cottage. She must return to her bed.

She ran out of the door, down the path and vanished.

CHAPTER SEVEN

Mary stopped her sobbing as soon as Anne left.

She stood up, brushed down her skirt and said, "I think that you should leave now John. You are a stranger here and you need to go. You are not helping any of us. Please go."

Mary walked towards the door and held it open. She stood erect, with the dignity of any high born lady. John smiled at her and walked out of the open door into the sunlight and into the street. There was no sign of Anne Gunter anywhere. He walked quickly past the stone walls and the Rectory barn, rounded the corner and stood on another road which crossed the High street.

John looked up and down the road and saw no one in either direction. He idly wondered where the people of the village were this morning, but his attention was suddenly arrested by the sight of the Church which lay beyond the Gunter house. The Church was a beautiful sanctuary, inside which John wanted suddenly to be. There he would find peace. He went inside, chose a front pew where he had a good view of the altar and was soon on his knees in prayer.

John hadn't prayed that much in a church recently. At home, he had spent a lot of time in Harford Church, but that was because it was on the edge of Dartmoor and all the Prideaux children liked to scamper and ride over there whenever they were not required to work on the farm. He liked the smell in there, a mixture of moss and damp even on the sunniest of days.

The church felt old and once inside it was easy to feel close to the men and women buried there. In granite tomb lay Thomas Williams who had been Speaker of the House under their Great Queen Elizabeth. He had been a favourite of hers and she sold him the Manor of Stowford from her own lands. The Williams and Prideaux families were joined by blood and land.

Harford Church was cosy and comfortable. John knew the families of most of the people who worshipped there and who were buried there. Here in North Moreton church, he knew no one and he wondered what he was doing here, sat in the church, mulling over the events of the past few hours. John looked at the pictures depicted in the stained glass windows and the embroidered kneelers and felt homesick again. Surprisingly, tears welled in his eyes as he thought of his family going about their familiar business at Stowford. Thomas, his elder brother and heir to the farm, would be bossing about his brothers and sisters as though he were Lord of the Manor.

But it was John that everyone expected to be famous and rich.

What a responsibility.

He sat head bent and eyes covered with his hands as he prayed quietly. Suddenly he was conscious of footsteps behind him.

"Hello," said a voice.

John looked up and saw a vicar looking at him. He seemed kind and John smiled at him.

"Hello young man," he repeated. "What are you doing here so early in the morning?"

John wondered briefly whether or not he would be in trouble with the vicar, but considered that he probably wasn't.

"I am on my way to Oxford, sir. I have an offer of a place at Exeter College and so have walked from my home on Dartmoor."

"Is it usual to walk through North Moreton on your way to Oxford? It seems a little off the track." asked the vicar.

"I did get side tracked sir. I helped someone and have ended up in a pickle." John tried to keep the quivering from his voice.

"It's often the way young man, even the Good Samaritan had problems I believe. Who did you help and why the trouble now?"

"A young girl called Anne Gunter, she lives at the Rectory."

"Yes, yes. I know who you mean. Have you met her father?"

"Yes, he was very angry. He threw a rock at me."

Thomas Heard sat down next to John and asked him to tell the whole story. When John finished, eyes sparkling with emotion he felt as though he had given a full confession to God. The relief was wonderful.

"I think you are overtired John and this morning has taken more out of you than you expected."

"It is probably because I am so far from home and have so much to do once I get to Oxford and then there is the rest of my life to get through. Just at the moment it feels too much."

Thomas Heard smiled and said, "There are some things I can tell you, which may or may not help you understand something of what has gone on. Perhaps then you can continue with your journey to Oxford."

"What kind of things could you tell me? Why would you tell me anything? I'm just passing through."

The vicar smiled at the young man and answered, "Because someone outside of this village ought to know what sort of despicable things that man does to people."

John drew in his breath sharply. This was grown up talk and he wasn't really sure whether he wanted to hear about it. But Master Heard didn't appear to be giving John a choice. Thomas Heard patted his young visitor on the back and was about to begin his tale when they were interrupted by the entrance of another man. This man stood calmly beside the men and smiled at them. Thomas stopped his narrative and half stood up. He seemed confused to see this visitor.

"Hello Master Holland," he said, "I didn't know that you were in North Moreton."

"No one does yet, I only arrived this morning. My wife is very near her time and I want to be here."

"Yes of course sir. Mistress Holland is looking very well at the moment, I saw her only two days ago." Reverend Heard was deferent to this stranger and that interested John. John liked to notice how people reacted with each other and what lay behind it.

"I hope so Thomas," he said. "Mistress Holland is important to me and she likes to be with her family at these times."

"That is understandable. A mother is important at this time, as are all her family."

"Yes, yes, it is useful to me to be able to continue with my work and studies without interruption."

He became aware of the young man sitting next to the Rector.

"And who is this with you Thomas? I don't recall seeing him before."

John blushed and was ashamed to do so.

"This young man is on his way to Oxford and has only stopped off to be a Good Samaritan he tells me."

"I am impressed young man! Our Lord rewards those who help others. Why are you going to Oxford? I live there myself and it is a wonderful city."

"I am on my way to Exeter College sir. I am to work in the kitchens to help pay my way. My aunt, Lady Fowell has helped to arrange it." John suddenly felt as though he must make it clear that he was not a common man and had good connections.

"Then we shall be meeting often for I am Regius Professor of Divinity and the Rector of the College." He did not say this any boastful way, but as one who is stating a fact.

John didn't know how to react. The man in front of him was important in his own right and to John's future. He decided to be bold. Standing up, he leant forward and shook Master Holland's hand.

"I am happy to make your acquaintance sir. I hope that we can be friends."

Thomas Holland was slightly taken aback by the confidence of this remarkable young man, but he was impressed. He returned the handshake.

"I'm not so sure that we can be friends just yet, as there is a lot of space between us at Oxford. However, I always place myself available for any student who requires help and advice. I am also a believer in solid hard work, so if you are a worker we shall get on. It is imperative that a man study and then study some more if he wants to get on." Thomas Holland looked intently at John Prideaux, but with kindness.

Reverend Heard smiled.

"Master Holland has reached his high offices through hard work and piety John and will have us all study as hard if he had his way!"

"Oh! I'm sorry Thomas. I didn't mean to upset you or the boy. But education helps free a man's soul and if he understands the Scriptures and stays away from popery and idolaters, then he will be welcomed into the Lords Kingdom. I hope that I haven't upset you ……."

"Prideaux, sir. John Prideaux."

"Sir John Prideaux?" asked Thomas Holland. "I know of a Sir John Prideaux who used to live in Devonshire."

"Yes he was an ancestor of mine. But I am just plain John Prideaux." John thought that this man may be high powered, but was nice. Meeting him was a stroke of luck. Perhaps God had led him to this village in order that he could meet Master Holland.

"That is splendid! We have other Prideauxs at Exeter now and many before you. A proper old West Country family I know."

John felt good and perhaps a little smug to know that his family was well known so far from home. It would be nice if he discovered that beyond small town gossip, a man could be just that, a man.

"Thank you very much sir. I shall look forward to seeing you. When are you returning?"

"Not for a little while, once my wife has had her… well we don't need to talk about that. This is my fourth you know! I'm very happy to be blessed this way."

Thomas Holland twinkled and looked very happy and excited. John thought, but did not say, that Master Holland seemed very old to be having children. He must be 60 at least.

"Now, before I go to the Rectory, I want to talk to you about something I recently read and translated. There are three different possibilities and I need your opinion..." He took the arm of the Reverend Heard and led him up the aisle.

John was left on his own, wondering.

He wondered how he would act when he met this great Thomas Holland again in Oxford. He also wondered who had done what to whom, but felt ashamed for doing so. It was highly unlikely that he would find out now and he resolved to set himself back on the road to Oxford. He picked up his bag and threw it over his shoulder and with a dip in the direction of the altar, made his way towards the main door. It was only as he was lifting the heavy latch that he remembered Anne Gunter telling him about her sister having her fourth child at home at the Rectory. Thomas Holland was married to Anne's older sister. There must be almost forty years between them. That really wasn't right.

He walked out into the churchyard and on to the street. Not for the first time, he wished that he had never left home. It's one thing hearing that other villages and towns have funny ways and quite another to discover that it were actually true.

The day hadn't quite warmed up, the grass was still wet and there was a smell of damp moss, which put him in my mind of Harford again. John rubbed his face with both hands and felt tired and dirty. Still a long way to go and he needed to find food so he could stride back on his journey of monotonous steps that would hypnotically connect him with his goal at Oxford.

At least now he had an influential friend, always a bonus. That wasn't going to help him find food today though – or was it? Taking his courage in his hands, John turned round and walked into the church. He saw the two Thomases talking intently and he said,

"Excuse me, but do you know where I can buy some food for the rest of my journey please?"

The two men looked at him and John feared that they had found his question an insult. After all, many were starving and finding it harder to share.

"I have money, sir. I am not asking for charity."

Thomas Holland answered, "If we cannot provide charity John Prideaux, then I don't know who should! But I acknowledge that you wish to pay your way."

"My parents would never forgive me if I did not pay. We have never accepted anything that was not paid back sir."

"I understand John, my parents are the same. Here take this note to the kitchen door of the Rectory and speak to Mistress Gregory the cook, she will let you have some food." He scribbled a note and handed it to John.

"Round to the back of the house?" asked John.

"Yes. Go through the fields at the back of the church and you will see the Rectory kitchen garden on the right. Go that way and you will not have to walk down the drive."

"Thank you." John wasn't very sure about going round to the back door either. Brian Gunter had made enough of an impression on him to last a lifetime.

"Go on. Off you go!" said Reverend Heard. "We are busy and you will be there quicker if you set off!" They both laughed at this joke.

John walked outside and around the back of the church. Once out of sight he put down his bag and opened the note which Rector Holland had given him.

He read,

John Prideaux is a student of mine at Oxford and I would be very much obliged

If you could provide him with enough food and drink to allow him to reach Exeter College

I shall be arriving later this morning.

Please let my dear wife know that I am on my way,

Rector Thomas Holland

He folded the note and felt happy that a stranger should show him so much kindness.

John moved swiftly across the grass towards a stone wall. He noted that some men were working in the fields and was glad that there was some life about. Finding a gate hidden behind ivy and late purple clematis, he pushed it open and stepped into a large kitchen garden. At one side stood a glasshouse and everywhere else were row upon row of fruit and vegetables. Apple, pear and damson trees and against a brick wall, what appeared to be peaches. John had seen all these at Lukesland back home.

Home.

He noticed that an old man was moving amongst the rows, but he did not raise his head and acknowledge the young visitor. John knocked gently at the back door and waited.

No one came.

He knocked louder.

No one came.

He pushed the door and arrived in a cold hallway.

There was no one about.

At the end of the hallway he could see what appeared to be a cook at a large kitchen table. She was clearing away items from its floury surface. She wiped her hands on her apron and walked towards the hallway. For some strange reason John darted into a side door when he saw her coming towards him.

CHAPTER EIGHT

As soon as he was nicely concealed behind a storeroom door, he began pulling faces.

Why on earth had he done it? He didn't even know this cook woman and yet the sight of her had caused him to go into some sort of self-preservation mode. That didn't make sense! He tried to stop thinking in case the cook could hear him.

What?

His manic internal ranting was stopped temporarily as he realised that the cook was in the storeroom next door. In the wall separating the two rooms was a metal grille and through this he could see what the woman was doing. Upon a shelf were various bottles and jars. The cook was pulling different ones down from the dusty shelf, looking at them in turn and putting some back. Eventually she appeared to be happy with her choice and put the items into the small straw basket she carried. The basket was tied around her waist and covered by a voluminous apron. She dusted herself down, looked around to make sure that she had not been seen and walked out of the door.

John put his head out of the door and watched her go back into the kitchen. He decided that he had better wait for a few minutes before he followed her and made his request. John would have dearly liked to go straight out of the back door, but the need for food and supplies was more important. He must reach Oxford and start his education. A feeling welled over him which almost took his legs away. The feelings of homesickness had been creeping up for a few days and now the panicky thought that unless he got food soon, he would not make it to Oxford and would most assuredly never make it back as far as Dartmoor. He felt lost in an unknown land.

He was alone.

John was one refusal of food away from ending his days on the roadside, starving and dirty. Once he became too hungry and weak, he would stop washing and looking presentable and then no one would even speak to him.

One meal away.

John noticed that someone else had entered the kitchen and was talking to the cook. Not just talking, he had his arms around her and was pulling her towards him. She seemed to resist for a while, but not for long.

The man was Brian Gunter. He held her arms behind her back and was making an attempt to kiss her.

"Now Lizzie, you can spare a kiss for me can't you?"

"Someone will come in and catch you, Brian. You don't want you reputation ruined any more than it already is do you?"

"Ruined? Me? That will be the day my girl. I am Brian Gunter and no one can ruin me." he declared with feeling.

"Perhaps someone like me will," said the cook.

"How do you imagine that you will be able to do that?"

"I can start letting the right people know about this tithe business of yours. It's not quite such an honest deal is it?"

Gunter seemed to hold her arms more tightly, for John saw her wince. He put his face nearer to her and growled, "You cross me woman and I will kill you. I promise you that." He dropped her arms, spat on the floor and left the kitchen.

The cook put her hands automatically on the basket around her waist and looked after him. John coughed and she wheeled round and glared at him.

"What the hell are you doing in my kitchen, boy?"

"Erm, sorry Mistress, I wanted to erm…. I have a note," he passed the crumpled piece of paper to her.

She took it from him and read. After finishing it she looked at John.

"Well this is not usual. This is not Rector Holland's own house you know."

"Yes I know. I said I would pay. I need to get to Oxford. I would be very much obliged if you would let me have some food."

"Pay? Yes I can take the money from you. I will see that Mistress Gunter gets the money."

"Alright," said John, who was not entirely sure that the Gunters would be seeing any of his money.

He handed over a few coins to the woman and she pocketed it with as much finesse as the old woman on the road a few days ago. He stood quietly while the cook put together some new loaves and cheese. He looked around the room and noted that it was a nice place to be.

"You keep a nice kitchen, Mistress Errr…"

"Mistress Gregory," she answered.

"Yes, Mistress Gregory. It reminds me of home. My mother spends a lot of time in the kitchen and so does my grandmother. It's very warm and smells lovely. I miss it very much," he added sadly.

Mistress Gregory stopped her wrapping and looked at the young man. She wasn't so harsh really. She opened the cloth that she had been putting the bread in and added more loaves, cheese, apples and biscuits. Two bottles of wine and a small joint of meat made up the parcel. John had a problem fitting in it his bag.

She didn't hand back the money however.

"Thank you very much Mistress Gregory. I am very much obliged for this. It will help me a lot. I don't know what will be greeting me at Oxford and to be honest I'm nervous."

"Don't be frightened. Oxford is full of the same kind of people you find on Dartmoor."

John doubted that, but smiled at the woman and thanked her again.

"Off you go," she said. "Before he comes in again."

John repeated his thanks and went outside. He pulled the cloak around his head and shoulders as the rain started. The clouds foretold another long spell of heavy rain and he dropped his shoulders and made his way back to the Oxford Road.

Elizabeth Gregory watched the young man go and as soon as she was alone, took out her bottles to look at them again. She took a small bowl from the dresser and placed it on the table. She poured a few seeds from one bottle and poured a little vinegar onto them and began to grind the two into a paste. This took some effort on her part, but once the paste was smooth, she stood back and admired the result. Elizabeth lifted the bowl to her nose and sniffed.

She frowned and then opened a small jar which she had retrieved from her skirt pocket and not from the basket. It was full of seeds and Elizabeth hesitated before she placed a few seeds into the mix. She ground these into the paste until it turned green and smooth. She did not sniff this concoction. What she did was to add it to the pie mixture in a large mixing bowl at the other end of the table. She noted with dismay that the green colour remained. So she added some black treacle to the mix in order to eliminate it. She poured the whole concoction into a dish and put it into the oven. She smiled and began clearing away the bowls.

As she was completing this task, young Sarah came into the kitchen and said, "That's my job Auntie!"

"I know my dear, I thought that you had a lot on your plate today and I decided to help you out."

"You don't usually do that!" Sarah was surprised because in truth she didn't think that her Auntie had ever done a job on her behalf. But she had no intention of questioning her any further.

"No I don't, but there's nothing wrong in being kind every so often is there?"

"No Auntie."

"Open the door of the oven and turn round the cake that's in there to save it from burning on one side. I'm serving it up for his lunch."

"What's in the pie?" asked Sarah.

"It's a secret recipe from my mother."

"What's in it though?"

"Never you mind. Go and get the table ready for lunch. There will only be Gunter in there eating, the others are having their meals in their rooms. They don't mind causing us trouble do they?"

Sarah laughed and left to sort things as instructed. Master Gunter was notoriously irritated if his meals were upset. Although it had to be acknowledged that he got irritated about most things.

By the time Sarah had finished setting the table, Brian Gunter entered the room.

"Why are you only setting one place, girl?"

"Because err, because Aunt, err, I mean Cook said that there is only you eating lunch here today." She was holding firmly onto the knives in her possession, hoping against hope that she would not let them slip through her fingers and crash to the floor.

"Err? Stop erring your stupid girl. Answer me properly."

Sarah wasn't sure how to respond to this and stood as still as she could manage. Brian Gunter was so unpredictable that he was capable of anything.

"Set the table for six people. Today we shall have a good lunch."

"Six?" The word was out of her mouth before she could stop it.

His face darkened and Sarah scurried from the room to let her Auntie know the change of plan.

At luncheon, when the full complement of guests had made themselves comfortable around the huge oak table, the atmosphere was not light.

Anne and her mother were quiet and subdued. Susan Holland alternatively leant back and then forward in her chair, moaning and rubbing her back. Thomas Holland carried a calf leather bound book and spent most of his time referring to it and sometimes nodding to his host in response to a comment. Harvey Gunter the heir, paid little attention to the group and drank copious amounts of wine for so early in the day. He had matriculated at Brasenose College seven years previous, but had spent most of the time drinking and gambling and never finished a degree. Brian glared at them all, disapproving of his family en masse and individually.

Sarah brought out the meal, including the pie made recently by Elizabeth Gregory. There was a joint of meat, cheese and pickled fruit. This she laid down the centre of the table, wishing that there were other servants in the house.

"If he thinks I'm waiting on his awful family, he can think again," Elizabeth had said to her when she asked her aunt for help. "It's bad enough cooking for the idiots." She dropped the joint on the tray and pushed it towards Sarah.

Now Sarah stood at the edge of the room by the door. She had tried to leave, but Mistress Gunter asked her to stay, "In case we need you dear." So it was hard to go.

Sarah watched how the family acted with each other and noted how unfavourably it compared with her own family. Suddenly her musings stopped as Brian Gunter banged loudly on the table.

"What's the matter with you all? This is a family lunch. We should all be enjoying ourselves, chattering away as though we love each other!" he shouted.

Everyone looked up at him, with the exception of Thomas Holland who continued his reading in oblivion of the change of atmosphere. Anyone who knew him well would agree that this was normal behaviour.

"I think we have all had a couple of busy days haven't we?" Mistress Gunter looked around the assembled people and smiled, as ever trying to calm the atmosphere. "Let us all carry on with our meal and enjoy each other's company. How are you feeling now Anne?"

"I am perfectly well mother. My head aches a little, but I'm sure it will be better soon." She rubbed it as if to help the healing along. Anne dropped her gaze to her plate and said no more.

Thomas chose this moment to join in the conversation and asked Anne, "What happened my dear? Have you had an accident?"

Anne looked up and her eyes darted from Thomas to her father. Brian glared at his daughter, daring her to say anything that would cause trouble.

Anne looked her father directly in the face and said, "Dear brother, I slipped and fell at the top of the stairs this morning and felt sick and faint afterwards. After lying down on my bed and my father rubbing my head and hands, I am feeling much better now."

"Oh, I'm sorry that you had a fall Anne, but glad you are better now." Thomas returned his concentration to his book.

"Eat your food Anne, you are picking at nothing there." Brian leaned over to the pie, which had remained untouched by everyone and spooned a huge portion on to his daughters' plate. "No one is eating this, you have some Anne."

"That's because there is green stuff coming out of the side of it. I don't think that Ma Gregory was at her best this morning. The meat's alright though, I like that. I like meat." Harvey Gunter took another large slice and shoved it into his mouth. He was looking slightly the worse for wear after the many glasses of wine he had indulged in.

Brian prodded the food with his knife and said, "Eat it Anne. We don't want you fading away."

"I'm not very hungry father. I don't want anything else to eat," she said quietly.

"But you will eat it," said her father.

"I don't want it."

"You will eat it." Harvey took a large piece of pie on a spoon and handed it to Anne and held it to her face.

"You have had a few falls recently Anne. Is there something else the matter?" Thomas Holland said, not taking his attention away from his book.

"She doesn't eat enough food. That's what the problem is. Eat this pie Anne," said Brian.

Anne took the spoon from her father and ate some of the pie. She pulled a face, "It tastes disgusting," she said.

"I told you that the cook wasn't at her best today. I'm not having any of it," said Harvey.

"No one has asked you to have any," said Susan, who had been moving a piece of meat around her plate for the last few minutes.

Anne ate the rest of the pie on her plate and slammed the spoon back down. Suddenly she pushed her chair back from the table and stood up. She spun round and screamed and then threw up all over the floor and collapsed in a vibrating heap. There was green froth coming from her mouth.

Thomas Holland got up and went towards her. He couldn't get too near because her limbs were thrashing about wildly. He saw her eyes roll back into her head showing only the whites.

"What's the matter with her, Thomas?"

"She seems to be suffering from the 'mother' Brian. She is coming to the right age."

"Thomas, I want to go back to my room now, please help me there," said his wife.

Thomas left Anne and went over to her, "Come on my dear, I will take you up. We don't want the baby upset."

As they left the room, the others heard Susan say, "Bring me some food up Sarah. Cake and cream and sweets will help me feel better."

Sarah bobbed a small curtsey and followed them out of the room.

Anne was still shaking and foaming on the floor and the remaining guests watched her. Brian pushed his chair back saying, "Harvey let us go and drink elsewhere, while these women sort out the mess."

Mistress Gunter waited until the men left the room and got up and checked her daughter. She saw the green vomit and foam and winced as some of it landed on her skirt.

"I am sorry Anne. I cannot deal with this anymore. It's too much for me." And she left the room.

By the time Elizabeth Gregory came in and found Anne, the vomit was cold and beginning to set and discolour around Anne's mouth and clothes. Anne was unconscious and grey and the table upset and messy.

Elizabeth looked at the pie with only one piece taken from it and knew exactly what had happened.

"He was supposed to eat that Anne, not you. He is usually the only one to eat pie, never you. I wanted him or your horrible brother to eat it."

But Anne could not hear her. Elizabeth moved away from Anne and took the pie from the table and threw it out of the window. Then she came back to the girl and used the napkins from the table to wipe her clean. As soon as Anne was looking better, Elizabeth helped her to sit up.

"Here Anne, have some of this wine, it will help to bring your colour back."

"I don't like wine."

"It's not for drinking Anne. It's to make you feel better. I am so sorry."

"Sorry? Why?"

"I am sorry that you have been so ill."

"I feel poisoned Mistress Gregory. That's how I feel."

"You weren't poisoned by me Anne. Come on, let's take you up those stairs and get you properly cleaned up and settled."

Elizabeth Gregory helped the girl up the stairs and into her room. She helped her undress, folding the stained clothes as she did so.

"I will wash these for you Anne, we won't bother anyone else. Here is a clean nightgown. Get into bed and I will personally make sure you are not bothered again.

"Where is that young man who came into the village with me this morning?"

"He has gone off to Oxford now, I sent him with some food."

"Will you teach me how to do it Elizabeth?"

"Teach you what?"

"You know."

CHAPTER NINE

Sitting around the big dark oak table with his teachers, William Helme and Thomas Holland and waiting for the Gunters to join them, felt very strange to John Prideaux.

It was less than two years since he had asked for food from Mistress Gregory and met Anne Gunter roaming around the fields. But now John Prideaux, a second year student at Exeter College, Oxford was sitting at the Gunter family dining table with two men who were welcome at most good houses. John did not feel in awe of them, he wanted their jobs one day. So he was sticking close.

Back then, when he finally arrived at Exeter College tired and nervous, he had made the arranged contacts and was soon working in the kitchens serving other students. Master Helme had been impressed with John's piety and hard work in those early days at the college and part way through October, he accepted him as a student. John Prideaux had been so proud and read and learned and prayed every spare minute.

He knew now that you get everything you want if you concentrate hard enough on prayer and study. John Prideaux had been made most welcome at the Holland house and subsequently remained aware of the goings-on, back in North Moreton via the constant gossiping of Susan Holland.

"Are the family to join us soon, Thomas?"

Dr Helme had agreed to come to the Gunter household under protest, because he had much to occupy his time back in Oxford. He had not really wanted to become embroiled in these recent dramas. To be asked to take sides in a potential murder case was not going to do his career much good he thought, as he continued to fiddle with the little doll he had found on the table.

"Yes, I am sure."

Thomas Holland wasn't so sure however. As time went on he was becoming less enamoured of his father in law. His two brothers in law weren't so reliable either. Always arguing and suing people, shouting and causing fights where there was really no need. If it weren't for his wife insisting that she give birth to their children at North Moreton with her mother present, then he would have had his family remain in Oxford. There he could read his precious books, study and remain in a calm state of mind. Here there was constant shouting, arguing, and tales of who fought who and….

His musings were interrupted by a loud bang on the table. Coming back into this reality, Thomas saw his father in law Brian standing alongside him, hands on hips and a huge grin on his ugly face.

He had been drinking.

"Well, well, Thomas! You have brought some of your fine Oxford friends with you! Have you told them what is happening?"

"I have told them something of the story. I am not aware of most of it. We are here to advise and help where we can." That was not technically true as he was here because Susan had said he must. She had nagged and nagged,

"Thomas you must help them! Those rotten villagers are determined to cause trouble for Papa and Harvey and William. They will have them in gaol if they can! Or worse!"

"I am sure that will not happening my dear. The inquest decided that there was no case to answer," he answered in what he considered to be placatory tones.

"But they are trying to get a court hearing, Thomas." Susan was lying across the bed at the time, the babies being taken care of by one of the nurses.

"I am too busy to go back again to The Rectory," he said.

"Again? Why again? Are you saying that we go too often to my family Thomas? My own blood?"

Thomas could feel yet another conversation slip away from his control.

"No, not all my dear! I am glad that you feel so close to your mother."

Susan fiddled with the bedclothes. "There is also another point to consider Thomas."

"What?"

He worried about what was coming next.

"If any of my family goes to gaol for this or anything else, it will not go down well with the College will it? Your career will be in ruins and we shall lose our home and we shall have to go and live with my family in North Moreton anyway. Only it won't be the same there because Papa and the boys may be in gaol or hanged and there will be no one to keep us and we shall all end up starving to death. Your wife and your babies starving to death!"

If nothing else, Susan Holland was very good at making a point. She now had her husband's attention and so, during the next week Thomas asked his friend William and the clever young Prideaux to accompany him. He did not want to involve anyone else who may delight in his problems and report the trouble to others. He could lose his job if there were too much information in the public domain. So here they were, none of them knowing exactly what they were expected to do. They were apparently on the same side as a rather objectionable country squire and his arrogant sons.

Happy days.

"Where are the drinks? Where is the food?" asked William who enjoyed both.

"Sarah! Sarah! Bring us food and drink! Now!" Harvey came back from the door through which he had shouted and slumped down next to his brother in law, grinning inanely. Sarah was now in charge of the kitchen and the house, following Elizabeth's recent departure from their household. She was finding it very difficult and unbeknownst to her employers was also soon to leave and begin work at another house. In the meantime, she did as she was told and put up with the innuendos and gropes and rubs and vowed that one day she would get her revenge.

She was willing to wait.

As it was, she passed on everything she heard and saw to her family, so that it could be used to the advantage of the Gregorys in their battles against the Gunters. The Gunters did not appear to have realised yet that this was happening. Sarah hoped that they never would.

John Prideaux looked around the group in the room and worried a little about what was coming next.

"Do I know you?" John looked up as Brian Gunter barked the question at him.

"I – I don't think so sir. Unless you have seen me when visiting Master Holland at Oxford. I have been in the Holland lodgings from time to time."

"Yes, well I expect so. It's just that I feel as though I remember you from here." Brian Gunter had not got to where he was, by missing small points of potential interest.

"I don't think so sir. I have never been here."

Dr Holland shot a glance at John, knowing full well that he had first met his protégée at North Moreton. Gathering that he had a good reason not to mention the fact, he let it be. Gunter was not the kind of person to chit chat with.

"I'm still sure that I've seen you around here. Now then Holland, what are we going to do about this bit of a problem we all have?"

Thomas decided not to mention that the problem was the Gunter's problem alone. He didn't imagine that for one minute he would believe it – or care.

"I think it is probably best that you tell us about it in your own words. Calmly and clearly," he added.

"I can tell you straight away what happened," said William Gunter. "Those damn Gregorys that's what. Damned trouble causing idiots. Papist devils. They won't let this drop if we don't stop them. They will cause trouble for us all."

At this moment Sarah arrived in the room with a wheeled trolley upon which was meat, bread and jugs of mead. John hoped that his face did not show disappointment in the offerings. He was not a fan of this type of fare, preferring only light food. As Sarah passed around the gathering with the trolley, she noted that John was the only one to refuse. She also noted what was being said, having determined as soon as she heard about this meeting to pay attention to everything which went on.

She liked the young John Prideaux and was trying her best to attract his attention. It wasn't working, so she finished her serving and left the room.

"I think it is best that you tell us what happened that day in your own words Brian," Thomas asked his father in-law.

"But we saw things as well as he did. I mean we were all involved. We know what really happened." said William petulantly.

"But if we hear just one opinion at once, we shall be able to make a judgement." Dr Helme interjected.

"Are you trying to say that we are lying? That we are making it up? We haven't done anything wrong. It's all the fault of those damned Papist Gregorys!" Harvey repeated the earlier claim and John wondered idly whether this was the line they had decided to take. Stoke up the anti-Catholic feeling and get sympathy from the audience. But if these Gregorys were really Catholics, then John could not take their side. Not after that dreadful Queen Mary.

He suddenly remembered that Mistress Gregory had been very kind to him that day two years ago.

Hmmmm.

They were interrupted again by the entrance of Sarah into the room. She carried a tray containing a jug of cloudy liquid and some bread and cheese.

"I thought that the young man might like this to eat and drink. I notice that he didn't want anything of the other food. Perhaps someone else would like some?" she stuttered.

"Oooooh!" said Brian Gunter at his maid.

The girl coloured up, John smiled at her in gratitude and she fled the room.

"You've made a conquest there, young Prideaux," noted Harvey.

"She is just a helpful servant, I would think," he answered reasonably.

"Keep clear of her, boy," said Brian. "She's not up for games."

Dr. Helme had now had enough of this line of conversation and did not intend to let his charge suffer any more of it.

"Perhaps we can get back to the point of our meeting Master Gunter. We have to be back in Oxford by tonight." He looked at Holland and suddenly felt sorry for him for having this family as his relatives.

"Tell me father in law, what happened that day," asked Holland.

"None of it was my fault, I can tell you that for nothing," said Brian Gunter petulantly.

"We aren't saying that it was, but would like to know your account," answered Holland quietly.

"I was watching them running down the street and making sure that they weren't damaging the wall. I sent Tailor and Watts to sort it out. Then there was half the village coming pushing this way and that."

"I was with them and we were just having fun!" added William.

"Where were you, Harvey?" asked Holland.

"I was drinking and talking to Susan Field," he said and sniggered.

"So you didn't see what happened?" asked Holland, who was becoming increasingly aware that he was in charge of questioning.

"I had my hands full. I heard all the shouting while everyone was fighting up the street."

"Whereabouts were you?"

"Behind the Bear Inn, she likes it when we nearly get caught out," he sniggered again.

"Don't you go getting another one with child, Harvey. I don't fancy buying off another little baggage. He's such a man," said Brian turning to the men around the table. If he was expecting admiration, he was disappointed.

"And where were you Master Gunter?" interjected Dr Helme. He disliked this family and wanted to find out exactly what had occurred and report back to Edward Dunch, Lord of the Manor. But he was keeping that little gem of information to himself.

"I was standing outside the gates of my own property Dr Helme. I was with my servants and wanted to make sure at none of that rabble got into my property. I didn't want the womenfolk upset."

"I had heard that you had previously been in the Bear Inn and suggested that an argument would be sorted out with the match," said Holland.

"I don't know where you heard that rubbish. I was in the Bear Inn before, but everyone was just having a drink and a laugh."

"And there wasn't an argument there?"

"No there damn well wasn't!" Brian was getting angry and his face was beginning to turn red.

"I thought there was trouble with William Gregory?" asked Holland.

"I thought you were on my side? You married to my daughter and all?"

"Of course I am Brian. I need to know all the facts so that we can put up your defence if it comes to it."

"Father, listen to Thomas. He knows what he's talking about. He won't care what went on, he just wants to know," said William.

"Perhaps you could tell us, William," said Holland.

"Gregory did start on about the payments he was supposed to make to my father and was refusing to pay anything. He said that our family were thieves and liars and he didn't see why he should pay us for their hard work and he wasn't the only one to think it."

"And," interrupted Brian. "I told him if that was his attitude we could go straight to law and I know my rights and would see him in court and in gaol before I let him off any money."

"And was that the end of the matter?" asked Helme.

"Pretty much. They know that I stick to my word."

William Gunter continued, "Then they were all talking about the match and after a few drinks, off they went."

"Were any of you playing the game with them? Any of the Gunters?"

"No, we weren't," said Harvey. "We don't play stupid games like that. We've got better things to do."

"But you were watching?"

"I told you I was making sure those Gregorys didn't damage any of my property. They wouldn't be above coming in and stealing my stuff," said Brian.

"And did anyone try and come into your property?" asked Holland.

"Richard Gregory did. He left the crowd and came over to me and started the argument again. He must have been determined because they had only just left the Bear Inn and someone tripped him up and he thought it was John Field and they started to fight," said Brian.

"I came over then because I didn't see why that bloody Gregory should start picking on my father and told him so and then I got attacked by his stupid brother!" said William.

"Then my men tried to get them off William and me and they all started fighting," joined in Brian.

"And what of the football match?" asked Holland.

"They were all shouting and watching what was going on. The Gregorys were attacking us and then the rest of their family started joining in and we were getting outnumbered. So I took out my dagger and I bashed them both on the head!" Brian Gunter grinned from ear to ear.

"Bashed the Gregory boys?" asked Helme.

"Yes I did! Bloody cheek trying to cause us trouble. But they didn't much feel like causing trouble after I hit them both!"

"So you were aware that the blows you gave them caused them to suffer?" asked Holland.

"Of course I did!" Suddenly Brian Gunter realised where this line of questioning was going. "I just wanted them to stop attacking William and gave them a bit of a clip round the ear."

"But both men died from that clip round the ear, Brian and although the inquest did not blame you, the Gregorys want a formal prosecution. You are going to have to be sure of your facts," said Holland.

"John Sudbury and Robert Adams are both a pair of liars. They owe me money and goods and want to cause trouble. Robert Gregory is as bad as the rest of them." Brian smashed his fist on the table and John Prideaux was knocked back with the force. Up to now John had been listening, finding that his mind could work things out better when he didn't talk.

"Nevertheless Brian, they have a valid story to tell and theirs is different to yours," added Helme. He didn't want to reveal that Edmund Dunch was interested in seeing Gunter prosecuted and out of his hair.

"What do they say?" growled Harvey. "I will soon see them change their minds!"

"They say that you instigated the argument at the Bear Inn with Gregory and when they were running with everyone by your property, you sent your men in to cause a fight. Then after you, Harvey and William were challenged by the other Gregorys, you hit the boys over the head until they fell."

"That is complete rubbish. There wasn't any blood on them and no marks."

Thomas Holland felt that, in spite of his bluster, the threat of the Abingdon Assizes had rattled his father in law more than he was likely to admit.

"It is also said," added Helme. "That you went to the Gregory house when the boys were dying and threatened them."

"I did no such thing! I went round to see if I could do something to help, that was all."

"Who has been filling your heads with this nonsense?" asked Harvey.

"It's all from the evidence which has been presented to the Summer Assizes," answered Helme quickly.

"We managed to see the coroner's inquest through well enough," said William. "There won't be any problem with a grand jury."

"Shut up William," instructed Harvey. "We don't need to tell everyone everything."

"I'm not Harvey, don't you start bullying me. It won't work."

"I'm not bullying you! I can't say a thing to you without you jumping down my throat. Why, I could do for you!" said Harvey Gunter as he lurched across the table at his brother.

Thomas Holland stood up and said, "Boys! Please! Let us maintain decorum." Sometimes he thought that the only thing that separated this family he had married into and the rabble in the street was their money. When he saw Susan Gunter that first time in Oxford, standing by her rich and well-connected father, she had seemed so sweet and innocent and he fell in love there and then. Now he was stuck with this violent and brash family whose blood ran through the veins of his children. His Puritanical leanings had to be brought fully into play whenever he had dealings with them. Today was one of those days. He leant across the table and poured himself another drink. He caught the eye of his charge John Prideaux and smiled.

"Go and have a word with the maid, John," he instructed on impulse.

John nodded briefly and left the room.

"Where's he going?" asked Brian Gunter.

"He needs to relieve himself," said Holland. "Now tell me what happened when you called at the Gregory's house after the football match."

John was grateful to leave the room, finding the argument and dramatics claustrophobic. He made his way along the hallway and turned into the doorway to the kitchen. He was about to lift the latch when he heard a familiar voice behind him.

"Hello John, I see that you have rapidly made good connections at your college."

It was Anne Gunter, now fourteen years old. She was a young woman and looked beautiful as she stood on the staircase, hand resting gently on the rail. He took his hand from the latch and moved towards her. She held up her hand signalling him to stop.

"Hello Anne, how are you? You look really well."

"That is a very pretty compliment John. I am very well, thank you for asking. Are you here to find out why my father murdered those young men?"

"You think he murdered them?" he asked.

"I know he murdered them. My father and my brothers for that matter hate the Gregorys and will do anything to harm them." She sounded so matter of fact.

"Why do they hate them so much?" he asked.

"Because the Gregorys and the other farmers don't like the way my father takes money from them. He is an outsider who has got the right to take some of their profits for no exchange at all. And he is cruel and he struts about the place as though he owns it. No one likes him, so he hates them."

"You sound as though you don't blame them."

"My father has no redeeming features John. And if he catches you speaking to me, he will make you suffer. I suggest you talk to Sarah and find out what you need to know and meet me later. We can meet on the lane to the Pepwell cottage. No one goes there."

"The Pepwell cottage?" he asked.

"You took the girl back there after you met her mother."

"I know. You want me to go to the cottage?"

"No. Just the lane. Thomas will stay here for supper tonight. I will make sure of that. Then he will drink with my father and that is the time you will leave and meet me."

Anne turned and skipped lightly up the stairs and onto the landing. John turned back to the kitchen door and lifted the latch.

Sarah was crouching in front of a door at the far end of the kitchen, which John estimated must look into the dining room. She was so intent on her task that she didn't hear him enter the kitchen and almost jumped out of her skin when he said hello.

"Oh sir! You made me jump. Do you need something? Shall I get you something?" Sarah stood up so quickly she looked as though she was going to faint.

"Does your Master allow you to listen at doors?" asked John.

"No sir, I wasn't listening, I was looking for something. I dropped my ...."

"Spoon?" asked John, noting the one Sarah held in her right hand.

She looked at it and answered thankfully, "Yes."

"Do you know what we have been discussing, Sarah?"

"I know that Gunter has been lying about what happened. He murdered my cousins and he's going to get away with it."

"Could you tell me what you know about what happened?"

"I can, but why do you want to know about it?"

"Perhaps you know that there is to be a hearing about it at Abingdon?"

"Yes, my father and uncles want him to be prosecuted. I saw some of it that day you know."

"Perhaps you could tell me then. Shall we go through the kitchen door and outside?" He was conscious that any of the Gunters could catch him talking to the maid. If they went outside at least he could pretend that he had gone to relieve himself out the back.

"We could go into the kitchen garden," she said. "I need to get some vegetables from there."

The two went out of the door via a small corridor and were soon in the garden. John noticed that he could see the church and his mind went back to the night he was last here, needing help.

"What happened to the cook?" he asked suddenly.

Sarah seemed surprised with the question and asked, "You knew my auntie then?"

"I didn't realise that she was your auntie, but she was quite kind to me years ago when I needed some help."

"She can be kind, but she can be a cow," said Sarah.

"So did she leave recently?"

"She left before the murders, if that's what you mean. There had been lots of arguments between the families and she couldn't stand it anymore."

"What kind of arguments?"

"To do with money, I think. I'm not really sure why. Something to do with tithes. Master Gunter suggested tithing them on branches they cut in the winter for the animals. There was always arguing and fighting."

"So what caused her to leave then, in the end?"

"There was a massive argument one day. Auntie came to work and she had a face like thunder. She said that someone had been spreading gossip about her and she was going to put a stop to it. She said that she knew things about Gunter that he wouldn't want getting out and she was going to let him know. She said that she wanted people to know how he treated his family and the things he has been stealing."

"That all sounds quite dramatic. Do you know what they actually argued about?"

"It didn't happen here. Mistress Gunter caught her as she went crashing into the hall and made her come back into the kitchen. Then Auntie was talking about Mary Leaver and Peter Field and catching them up the lane to South Moreton. She said that she thought Master Gunter had been with her too and Mistress Gunter slapped her and told her to leave the house before she did something they both would regret. Then Auntie said she needed the job because of the debt her husband owed the Gunters and that if she didn't work it off, they might lose their farm and Mistress Gunter said that she didn't care, she wasn't to stay in her house a moment longer. Then Auntie said if they tried to do anything about the debt, she would tell the courts about what she knew and that would be the end of that."

"So, your Auntie left that day?"

"Yes she did and I won't be long following. I've got another place. Oh! I haven't told them yet, you won't say anything will you?"

"I won't Sarah. I won't tell on you." John was used to young girls finding him attractive. He used the fact when it suited him, but had interest only in getting on in his life and not in marrying. The girl he intended to marry would be a special lady.

"Would you like to speak to my auntie?"

"Yes I would. Where does she live?"

"She lives the other side of the church along with most of the Gregorys, in different cottages. That's Auntie Elizabeth there now. Standing at the back of the church looking at us."

John followed her gaze and saw the cook from two years previous, hugging herself and shaking. He patted Sarah on the shoulder and said, "Best go back in. I will go and talk to her."

John made his way through the kitchen garden and into the graveyard. Elizabeth stayed where she was and as he got closer, he noticed how pale and ill she looked.

"Hello Mistress Gregory. Do you remember me?"

"Have you come with Master Holland to see that Gunter?"

"Yes I have. I'm John Prideaux. I study with Master Holland at Oxford. I've come with him and Master Helme for a visit."

"I hope you are trying to find out the truth about Gunter murdering my cousins. And yes I do remember you. You came for food a couple of years ago, didn't you?"

"Yes I did and I thank you for giving me some. Would you like to tell me what happened that day? Perhaps I can make some sense of it?"

Elizabeth suddenly looked cold and said, "I will tell you, but I doubt you will make sense of it. I have set something in motion already that will damage that arrogant man. That murderer. But it's a long game I am playing. A long and dangerous one."

John felt himself shiver when she spoke. Although summer and a warm day, the churchyard had become suddenly dark and cold and the church itself looked menacing.

"Is there somewhere we can talk, Mistress Gregory?" he asked. "In the church perhaps?"

Elizabeth looked terrified. "No!" she replied. "We can walk along here to the back of the Bear Inn and then go our separate ways."

"I will do that, but we should walk slowly if you are to tell me everything."

"I will speak quickly," she said.

John could not help but smile at this and beckoned her forward. He glanced back at the Rectory, but saw nothing out of the ordinary. He would have to feign sickness when he finally returned to the Gunter's house. He was yet to decide whether he would tell Master Holland all he found out. Master Holland was a good man, but married to a Gunter nonetheless and John Prideaux believed in the absolute truth. His immortal soul was far more important to him than anything.

"Sarah tells me that you know something about Brian Gunter and other women?"

"Sarah talks too much. But yes he does have other women. For my part I'm ashamed to say, I was one of them for a while. I was trying to save my husband's properties."

"I see."

"I don't think that you do. You are far too young. It has nothing to do with love of my husband. I have no intention of losing my rights when he dies. I'm a Leaver you know and I wished I had stayed one. These Gregorys are almost as bad as the Gunters and they lose and make money all the time. When the Gunters came here and took over the tithes, the Gregorys were furious. They intended to get them back."

"They were upset with Brian Gunter?"

"Not Brian, his brother Edward. When he died he left it all to Brian. Edward managed to blackmail some judge or someone and got the Rectory. I remember him living here when I was a girl."

"So there has always been bad blood between them?

"Yes. But Richard and John didn't deserve to die, they were nice men. Typical Gregorys and always ready for a fight, but nice. I liked them."

She shivered again.

"Are you cold?"

"No. I feel as though trouble is on its way. I've done some things that may come back to bite me."

"Such as?"

"Doesn't matter. That day there were quite a few people at the Bear and they were all getting really drunk ready for the ball game. There's always fighting at the game, but they want it and expect it. Suddenly Brian came in with his boys and his servants and started accusing William, my brother in law of not paying him and he argued back and everyone took sides and a fight started and then they were told to leave."

"Were you there?"

"Not at the Inn, I was told what went on. Brian wanted the lands that William has on that side of the church," she said pointing to the east.

"Do you think that he will do anything to get them?"

"And the Gregorys will do anything to stop him. They are all as bad as each other. The innkeeper threw them all out onto the street and they fought and chased each other down towards the Rectory and it was hard to tell if it was still a fight or a game. I was watching them from the other side of the road. Then William and Harvey Gunter really started laying into Richard Gregory about his father William being a thief and a liar and Richard fought back and punched William Gunter square in the face. Then John, his brother and John Field my brother, came to help and punched William Gunter in his face and they were all on the floor."

John tried to keep focus with all the names and the part they played in the story. It was complicated.

"What happened next?" he asked.

"Brian started shouting and screaming like he usually does and told Simon Watts and John Tailor to go and help his boys."

"Who are they?"

"His men. They will do anything he says."

"His men?"

"His thugs who will do what he tells them to do. Whatever he wants them to do," she added with emphasis.

"And they joined the fight?"

"Oh yes they did. With staff and dagger. They are big, heavy men and they began kicking the others out of the way. That meant that anyone who wanted to help the Gregory boys backed off. There were a lot wanting to help but they know what those two are capable of. Then they held Richard and John by the arms so that they couldn't move and Brian Gunter came towards them now that they were held securely. He's a coward. His two sons started saying things to them while they were being held and then kicked and punched them in the body. Richard and John were very brave and shouted all sorts back, about what they were going to do once they were free and how they would let the authorities know. Then Brian took out his dagger and hit them very hard on their heads. He said that he would shut them up. And he did, because they didn't say anything else. They just slumped forward and the men dropped them onto the ground. William and Harvey Gunter kicked them a few times again until they were stopped by their father."

"Didn't anyone come to help them?" John was shocked by this tale. But his experience of the family Gunter led him to believe Elizabeth's version of events to Brian Gunter's tale.

"They were scared and stunned I think. Brian threatened them with some of the same and he also said that he would ruin their livelihoods. They know he can do it because he's done it before."

"So you are convinced its murder and not an accident?"

"Of course it was murder and everyone else knows it. You know the Gunters even came round to the house and threatened them all again? The men were lying in their beds with a dreadful fever and their family weeping over them and the doctor not able to help them and he came round to look at them. He threatened the men who had not even opened their eyes or spoken a word since the attack.   Brian Gunter told them he would give them more of the same right there and then. And my husband Walter heard William Gunter say to John as he lay there on his deathbed, that he wanted him to get up so that he could fight him again. He said if anyone told, he would make sure that they would receive the same."

"Is that why the inquest called it divine intervention?"

"They were scared. They felt forced to say that no wound caused their deaths. My cousins took two weeks to die and it was a horrible death. John had been a friend of Edward Gunter you know. Brian wasn't even bothered about that."

"It seems that some of the family want to see justice done at the Assizes."

"I know about that. But they have already been threatened by the Gunters. He will pull something out of the bag, he knows too much about people. He keeps secrets and will get out of it somehow."

They had arrived at the rear of the Bear Inn and Elizabeth was ready to part company.

"I hope you can get justice for my family, you seem well connected yourself. His daughter Anne needs protecting from him too and some other young girls around the village. I remember when I was young…" She stopped talking.

"Remember what Mistress Gregory?"

"Nothing," she replied.

"Remember what?" asked Harvey Gunter who had made his way towards them from the Bear Inn without their noticing.

"Nothing," she repeated and walked away from the two men.

"You cause trouble again and we will see that you live to regret it!" he shouted after her.

"Don't you like the woman?" asked John.

"No I don't and you shouldn't either. She's a trouble causer and a gossip. Why were you talking to her? We missed you back at the house and I was sent to look for you."

"I felt ill," said John, "and I decided to go for a walk around the church. I met your old cook and she told me that if I walked along this little track and came through to the back of the Inn, I could walk back down the street to the Rectory again. I was hoping that the air would help me."

"And has it?" he asked suspiciously.

"A bit, but I'm still feeling poorly. I ate some meat this morning which I felt was too old and I think it has affected my stomach."

"You know Elizabeth Gregory do you?"

"No, why do think that?"

"You said our old cook."

"Oh I see, she told me that. I don't think that she likes your family very much."

"We don't like her either. She's a witch they say."

"A witch?" John asked incredulously.

"So they say. Her Leaver mother was supposed to be one and her aunt had a daughter who is called Agnes Pepwell and she's a witch too. I think they should all be hanged or burned."

"That's quite a serious accusation."

"It's not an accusation. It's a fact," Harvey replied.

CHAPTER TEN

When John arrived back at the Rectory with Harvey, he wasn't sure if he was really feeling ill or not. They did not speak a word on the short journey along the High Street and in through the gates. They had passed several villagers and every one of them looked at Harvey Gunter for only a moment before dropping their heads and scurrying away. John was sure that some people, who had been walking up ahead, vanished once they came within their vicinity. It was quite draining. Today had been draining and he still had things to do. Was it the village or the people?

They had walked in the footsteps of the football game from the Bear Inn to the Rectory. They passed the place where the murderous attack occurred. Harvey Gunter didn't seem to notice. He strode on, swinging his silver topped stick and whistling. He used it to open the front door and as he did they almost crashed into Sarah. She squealed and Harvey hit her on the behind with the stick.

"Drinks girl! Fetch us drinks!"

She scampered off in the direction of the kitchen and Harvey said, "That girl will have to go. I'm sure that she is spying on us."

"Why would she want to do that?" asked John.

"Because everyone wants to know what we are up to."

He pushed open the door into the dining room. The other men were preparing to eat supper.

"I found him at the Inn," announced Harvey to the group.

Master Holland and Helme looked aghast. John stepped in quickly to ease their worries.

"I was on the little lane at the rear of the Inn. I had walked there from the churchyard as I have been feeling unwell."

"And how do you feel now?" asked Thomas Holland.

"I am feeling better than I did," he answered. "But I am not feeling quite right. Would it be of great inconvenience if I went outside again after supper?"

"No, I'm sure it will be alright John. We shall be staying here tonight and leaving early in the morning. Perhaps have your walk and retire early. I believe you are staying in the barn, there are some servants quarters there."

"Thank you," said John.

"You seem to be doing a lot of walking for someone who is so ill," noted Brian as he looked at the young man with renewed interest.

"I have always walked sir. I walk to think, to make myself better."

"He even walks while he studies," said Dr. Helme.

"He is known around our college as a very pious man who can walk, pray, study and pass the time of day all at the same time. He is much admired."

John blushed at this unexpected compliment. He sat down at the table and took a little of the vegetables and a piece of cheese. He ate slowly while the others chattered away. They talked about London and Oxford and how the old Queen was never to be seen these days and who would take the throne when she died? John remembered the stories told to him by his parents about Thomas Williams, a relative who had let them buy Stowford House and Farm. He had been Speaker to Queen Elizabeth and a good friend of hers. She had allowed the Williams family to purchase the Dartmoor lands from her. He had tried to persuade her to marry all those years ago in order to provide England with an heir when she died. But the strong woman had not wanted to defer to a man who would become her King and decided to reign alone. Sadly Thomas Williams had died while on a visit back home and he was never able to follow up his insistence.

He was not going to tell them the story however. John didn't approve of gossip. Yet here he was, listening to the gossip of maids and farmers wives. Hopefully, if he solved this murder and brought the perpetrators to justice it would be worth it.

The party at the table were becoming merry with drink and John was surprised to see that his masters could join in with such fervour. He hadn't seen that before and wondered if the Gunters had given them stronger drink than they were used to. At least it meant he needn't excuse himself when he decided to leave.

"Enjoy your walk!" shouted William Gunter as he left the room. John gave a half smile in response.

He felt happier as soon as he walked down the drive and crossed the street. He needed to head west and retrace his steps of two years prior. The small track on the right was easy to spot and after looking quickly up the street he went down there. Why he was checking he couldn't have immediately explained, but he suspected that he felt embarrassed about being seen walking down the Pepwell Lane. It was a light night and warm, but the rain took the edge off that. Making his way through the wet overhanging branches and the overgrown hedgerows, he felt as though he was walking into another world.

An unreal world.

And here was his young friend Anne Gunter. Was she his friend? He would like to think so.

"Hello John. Are you enjoying yourself at my father's house?"

"He seems to be entertaining my teachers. But I have to say that your father and brothers seem to me to be soulless men."

"That, I can't dispute John. I agree with you. My father terrifies me and he is supposed to love me. He is a bully and my brothers are the same. I would call my sister Susan a bully too. She certainly bullies that husband of hers. They all have terrible tempers."

"Do you have a terrible temper, Anne?"

"I have a temper. That I can't deny. But I put my energy to different uses."

"I have been speaking to Elizabeth Gregory and she tells me that your father murdered those men."

"Elizabeth Gregory can be a liar. She tried to poison our family on more than one occasion. I found effigies of us all in the kitchen chimney. She has also become very friendly with Agnes Pepwell. She's a witch you know and a relative of Ma Gregory."

"I don't think that it helps to accuse people of being witches. It can end up with people paying with their lives and their livelihoods. I am not so sure that witches abound quite as much as is thought."

"Then you are an innocent, John Prideaux."

"And you are a fourteen year old girl with little experience of the world."

"That was a horrid thing to say. Just because you have had little experience of witches, does not mean that they don't exist."

"I believe that they do exist, Anne. I just don't think that there are quite as many about as people think."

"I am telling you that there are at least two living here in North Moreton. Perhaps more. Witches tend to stick together. Like bullies." She smiled and John realised that he knew little about this young woman.

"What can you tell me about the deaths of Richard and John Gregory?"

"I can tell you very little. I know there was an argument in the Bear. There's always an argument in the Bear. Then a lot of silly drunken men fell out of the Inn and fought and played down the street. Then another argument broke out and my brother tried to stop it and then my father somehow got involved and accidently hit them on the head."

"Accidentally hit two separate men on the heads in a scuffle with blows that killed them?" John was incredulous.

"There is no proof whatsoever that the men died as a result of being hit by my father. And if you repeat that away from here, expect my father to sue you."

John was shocked that Anne defended her father so strongly. He had been of the opinion that she didn't like him. But there was something different about the girl since their last visit. She seemed much wiser somehow. Anne dropped her gaze to the floor in a sweetly innocent way and he immediately felt guilty for having the thoughts he had. He walked towards a wall, intending to sit out of the rain and turned to ask her to accompany him. He saw that she had raised her head and was no longer sweet. Her eyes were dark and evil looking.

He shivered.

"Shall we move out of the rain?" he asked.

"If you like. It doesn't bother me."

"So you are convinced that the deaths were accidents, Anne."

"I am. Elizabeth Gregory was dismissed from our house and that means her husband still owes my father money. He is in considerable debt to him. I don't know how they will ever pay him back. They need to earn some money desperately or they will lose their home."

"That's quite sad. Would your father see them homeless?"

"He wouldn't care. He only takes responsibility for the things he is interested in. That's mainly money."

"And bullying."

Anne looked at him and her eyes flashed dangerously.

"And bullying," she repeated.

"How have you been keeping since last we met?" John asked her.

"I have been growing up and learning some things and planning my future." Anne was sitting on the stone wall and resting her feet on one of the blocks which made it up.

"Do you study your Bible?" he asked. John was of the opinion that the answer to all problems could be found in the great book.

"You are funny John! The Bible only reveals its secrets to those who know how to read it. Everyone reads it as though it were a story. But they have to have the proper development of mind in order to understand it properly."

John Prideaux, a pious studier of religious texts and academic pamphlets was aghast at this observation. He had been reading something similar in a book he had borrowed from the college library which talked of the hidden meanings in the Bible and how these meanings depended upon the reader's state of mind.

"Are you talking about learning from the Bible only what you think you can learn?" John hadn't quite understood the book he had read.

"I am saying that we live our lives from our minds not from any books. Bible or not. But the Bible was written by people who understood the power of the mind and so if you read it from that level, you learn different things."

"You should come to my college and say that," he said.

"Are you trying to make fun of me, John?"

"No! Not at all. I meant exactly what I said. That your views might make an interesting debate. Most people at my college like a debate and they would certainly have one with you." He felt as though he was digging an even bigger hole for himself.

"Would you like to visit Mary?" asked Anne.

"Mary? Mary who?"

"Mary Pepwell. You remember the young girl you met last time. The one with the dirty looking mother."

"Yes, I remember her of course. Do they still live in the cottage?"

"They do. Let's go down there." Anne took his hand and led him through the trees until they reached the cottage. It didn't look much different from the last time he had seen it. Except perhaps it was more tumbledown than he remembered. There was no one about on the lane and in the little field which surrounded it, but there was smoke coming from the chimney.

"Are they in?" John asked.

"Don't know and I don't care," answered Anne as she went ahead of him and pushed her way through the gate. John noted that this was barely hanging on its post. Surrounding the cottage were piles of sticks and he saw a pig in a tiny pen at the back. John felt sorry for pigs. They had a rough life.

Anne didn't bother to knock at the door. She merely swept in and shouted "Hello! Anyone in?"

John followed her, but felt very uncomfortable about it. The kitchen was as he remembered it. Herbs hung from the low roof and pots and jugs around the surfaces. There was a recently dead rabbit on the table not yet skinned, but with blood dripping on the floor from its mouth. John would find it very easy to become a non-meat eater. He hated the killing of animals.

"They are usually in at this time. Hello!" she shouted again.

There was a noise in the back room and Anne pushed her way in.

"What are you doing Mary? Come out from there!"

John walked towards the room, when suddenly Anne stepped back smartly. She turned to John as she did and said, "Mary doesn't look too well."

John barged past Anne and entered the room. Mary lay slumped on her scruffy little bed and was covered in blood. He went towards her and crouched down. He picked up her hands and saw that they were bloody, scratched and sore. Her face was also scratched and her lips were sore and cracked. Her hair was matted and her clothes filthy and she stank. John was used to the smell of poverty, but there was another smell here. Almost of death.

"What is the matter with her?" asked Anne.

"I'm not sure. Has she been attacked? Is that likely?"

"Shall I throw some water on her?"

"No! But you can fetch some water. Is there any hot water on the stove? We should clean her."

Anne went reluctantly back into the kitchen. She returned eventually with a bowl of milky warm water and a grubby cloth.

"You should clean her," suggested John.

"You must be joking! I'm not touching her. I might catch something!" Nursing was evidently not one of her strong points.

"I can't touch her. It's not right!"

"I am here to swear that nothing wrong took place. You trust me don't you?"

"I suppose," he answered. Though he didn't know why he should trust her, he hardly knew the girl. But he cleaned up Mary Pepwell as best as he could and gently tapped her face, hoping that when she came round she didn't scream.

She did come round and she didn't scream.

"Oh hello sir! You've come back!"

"You remember me?"

"Of course sir. You helped me that day. I won't ever forget that."

"She likes you!" said Anne and laughed.

Mary remained staring at her saviour. John hoped that helping a girl twice did not count as an engagement out here.

"What happened to you Mary?" he asked her.

"I was helping at the farm last night and someone grabbed me and bashed me about. They said I was a witch just like my mother! They said it was my fault that those men were killed. How can it have been my fault? I was there watching, but I didn't do anything. I swear!"

"Which farm?" asked Anne.

"The farm by the church," she answered.

"Who attacked you?" asked John.

"I expect she couldn't say," interrupted Anne. "And if she could identify who did it, well she wouldn't dare say in case she was attacked again. Isn't that right Mary?"

"Yes Mistress," answered Mary. Her eyes were very wide and John thought that she seemed scared.

"So you have no idea who attacked you? Have you reported it to anyone?" persisted John.

"Who would she report it to?" asked Anne. "No one would listen to a girl like Mary. Would they Mary?"

"No Mistress," agreed the girl.

"Where is your mother?" asked John, less concerned for Mary than the thought of meeting that old crone again.

"She is about somewhere sir. I don't know when she will come home. It could be anytime at all."

"Perhaps we should make our way back then," he said to Anne.

"Oh! I thought you might want to ask Alice Pepwell what she thought about her cousin Elizabeth."

"I think that she is a filthy liar," spat the old woman as she crashed her way into the kitchen.

John jumped up from his crouching position, hit his head on a beam and almost fell down again. Anne Gunter did not seem bothered at all and remained leaning against the wall.

"We didn't hear you come in," she said.

"Didn't you? You should pay more attention Mistress Gunter and then perhaps you wouldn't get yourself into so much trouble."

"Don't you dare speak to me like that you bitch," answered Anne nastily.

Alice Pepwell sneered at her and turned her attention to her daughter.

"What's the matter with you?" she asked.

"She says that she has been attacked. We have cleaned her up as well as we could and I don't think that there is any permanent damage," said John.

"I didn't clean her up," said Anne. "This college man is the one with the conscience, not me."

"Attacked?" said Agnes suspiciously. "Who would want to attack you?"

"I don't know. I was probably mistaken."

"And why are you two in my cottage anyway?"

"We were taking the evening air and found ourselves here," said John.

"Were we John? I came here on purpose because I wanted to see if Agnes Pepwell had anything to do with the Gregory's deaths you are so interested in. What do you know about the deaths?"

Agnes glared at the young woman and answered, "I had nothing to do with those deaths. If Elizabeth Gregory has been saying that I have, then I shall go straight round to her house and see her now."

"She hasn't been saying you had anything to do with the deaths. In fact I think she believes someone else is responsible," said John.

"He means my father when he says that. Probably my brothers too."

"What do you think about it, Mistress?" said Mary.

"They may have been and may not have been. We all know though that those two men weren't as good and kind as the family Gregory would like them painted."

"That's very true," said Agnes in a rare moment of agreement with her better.

"Why? What had they done?" John was genuinely interested because up to now he had believed that the men were innocents, caught up in the Gunter bullying.

"They were as bad as the Gunter boys. Always fighting and causing trouble. One family always threatening the other," answered Agnes.

"It sounds like the only thing missing is the love of a young girl," said John. "Like the Capulets and the Montagues."

"That will be me then," said Anne, running her fingers along the wall.

"You shouldn't have let him talk to you and walk with you," said Agnes. "That way he wouldn't have got interested. You got them killed Anne, whether you admit it or not."

"Thank you for coming to a completely wrong assumption. It is not my fault if he wanted to follow me about the village. I didn't ask him to fall in love with me."

"You seemed keen enough on getting that potion from me," answered Agnes.

Anne looked abashed for no more than a second and then became the haughty daughter of Brian Gunter.

"You should mind your manners Agnes Pepwell. Get that filthy daughter sorted out and if the pair of you don't clean this filthy hovel up, I shall see that my father has you evicted."

She pushed John in front of her and before he knew it, he was outside in the dirty yard in the rain with a scowling young woman. She didn't look quite as pretty now.

"What was all that about?" he asked Anne.

She looked at him as if wondering whether to tell him or not. She decided against it and said, "Nothing."

Agnes came out of the back door, dragging Mary with her.

"I want you to have a good look at this young girl, John Prideaux. If I ever find out that you did more than clean her up, I will make you suffer. And I can make you suffer."

"I don't understand," asked John. "What do you mean?"

"Mary has just told me that it was you who rubbed her all over with a cloth while you made Mistress Gunter watch." Her face had crumpled even more than before and he was aware that the lines were traced with dirt. That dirt was old and he suspected impossible to remove.

"I didn't rub her all over as you say. I merely provided her with a cloth and warm water to clean her own wounds. We had no idea how badly injured she was."

"And I have no idea how she got injured as she did. She was alright when I left her this morning and I get back and find you two here and her all bloodied."

"Ask her," instructed John.

Mary looked frightened and said nothing.

"I already have. You had better get on your way college boy and stop asking stupid questions about things that don't concern you."

John Prideaux decided that this was probably good advice and caught up with Anne who was walking quickly away. There was proper summer rain now, not a mizzle drizzle. The precipitation meant that all the hedge branches were dropping down and almost meeting in the middle. His clothes were soaking wet as he pushed his way through. Anne didn't seem bothered and John noticed that the dress she wore seemed to repel the water. That didn't seem normal. By the time they got to the end of the track and were back on the street, John was soaking wet and Anne looked every inch the young lady.

That can't be right.

As they made their way back to the Rectory, John was wondering if he was wishing himself into a proper illness. Anne seemed to notice his discomfort and said, "Have a drink of this." She handed him a flask containing an orange liquid. John wrinkled his nose.

"Don't worry, John. Nothing menacing. Just some mead I carry it around with me in case I am feeling faint. Look, I'm drinking some. It's quite safe."

"It's not that, I just..." He felt stupid and took the flask from her and took a swig. It tasted nice and he quickly felt better.

"What was that story about you and the dead Gregory men?" he asked.

"Richard Gregory had taken a fancy to me and used to follow me about the place when I walked. I gave him no encouragement, but he persisted. My father caught him once and threatened him if he did not leave me alone. "

"Did he leave you alone?"

"I'm capable of looking after myself, John Prideaux. "

She smiled prettily at him and John thought how much older than her age she acted.

"I'm going home first," Anne informed him. "I don't want to be seen with you. I don't want to start another fight."

Without waiting for his answer, she swept away from him. John decided to walk on past the end of the High Street and perhaps visit the church to ensure that he did not meet any Gunters. No, he didn't fancy that.

It was almost dark now and John longed for the sanctity of the church. After seeing so many people who were less than wholesome, he wanted to have a few private words with his God. As he made his way to the church gate, he passed the gate in the wall of the Rectory. He found himself tiptoeing past this doorway to the rectory garden, perhaps in case someone waiting for him the other side would hear him.

He left the street and walked through the church gate. From there he was soon in the little church and he immediately felt calmer. He felt colder from the damp of his clothes, but he walked to the altar and the soft candlelight and forgot all his troubles at once. He took out his Bible and made himself comfortable at the front of the Church.

He was still here when the birds woke up at dawn the next morning. He was lying on the front pew and was covered with blanket. He got up quickly, bowed reverently to the altar and left by the side door. There was no one about in the churchyard, or on the track beyond. He thought quickly about whether to leave by the front, walk down the street and appear up the Rectory drive, or go through the churchyard and kitchen garden. He chose the latter and was glad of it as he could see Sarah busying herself in the kitchen. Hopefully he would be given a warm drink and some food.

CHAPTER ELEVEN

"We are very impressed that you have taken your Holy Orders, John." said Anne Gunter.

They were having lunch at the Holland lodgings at Exeter College in Oxford. Although this event was generally a regular and sedate occasion, today's party was full of gossip and news. As the years progressed, John Prideaux spent a lot of time with the Hollands and by default the Gunters. Once she reached 16, Anne was allowed into Oxford to visit her sister and often helped her with the children. Anne didn't particularly like children, but found that it was a good excuse to stay in Oxford. She loved the colleges and the houses and the clever people who arrived at the Holland rooms and talked about subjects of which she had little understanding. She loved the countryside and the city walls and the gates and the churches.

She found however, that she was gradually becoming more knowledgeable. At home she could learn about herbs and flowers and sewing and music. And the extra skills her mother and her friends taught her. In Oxford she learned about politics and philosophy and the law. She liked John Prideaux. He was kind and friendly and didn't treat her differently to the men. And he was moving upwards in Oxford society and Anne approved of that. He would make a good husband.

Whether John was aware or not of her intentions, he did not let on and continued to act as if she were a sister.

"It's good news for us all," acknowledged Thomas Holland. He was very pleased with his protégée and he and Dr. Helme had high hopes of the young man. In these turbulent political times, it was good to have someone close who they had trained themselves.

"I am honoured and proud to have received my Masters and then to be accepted by the Church," said John.

"What did your parents and family say when you visited them this summer?" asked Anne.

"They were most pleased and insisted that we went to Harford Church, a lot, so we could thank God for everything!"

"They would have been happy to hear all the news from London and Oxford. Did you tell them about the Coronation?" asked Anne. The rest of the company were used to the constant questions from Anne and cared not in the least.

"I did indeed. My family were great supporters of our Queen and interested to see that we now have a Scotsman on the throne." He did not feel it appropriate to add that they did not approve of the Scotsman on the English throne.

"You left soon afterwards, didn't you?"

"And returned only yesterday. So much of the month is spent in travelling there and back, but I recover very quickly."

"You didn't walk this time?" asked Anne.

"No! I haven't walked the journey since I arrived here six years ago. Do you know that I keep those leather clothes I first had, in my cupboard? At the back, but if I am ever feeling too proud of myself I go and look at them and remember how difficult it was for me to get here."

"That is nice to hear. You are not from a humble background, but like to portray that you are," noted Holland.

"I don't think it really matters where a person comes from. On my way home this time, I travelled through Ashburton where I went to school. I stopped at the Exeter Inn and heard the tale of how Raleigh was arrested there, just before the Coronation. The townspeople were most upset about it," said John.

"It has been the fate of many well connected men to end their lives in disgrace," noted Susan Holland.

"Some quite unnecessarily," said John.

"The old Queen was in love with Raleigh and was furious when she found out he had married without her permission," said Susan Holland.

"Don't gossip about things you know nothing about," retorted her husband.

His wife glared at him, embarrassed that yet again he was rebuking her in public. It was so unnecessary and unfair. She didn't gossip, she only quoted things her friends told her.

She said petulantly, "I know someone who knows Raleigh's wife and she has given me the information and what's more, many of the public knew it too!"

A maidservant entered the room, bobbed a curtsey and handed a note to Thomas Holland. He read it and his face altered.

"This is terrible news," he announced, unusually animated.

"What has happened?" asked Susan.

"There is plague in North Moreton," he said. "It's at the Adams' house."

Anne and Susan looked at each other and Anne said, "Oh no! Are we to go home and warn the family?"

"Don't be stupid Anne, if we go home now, we shall put ourselves in danger. We must stay here until it is all over," said Susan.

"Here in Oxford?" she answered.

"Yes indeed. You will have to stay here."

"The rest of your family are making their way here too," said Thomas. He sounded dejected.

"Well they can't all stay here!" said Susan with feeling. Her father and two brothers drinking and carousing around the house would be beyond endurance.

"No indeed not. Perhaps they will stay in lodgings elsewhere." Thomas was thinking of his studying and did not want to be upset for weeks on end.

There followed several hours of shouting, beds being made and moved around and orders given to the kitchen to arrange for increased supplies and extra linen. Susan reflected and decided that they should fill their larders in case the plague reached Oxford too. She had dreadful fear and anticipation of four extra mouths to feed for months on end.

Two days later, their parents were installed at the Holland residence and William and Harvey at friends. The Holland house was now a very crowded one. At lunch, when everyone was settled in, Brian regaled them with the latest news from North Moreton.

"It seems that some wretched boy called at the Adams' house for food or something. I'm always telling everyone to leave these dreadful people alone. Let them starve. But no, they decided to feed him and it turns out that he had the plague. Caught it on his travels and now they've all got it at the house. Old Robert Adams won't survive they say, he was hit badly."

"That's truly dreadful," said Anne.

"Well that's not the end of it. Two sons and three grandsons have got it and his wife. One of the servants is dead already, the stupid maid who fed him and the other servants are sick too. They aren't allowed out and food is put by the door," said Brian.

"They had to sign a document swearing that they would pay for everything they are being supplied with. Their land is already going to rack and ruin and they've only been sick for a week," added Mistress Gunter.

"Who is looking after the Rectory and its interests, mother?" asked Anne.

"I left the maids in charge of the house and the men are carrying on with the farm and the grounds. Anyone who doesn't will face losing their places."

"Well done father. But, I hope this bout of plague doesn't last too long," said Susan.

"Had enough of us already?"

"Of course not father! You may stay here as long as you want."

Anne stared at her parents and felt confused. She had expected to go back to her home and now she was to stay in Oxford. That was good, but she didn't want her parents here, checking on her movements. When alone she could talk to John Prideaux and the others she had befriended, with little interference. Her father would not allow anyone near her. This plague could last for months and months and that would limit her a lot. She had high hopes of making a good match and being able to leave her family once and for all. A match that even her bullying father could not disapprove of. He would marry her to the man who could supply him with more business opportunities, whether he was nice or not. This plague had not been in her plan. She must think.

"I am feeling a little unwell," she announced. "May I leave the table, father?"

He stared at her and said, "No, you must stay."

Her sister interfered and said, "Father, this table is run by my husband. Should he not decide whether Anne may leave or not?"

This was difficult. An awkward silence followed while the matter was considered by both Thomas and Brian.

"Perhaps you should remain at the table until everyone has finished their meal," said Thomas. He thought that if he must entertain his father in law for several weeks, they ought to begin calmly. He didn't want to argue with him. As it was, he had to endure scowling from Anne and his wife glaring at him.

Anne resolved to think through her problems while she was being forced to sit and stay. Honed from her childhood was her skill of withdrawing completely from the situation she was in. She thought about her friend John Prideaux. She had decided to marry him, noting that her sister Susan was quite happy in her marriage. A learned man seemed to be content to leave his wife alone, while he performed his college and religious duties. The trouble was that John did not seem too keen on marriage just yet. He told her stories of how ambitious he was and a family would only hold him back. He was certainly making substantial connections the longer he was in Oxford. Sometimes she would tease him about how they first met and how innocent he was. He would remind her about what a child she had been and what a little lady she had considered herself now.

Neither mentioned her father and the abuse she had suffered at his hands.

If John lived at North Moreton or she lived permanently in Oxford, she would be quite happy to sit and be his friend until he felt ready to settle down. He would be in her social circle and she could ensure that no other woman could catch him. But these latest developments were putting the anchor on that idea. Her father would slow up her game. She needed to find some way that she could get his attention. Not just his attention, but his academic interest too. Yes, a way would have to be found.

Turning her attention back to the room, Anne realised that she was on her own. Her family had left and the table was being cleared away by the maids.

"Where is everyone, Mary?" she asked.

"Mistress, everyone left a little while ago. You were asleep, so they told us to clear away so long as we didn't disturb you. Was that alright Mistress?"

"Yes Mary. Absolutely fine."

Anne got up from her chair and swished out of the room. So she had gone into one of her trances again. She needed to be careful about that.

The hallway was silent and she stopped another maid and asked, "Where is my father?"

"He went out Mistress and he said he wouldn't be back until late. The master has left too and the others are in their rooms."

"Thank you," said Anne and opening the front door, she crossed the grass and went into the street through the college gate.

This summer afternoon the streets were still busy from the market and Anne could lose herself amongst the crowds. She wanted to walk outside the walls and into the lanes beyond. She thought vaguely about the anonymous people who walked towards her and how they knew nothing of what went on in her mind. And equally, how was she to know which one of these travellers, poor and rich alike could be carrying the germ of the plague? It had reached North Moreton so quickly after London and she had heard such dreadful stories of the deaths from its last visit. But to be honest she didn't intend to catch any illness, she was a healthy girl and intended to stay that way. No, she was certainly not going to worry about it.

But in spite of these thoughts, she did move more quickly and tried as best she could to keep her skirts near to her so that they touched people as infrequently as possible. She didn't like people and their thoughts, never mind their germs. Sometimes if she touched people she could feel as they felt and heard their thoughts. That was unpleasant to her. She knew when her father intended to beat her, hours before he actually did. She heard his mind beginning to get angry and knew exactly what would be coming next.

Then, as if she had been creating his bodily form, Anne noticed her father talking to someone alongside the walls at the turnstile. They were in deep conversation and Anne could see that her father was angry. She wished that she had worn her cloak so that she could hide her face from recognition. But she hadn't and her father looked up as she approached them. His face reverted to its well-recognised purple colour and he growled, "What are you doing out of the house without a maid or your mother?"

As she often went out on her own, she wondered why he was making this accusation and assumed that it were to impress the man he argued with.

"I am only taking the air, father," she answered quietly. "I was feeling unwell after lunch and wanted to walk in the woods and by the river so that I could regain my health."

"Always walking, always out of the house!" he answered impatiently. "We must find you a husband who will put you to sit."

His companion had noted the lovely young woman and saw his chance.

"This is your daughter?" he asked. "Please, introduce us!"

Brian held his temper and said, "Master Field, I wish to introduce you to my daughter Anne. She is 19 years old and a credit to our family. Anne, this gentleman is a close relative of the Field family at North Moreton."

Anne bobbed a little curtsey. "I am pleased to meet you sir. Do you live here in Oxford?"

"For some of the time, Mistress Gunter. I mainly stay in London," he added.

"I hear there is plague there too," commented Anne, realising immediately that was probably not the best thing to say to a stranger.

"There is a lot of plague there, Mistress Gunter and many people are dying. I do not intend to go back yet awhile. I am sorry that it has reached your village and I hope that your family is safe."

Anne nodded at him and started to walk away.

"Where are you going Anne?" asked her father.

"For my walk, father. I always walk."

"Not now you don't. Get back home and wait for me there."

"Do you mean North Moreton, father?"

His face almost turned black and he said, "You know exactly what I mean Anne. Do as you are told before I slap you."

She curtsied and turned for home. Richard Field smiled and winked and she blushed. Men found her attractive, she could tell and she meant to use that to her advantage. Her father would want to gain in some way or other from her marriage and she dreaded what sort of man he would try and line her up with.

She walked away from the Turl and turned towards the North Gate. It would be busier there by the church and so perhaps she could lose herself. As she arrived at the church she bumped into John Prideaux. He was dressed in attire befitting his new position and he looked quite bewitching.

"Hello again Anne! What are you up to?"

"I was out walking John. I was going to go to out into the countryside but saw my father and some man and he told me to go home."

"Are you going home?"

"What do you think?" she asked.

"I expect you are going any place other than home. Would you like to walk with me? I have to take some papers to Lincoln."

"Yes please," she answered and turned on her heels again in order to accompany him.

"My father was talking to Richard Field over by the twirling gate and they were arguing. My father was cross that their talk had been interrupted."

"I hear that your family are keen to build some houses on land outside the wall."

"I know that he bought some land with cottages and he wants to knock them down and build bigger houses, but are you saying he wants to build on other land?"

"So I hear. He won't be allowed to just knock places down as he feels like it," said John.

"Not unless he makes the right contacts," answered Anne. "He generally does, when he wants to do something."

"His deeds will catch up with him Anne. They catch up with us all eventually."

"My father's deeds are going to catch up with us?"

"You know exactly what I mean Anne Gunter. We must be careful and watchful of everything we do."

"I thought we need to be careful of everything we think," said Anne.

"Our Lord always provides everything we ask of him."

"Whether we do it through a priest or from our own mind?"

"He is capable of hearing us wherever we ask."

They walked slowly down the street and John regularly nodded to acquaintances of his.

"So my father will get his way?" asked Anne.

"It's more complicated than that," he answered. "In order to get his way, he wants others to lose out. So eventually, one way or another, he will lose out too."

Anne considered this point and said, "He is thinking again about marrying me off to one of his business partners and the thought of that scares me."

John didn't answer immediately. He knew that Anne liked him, but he couldn't see her in that way. He saw her as a sister, not a wife. Her family were trouble and if it wasn't for Thomas Holland, he wouldn't be anywhere near them.

"I'm sure that everything will work out in the end," he answered consolingly. Although now a priest, he wanted people to know that they could sort out their own problems through God and not expect the priest to do it for them.

"Then I will do something for myself," she answered. "I will make happen what I want to happen."

Anne had stopped in her tracks and John felt awkward carrying on with his mission. But standing here while she scowled, made it appear as though they were having a liaison. It really wouldn't do.

"I must make my appointment now Anne, I'm afraid. I am late already."

Anne felt the situation moving away from her, but she said, "Goodbye John." and she walked away. She decided to walk towards the ruins of Oseney Abbey and stare at it for a while. She found that to be meditative and relaxing. As she walked, she prayed steadily that she would be rewarded very soon with John as her husband and her father to die or at least be shamed and lose his status.

As it was, Anne was arrested from her prayers when someone grabbed her arm firmly and a familiar voice growled, "Home, I told you. Why are you here? Are you meeting someone?"

"No, father. Not at all. I was walking and I bumped into our friend John Prideaux and walked and talked with him a way."

"Our friend? I don't know that he is our friend. He may be Holland's friend, but he isn't mine."

"I hear that Master Prideaux is close to the King," she said.

If she had wanted to raise the interest of her father in her target husband, then her comment worked perfectly. Brian Gunter kept hold of her arm and marched her back to the Holland's. Once there he pushed his way past the maid, who was trying in vain to answer the door in the manner she had been taught by her mistress.

"Susan! Susan! Come down here now!" he shouted up stairs.

Susan's flushed face appeared at the top of the stairs.

"What has happened father? Is it Thomas? Not one of the children?"

"What are you talking about woman? No one cares about the children. Now, is it true that this Reverend Prideaux is close to the King?"

Susan stared at Anne, who shrugged her shoulders as if resolving herself of any responsibility of the news leak.

"I'm not sure. You will have to ask my husband about that. What does it matter?"

"Stupid woman, of course it matters. Connections are everything in this modern age and I have worked very hard at making sure I have the best connections. It's because of that, you ungrateful lot have fine houses and clothes and much money. Now, invite that Prideaux man round for dinner. I have plans for him. Anne, go to your room and brighten yourself up. You look like a street girl with your hair all over the place."

Anne ran up the stairs grinning. Her sister followed her into her bedroom and said, "What have you been telling him? I know you are after that priest, but don't drag my husband into trouble."

"How have I done that?"

"If father starts telling everyone about the King thing, they will ask who told him. Then he will say you and you will say me and I will have to say that Thomas told me. So don't tell father it was me, or I shall tell him things about you."

"What sort of things? I don't get up to anything. I am almost twenty years old and nothing has happened to me. No husband on the horizon and no future planned."

"But you have had plenty of scandals haven't you?"

"Scandals? No!"

"What about the Gregory men? You led them a merry dance, chatting with one and then the other. Skipping along in front of them making sure your breasts jumping about and almost fell out."

"Don't be so rude!" objected Anne.

"You made sure that your bodice laces weren't done up tight enough and then you ran along the street playing the little girl. Why were you surprised that men looked at you? You did it on purpose!"

"You are disgusting Susan. I lace up my dress tightly. If it comes undone, it does so of its own accord."

Susan grabbed hold of Anne's bodice and twisted it tightly.

"I don't expect for one minute that father will believe that and you won't want me to tell him. So don't gossip about my husband and John Prideaux. I am not ruining my life for you or anyone else."

Anne, used to violence, was not impressed and twisted her sister's wrist until she let go.

"Then help me catch this priest, sister."

CHAPTER TWELVE

Anne looked out of the window at the students making their way in and out of Exeter College. There had been very few people around the colleges these past few months. After the plague spread from London, anyone who had anywhere else to go left to join families who lived where there was no disease. And because this happened all over the country, the plague itself was spread even further. Many had returned to their homes in the West Country.

John Prideaux was among the escapees there.

Now, as the winter was nearing its end and reports of deaths abating, the students and the great and the good were beginning to return to Oxford.

There was still no sign of John however and lately she feared that he may never return. She knew that he would want to come back to Oxford to pursue his career. But she dreaded that he had been persuaded to stay in Devon or worse, had become ill. This plague had meant that her scheme with regard to marriage had been sadly delayed. Her father was more interested in preserving an increase in his business interests by buying up cheap property and tithes where plague had brought various families to their knees.

Anne had been left in Oxford with her sister, mother and Thomas and the children. They remained within the confines of the college and food was brought to them.

They were safe and well, but bored and extremely stressed from lack of exercise and diversion.

They heard that 30000 people had been killed in London these past six months and thousands more in Oxford and elsewhere. In North Moreton, many dear friends and neighbours had lost their lives. Most of the Adams family and their servants were dead and the poor vicar, Gilbert Bradshawe had lost his wife and his three children. He had spent a good part of his time helping people around the village and all the time his family had suffered and died alone.

All those petty neighbourhood arguments no longer mattered, for God had sorted it out. Though Anne was at a loss to understand what sort of God would allow this to happen. She would dearly have liked to speak to John about it. He would make sense of the problem.

Now, the students were slowly returning to the colleges of Oxford and gradually day by day the streets were filling up with people. Anne was desperate to go out, but was under strict instructions that if she did, she was not to return to the Holland house. There was to be no plague here.

She had not missed her father or her brothers. That was one blessing from the whole experience. There had been no male Gunters drunk, argumentative and shouting. Even Susan had been relatively calm when not nudged into arguments by her brothers. Her mother spent most of the time talking about how dreadful it all was and the world was coming to an end and if they did not pray constantly they would all die. Lately, mother had been crediting herself and her potions, with keeping them all alive.

Perhaps she was right. Perhaps God had decided to save the Gunter family because they were special and he had work for them to do. That seemed highly unlikely. Unless of course, Satan was now in charge. Since their self-imposed quarantine, Anne had suffered no trances, no out of body experiences and no insights into other people's minds. Perhaps if Satan was running the world now, he didn't need to make her suffer in that way.

So without her guide John Prideaux, Anne read books brought from home and pamphlets and books she found around the Holland library. She understood and enjoyed them all and secretly wished that she could be allowed to study here at Exeter College. Instead she was more determined than ever to marry a learned man who was preferably John Prideaux. She would make him help her to learn. She took another drink from the flask her mother had given her.

Some of the young students looked at Anne and smiled and winked. They could not fail to notice the pretty young woman who appeared constantly at Dr Holland's residence. More than one of them would have liked to know her better, but the chances of that were slim to none. Anne showed no interest in any of them.

She dared to open the window a little, finding it stiff from lack of use throughout the winter and horribly covered in spiders and cobwebs. She leaned out and took in a deep breath. Oh how she missed the walks and the river and the freedom. She closed her eyes and breathed in deeply. Her fingers stroked the rough stone under the windows and for a moment she was lost in her daydreams.

"Hello Mistress Gunter! Fast asleep are you?"

Her eyes opened wide and she said with no decorum, "John. Oh John! I have missed you so!"

He beamed at her and said, "I have missed you too Anne. How are you and all the family?"

"We are all well John. A lot of people have died, but we are all safe. What about your family?"

"They are well. Our town has avoided the plague but several people I know have suffered. It has been a terrible time, but I think the worst of it is over now."

"So long as someone doesn't spread it again. That's the trouble. It only needs one person to keep it in their body for a bit longer than the others and they can re-infect people with it later on. But we don't feed waifs and strays at the doors anymore and will no longer talk to dirty, common people."

John laughed, "Well I hope that keeps you safe Anne. But a lot of rich and important people have died these past few months you know."

"Only because of the dirty, common people starting it," she reasoned.

"Well, perhaps so. Now, I have a lot of catching up to do."

"Are you behind in your studies John?"

"No, not really. I studied a lot at Stowford."

He rubbed her head, as he would a little girl and said, "See you soon, Anne Gunter."

She watched him walk away from her, even going so far as to lean out of the window so that her eyes could follow him around the corner. Anne knew that she was still in love with the Prideaux priest and as she closed the window, she thought up a scheme to catch him. And this time she meant business.

John Prideaux swept through the courtyard towards the main hall. He had missed Exeter so much and felt his heart lift when the city walls had come into view on his way back. After his trip back to Stowford House, he realised that he now considered Oxford his home. He felt like skipping all the way through town and up Turl Street. When he saw Anne Gunter he was filled with the happiness and excitement of seeing her healthy.

Stowford was exactly the same as he remembered it. His brothers and sisters were always so pleased to see him and would stop their jobs as soon as they saw him arrive. On the ride across country, the roads and villages had been much quieter and there had been little or no chance of obtaining food and lodgings anywhere. His servant swapped horses at the usual stops, but they had laden the carriage with food at Oxford and hidden wine in crates under the seats. He took a decent amount of money and several presents with him which he intended to give to his parents. They had the big house and the farm and its lands, but the years of bad harvests and the subsequent poverty of their neighbours had meant that there was less money around in that area.

His elder brother Thomas would be taking over Stowford when their father died, but currently lived at Church house by the Ivybridge since his marriage to Blanche. It was here that he always made his first and last sighting of his Prideaux family. The family sat on the bridge and waved him off on that first day, seven years ago and on every visit since.

It was early in October that his carriage pulled up outside these familiar houses and John got out. He walked around Church house to the back. He waved to the wife of his father's cowman who lived in the cottage next door. This was also under the tenancy of Stowford House.

Blanche Prideaux was pleased to see her brother in law and embraced him heartily.

"We are so pleased to see you John!"

As she held his arms and stepped back from him, he noticed that she was with child.

"Showing a bit since your summer visit isn't it? We are happy to announce that an heir will arrive in the New Year!"

They embraced again and Blanche asked, "Do you want tea and cake? Or anything stronger?"

"I would like to freshen up and then I shall go straight to Stowford to see my parents. Would you like to come up in the carriage with me?"

"Yes I would! It's not too wide for the lane is it?"

"No, it will get as far as the house but won't get me to church. We have scraped through some very narrow roads on the way down here," he laughed.

"That's a shame. Agnes would like to ride to Harford Church in that carriage."

John considered the carriage to be nothing more than a fancy cart, but he had been living in Oxford for a while now and had different expectations to his family. Narrowly missing the banked sides of the lane and the tall hedgerows, John and Blanche clattered into the winding driveway of Stowford House. Dogs started barking as soon as the wheels touched the cobbles and by the time they reached the front of the house, most of the occupants were standing at the front.

His mother was one of the first out and she beamed when she saw him.

"We got your letter only yesterday and have been looking out for you. You are quite well and safe John?"

"Quite well mother. The plague has not touched me and we have seen no sickness on our journey here. Now, my driver Philip is also my servant and will need a place to stay."

Agnes nodded at the servant and he smiled back.

"Servant, John?"

"And bodyguard. He's a good man and necessary these days."

"Well I am glad he is here to help you," said his mother.

"Unload the bags and take the horses to the farm would you please?" instructed John.

This done, John and his brothers helped carry the luggage into the house. They were happy to note that there were trunks in addition to his luggage and that could only mean presents. They lived in a beautiful house and were a very privileged family, with a good name and connections. But they all loved the things that John brought back with him every time he returned. John Prideaux was very generous to his family and they loved him for it.

"Have you got rocks in these trunks, John?" asked Thomas.

"Yes, special Oxford rocks. I thought you would all like one for Christmas," he said.

They laughed and allowed John to supervise which trunks would go up to his room and which would go into the kitchen.

"Food for John," said his mother and she began preparing it, while shouting instructions at the maids.

It wasn't long before his father, also named John, came into the kitchen. He had been summoned by one of the men when the carriage arrived.

"Are you all alright John? We have been very worried about you with all that sickness up there in Oxford. I see you have brought a man with you, he hasn't got any disease has he?"

"No, father. We are both quite well and haven't had any contact with any plague victims. Apart from changing horses, we had no contact with anyone on the way down." He did not like to tell them about the people they saw around Oxford who obviously had the sickness and wandered around the roads, raising their arms and begging for help. He knew of some travellers who had run these people through with swords and left them for dead. Better than them infecting healthy people, they would say. There was a valid argument that to die by the sword was better than dying by plague, a dreadful and cruel way to go. As it was, he and his servant Philip had galloped the horses past and tried not to listen to the cries of the women and children. They knew that someone from their own village would deal with the sick people, one way or another.

Whenever they could, they ran the horses and carriage through water in order that the wheels would be cleaned. They hoped that the water would not affect any people who would later drink from it. They had seen no sick people since reaching Devon and John felt safe in telling his family that they were free from infection.

"I am glad to hear that my boy, we have not been travelling to the markets or to visit our family and friends lately. There will be some people who won't be happy that you have travelled here as it is."

Agnes glared at her husband, for although she knew that what he said was true, she didn't like him telling John. She was proud of her son and his achievements and relished the little time he now spent with his family.

Her husband bridled and said, "Not that they would say that to me. I would tell them straight." He too was incredibly proud of his academic son. He was proud of all his children for their different skills and loved them all. Their first son John had lived only a few weeks and he and his wife suffered greatly at his sudden and unexplained death. A local wise woman said that this boy would return to them a few years later and they would know because of his smile soon after he was born. She also said that his hands would be held together in prayer. They listened to her but thought nothing more of it until John was born in apparent prayer, hands together and eyes closed.

John had taken the decision to name his eldest after Sir Thomas Williams who had sold them the lands here at Stowford. It was lucky that Thomas was also the name of various Prideaux uncles and cousins. They named the next boy Johan after his maternal grandfather and the next Henry after another paternal uncle. A daughter named after her mother was born before the second John arrived. The following five surviving children were named after another maternal uncle and various members of the family. They had seen two further children into the world, but they had died soon after birth. It had been thought that Henry would also die, but he had rallied and survived, although he did not have the mental abilities of the other children. He was a little slow, but kind and was also the most handsome of the family.

John and Agnes were proud of their family and excited about the prospect of the new arrival for Thomas and Blanche and now John was home, life was splendid.

"I may be staying here for a few weeks I'm afraid," he informed his father.

"That's fine son, we shall be glad to have you here. There is plenty of work to be done and we can always do with an extra pair of hands."

"I was rather hoping to continue with my studies," said John.

His father pulled a face and his brother Thomas did too. They loved having John here for visits and holidays, but really he must be prepared to help around the farm if he was staying here for such a long time. No one here had time to wait on him.

Agnes said, "I'm sure that John will be helping wherever he can."

The Reverend John suddenly became aware that he was the centre of silent attention and looked up.

"Of course I shall be helping on the farm!" he said. "I shall continue with my studies in my own time. Now where are my trunks? Let's look inside them, Elizabeth," he said to his youngest sister.

He handed a purse of money to his mother and said, "I'm sure that you can find a use for this mother."

Agnes took the leather purse from her son and made it disappear amongst her clothes. The other trunks were opened and on the kitchen table they piled wine, cloth, a large quantity of candles and a big leather Bible.

"I thought you might like this, father. It was printed in Oxford," he said as he handed it to him.

"Thank you son," he answered and he moved his hand lovingly over the beautiful book.

"Please share the gifts around the family as you see fit mother," he said.

So it was done.

Christmas was an extra special occasion that year. It was in styled in honour of the old Queen, certainly no one yet cared about the new King and the Prideaux and the Williams family at the Manor had plenty to remember about her. The lands upon which they lived and farmed had been sold by her, to Thomas Williams in recognition of his support.

An oak tree stump had been dragged by oxen to the house earlier in the year. It had dried out nicely and on Christmas Eve each sat upon it and told a story about either the old Queen or a ghost. There were memories of seeing the navy at Plymouth and the Armada and the beacons that were lit to warn of its approach. John told a story about the Queen which one of the porters at the college had told him about her visit there. After the stories, the log was lit and as the fire roared, they ate and drank and danced and sang. The house was decorated inside and out with holly and ivy and any greenery they found. Candles hung amongst the boughs and candied peel and pine cones added to the scents. They ate goose and cream and cakes and pies. Neighbours arrived and left and it was wonderful.

The plague had apparently reached Exeter, but never Stowford and the Prideauxs on the whole, remained safe. They lost a few cousins and there was sadness for that.

The tales were terrible, with plenty of stories about murders occurring all over the land as people became scared of catching the plague. Some took the opportunity to sort out old feuds by stabbing, hanging and battering anyone they believed to be spreading the plague. Or they said that they were.

Some Puritans were saying that the plague was God's punishment for worshipping ritual instead of the Lord. But many of them died too. Sometimes John preached at Harford Church, where even the cold and the damp which came straight from the moor and in through the church door, could not curb his enthusiasm when he preached God's word.

John Prideaux believed.

He really believed.

Not because his mother was a pious woman, but because his studies at Oxford had made him realise that a man was in charge of his own redemption and everything he thought and did had a consequence. He felt that the Bible was the handbook of freedom and as he spoke to the congregation, he made them believe it too. Until of course, they walked outside and gossiped with their neighbours and forgot the sermon during their journey home.

The longer John remained in Stowford, the more his family saw how much he had changed. Those short visits had not let them realise that fact, as much as this one had. Their son and brother was a special man, but a changed one. When he left in March, there was much sadness. His servant had made a friendship with one of the girls in the village and had made promises to return. He had no intention of so doing.

John had been receiving attentions from Mary Dawe, the elder sister of Arthur who had married his sister Agnes. He wasn't interested in a marriage to a homely girl with ambitions of babies and a regular day.

He wanted a girl with spirit, wit and brains.

Johns mind had been turning to Anne Gunter a lot lately.

On his last day, John enjoyed the familiar routine of his entire family coming to the bridge at the junction of the Harford road and the Exeter road to wave him off. His mother cried and his father looked serious, but smiled. His brothers waved and his sisters sobbed. The only difference on each visit was the increasing quality of his clothes and transport.

"You have a nice family sir," said Philip.

"I do have a nice family, thank you Philip. I shall miss them, but we must return to Oxford."

"At least this time we won't have scary, half dead people trying to get into the carriage."

"No Philip. We do have our blades available ready in case of attack, though."

"Yes we do sir. I shall use mine if necessary."

But it wasn't necessary. They were bothered by no one. March was kind this year and the wildflowers waved in the hedgerows and the leaves were already beginning to unfurl. Birds twittered and John noticed men and women working in the fields.

Yes, God was back in his heaven and England could begin to grow again.

It looked like 1604 would be a good year.

CHAPTER THIRTEEN

"You are looking pleased with yourself," said Susan Holland to her sister.

"John Prideaux is back," Anne answered simply.

"And if you are going to catch him," said Susan. "You will have to get father onside. How do you intend to make that happen?"

"I will find a way," Anne answered. "I will make such a nuisance of myself that he will be glad to get rid of me."

"Well you will get your first chance this afternoon. They are all coming for dinner."

Anne smiled and rubbed her hands together with excitement. She must strike soon, before John got his feet under another Oxford table.

At dinner there was constant noise because the entire family were present. Everyone talked about their own experiences of the plague and their problems. There was plenty of gossip and Anne was finding it difficult to bring her own subject to the table. Susan seemed to realise her difficulty and said, "Anne saw John Prideaux today."

Brian Gunter held the roast chicken he was devouring in front of his mouth. Fat dripped from his chin and down the front of his clothes.

"John Prideaux is it? Back from Devon. He has met the King, hasn't he Thomas?"

"No idea, but I am going to ask him to help with the new Bible. We have already been given our portion to do and I think he will be invaluable in the new translation. John is a good man, Brian."

Brian Gunter put the chicken onto his plate and wiped his face with the back of his hand. Anne watched his expression and his continued silence began to attract attention from the rest of the table. By the time he spoke, the whole family were looking at Brian Gunter's face. Even the maids had stopped their busyness and waited for the big announcement which they felt sure would be happening at any moment.

"That's very interesting," he said and then with no hint of irony. "I have been thinking of going into printing, Thomas. You could pass the Bible job my way."

"I doubt that I will have any influence there at all, Brian. The King has his own ideas," answered Thomas. He hated it when Brian got a scheme into his head.

"Well you know the King, so you can talk to him on my behalf. You don't want the family to starve do you?"

These claims had no basis or foundation in reality, but that wasn't going to stop Brian. Amidst the mumblings of Thomas, Brian continued.

"So when are you seeing the King again? You will be talking about the translations, so you could bring it up then. Or you could talk to Helme and the others. I'm going to see a man about a press tomorrow."

The matter, apparently settled meant that the family could carry on with their meal. Anne did not and while pushing the food around her plate, pondered how she could bring the marriage question into the room. Whenever she felt anxious, food and drink began to make her feel nauseous.

She was feeling nauseous now.

"What's the matter with you girl? Always the pale face, are you getting your maiden's problems again?"

"Father!" she exclaimed helplessly.

"Master Gunter! There is no need to speak about such things!" warned his wife.

Brian did not look abashed, merely answered, "She is my daughter and I shall do as I please."

And he carried on eating.

Anne felt light headed now she was under threat from her father. No matter how brave she felt when he wasn't around, it still only took a few words from him before she was useless again.

"Got your heart set on this priest have you girl?"

"No father," replied Anne and wondered why she sounded so sulky.

"I think it would be nice to ask John Prideaux to dinner one evening this week. He can tell us about his trip to Devon and you can ask him about the new Bible," said Susan and she winked at her grateful sister.

"Get it done then," said Brian. "Now, you boys, I want to talk to you about some old gits who are refusing to pay their dues. We will take the men and make them pay. Just because a couple of them died of the plague, they think I should give them more time. Well we all lost family with the plague and I'm not asking for any favours am I?"

"We didn't lose anyone with the plague," said his wife, unusually brave due to the red wine she had been drinking.

He glared at her, but before he could answer, their son Harvey said, "Shut up mother. Women don't understand business, so keep your nose out."

With the rising tension in the room, Anne felt her nausea rise in sympathy and she held her hand in front of her mouth. She began to gag.

"Get out of the room," ordered her father. "Before you ruin our meal."

Anne ran out of the room and just made it into the hall before she threw up her meal. One of the maids looked at her in disgust.

"Clean that up Mary. Before my father sees it."

"Yes Mistress," bobbed Mary.

It was another week before John Prideaux was able to attend the Holland house. Although he and Holland worked together, the recent mass return to Oxford meant that there was a lot of catching up to do. He had attended meetings with many people. This day, he was telling the Gunters and Hollands about one of the meetings while at dinner with them.

"And you see Mistress Goodwin is the daughter of Dr Rowland Taylor...."

"Who is that?" asked Brian Gunter, already bored.

"The martyr, Dr Taylor! Surely sir, you have heard of his bravery?"

"No," answered Brian, hoping against forlorn hope that he would not have to hear about Dr Taylor's bravery.

John continued, "Even at his death he called over his wife and two of his children and gave them a very pretty speech about his faith in the Lord. Then they watched him burn as he prayed!"

Anne was a bit stunned and asked, "He made his children watch? Did he take long to die?"

"It took a great deal of time and in the end, an observer came forward and hit him over the head, cracking it open and ending his suffering."

"And his family saw that? Mistress Goodwin must be either a very strong person or an unfeeling one," commented Anne.

"Perhaps he didn't mean to kill him," said Brian.

"You mean like you, with the Gregory boy's?" asked Harvey.

"Exactly like the Gregory boys, I never meant to kill them."

"But kill them you did," said John, now peevish because no one was as enamoured as him about Mistress Goodwin.

He persisted, "and her daughter is as fair as she, although a little weak, she has been taught the stories of her grandfather's life and death."

"How old is their daughter?" asked Anne, suddenly alert. "Is she old enough to make sense of what she has learned?"

"I think so. In fact I know so. She is one year older than me. She has the sweet nature of a woman who truly believes in redemption and knows that her beloved grandfather is now with his Lord and awaits his family."

"Do you believe that only those who have suffered can find salvation?" asked Anne.

"I believe that suffering strengthens a person when they accept the Will of God," answered John.

"Absolute rubbish," shouted William Gunter, "I believe that God rewards those who look out for themselves. This Goodwin lot are probably nuts. Being made to watch that burning won't help!" He laughed at his joke, although no one else did.

"Do they live in Oxford?" said Anne. By now Susan Holland was watching her sister, noting that the questions, although seemingly innocent, were gaining information about John Prideaux's intentions towards this potential angel.

"No sadly, for I would like to speak more to Mistress Goodwin about her father. They spend a good deal of their time travelling between London and York due to Master Goodwin's commitments. They will be leaving again at the end of the week and I shan't have time to meet them before then."

"Oh dear. That must be quite upsetting for you," sympathised Anne.

Susan noticed her sister's wry smile.

"But they will be back in a month and we've arranged to meet for dinner and talk further."

When Susan looked up from her meal, she saw that Anne was no longer smiling.

During this little exchange, the other members of the party were talking amongst themselves. They had averted their attention from John, in the hope that he would soon shut up about the brave Dr Taylor and the wonderful Goodwin family.

"You see, he has gained his BD and DD and is at Christchurch, he is much older than me, more like my father's age, but you see he does have connections with the King. He was a sub-almoner to the late Queen," continued John, with his less than subtle name dropping.

This last comment brought some attention back to John, although he had no idea why that would be.

"Perhaps you should invite the Goodwin family over for dinner!" said Brian with blatant disregard for the fact that they house they stayed in and the table they ate from, belonged to Thomas Holland.

Thomas, who years ago had given up on being master of his own household when the Gunters were in residence, said helpfully, "I know William Goodwin and find him to be a genuinely kind and pious man. It is no surprise to me that his wife is from such good stock, nor that he has a daughter as good as you make her sound."

"So we may ask him here to dine with us?" asked John, forgetful that he was a guest also.

"I would be honoured to have him eat with us. I have dined with him several times on college business," said Thomas.

Susan Holland, now aware that her sister was shifting in her seat asked, "It seems from what John tells us, that the Goodwins are leaving Oxford for a while? Is that not correct?"

"It is true, but they will be back soon and I'm sure we can arrange something then," answered Thomas.

Anne raised her head and flicked her eyes gratefully at her sister. For once they were working in sisterly union.

"Then we must invite them here and see these wonderful people in the flesh!" said Susan enthusiastically. "and we shall discover what wiles this girl is using and stop her," she said in an aside to Anne.

Anne smiled.

"Do you remember when Mistress Gregory worked for us?"

"I do," answered Susan. "She doesn't anymore though."

"No, but she taught me some things when she was here," whispered Anne.

"Like what?" asked Susan.

"Like ways to make people do what you want."

The two women jumped up from their chairs as Brian bellowed across the table, "What sort of wench scheming is going on over there?"

"Nothing father!" said Susan and Anne together.

"Better not be," he warned. "I have got enough trouble with your mother!"

Mistress Gunter stared at her husband after this unsolicited assault, but decided to ignore it as it was not the first time it had happened. Anne put her napkin to her mouth and told Susan to meet her in her bedroom later. Her sister smiled, nodded and agreed.

Anne smiled at John and tried to engage his attention several times, but he remained in deep conversation with Thomas Holland. He eventually left at almost midnight without Anne making any headway with him at all.

When she and Susan talked in Anne's room when everyone else had gone to bed, they felt closer than they had since they were children. Tucked up in the small bed with candles burning in holders on the table, they nibbled some sweet biscuits taken from the kitchen.

"So what do you want to tell me about Ma Gregory?" asked Susan.

"She told me she was a witch," answered Anne.

"A witch?"

"Yes!"

"I thought Pepwell was a witch, not Elizabeth Gregory."

"I'm just saying what she told me, but I did see her do some things which made her look like a witch," said Anne.

"What sort of things?"

"She mixed up potions and made little figures," Anne answered shyly.

"You never mentioned that before."

"No. I didn't."

"Father will be furious."

"Are you going to tell him?"

"Probably not," answered Susan.

The two women lay quietly side by side until Susan broke the silence.

"Did she teach you anything?"

Anne finished her biscuit and lay down a little further in the bed.

"Of course," she answered.

"Then tell me. I want to know."

"She taught me how to mix certain herbs that make people sick or tell the truth or do what you want."

Susan turned onto her stomach and said quietly, "Did she tell you about potions that - you know?"

"What?" asked Anne, although she guessed that she probably did know what her sister meant.

"Potions that could make men fall in love with you and the potions that make them want to lay with you all the time?"

"She told me about the love potions, but the other one? She said that was for married women."

"I wouldn't mind knowing the recipe. Thomas is so academic these days and has little appetite for fornication. I shall have to choose a young lover from the boys in the college," mused Susan.

"Susan! What about the children?"

"The children? What about them? The maids take care of them. It's the easiest thing in the world to turn out a child. I have no idea where this idea that they are special comes from. Thomas just keeps giving me 'another little gift from God' and that's it. Now we have so many, he says that we should refrain from our marital obligations as there is not enough money to feed any more. But I've heard that there are ways that you can enjoy yourself, without a gift from God."

"Susan, you are terrible! "

"But, did she tell you anything?"

"No, she didn't. Why? Do you already have a young man in mind?"

"I have a few young men in mind, Anne. If you weren't so stuffy I could put one or two your way. It's amazing what these men know. It's something to do with the books they read here. Apparently there's this particular book which tells men what to do to women to make them have more pleasure than they know is possible."

"You can do that with wine," answered Anne.

"No Anne, not like that. I think I need to tell you some things that mother never will."

When Anne had been given the details of what a husband expected from his wife, she felt a little unnerved.

"No wonder mother didn't tell me about that. It's horrible!"

"It can be quite nice. Thomas has always been kind to me and never hurt me. I just want some more fun. Do you think that we could ask Ma Gregory if she knows?"

"I suppose so. But I'm not so sure how friendly she would be towards us since father killed her nephews."

"He did kill them didn't he? Father and our brothers are becoming more dangerous the older they get. I'm safe here in Oxford with Thomas, but you must watch your step if you go back home and remain under their protection. Father is not above selling you to the highest bidder in one of his business deals."

Anne looked at her sister.

"Do you think he would do that really?"

"Yes I do Anne. All he thinks about is money. His children are only possessions. Mother is too. He thinks we should all do what he says."

"He still hits me when he gets the chance. It's just that while I've been in Oxford, he can't get to me."

"No, this plague has been a blessing in some ways hasn't it? It has kept Father and William and Harvey away from us and my darling husband has been so busy with his books. I'm glad my children are safe though. I wouldn't like to lose any of them," she said.

"I'm sure you wouldn't. I don't think that I will ever have children," added Anne.

"Really? What makes you think that?"

"A feeling in my heart. I will probably die young anyway. I've got a feeling about that too."

"That's a bit grim Anne. But apart from that, I want you to ask Mistress Gregory about some more potions. Especially that one for pleasure."

"Is the woman or the man supposed to take it?" asked Anne reasonably.

"Do you know, I have absolutely no idea?"

"That's funny!" answered Anne.

"We will get a love potion for John Prideaux too and work out how we are going to make him take it."

"He seems a bit keen on that woman doesn't he?" asked Anne.

"Well, we can soon put a stop to that," said Susan with feeling. "I don't know of any woman who is a match for me."

Neither did Anne and she smiled, happy that her sister was going to help her this way.

"Of course, there will be nothing doing if I don't get that potion from your friend."

"I don't know if I can!" she protested.

"If you want John Prideaux, you will," Susan answered simply.

They both jumped at the hammering on the door and pulled the covers higher over their bodies. The door swung open and their father stood in the doorway, holding a candle.

"What the hell is going on in here?" he bellowed.

"Nothing father!" answered Susan.

"Is there a man in here?"

"Don't be ridiculous!" said Anne.

Brian leapt across the bedroom floor, showing his undergarments as his night coat billowed. He raised the candle above his head and shouted, "you harlot women!"

The women wasted no time and jumped out of the bed before he could reach them.

They were screaming.

Thomas Holland arrived outside the door and held his wife tightly as she ran into his arms.

"Tom. Oh Tom! My father is trying to hit us! Please stop him."

Anne hung onto her brother in law's arm as Thomas Holland said, "I will not have this behaviour in my house,

Brian. Unless you act like a gentleman, I shall have no alternative but to ask you to leave."

Brian's face was beetroot. But aware of how he looked and the fact he was in someone else's house, caused him to lower the candle holder and place it on the table.

"I am sorry Thomas. I believed that Anne had a man in here with her."

"Why father? I never do any such thing!"

"Nevertheless," he said with as much dignity as his current attire would allow. "Tomorrow you leave for North Moreton with your mother and you will oversee the house and make it fit for your brothers and me to return to."

He stalked out of the bedroom and made his way to his own room.

Thomas Holland, glad of news that he may soon be getting his house back to some sort of normality said, "I think that is an excellent idea Anne."

He took his wife's hand and escorted her to their room. Susan turned to her sister and shrugged her shoulders. What could she do? She seemed to say.

Anne dropped her head, conscious now that she would not be seeing John Prideaux anytime soon and she would have to find yet another way to catch him.

CHAPTER FOURTEEN.

Anne stared out of her bedroom window at the churchyard beyond.

She watched the vicar Gilbert Bradshawe talking to a man who was digging another grave. She didn't know who the grave digger was, for their usual one had died during the plague. This stranger was from the West Country somewhere and had walked to the village on his way to Oxford a couple of months ago. Just like John Prideaux, she thought.

Anne and her mother had been sent home after the dinner with John Prideaux. Father had been especially horrible that morning and insisted on their returning to North Moreton to sort out the house. It had been difficult to decide whether he had been embarrassed at entering their room and making a fool of himself, or whether there was an ulterior motive.

Nevertheless, Anne found herself back in her old home that afternoon and could see no way that she would meet John Prideaux any time soon. Susan had hugged her and whispered, "We will work something out. Don't forget our bargain!"

Anne wasn't very happy about the supposed bargain, but did intend to find a reason to meet Mistress Gregory. It would have to a careful meeting, without her mother or any of the staff knowing.

Gilbert Bradshawe appeared to be unhappy with the standard of grave digging and berated the man, who leant on his shovel and listened impassively. The grave was quite near to the church and she wondered if it was for another of the Adams family. Several people in the village were still ailing after the plague, its effects lasting long into the year although the plague itself was no longer around. It was strange to see some of the previously fit and healthy villagers, now bent and pale and depressed.

The vicar, in spite of losing his family had a continuing faith in God and maintained normality at all his services and his ministrations. He was a man who was trying his best to bring peace and harmony to the devastated village. He looked across at the Rectory and waved at Anne. She waved back.

"Anne!" shouted her mother from the hallway outside her bedroom.

"Yes mother. What do you want?"

"I'm going out for a while. I will be back later this afternoon."

"Alright mother. I might go for a walk myself. See you later."

At home for only two days, both women were bored with their new surroundings. Neither would admit to the other where they were going and neither would ask.

Anne heard the door slam as her mother left the house and she made her way to the front window so that she could watch her walk down the drive, past the barn and out onto the street. She would give her a few minutes and then leave herself. One of the maids came up the stairs behind her and bobbed slightly when she saw Anne. This new maid, an 18 year old girl from one of the tiny cottages in an outlying village, was scared of her mistress. Her entire family had died in the plague and she had been looking for a live in job. Prior to working at the Rectory, she had seen Mistress Gunter walk serenely around North Moreton and thought her beautiful.

"Good morning Mistress," she said.

"You do not speak to me unless I speak first. Now, I have forgotten your name."

"Sarah, Mistress," answered Sarah.

"I thought we already had a Sarah?"

"She left, Mistress."

"Well we can't have another Sarah. You will be called..." Anne looked at a painting on the wall for inspiration. The painting of flowers in a vase gave her an idea.

"Rose or Rosemary. I shall let you choose." Sarah was confused, but answered, "Rose, Mistress."

"Well Rose, I shall be going out for a walk now, but don't be using that as an excuse to laze about. I will check your cleaning when I return."

"Yes Mistress."

Anne pulled her wool shawl about her shoulders, and skipped down the stairs. Rose, formerly known as Sarah, mimicked a spit at her as she went and pulled a very ugly face. Anne Gunter had made another enemy.

The weather outside was bright and sunny, but the cold wind made Anne glad she had the shawl. She wrapped it tighter around her shoulders and walked towards Elizabeth Gregory's house. She met no one on her journey and the back door of the farm was answered by Elizabeth herself.

"Good afternoon Mistress Gunter, I heard you were back. You managed to miss the plague then. None of your lot got affected I see."

"No, we have been very lucky Mistress Gregory. We are all safe."

"Your father included?"

"My father included."

"Pity that," answered Elizabeth.

Anne felt awkward because so far there had been no offer to enter the Gregory farmhouse.

"I wondered if I may come in and visit with you."

"Why?"

Anne blushed and said, "I wanted to have a word with you about some remedies."

"Remedies?"

"You know, like the ones you showed me before that could make people better."

"I thought you said you were feeling alright?"

"I am. I am. Look, can I come in please?" asked Anne.

Elizabeth took sympathy on the girl, after all it wasn't her fault that her father was a fool was it?

"Come on in then. You are lucky today. Everyone is out and won't be back for a while. I can't answer for what might happen if one of the men catches you."

"Are they ever going to let it drop?" asked Anne as she sat down on one of the kitchen chairs.

"Your father killed two Gregory men and got away with it," mused Elizabeth.

Anne opened her mouth, ready to argue but decided against it.

"You must want some remedies really badly to shut your mouth like that."

"Not particularly. I don't want to argue, that's all," she answered.

"It's a bit of a difficult subject to drop, when the Gunters get away with the murder of my kin, but it's also known that they get away with murders of others too."

Anne decided to keep quiet again as she could see that it was highly likely that her statement was true.

Elizabeth put a wooden beaker in front of her former mistress and poured a dark liquid into it from a large jug.

"What's this?" asked Anne.

"Only wine. You will be quite safe with it. Now what are these remedies you want to know about?"

"It's not me really, it's for my sister. She wants a potion that will make someone fall in love with her."

Anne thought that honesty was called for here, if for no other reason than she didn't want Mistress Gregory to think that she was in love with anyone. She didn't want her to know about John Prideaux.

"Got a young man in your sights then have you? Someone you met in Oxford? Can't see it being anyone here. No there's no one in this village you have your eye on."

"I don't have my eye on anyone in Oxford, or anywhere else," she lied.

"I see," answered Elizabeth with no hint of irony. She poured more wine into the beaker in front of Anne and continued, "and why do you think that I should know about such things?"

"I told you, you showed me some potions years ago and my sister wants some now. I am willing to pay, well she is," added Anne.

Elizabeth sat down and dusted the table top with her hand. A few crumbs fell to the floor and she looked at them disapprovingly.

"So will you help me with this?"

"Do I have a choice?" answered Elizabeth.

"Of course you have a choice, but I hope your choice is to help me."

The women looked at each other carefully. Anne was deciding whether to be the superior class of woman she was and demanding obedience while Elizabeth was wondering whether she could get away with slapping the

Gunter girl hard. Elizabeth knew that Anne's mother was not as high born as she liked to pretend and if she guessed correctly was currently in the arms of the vicar. She decided to play a longer game and answered.

"I can make a potion which will make a man want you, but you have to be in his presence if you want it to work. It won't work on a distant man," said Elizabeth then added. "There is a way to do that, but you need to be a bit more advanced with your skills. Or I do."

Anne felt her curiosity arise.

She asked, "Do you know someone who is more advance in their knowledge?"

Elizabeth became quiet as she thought over this request.

"I don't think you are ready for that yet, Mistress Gunter. I will let you have a love potion, but you must pay me for it."

Anne brought out her pocket and handed over a few coins.

"Will that do?" she asked the former maid.

Elizabeth examined the coins, threw them in the air and closed her fingers around them before hiding them in her skirts.

"Follow me," she said and Anne did as she was bid.

The room behind the kitchen was neat and tidy and there were many framed pictures on the walls. The furniture was solid oak and had been polished until it shone. The curtains of heavy weave were a bright red and were beautiful. Anne couldn't stop herself walking over to them and stroking the fabric.

"These are lovely Elizabeth and the paintings, who did those?"

Elizabeth reddened slightly and answered, "I did. I have a talent for painting which I got from my mother. My husband frames the paintings for me."

"You should sell them," said Anne, meaning it more than she expected to.

"No one is going to buy my work. I'm not a Lady," she answered with more than a hint of irritation.

"They might if someone in the village hung your work on their wall," reasoned Anne.

Elizabeth made a disapproving noise and continued her progress to the back of the room. Opening a drawer in a large black chest, she pulled out a box and using a key from her bracelet, she turned the lock until it clicked. Anne moved forward and saw several small bottles and flasks and smaller boxes of crushed herbs. Elizabeth picked a flask and shut the box and the drawer.

"Here you are Mistress Anne. Only a few drops in a drink and watch out. You will need to keep one hand on your drawers after it has been drunk."

Anne went bright red and said, "There is no need to speak to me like that. I want two bottles, not one."

Elizabeth stared at her and said, "Two?"

"Yes. They aren't for me and I won't say where I've got them from, but I want two please." She put her hand in her pocket and brought out more money. Elizabeth didn't think for too long, money was tight as usual. She turned back to the drawer and repeated her recent act and handed her another bottle.

"Thank you Elizabeth," said Anne as she put the bottles inside her skirts.

"Now you had better get off because the men will be home soon and I don't have high hopes of your chances if they find you here."

"I will go. Thank you very much. Look, is there any chance that you will introduce me to the person who knows more than you?"

Without hesitation Elizabeth answered, "No, never."

Anne smiled and walked out of the room through the kitchen and into the back garden. As she left, she saw Master Gregory making his way down the road on his horse and so she hid behind a tree until he had passed by.

"I just hid behind a tree," she said to herself and laughed. She made her way along the road in front of the church and through the side gate into the Rectory. Walking towards the door she noticed her mother returning too.

"Hello Anne, have you had a nice walk?"

"I have mother, what about you?"

"Very nice, thank you."

"Lunch will be ready I should think," said Anne.

"I hope so."

The women went to their rooms and Anne hid her flasks amongst the clothes in her drawer. She went downstairs and ate lunch. When Rose came in with the food, she stared at Anne who glared back. Rose put the plates down with a bang and ran out of the room. Anne laughed.

"What's the matter with Sarah?"

"She's called Rose now. I thought it was too confusing with us having had a Sarah before."

"Did we? Oh yes I had forgotten that. So it's Rose now is it?"

"Yes it is. Mother?"

"Yes Anne."

"I heard someone say that there is someone in the village, or it might be more than one person, I'm not sure which."

She had her mother's attention, but was suddenly embarrassed that she had.

"What are trying to say?"

"I was wondering if there was someone who had special powers. Like a witch."

"Nonsense! Don't ever let you father hear you speak like that." answered Mistress Gunter with fervour.

The meal continued in silence. Anne, now feeling stupid thought that she should have kept quiet.

After lunch, mother left the house and Anne went upstairs. The freedom they had when there were no menfolk about was wonderful. They could do what they wanted, when they wanted. Such a simple freedom.

Back in her room, Anne took out the flasks and looked at them. She opened one and then the other. Both contained liquid of a muddy brown colour which smelt of vinegar, one more so than the other. She had decided while at Elizabeth Gregory's house to use one of the flasks herself and refrain from telling Susan that she had. She was going to make John Prideaux fall for her before he married that woman he had been going on about. She sounded wet and boring and John deserved a woman like Anne. She didn't know why her mother had answered so abruptly. Anne had only been trying to find out if there was a secret witch. Everyone knew about Agnes Pepwell, the scruffy and revolting sister in law of Elizabeth Gregory. Anne's mother must be frightened about how her husband would react and that was a good enough reason.

Anne examined the bottles again and decided that hers would be the largest one. As she noted that the bottle must hold as much as a beaker, she realised that she had no idea how much to take.

"I will try just a few drops," she said to herself.

She dripped a few drops into her mouth and suddenly thought. "Am I supposed to take the potion or give it to him?"

Anne wished it had been him who took the potion, for within a few minutes she felt sick and dizzy and lay down on the bed. The room was spinning round and round and she closed her eyes for respite, but there was none.

She tried to get up but had no strength. She felt as though she was paralysed from the neck down. She could see the room but not feel it. At the other times when she floated to the ceiling during her father's escapades, she could see everything from her vantage point. Now she just felt pinned to the bed, her mind racing in panic and her body incapable of movement. She felt nauseous and wanted to throw up her lunch, but daren't because that she knew if she did, she would surely choke.

What to do?

Her mother walked in without knocking and when she saw her daughter lying there wild eyed, she ran to her side.

"What is the matter with you, Anne?"

Mistress Gunter shook her daughter for a few seconds before realising that this was doing nothing useful and so she stopped. Green foam frothed from Anne's mouth and her arms pointed straight down and rigid towards the end of the bed.

"Anne! Anne! My daughter, please wake up!"

Anne was hysterical in her mind. Could her stupid mother not see that she was totally unable to move or respond? The most Anne could do at the moment was force the vomit she had brought up from her stomach out of her mouth with her tongue.

Mistress Gunter took a cloth from the stand and dipped it in the bowl of water. She gently wiped the green foam from her daughter's lips. Once clean, she pulled a fur blanket over her and rubbed her arms while under it. Then she shouted the maid and ordered wine. Once the wine arrived, she raised her daughter's head gently and poured a little into her mouth. Rose had remained to help and was currently standing open mouthed at this bizarre scene.

"Get out Sarah or Rose or whatever you wish to be called. Leave us now. I shall call if I need you for anything else."

Rose bobbed and left quickly. She did not go too far, hoping that there would be something else happening, which she would be able to report as gossip later on. She didn't have to wait long.

As the wine took effect Anne felt a slight shift in her mind-set. Her arms and legs relaxed slightly and as she began to breathe a sigh of relief. There was a funny taste in her mouth.

Anne was suddenly aware of her mother's worried face over hers. She tried to get up but felt weak and wobbly.

"Anne! What happened?"

"I felt ill." Anne didn't want to mention the drops she had taken. A love potion? She couldn't admit to that.

"You just had a seizure!"

"Did I?" She looked around and realised that she was no longer on her bed, but curled up under her dressing table. Her dress was covered in green vomit.

"My head hurts," said Anne and she put her hand to the sore spot.

"You were rolling all over the place and your legs were spinning round and so was your head and you were spitting out green blood!" said the maid.

"Go and fetch some hot water and soap and bring some towels from the chest and do it now!" ordered Mistress Gunter.

"My tongue hurts too," said Anne, while feeling very disorientated.

"Let me look," said her mother.

"You have bitten your tongue. It's going to be very sore," she informed her.

"Is it? It feels sore now."

"Did you take something Anne? You can tell me."

"No! Like what? No!"

"Alright Anne. We will clean you up and put you to bed. Do you think you can rest?"

"I want a drink and a wash first."

Rose and Mistress Gunter cleaned Anne, gave her a drink and put her to bed.

Anne felt much better and vowed to herself that she would not take any more potions. Why would she have had such a terrible reaction? She closed her eyes and moved a little further down the bed.

"Oww!" she said. Putting her hand under her body she pulled out a pin which was caught in her nightdress. The surprise on finding it caused her to sit up straight. A noise outside her bedroom window made her look out.

There was Agnes Pepwell staring at her and laughing.

Anne stared back as the vision faded. Then she remembered that she was on the first floor.

CHAPTER FIFTEEN

Thomas Holland had been trying to spend as much time as possible working at the college.

There hadn't been a day in the last year without a Gunter of some description staying at the house. Once the ladies left for North Moreton, there was no restriction on the behaviour of the men. Drinking, shouting and fighting had been some of the events the Hollands had put up with. There was almost a permanent breakdown of familial relationships when Brian brought back two women who were definitely not ladies to the house. Luckily a maid brought the situation to the attention of her master and the group were sent on their way. Although Brian had left reluctantly and he threatened Thomas with the law, the evening was never referred to again by anyone. Brian Gunter having thought better of attempting to bring a case against Thomas.

Brian's constant escapades began to take a toll on him and by midsummer he took to his bed at the Holland's. The maids had to answer his every call and often left in tears. Thomas found it intolerable and complained regularly to his wife. Susan promised to speak to her father, but would come back downstairs with the news that he would be stopping a little longer until he felt better. The Doctor was called and he announced that Brian Gunter was suffering from a deep rooted infection. He told Thomas Holland that the infection had most likely been caught through dubious sexual activity.

Thomas was paying the bill, not Brian. Brian rarely paid for anything.

"Girl! Girl!" was a regular cry from the depths of his room. The maids were taking longer to answer the call each time.

"Come over here girl," he would say as they entered. Once obeyed, he would grab their arms and pull them onto the bed, touching and rubbing them roughly while endeavouring to release breasts from their coverings. The maids of Oxford were not as passive as the maids of North Moreton and screamed and slapped. It wasn't long before Susan sent only the male servants to deal with her father's requests. She didn't want to lose any more servants.

A week after Brian fell ill, a note arrived from North Moreton informing them that Anne too had fallen ill and was lying in her sickbed.

"Nonsense!" said Brian. "She must be suffering from women's problems and wants to outdo me with her sicknesses."

"Women's problems, father?" asked Susan, hoping to embarrass her father and pay him back for his behaviour of late.

"The mother, hysterics. That's all. As soon as we get her married off and a husband regularly sorting her out, those hysterics will soon stop."

His daughter coloured up and Thomas took a deep breath in order to not to scold the man.

"I think that we should send someone to check on Anne. Mistress Gunter would not have sent word if the problem was not serious. Shall we send Susan and the children back to North Moreton to see her?" asked Thomas.

"I don't want to take the children if there is illness back at the house. We have only just kept them all safe from the plague."

"The children can't catch what your sister has. All women fall ill in that way without a man to give her regular servicing," said Brian, winking at his son in-law who used all of his patience to conceal his disgust.

"I shall visit my sister and make sure she is well, but will leave the children here. I shall take a maid and perhaps you could organise someone to ride with us and keep us safe?" Susan was thinking about one of the senior boys she had been flirting with of late.

"I will send John Prideaux with you. I need him to do some work for me at Abingdon." Thomas was thinking that John could keep an eye on his wayward wife and hopefully report back. He had recently become more suspicious of her fidelity.

Susan was not perturbed by this bit of news, knowing that her sister would be more than pleased to see the young clergyman. She would probably be out of her sickbed quick enough.

Susan left the room and called on her maid.

"You are to make sure that a note is delivered to the Rectory at North Moreton informing them that we shall be traveling to visit my young sister Anne, under the guardianship of John Prideaux."

Susan had a pretty good idea how this news would affect her sister. She would no doubt get up from her bed and make herself beautiful enough to meet John and charm him. She was wrong however. As soon as Anne heard that John would be arriving she decided on a plan, the embarking of which would alter the path of many people.

Susan ran up to Anne's room as soon as she arrived at The Rectory. She was surprised to see her lying on the bed looking grey.

"I thought you would be up and about when you heard that your beau was arriving with me."

"I thought that I might have more attention from him if I still was ill," she said honestly.

"My, my, you have changed Anne. Did you manage to get me that potion I asked you for?"

"Yes I did, I got it from Ma Gregory. I took some and this is the result. I've been so sick Susan. I fainted and threw up and had seizures. It happened directly after I took the potion."

Susan laughed loudly.

"You silly girl Anne! You don't take the potion. You give it to him! You didn't take it directly did you?"

"Yes," nodded Anne sadly.

"No wonder you have been ill. You are supposed to put it in a drink or food or something. Didn't Gregory tell you that?"

"No," answered Anne.

"What a cow she is!" said Susan. "I know she makes potions, but it sounds like she is a witch as well as Agnes Pepwell."

"I saw her at my window the night I took the potion. She was at that window." Anne pointed to demonstrate.

"That's not possible!" said Susan.

Their conversation was interrupted by their mother, who gently knocked on the bedroom door and said, "Reverend Prideaux has asked if may come and visit with you for a short time before he travels to Abingdon."

The women giggled and Susan helped to rearrange Anne until she looked suitably attractive and vulnerable. John Prideaux came into the room and both women noted that he had a high colour to his cheeks and knew instantly that he was either excited or nervous about seeing Anne.

"How have you been keeping Mistress Gunter? I was sorry to hear that you have been so ill. Have the doctors got to the root of the problem?" he asked.

Anne answered quietly, "Not really. But hopefully I'm on the mend now."

"I am glad to hear that. You are looking quite well, if a little weak."

"Thank you for your good wishes, Master Prideaux."

Susan suddenly said, "Will you excuse me for a minute or two? I must ask my maid to do something for me." Before they could answer she had slipped out of the room, leaving the pair alone.

"How is your life in Oxford, John? I find that I miss the city now I have returned to North Moreton. In fact it's quite boring."

"I am sorry to hear that Anne. I do miss our chats."

Anne felt emboldened to speak up. "Have you seen anything of Mistress Goodwin lately?"

"No sadly, she left Oxford with her family. Her father has a mission elsewhere."

"Let us hope that they are able to return to Oxford soon."

"Yes indeed."

Both were unsure where to go next with this conversation but Susan soon returned with a maid, carrying wine. The tray was put on a table by the window and Susan casually asked her sister,

"Where is your medicine, Anne? The potion you were telling me about? I can put it in your drink."

Anne's eyes widened and she pointed to her dresser.

"In there. In the flask."

Susan smiled broadly and went to the dresser. She put two drops into a beaker of wine and then added another two. She handed this to John and handed another to Anne and winked at her sister.

They all drank their wine. John's face coloured more and he smiled broadly.

"I must be on my way soon," he informed them and started to get up. He soon sat down and he leant forward. He threw up all over the floor and carried on retching without restraint. Susan ran out into the hallway and shouted for a maid and Anne jumped out of her bed in order to avoid the spray coming from the mouth of the focus of her heart.

"Oh, I am so sorry. I don't know what the problem is. Was there something in the wine?" He spluttered the words at them.

"We are alright, aren't we Anne?" said Susan.

"Yes we are. Do you want to go outside?" John was still retching.

"I don't think that I will be able to go outside. I don't think I can get up from the chair."

The maid ran in and squeaked and ran out again. She thought she would need the large bucket for the mess in the room.

By evening, John was in bed in a spare room and Anne was dressed and downstairs.

"I hope the Reverend is feeling better by the morning. I don't want another sick person in the house," said Mistress Gunter.

"I'm better now, so don't blame me."

"I'm not blaming you, Anne. I just don't like sickness in the house."

After dinner, Anne and Susan went to Susan's bedroom and discussed the dramas of the day.

"Did he fall ill in the same way you did?"

"Yes, the same way. Horrid isn't it?"

"I think Ma Gregory must have been trying to poison you. We shall visit her tomorrow and see what she has to say."

The next morning they left John in bed trying to recover from his ordeal and the women walked through the village to meet with Elizabeth Gregory. She opened the door and her face fell when she saw who was standing on her step.

"What do you two want?" she asked nastily.

"We came to ask why you gave Anne poison."

"I haven't given her poison. What are you talking about?"

"That potion you have me last week has made me very ill and also a guest in our house accidentally took some and he is ill too," said Ann.

Mistress Gregory leant against her door.

"I understand now. You took the potion yourself first and then gave it to a man you want to attract and you gave him too much. That's what it sounds like to me."

"We don't care what you think Mistress Gregory, but if you don't give us the correct potions we will start causing trouble for you."

Anne wondered vaguely what trouble Susan intended causing the woman, as it was highly unlikely that they would be telling anyone else about this particular problem. Elizabeth Gregory waited a minute and then stepped back and beckoned the women in. This time there was no stopping for drinks and they went directly through to the parlour. Elizabeth opened the drawer and looked at the flasks. Suddenly she turned to the women and asked, "Did you bring me the other flasks back?"

"No," answered Anne. "We threw them away."

They hadn't of course. Last night they decided to keep the other potions and use them in some other as yet undecided way. Elizabeth continued to stare at the women knowing that they were lying to her but was unable to do anything about it. She took out two further potions and handed the flasks over. These potions were an orange colour and the flasks were smaller than the previous two.

"Thank you Mistress Gregory," said Susan as she put them in her pocket. "Do you need payment for these?"

Elizabeth answered, "Tell your mother you have been to see me and we will work something out between us."

"I'm not going to tell mother anything. I would rather that she didn't know anything about this," said Susan.

"Good luck with that," answered Elizabeth. "You might find that she already knows."

Although they found the comments strange, neither replied.

"Is it that priest you are interested in Anne? He comes and goes into your life; almost like you two were meant to be together." She smiled and Anne couldn't work out whether Elizabeth Gregory was being friendly or nasty.

"I thought I saw Agnes Pepwell at my window the night I took the potion," she said suddenly. "Then she vanished."

"If she did that, then she is a witch," added Susan.

"Most people think that anyway, don't they?"

Susan shrugged her shoulders in answer and the women left the Gregory cottage.

"I think she's a witch too," said Susan.

"I think she's a bitch!"

By the time they arrived back at The Rectory, John Prideaux was in the hallway, dressed and ready to leave.

"You are feeling better now?" Anne asked him.

"Yes. I am, not fully recovered I think, but I have to go to Abingdon and commute some business for Master Holland. I shouldn't like to fail in my task." He seemed nervous, but perhaps that could be explained away by his recent illness.

"Are you recovered enough to make the journey?" asked Anne.

"I am well enough to travel. The fresh air would do me a lot of good."

Before the women could make any further comments, John Prideaux was out the door and walking down the drive.

"He was acting oddly," said Susan.

"I thought that," agreed Anne.

"You know, that man is such a goody- goody that I think the only way to catch him is by letting him see your titties!"

"Susan!" said Anne, although she thought that it was an excellent idea and one which she was more than willing to go through with. The women walked back into the house.

John Prideaux scurried down the drive and out onto the road. He wanted to get away from The Rectory as soon as possible. He was thinking that he wouldn't be coming to North Moreton again if he could help it. There was always a drama there.

Now he must walk back to Abingdon. They had taken a carriage to North Moreton, but he must walk and hopefully get a cart to Oxford as soon as he had completed the business he had agreed to do. Although under orders, John had been more than keen to visit with Anne Gunter. He often thought about her when he wasn't expecting it. When he was halfway through some writing or lecturing, her face would appear in his mind's eye and he couldn't remember what he was supposed to do next.

Seeing her lying on her bed had made him glad that her sister was there as he wasn't sure how he could have coped on his own. She looked so small and vulnerable and attractive as she lay in bed. Perhaps it had been the heat of the room, or the length of the journey, or perhaps it was God punishing him for his carnal thoughts. Whatever it was, he had never felt so ill in his life. If this was what the plague felt like, no wonder people wanted to die.

When he had been left sleeping in one of the spare bedrooms, he heard knocking and called softly, "Come in."

No one did come in however and John half sat up when he heard further knocking. It seemed to be coming from the window and there he saw the old woman Pepwell, who he had met that day years ago when he first travelled through North Moreton. She was sitting on the windowsill and grinning at him.

"I remember you," she said. "You are the man who wants to rule Oxford and tell everyone how to live their lives."

"I don't want to do any such thing." John rubbed his head and tried to work out whether or not he was still asleep.

"Of course you do. And you have the ability to do it. Do you want me to tell you how?"

"I want you to tell why you are here in my room. You are not a maid are you?"

The old hag crabbed towards him and he pulled the cover to his chin as he had done as a child. John Prideaux was frightened.

The dirty, toothless mouth appeared huge as it neared John's face,

"You must plan your own way to fame and fortune," she said. "That is the only way to succeed."

"I don't know what you are talking about old woman. God decides whether we shall succeed or fail."

"Really? You are a fool, priest if you believe that. God doesn't care. He kills the good as well as the bad. He saves the bad as well as the good. What you need is a person who can tell you how to get past all of your rules."

"Get out, you foul woman." John shouted.

The hag sat on the bed and he could smell death and sweat and alcohol.

"You would like to know though wouldn't you? And don't be thinking that girl you fancy is so sweet and innocent. She takes after her mother and her mother is one of us."

"What do you mean, one of you?"

Agnes Pepwell laughed loudly and her eyes reddened and she seemed to grow in size. John heard himself squeal and he moved further up the bed and pulled the cover over his head. Feeling suddenly ashamed that he had not had faith in his God, he dropped the cover, ready to face this witch. But she had gone and he hadn't heard any door open or close. She must have vanished. He needed to leave this village and get on his way. He put his few belongings together and decided to leave the house immediately. A maid met him in the hallway and he asked her to give him some bread and fill his flask with water. This she did and added cheese and apples when she found out he was to walk to Abingdon and then on to Oxford.

"If you hurry to the Inn sir, I know that they are leaving in the cart for Abingdon this morning and you can get a ride there. But you must hurry, they will be leaving soon."

Anxious to get a ride out of this crazy village, John didn't want to speak to the Gunter women when he met them on the drive. It was true that Anne looked beautiful as she giggled and skipped with her sister, but he had been properly scared and didn't want to show that he was.

He had hoped that they might spend a little time on their own, where he could have said things to her which would make her understand that he liked her and that as soon as he had finished his studies and established himself, and then he would consider taking a bride. But he couldn't imagine that such a vivacious girl would wait for him. He had even considered that he might marry earlier than he planned if it meant keeping a girl like Anne. There had been some expectation of the part of the Goodwins that he might marry their daughter. It was true that she came from a pious family and her grandfather had died for his faith and surely he would be nearer to God married to Anne Goodwin. But he would be nearer to Heaven married to Anne Gunter.

He ran up the road and soon reached the Inn, where he saw the cart was thankfully still standing outside, with the brown cob patiently waiting. John stroked the horse and called to the innkeeper, soon discovering that he was more than willing to give him a lift. He would be glad of the company he said and some extra cash.

John jumped on the cart to wait and while there he looked around. No one was about save for a large rodent with a long beard sitting on the wall of the Gate House and it was grinning at him. He closed his eyes and repeated The Lord's Prayer over and over.

CHAPTER SIXTEEN

"This trip hasn't gone as well as I hoped," said Susan to Anne as they went back into the Rectory.

"No it hasn't," agreed Anne as she sat down on the settle by the fire. She poured drinks and passed one to Anne.

"What shall we do?" asked Susan.

"I think I'm really in love with John Prideaux. I mean really in love."

"How do you know?"

"You tell me. You are married and have five children. You are in love aren't you?"

Anne was shocked by the power in the laughter coming from her sister.

"Love?" she said. "You have answered your own question without realising it. I'm married and have children. I'm not in love! I have security and can do as I please."

"Were you never in love with Thomas? He is so nice to you!"

"He is nice to me. But he doesn't make me excited and he hardly ever wants to touch me. I only got pregnant by lying down, lifting my shift and asking for a baby!"

"Susan!" Anne was shocked. Susan had never talked to her like this before.

"Why do you think I want that potion? Thomas has never made me feel like Richard did."

"Richard?"

"Richard Gregory."

"He's dead!"

"I know."

"Did father know about him?"

"And killed him you mean? Maybe. I've wondered that many times. But if he did, he hasn't said anything about it. And I'm certainly never going to ask him."

"No," agreed Anne.

"But there are some lovely young men at the college and I need to give them a bit of encouragement with that potion. They are hardly likely to take a chance with me otherwise."

"What is it you want them to do exactly?"

"Do you really not know, Anne? Have none of the village boys ever touched you?"

"No! "

"Perhaps I should let you watch me with one of my beaus," suggested Susan.

"Don't be a ninny, Susan. That is never going to happen," answered Anne, more interested than she thought she ought to be.

#

By the time her husband arrived home, Elizabeth Gregory was in a foul temper. Those Gunter women annoyed her every time she saw them. It wasn't just that they were rich and beautiful. It was the fact they could do what they wanted, when they wanted and could wear wonderful clothes and stay in some of the nicest houses in the county.

Perhaps it was also because she was soon to have another child and their rotten, scheming, two faced, bullying father was responsible.

Walter pushed open the kitchen door noisily and slammed it with his usual fervour.

"What's for lunch?" he asked.

"There is some beef and some cheese on the side over there. Eat that."

"What's the matter with you? Always naggy and always nagging me lately. I can't make head or tail of you, woman."

He walked over to her at the sink and put his arms around her, "Oh Lizziebits, you feel so lovely, shall we go upstairs? There's no one about. I'm sure your titties are getting bigger by the day."

He was rewarded with a slap around the face.

"Are you calling me fat?" she asked.

Walter never knew how to answer trick questions like this and took his hands away from his wife.

"Well?" she questioned again.

"I think you look beautiful. Same as always," he answered, edging towards the door of the kitchen.

"Get out of here. Ever since I married you I have had bad luck. I wouldn't have been here at all if your stupid mother hadn't threatened to hex me if I didn't marry you. I have had enough of you all." She threw a pot against the wall and burst into tears. Walter grabbed some food as previously directed and left the room. He decided that he would stay at the Inn tonight and keep out of his mad wife's way.

As soon as he left, Elizabeth stopped crying and began to clear up the mess she had made. It was a pity that she couldn't clear up the mess she was in. The thought made her sit down on the floor and she moved her hands around the contours of her body. It was true that she was getting fat and that her breasts were the size of a cow's.

She and Alice Kirfoote had gone to stay in Reading during the worst of the plague and Brian Gunter visited the town from time to time. In boredom they had come together again in a furtive and dirty way and the result was this. Another pregnancy. She hadn't told Brian and didn't really know why she would. Brian wouldn't do anything about it and Walter would throw her out. That was never going to be a help to her or her child. Then there was Anne Gunter, a fellow initiate and someone she did not want to cross. And this baby was a Gunter child. She knew in her heart that she would have to keep her secret or face dire consequences. Giving young Anne the false potion had been a good joke and one which she deserved. The new one would turn whichever man they gave it to into a sex crazed animal and they wouldn't want to try it a second time. But if Anne's mother found out what she had done, there would be hell to pay.

She looked out of the window and saw Gilbert Bradshawe walking by the hedge which led to the track from the Inn to the back of the church. He looked tousled and was endeavouring to brush down his clothes as he walked quickly towards the church. Elizabeth soon saw the reason why. Following him at a more leisurely pace was Mistress Anne Gunter.

"You crafty old bat," said Elizabeth. "He is way too young for you! Been using some of the potion too have you?"

Elizabeth grinned. She had the upper hand for once and intended to use it to her advantage.

#

Anne Gunter found her two daughters sitting in the garden when she got home. She was a little surprised to see them as she slipped through the side gate which separated the garden from the church yard.

"Hello mother," said Susan. "You just missed Master Bradshawe; he waved to us as he went past."

Mistress Gunter coloured up, not knowing whether her daughters had guessed her secret or not. She sat down at the table and reached for a drink. While putting it to her lips, she tremored slightly and spilled the drink down the front of her dress.

"You alright mother?"

"Yes I am."

"You look a bit flustered, that's all," said Susan, eager to push her mother as far as she could.

"I am not flustered Susan. I said I am fine. You are looking better Anne!"

"I feel better mother. But John has left us in a rush this morning."

Mistress Gunter put her drink down and looked genuinely surprised.

"Why?"

"He just said that he had to go to Abingdon and then back to Oxford."

Anne looked at her daughter with new eyes.

"Are you in love with the priest Anne?"

"Yes I am mother. I have only recently realised how much."

"Does he love you?" she asked reasonably.

"I think he likes me. But I don't think he loves me. I want him to love me," she added.

"Well, let's see what we can do about it. "

The girls nudged each other. If their mother was on their side, the solution couldn't possibly be far away.

They were interrupted by the voice of Gilbert Bradshawe saying, "Good afternoon ladies. I hope you are feeling well now Anne. I have been worried since I heard the nature of your illness."

"What have you heard about me?" asked Anne, returning to her haughty Gunter attitude.

"That you have been suffering from the falling sickness. My cousin suffers with that and I know how distressing it can be. There are doctors who can help you," he said.

"Get away from my women, Bradshawe. If I catch you near my wife or my daughters again, I shall do the same to you as I did to that Gregory bastard who wanted to touch Susan."

The Gunter women turned round sharply to see their father, red faced and obviously full of drink, standing on the path. He didn't look pleased. Bradshawe paled and walked swiftly away. Mistress Gunter endeavoured to keep her cool and said, "We weren't expecting you back from town yet my dearest husband."

"No you weren't were you? I saw you with your skirts around your waist and the vicar between your legs." He walked over to her and hit her hard on the side of the head and she fell to the floor.

Her daughters ran to her and held her head and stroked her face.

"Father, how could you do this? Why do you have to be such a bully?" asked Anne.

"Shut your mouth or I will do the same to you. I came back to see if you were better my dear daughter. I left my sick bed for you and here you are defending your mother while she talks to this supposed man of God who only this morning she was servicing."

"Father! You mustn't speak like that! My mother would not do any such thing!" Anne immediately jumped to her mother's defence.

Mistress Gunter groaned and stirred.

"Thank God, she is alive!" said Susan.

"I didn't kill her!" said Brian. He seemed pleased that he would not have to be facing the law yet again. He stalked back to the house.

Early the following morning, the three women mounted their carriage along with bags and trunks and potions and set off for Oxford. Susan had sent word to her husband that they would be arriving at their house to stay for a while. She was sure her husband would be pleased about that. As they drove, they talked.

"I don't expect father will encourage you marrying the priest now, Anne."

"No. He seems to have a problem with priests. I wonder if he will take it out on Thomas?" asked Anne.

"Your father is an idiot. I have known it for years, but I have no intention of allowing him to get away with it any longer," said Mistress Gunter.

"What are you going to do mother?"

"Set him up. He thinks he can get away with anything. But I am good at the long game, I have had enough practice. I have some friends that he doesn't know about, that you don't know about," she answered.

"People like who?"

"A few ladies."

"Are you a witch?" asked Anne.

"That's a funny question, Susan."

"But, are you?"

"When we get to Oxford, we will invite your Reverend Prideaux round for dinner or lunch and we can find an excuse for you two to be together and then you can work on him."

"And how should I work on him?" asked Anne.

"That will be my job. Mother can't tell us about that side of things. But I will."

#

That night, after dinner had been eaten and a letter sent to John Prideaux and the children kissed and patted, Susan and Anne lay on the sofa. Thomas was at the college and their mother had gone to bed early.

"So what should I do to get him to like me?" asked Anne,

"He already likes you Anne. All men like pretty girls such as you."

"Well if that is so, he hasn't done or said anything yet."

"This is where the extra bit comes in. I can't believe you haven't tried it on anyone else. It's important that you get him on his own. Then look directly into his eyes and find an excuse to get your body near to him. Preferably with your titties heaving and touching him in some way. If you can't get them near to his body, then make sure he sees them heaving or looking as though they may fall from your bodice at any moment."

"Oh! And what if that doesn't work?"

"Trust me, it always works. And when it does you will know what to do next."

"I hope so. I hope so."

"What do you think about mother being a witch?" asked Susan.

"I'm not sure that she is. I mean if she is. Why, are you?" said Anne, addressing her mother who had walked into the room.

"I think a little differently to most, I will agree with that," she answered.

"In what way?"

"Because I'm not just interested in this life, I'm interested in my eternal soul and its development and continuance," answered Mistress Gunter.

"So how does that work?"

"Anne, neither of you would be able to understand unless you studied the subject for years. And years and years. But I can tell you some things to do and some ways to act which will help you if you want."

"I don't know that Thomas would approve of that," said Susan.

"Or John," said Anne.

"Gilbert wasn't that interested in the beginning, but he soon came round when he saw what was possible," said Mistress Gunter.

"So you are having a love affair with Master Bradshawe?" asked Susan.

"A thing, not a love affair. A love affair is such a waste of time and energy. It should be saved for the women who want to make sure that her man's undergarments are presentable."

"Is that all love is? Neither of you are selling it to me," commented Anne.

"That's because we know about it. We will make sure you know about love and how exciting it can be. Then once you have it out of your system, you can learn how to enjoy yourself," said Mistress Gunter.

"You don't seem to enjoy yourself much with father," said Anne reasonably.

"I told you before. I have plans for your father. Sadly I haven't been able to do anything until recently. I needed to wait until you were old enough Anne. It's not easy to be without a husband and keep a child."

"I would have thought it was impossible," said Susan.

"Why have you both had so many children? I mean, if you don't like being married?"

"We don't like being married, but having children is the best way to make sure that you put a wall between you and your husband. You can always use the children as a reason to be out of his way," answered Susan.

Anne nodded, but remained unconvinced. The description of love and marriage and children made her understand a little better, the married women she knew and the way they acted. She was yet to learn about survival.

"I am not so sure that I want to catch John now," she said.

"Of course you do. Let's get your first love over and done with and then you can get on with your life," advised her mother.

"Susan has been giving me some advice."

"Has she told you about accidentally bending over in front of him? Not with your knees bent, just your waist and making sure your bottom is pointing directly at him?"

"This doesn't sound much like love either," said Anne.

"You rarely win a man by being quiet and graceful. By the time he has realised what you want, some other woman has caught him. Romeo won't keep coming for you, declaring his undying love indefinitely."

CHAPTER SEVENTEEN

When John Prideaux finished his errand in Abingdon, he stayed at an inn there and left for Oxford early the following morning. He was finding it difficult to remove the image of Agnes Pepwell from his mind and the sight of that thing on the wall. North Moreton was a very strange place and he didn't want to return there, ever. But he was more aware than anyone, that he kept saying that and kept returning.

He realised that he was missing Anne. He knew he liked her, perhaps even craved for her company, but this feeling was new. He felt addicted to her, palpitations and anxiety rising as he left her company. As he travelled to Oxford he felt as though he was getting further and further away from his heart. It was unbearable. He must find a way to speak to her again and see if she felt the same.

His wish was answered soon after his return to Oxford. Upon his return to his lodgings he was handed a note requesting his attendance at dinner at the Holland lodgings. He sent off a quick yes in response.

That was how he found himself sitting at the Holland dinner table in the company of Mistress Gunter, her two daughters and Thomas Holland. Thomas had smiled and nodded when John arrived at the door. He had almost given up on trying to have an opinion on who came to the house. He spent as much time as possible in the college library or his rooms. But he liked John Prideaux and if the family had a plan to catch him for Anne, then he didn't have a problem with that. He felt some sympathy for the young man who had no idea what was coming his way that night.

The meal went well and the company was happy and comfortable. All the personalities fit well together and John did not notice the glances the women gave each other from time to time. When the meal was over and Mistress Gunter said she was very tired and would go to bed early. Susan whispered something to her husband and within ten minutes, Anne and John were on their own, save for the maids who scurried around them clearing up.

"Leave the wine," instructed Anne.

"I am not so sure that we should be alone together Anne. I don't think it's right."

"We are hardly alone, the servants are about and the family are upstairs. Would you like to go for a walk?"

"No!" he said quickly, terrified that one of the other students would see them together. Why should that matter to him? Because he wanted to stay at the college without a stain on his character, that was why.

"Well, we shall stay here then." Anne was feeling awkward already. How was she going to act like she had been told? How should she actually begin?

"You left the Rectory in a hurry, John," she said.

"Yes, I knew I had to get to Abingdon and finish a job had been given."

"Nothing else? You looked so flustered."

John wasn't going to admit anything, he was too embarrassed. How could he admit that he had been in the presence of a witch at the Rectory? Worse, how could he mention that creature thing he absolutely knew he had seen on the wall? So he said nothing. Anne sat next to him and then moved closer.

"It's hot in here, isn't it?" said Anne.

"Is it? I feel alright." He suddenly realised he didn't feel alright, because as soon as Anne said it was hot, he felt hot.

"I'm feeling hot," continued Anne, not sure where she was going with this.

"Now I'm feeling very hot. It is most uncomfortable." Anne removed her lace shawl, folded it neatly and placed it on the arm of the bench. She passed her hand across her neck and down to the collar of her dress. She loosened the ties and fanned gently with her hand. She noted with satisfaction that John's eyes followed her every move. Perhaps there was something in this technique after all.

"Would you like me to open a window, Anne?" he asked innocently.

"No, that's fine." She wasn't that hot and if he went to the window she might have to start all over again.

"Are you feeling quite well now, John?"

"Yes I am, are you?"

"I feel very well," she answered and moved even closer to him. He stayed where he was, which was promising. She fiddled with the neck of her dress and accidentally opened it a little further. John's attention was still upon her. She crossed her legs in his direction and pointed her breasts at him, the movement exposing more flesh.

John moved towards her and as he was about to kiss her, the door flung open and in came the maid who had cleaned up the vomit.

"Mistress, will you be wanting anything else tonight? Will you be going up soon?"

The request was enough to make John jump up and answer, "I must be going now. Early morning, have to go. Thank you very much."

The maid bobbed and giggled. Anne was furious.

"I will call you if I need anything. How dare you interrupt me without instruction? I shall report your behaviour to Mistress Holland."

The maid did not appear to be to be worried about the threat and remained standing. John was now beetroot red as though he had been caught in the act of doing something really terrible, when he had only been considering putting his hands upon Anne's breasts and his lips on hers. He would have to go straight to the chapel tonight and pray.

"I will leave now Mistress Gunter. I apologise, I hadn't realised that it was quite so late. We were having such a pleasant talk." He left the room and the maid followed him out, giving only a glance to the young Mistress Gunter, who was scowling at her. She opened the front door and let him out into the night air. She was going to have such fun telling the others how she had almost caught them at it. Perhaps she should also tell the master, she was sure he wouldn't approve of these goings on.

Anne met her in the hallway and said, "What was all that giggling about?"

"Nothing Mistress. Nothing at all. Did you know that your collar has come undone somehow? You should fix that."

"Don't be so rude," said Anne and she ran up the stairs fixing her dress as she went.

That hadn't gone well at all.

#

When she was relating the tale to Susan the following morning, she was surprised at her reaction.

"That was quite good Anne."

"Was it?"

"Oh yes. He liked what was happening otherwise he wouldn't have acted so embarrassed when the maid came in. You will have to do that again. And don't forget, if someone actually catches him responding, then he will have to marry you!"

"I really enjoyed doing it you know. The acting and pretending to be someone else and then making that person react in a way that they had no intention of. And I want to do it to him again."

"Then we shall have to arrange another invite. Let's tell mother, she will arrange it."

They were disturbed by the sounds of shouting and crashing in the hallway. It seemed their father was back.

"Anne! Anne!" he shouted, "I have some news for you!"

Susan and Anne ran out of the bedroom and looked over the banisters. Two of the children who had escaped from their nurse scampered over to join them.

"What is it, father?" asked Anne.

"You are to be married!"

#

Mistress Gunter established later, when the dust had settled following a day of screaming, arguing and crying, that Brian had decided Anne should marry a cousin of the Dunches. It seemed Brian had a business scheme involving some land and a marriage to this cousin would seal the deal.

He seemed oblivious to all objections and could not see what the problem was.

"He is a Dunch. She would be marrying a Dunch," was all he would say.

"Don't worry Anne," said her mother. "I have a plan that should sort the whole thing out."

"What plan?"

"It would probably be best if I just told you what to do at each stage. If I tell you the whole thing at once, I am not so sure it would work quite so well. Do you trust me?"

"Yes mother. I trust you."

"Firstly, we need to have you pretend that you are not well. We will have you getting worse as time goes on and that should delay things nicely."

"I'm not supposed to meet this Dunch kinsman yet, am I? I've never heard of him."

"He has been away apparently, but we can put him off I think. You have to be patient." She kissed her daughter on the head.

"I can do that," she answered.

"I heard you have been to Mistress Gregory and coming away with jugs. Was that anything to do with your illness?"

"I think it was, mother. It certainly got John's attention though, didn't it?"

"There's an idea, little sister. You being properly ill got his attention. Perhaps that's the way to go. We will have you ill."

"But not just any illness. I shall teach you to have a different and special illness," said Mistress Gunter.

"What, some sort of witch illness?" asked Anne.

"Perhaps. You can either take a potion or we can cast a spell on you," their mother informed them.

"We? Who is we?" asked Susan.

"I have a few friends around the place that will help us out. We will scare off this potential husband of yours, Anne. If he is a friend of your father's, then he won't be up to much and probably won't treat you very well. No, we will get rid of him for you."

#

It was decided by the three women later that day that they should first ensure John Prideaux kept an interest in Anne and upon having learned from Thomas that he was currently in the college chapel rehearsing a sermon he was to give later that evening, they decided to visit him en masse.

The women linked arms as they walked towards the chapel. The wind suddenly picked up and their skirts and cloaks billowed behind them as they walked. The sky became black and a flash of lightening seared across the roofs of the college buildings. They pulled the wool capes tightly around their heads as the heavens opened and black rods of rain fell upon them. Students ran in different directions trying to avoid a soaking, but the women marched in a straight line until they reached their goal of the large wooden door of the chapel.

As they stood there, Mistress Gunter's hand on the latch, Anne turned round and noted that they could not see any of the buildings due to the heavy rain. The only sound was the drumming of water against the ground and the only light a faint candle light through the chapel window. The door would not open initially and the women had to push together.

"It's not locked is it?" asked Anne.

"It shouldn't be. I don't usually have any trouble getting in."

"Who is there?" The voice which shouted from the other side of the door was that of John Prideaux.

"It's me, Mistress Holland with my mother and sister. Let us in John, the weather is apocalyptic out here."

He opened the door easily and said, "The door wasn't locked ladies, it must have been jammed. Goodness, the weather has changed, come on in."

Mistress Gunter led the way and with only a slight hesitation as she crossed the threshold, was soon standing inside. Her daughters followed and they stood smiling at John, who was feeling unnerved although he couldn't explain why. Suddenly with no warning the candles blew out and they stood in darkness.

"Oh! What are we to do?" asked Anne nervously.

"There is a flame in the vestry, I will fetch a taper and we can restore light." John moved away from them and they could hear him shuffling along. The shuffling stopped and a door opened as he went in search of light.

"That was odd," said Susan.

"It felt as though someone came in behind us and blew the candles out!" said Anne.

"That's not likely," answered Anne.

"Isn't it?" said their mother.

John was busy lighting the candles on the altar and upon the metal candelabras. As his back was to the main body of the chapel, he could not see the shadow people and faces moving swiftly around the edge of the room, caught in the glare of the lightening which flashed through the church windows. The women could, but they did not bring it to his attention, feeling that he would not be able to take it very well.

"Mother? Who are those people?"

"Past souls, coming back for a look at everything."

"They don't seem very happy."

"They are still confused and have come to the place where they believe they will get the answers."

"And do they get their answers?"

"They aren't likely to here," said Mistress Gunter.

John came back towards them and he was smiling at Anne, although he probably didn't think that he was.

"Hello Anne," he said.

"Hello, Master Prideaux. How are you today?" said Anne.

"Very well thank you."

"We wanted to know if you will be free later this week for another dinner?" asked Mistress Gunter.

"Yes, that would be excellent!"

This was going well. John Prideaux was most definitely interested in seeing Anne again.

"We shall send a note with Master Holland," said Susan.

They made their way towards the door and the candles blew out again.

"Oh dear Reverend, you seem to be having trouble with draughts today!" said Anne.

A cold wind passed by them as they headed out into the walkway. The rain had stopped, although the sky was still dark grey. One or two students and traders had returned to the streets, but their heads were down against the strong wind which blew. Anne pointed to the sky just beyond the college.

"It's blue over there!"

"Yes, it appears to be only grey over us. I wonder what that means."

No one answered the question.

John waved happily at his friends, but brought his arm smartly back to his side as he thought he saw Agnes Pepwell standing next to the college hall.

"Surely not," he said to himself.

Mistress Gunter shouted, "We shall speak to you soon!"

"Yes!" he shouted back. As he looked over to the hall, he saw that Agnes had vanished, or perhaps he had only imagined her presence. He shivered and went back into the chapel, noting as he did that the candles were again lit.

He muttered to himself that today was yet another strange day. He had been very glad to see Anne and had appreciated her smiles. She really was a very pretty girl and he was reminded of the first time he had seen her all those years ago. Perhaps he would have a word with Reverend Holland about it.

He didn't have to wait too long, for Thomas called on him later that day.

"I wanted to have a word with you Master Holland."

"Did you Prideaux? I wanted to have a word with you too. I think we may need some help on the layout for this new Bible."

"Do you? I would be interested in that. Very interested. But no, that isn't what I wanted to speak to you about. You see I have feelings for your sister in law, Anne and I have reason to believe that she is interested in me. My question is, how do I approach her father?"

Thomas Holland looked surprised and said, "Approach her father about what? Marriage?"

"Well yes. Marriage."

"I think you should give up on those ideas Prideaux. The girl is to marry one of the Dunch cousins. You don't stand a chance."

CHAPTER EIGHTEEN

It was October before John heard anything more about the Gunter family. On learning that Anne was to be married, he knew two things. That he was jealous and also that he must get away as soon as possible. He didn't fancy Brian Gunter or his sons coming after him in order to prevent his pursuance of Anne. He asked for a sabbatical due to stress from overwork. Thomas Holland, guessing the real reason, agreed and gave him some advice on what he should study while away.

After spending two weeks with his family back in Harford and considering whether to move back home or remain in Oxford, John eventually returned. His persistent and growing ambition meant that he must return to the city. Although he stayed away from the Holland lodgings it took less than a day before he learned that Anne was back in North Moreton and was neither married nor likely to be. And she was ill.

"She has been suffering from fits for the past couple of weeks," Thomas informed him.

"Is it serious? Are her family with her? Why didn't she marry?"

Thomas looked startled. The rest in Devon didn't appear to have relaxed Prideaux much.

"I think it is serious, because my wife is down there with her, along with her mother. Brian is in London on a jury, but I know he is trying to get home as soon as he can. As for the marriage, I think whatever business deal

Brian had in mind fell through. Something like that. I try not to get involved."

"Oh. Do they need any help from us? Should I send a note?"

"No John. Don't do anything. I am sure if your help is required you will be asked for it,"

John conscious that he was sounding too effusive added, "I am sorry Thomas, I'm still a little highly strung, I know that the Gunter family will ask if any help is required."

He bowed his head slightly and left the room, Thomas watched him go and muttered to himself, "So, he is still in love with her. Brian will never approve of him."

John Prideaux walked briskly along Turl Street hoping that the people he passed could not see that his face was bright red with embarrassment. He hadn't realised that he still had such strong feelings for the young woman. But how was he to get to see her again? He could hardly call on her without invitation. He found himself chanting the prayer his father had taught him and he used on his walk to Oxford eight years ago. It gave him comfort and stopped the old habit of his mind repeating negative phrases over and over again.

John Prideaux would have felt much more relaxed if he knew how Anne had become ill.

When the women returned to the Holland lodgings that night and began to plan the next stage of their plans, they learned that Thomas had already told John about the tentative marriage plans. They also learned that John would be on his way home to Devon the following morning and there was little they could do about that without causing unwanted attention to themselves and ruining their long term game plan. It was decided to speak to him early the next day.

But John left on the early carriage and they missed him. They would have to wait until he returned and trust that his absence from Anne would encourage him to return single and not find comfort in the arms of a homely sort from Devon. Thomas could not be persuaded to send a note to have him come back to the college. Then two days later Brian told them that he no longer required Anne to marry the Dunch kin as he had discovered through closer enquiry that he was not an actual Dunch and therefore useless to his plans.

So the wedding was off.

With nothing to plan for and no one to see in Oxford any more, Anne and her mother decided to return to North Moreton. Susan wanted to come with them, but her husband insisted that she stay in Oxford and look after her family for a while. There were some occasions that he needed her to accompany him in order that he could maintain his position at the college. And the children really did need to see their mother more often. So she acquiesced and said that she would remain in Oxford for the time being, all the while thinking of ways she could escape. With all these recent events she had had to put on hold her romantic plans, but only temporarily.

Susan lived her day exactly as she pleased and had been having lots of fun these past few months with her family back and too and all the dramas. She didn't want it to end and was already planning how to continue. For what else was there to do for a young wife of an old Oxford academic?

Anne and her mother travelled back to North Moreton in silence, both contemplating the events of the past year. Anne especially was surprised to discover just how heartbroken she was about John Prideaux. She had considered herself to be in control of her feelings, she had had enough practice at control. And now there was a pain in her middle, an actual pain and her heart was racing constantly and she had begun to drum her fingers and wag her leg. Mistress Gunter told her that these actions were not those of a lady and she must desist at once.

Mistress Gunter decided that she would help her daughter catch this priest and get rid of her abusive, drunken pig of a husband at the same time. The project started not long after they returned home, when Anne was introduced into some of her mother's beliefs. Brian was in Reading trying to work one of his deals and was involving his son Harvey, now married and in his own house, but still following the Gunter rules.

The first time that Anne was taken to one of her mother's ladies sewing meetings, she was surprised to see Elizabeth Gregory and Agnes Pepwell amongst the circle. There were ladies from different walks of life who lived in and around the area and Anne recognised most of them. Most surprising of all was that the meeting was held in the church.

"We often meet here Anne; Master Bradshawe has no problem with that. He has sometimes joined in with us."

"I didn't ever know that you met here," said Anne.

"We don't always meet here. We have met in each other's houses, especially when the children were smaller. We could get away without the questions then."

During the meetings, wine was drunk and gossip made and the different classes mixed together seemingly without upset. The candles were lit and incense burnt.

"What about God?" asked Anne, incredulous that this was being allowed.

"God is everywhere, not just here Anne. But here we can connect with him much more easily. Here is where we have power."

This was confusing to Anne as she had been getting the idea that perhaps the group was against God rather than with him. Anne was particularly forward thinking in regard to the Bible and its teachings, but some aspects seemed so – unusual.

"Are you sure that God isn't upset about us all being here?"

Her mother laughed. "Why would he be upset?"

Anne was prevented from answering when Susan Dunch shouted, "Ladies, ladies! Please be quiet, the evening is moving on and we need to complete our business. Has anyone had any experiences they want to tell us about?"

Everyone shook their head, except for Mary Pepwell who said, "I would like to report something."

The ladies turned their heads in the girl's direction and silently listened to her.

"Last week I was walking through the meadow by the stream and saw Master Adams. The old Master Adams who died, not his son. He saw me too and waved. I waved back. He was wearing his best clothes, not the ones he was buried in."

"Did he speak to you?" asked Susan Dunch.

"He said good evening and waved. Then he walked back towards the churchyard and sort of vanished."

"That is excellent news," said Mistress Field.

"I saw Master Bradshawe's ghost wife walking through your garden the other week, Anne. She didn't look very pleased!" said Elizabeth Gregory.

Mistress Gunter glared at her and Anne saw that this ladies circle wasn't quite as cosy as the initial impression had seemed. Some of the other women giggled and some raised their eyebrows and folded their arms.

Susan Dunch said, "Enough ladies, lets continue with our praying, because that is the real reason we came here tonight."

The ladies made themselves comfortable on the pews, closed their eyes and faced the front. Anne joined in but didn't understand what was going on. Then the ladies began to hum. A deep soulful hum following a tune she had never heard before. She didn't join in the humming out of embarrassment but felt that listening with her eyes closed was very relaxing. Images came to her mind's eye of her life and her home, then John. John turned into a black bird and flew up into the sky over the chapel at Oxford. She watched him for as long as she could.

Suddenly she was brought out of her musings by her mother shaking her arm. Opening her eyes, she saw that the other ladies were leaving, or standing around chatting. What had happened to that time?

"I must have fallen asleep," she said.

"Perhaps you did fall asleep," answered her mother. "But did you enjoy yourself?"

"Very much. I will come again."

The meetings continued and Anne learned something each time. She learned not to fall asleep and hold on to the calm space between her thoughts. She liked the experience so much that she practised every day when away from the meetings.

The women took turns to host a meeting and when it was the turn of Mistress Field, Anne learned about holding on to the calm space and then projecting mentally what she wanted to happen. She found it very freeing. She was learning that she could have what she wanted in life if she mastered this skill. Some of the ladies appeared to have mastered their skill successfully and Anne heard rumours of flying and vanishing, although to date she had seen no evidence of either.

But the talk and the possibility was very exciting and Anne wanted desperately to know more. She was beginning to make sense of her own peculiarities and she asked each of the women for extra lessons so that she could learn quicker. Elizabeth Gregory noticed this and began to think of ways that she could clip the wings of these Gunter women.

One week, Gilbert Bradshawe called in partway through their meeting. He wasn't surprised or shocked, but sat down on of the pews and watched and listened. It wasn't the first time he had done it, conscious that what he was witnessing was not altogether acceptable but nevertheless both interesting and exciting.

"Creatures of the night," he said in a voice which was louder than he had intended. The women turned on him and slowly began to walk towards him. They had been standing in different areas of the church and this bizarre and hypnotic crowd moved as one in the vicar's direction. He was quite frankly, terrified.

Anne, shocked at what she saw, called to her mother, "What are you doing? What is happening?"

No one answered her, but Agnes said to Gilbert, "You know better than to make fun of us. Don't let us catch you doing it again."

Gilbert looked abashed and a little alarmed, but muttered something and left the church without saying anything further. The women laughed and made reference to his ignorance and his fear of them.

That night Anne followed him out and watched Gilbert walk home with his head down. He seemed disturbed as he scurried along. Anne didn't blame him as the scene she had so recently witnessed had been unnerving. She was finding it difficult to know whether the group was evil or silly or – something else. As the vicar scampered off around the corner, passing the gate to her own home, she felt a wind pick up suddenly and move the trees. The noise was terrific and she noticed the moon coming out from behind the clouds and casting an eerie glow over the muddy and rutted road. Anne was frightened and ran back into the church.

The women were listening to Elizabeth Gregory who was leaning against the altar and informing the group that they must now work towards a certain date.

"All Hallows Evening. That's when we shall bring it all together. Ten more days. If we do everything as we have practised, that will be the night to meet and see what we can raise up."

"Or who," said Mistress Gunter.

"I would like to see some of my relatives again," said Mistress Field. "Too many went out of the world too early with that dreadful plague."

"Me too," said another and there was general nodding.

"So, is that the plan? To raise the plague dead?" asked Anne, speaking before she thought.

The women looked at her and for a moment Anne was worried that they would turn on her as they had the vicar. But they didn't.

"It seems worth trying, don't you think Anne? We have all lost people lately."

"And not everyone died with the plague. I would like to see my husband's brothers and get the full story from them. That's my plan," said Elizabeth.

"Really? Is it Mistress Gregory? You want to bring shame on my family are you?" asked Mistress Gunter.

"You know what your husband and sons get up to Anne, don't pretend that you don't. I intend to get the truth about what happened to those boys. Not that we shall be able to bring it to the attention of the law. No. But at least we shall know."

"You idiot woman," answered Mistress Gunter.

"Ladies. Remember our vows. At these meetings we are all equal and must never bring negativity into the circle."

The ladies stopped arguing immediately and continued with the talking accompanied by more wine, before they began to leave.

As Anne and her mother left via the graveyard and walked towards their kitchen door, Anne said, "Mother, are you all witches?"

Her mother laughed and laughed, then took her daughter's arm and answered, "Not all, some are in training!"

"Am I in training?"

"If you want to be," answered her mother.

"I think I would like to be, mother. I want to have some power in my life. I want to be able to have the things happen that I want to happen. Not what I don't want to happen. Do you understand?"

"That is what we are training for. To be able to do what we want. If someone wants to stop us doing what we want, then we shall be able to stop them."

"By killing them?"

"No! Not by killing them. Where did you get that idea? I don't want to kill anyone. Well perhaps your father. But I don't think I would ever get away with that. I want to have influence on this man's world we live in."

Some of the other women shouted their goodbyes as they walked through the garden. The others were making their way across the churchyard towards the green.

Anne and her mother waved back. Anne was amazed how the usual society separations returned once the women were out of their meetings. Deference and bobbing occurred when any of the women met again and nothing was ever mentioned in the company of anyone who was not in the circle.

The servants were already in their beds and mother and daughter soon followed their example. Anne lay down and felt the spinning, dizzy head that she hadn't felt for a long time. She blacked out and then woke up with her mother staring into her face, eyes wide and terrified.

"Anne! What happened to you? "

"I'm not sure, mother. I felt a bit lightheaded and then I was like this. Did I have another fit? I haven't had one for ages."

"No you haven't. I hope you aren't going to be ill again."

"Oh mother! So do I! Please don't let me be ill!"

Anne cried while her mother began to clean up the vomit and urine which covered her daughter's clothes.

CHAPTER NINETEEN

With less than a week to go before Hallows Eve it wasn't looking good for Anne Gunter being at the planned event. When she wasn't throwing up, or having a fit, she was sat in the ladies private room.

She was losing weight and some of her senses. Mistress Gunter talked to her fellow ladies because this latest bout had begun immediately after their last meeting, but no one came up with any ideas. Not to her face anyway, there were several opinions behind her back.

"It was Elizabeth; she doesn't like either of them. I think she gave Anne one of her potions."

"I've heard that the baby she is carrying belongs to Gunter and not her husband," said another.

"Where did you hear that?"

"She was telling old Agnes about it when she thought no one was listening. But I was." This was from Mistress Field.

Elizabeth Gregory was considered to be a gossiping woman who would pick up on anyone's weak points and use it against them, so she wouldn't have been surprised to learn that there was gossip about her. But not that many liked Mistress Gunter either. They considered that she acted way above her station and her husband was a bullying pig.

There was a lot of gossiping in North Moreton.

Mistress Gunter was really worried about Anne this time. It had been one thing arranging a slight illness to encourage John Prideaux's interest, but Anne seemed properly ill. She gave her plenty of her remedies and potions, which Anne asked for often.

A message was sent to Brian who was doing jury service in London. Different doctors were sent for and by the end of the month, two had said that her afflictions were not of a physical cause. They said that meant she has been bewitched. An additional message to London announced this fact to her father in the hopes that he would return and offer some help. A note was sent to Susan at Oxford and this was how John Prideaux heard the news.

Everyone had different reactions dependent upon their relationship with Anne. Brian was wondering how he could make money out of the situation. Susan wanted to get back home and join in the excitement and John had two worries. He worried about Anne because he was still in love with her but he didn't want this kind of witch based drama to upset his career prospects.

Anne barely noticed the doctors, of whom there were several, because she had been almost comatose during this last bout of illness. Although constantly tended by the maids and her mother, she had fitted, fainted and vomited every day. Broth was brought to her five times a day along with milk and sometimes wine. Anything more solid lasted no time at all in her stomach.

All Hallows passed without notice in the Gunter household. It was several days later when Mistress

Gunter met Mistress Field in the street and she asked about young Anne when more news of the event was disclosed.

"So nothing happened until about midnight. We did all the usual stuff and when it started raining heavy we were about to go back home. Then Mistress Gregory says that she can see her Gregory kin outside the circle coming towards her. And then she says that they were calling your husband's name and saying he was their murderer!"

Mistress Gunter said, "Damn cheek. She can't go round saying things like that. Bringing our family's name down." She didn't want to lose her social position, which she surely would if Brian was convicted of a murder.

"No, I don't think anyone believed her. She's all over the place because her child is due anytime now." Mistress Field didn't want to be on the end of Mistress Gunter's temper, which was notorious.

"Well if anyone does start to believe her, you send them to me. I will put them right."

"I will Mistress Gunter. You can rely on me."

"Did anything else happen I should know about?"

"No. That was about it," answered Mistress Field. She had no intention of telling her about the events which happened after the apparent appearance of the Gregory brothers. Had they raised Satan?

The women parted company and Anne returned to the Rectory. Her daughter was in remission from her troubles and Rose asked her mistress to visit as soon as she came back into the house.

"Oh mother. What is the matter with me? Why am I so ill? The last doctor didn't seem to know what he was doing, even though he was very keen on trying to get my clothes off."

"Which one? Dr Cheyney?"

"No not him, he was nice. One of the others. Ma Gregory and Ma Pepwell came with him."

"They haven't been in the house Anne! Not to my knowledge. When was this? Sarah!" Mistress Gunter fired questions in different directions. When Brian was out of the home, she was far more assertive in her role as lady of the house. Chaos it may be at The Rectory, but everyone got on with their own jobs.

"Last night I think, or early this morning. I'm not sure. It was dark."

As dark as the circles under her eyes her mother wondered. Anne did look ill.

"Yes Mistress?" The maid had arrived quietly behind her.

"Anne tells me that Mistress Gregory and Mistress Pepwell were here with the doctor last night. Did you let anyone into the house?"

The girl looked confused and unsure how to answer. She gave it her best shot, "I don't think I let any visitors in here last night."

"This morning then. When I was out?"

"Not that I saw, Mistress Gunter. I didn't let anyone in and I didn't let anyone out."

Mistress Gunter stared at the girl and said, "Bring us some food here Sarah. Nothing too heavy."

Sarah bobbed and left the room.

"They were here mother. Really they were."

"What else can you remember about that visit Anne?"

"Not much really. They were here when I woke up."

"All three of them?"

"Yes I think so. I only saw the doctor at first, he was leaning over me asking questions and touching me. Then I noticed Mistress Gregory and I thought that you must have told her to come. She looked much bigger than when I last saw her. Has she had her child yet?"

"Not that I have heard. Did she say anything to you?"

"No. Well not to me, about me. She was saying to Ma Pepwell that she didn't think I could be long for this world and that it was judgment because of Richard and John."

"And what did Agnes Pepwell say?"

"She just muttered a lot and played with her cat. Or dog or whatever it was that she had with her. I wondered why she had an animal in my room, but no one else seemed to notice."

"That's very odd," said her mother.

"Yes. I feel so weak mother and so tired. I'm not going to die, am I?"

"No daughter! You are not going to die."

Sarah brought the food in and dropped the tray onto a small table by the window. She looked out on to the garden as she did so and commented that the vicar was staring at them from the churchyard.

"Is he?" asked Mistress Gunter and she went to have a look for herself.

Gilbert Bradshawe waved when he saw her and she waved back before she remembered that she wasn't alone.

"I think that Master Bradshawe wants to speak to me," she said and kissed her daughter before she began to leave the room.

"Did you let Master Prideaux know I am ill?"

"No. I let your sister know. She will tell him."

Sarah looked at Anne and asked if she wanted anything further.

"No, no Sarah I don't. Or is it Rose? I forget so easily just lately."

"It doesn't matter Mistress," she answered. Sarah Rose was pretty sure that Mistress Gunter would be dead soon, so it didn't really matter what she called her.

"I have found pins all over the bed again. Do you know anything about them? Do you drop them in my bed when you are changing the linen?"

"No Mistress. I never use pins. What kind of pins?"

"They seem to be ordinary pins. Not dress pins."

"If they were, you would be worth a fortune Mistress!"

"Especially if they were silver. My mother has some silver dress pins, but I don't."

"I have seen them Mistress. Those pins are beautiful. Are these the pins you mean?" Sarah picked some from the dresser.

"Those are the pins. Do you know I was pricked all over from them? Some had even stuck into me and I found some in my mouth. That's quite dangerous isn't it?"

"I would say it was dangerous Mistress. But you should go back to sleep now. Get some rest; it would be for the best."

Anne turned onto her side and faced the window and closed her eyes.

"You may leave now."

Anne tried to do one of the things she had been so recently taught at her ladies meetings about how to make what you want to happen more quickly. It was the basis of all spell work. Imagine what you want and believe it has already happened. She sent her mind to her middle and willed it to catch fire. Then she wrote her wish list in the fire. She wished for health and wealth and beauty. She wished that John would come to her and love her and she wished that something would happen that would help her to leave North Moreton and be independent. Anything.

It was very important that she did not write anything on the list that she did not want to come true. She went through the list again and had the fire burn through it. Now she could safely dream knowing that her wishes would come true. She dreamed of the Devil and the church meetings and then she dreamed that the vicar was burying her in the churchyard and she was covered with thousands of pins instead of soil.

She woke in the early evening and feeling a great thirst, took a long drink from the beaker on the table by her bed. She returned to a fitful sleep, but awoke again to see a group of concerned looking faces standing around her bed.

"Anne! Oh I didn't realise you were so bewitched!"

It was her sister Susan. Anne vaguely made out the others as her mother, her father and John Prideaux.

"Bewitched?" she asked, but couldn't recognise the voice that came from her mouth. She croaked and rasped her way through the question.

"Yes that's what you are daughter. We have it on the doctor's word now. And we know who has done this bewitching don't we?" Brian looked at his wife for confirmation.

"Do we? I don't think we are really sure if there has been any bewitching at all?" Mistress Gunter was still living in the residual freedom of the past few weeks.

"I think we are sure and we will be doing something about it." Brian glared at her.

The feeling of freedom was swiftly passing. Mistress Gunter followed her husband out of the room, leaving Susan and John with Anne.

"Anne. What has been going on? You look awful. Have you been taking those potions again?"

"What potions?" asked John.

"Just some remedies that the apothecary gave her in the summer," answered Susan quickly.

"Did they make you ill or well?" John asked Anne.

She didn't answer.

Susan wiped her sister's face with a wet cloth. Anne moaned a little and seemed to fall asleep.

"Mistress Holland, this is not good. You must get some help for Anne."

"I know that mother has consulted a few doctors and wise women and cunning men and they all say that her sufferings aren't of natural causes but that she has been put under a spell by someone."

"And who do they think has done it?"

"They say it's Mistress Gregory. I don't know if you remember her. She used to work here in the kitchens years ago and her husband's brothers were killed after that football match."

"There was talk about your father killing them."

"And my brothers. They were blamed too."

"Did they kill them?"

"I don't know how you can ask that question!" said Susan in mock horror.

John leaned back and laughed. Susan suddenly saw what Anne saw in him. When he wasn't looking studious and pious he was quite handsome. Susan found herself moving towards him and giving him her best smile.

"It's also supposed to be Agnes Pepwell. Do you know her? You can't miss her. She's a dirty old hag and she has a daughter who isn't much better than her. Some vagrant is her father. Of Mary that is, but Agnes is cousin to Elizabeth Gregory. It doesn't take long before you can relate everyone to everyone round here." She patted his knee and he didn't pull away.

John remembered his first meeting with Agnes as she carried that bag of sticks. Horrible foul woman. And Mary had said that she was a witch. And Agnes said she was a witch too. Yes he did remember seeing Elizabeth Gregory. She had given him food. Sold him food. At the same moment he realised that Susan's hand was on his knee, Anne sat upright in her bed.

"Anne, are you feeling better now?"

Anne's eyes were staring beyond them and she let out a long low monotone scream. The pair jumped up in shock.

Anne's head bent back and her wrists twisted so far round that her fingers almost touched her arm. The bedclothes slipped off and before Susan could cover her up, Anne's nightdress began to rise alarmingly up her legs.

"Anne! What's happening to you?"

Anne responded by jerking up and down on the bed. John ran out of the room calling for Master and Mistress Gunter. He didn't want to see anymore of Anne than he had already seen.

He stayed on the hallway while Anne's parents and two maids ran into her bedroom.

CHAPTER TWENTY

John wasn't allowed back into the bedroom again on that visit.

There was a constant flurry of visiting family and friends to Anne Gunter's room, all of whom came down with a story to recount.

John sat either in the parlour, or in the garden and he soon discovered that these were the usual places a visitor would come to mull over what they had just witnessed. Thomas Holland had sent word that John should stay on in North Moreton and report back to him as he was too engaged in the Bible translation and couldn't possibly leave Oxford. It was imperative, he said, that John brought back as much information as possible so that this could be passed on to the King. King James had a special interest in cases of witchcraft and the faking of bewitchment. He must not, in any circumstances let Brian Gunter know that the King was interested. Thomas would ensure that John's students would be taken care of. John promised via return letter to do as he was bid and proceeded to jot down in his notebook all that had occurred to date. All that he knew anyway, he must find a way to question others that knew more.

John had been quite shocked with what he had witnessed in the bedroom. Anne had shown signs of some kind of fit and many signs of what he had come to expect of bewitchment. Reading about witchcraft was part of his priest training and he had witnessed possession on more than one occasion. Some had been faked, but the symptoms which manifested themselves on this occasion, did not appear to be faked in any way.

A maid brought him some cheese and apple and bread and wine. She seemed distracted and had to return with a knife.

"It's Sarah isn't it?" he asked.

"Yes sir. Sometimes it's Rose."

"Rose? I thought that was a different maid?"

"No, it's me sir. Mistress Anne wanted me to change my name because she was getting me mixed up with another maid they had called Sarah."

"Oh yes! I think I remember her. She was maid here the first time I visited. She was a naive young girl."

"She used to like you sir. She told me. "

"You still see her then?" John asked with genuine curiosity.

"Oh yes sir. She is a relative of Elizabeth Gregory. A niece I think. Yes, a niece."

"Interesting. Now have you seen anything unusual happen with Mistress Anne?"

"Besides being bewitched?"

"Besides that, yes. I mean, who supervises her food and drink and who makes sure that any visitors to her room are seen first?"

"Is this to do with the law? Is that why you are asking so many questions?"

"Not the law. I'm just trying to get some information together so we can get to the root of the problem. So can you tell me anything?"

"The only people who visit Mistress Anne are her family and then lately all these doctors. And some neighbours the master is trying to impress for some reason."

"What about the vicar Reverend Bradshawe, has he been round?"

"Oh no, sir. He and Master Gunter don't get on and he isn't allowed in the house."

"Why is that?"

"Because he is a friend of Mistress Gunter," she answered simply.

"Mistress Gunter also said that Elizabeth Gregory and Agnes Pepwell were in her room with a strange doctor," said John.

"Mistress Anne has been unwell and gets easily confused," answered Sarah Rose. She went out of the garden and into the kitchen.

John learned from different visitors that Anne's symptoms were becoming stranger and more alarming. Her ankles twisted and her wrists bent back. She vomited pins and passed them in her water. Her eyes almost stood out on stalks and her belly swelled as though she were with child. These were not natural causes, these were signs of witchcraft.

A few days later, Elizabeth Gregory came to The Rectory. She was left on the doorstep and refused entry on the instructions of the family. John had been praying at the church and returned to The Rectory via the front gate. The road was frozen and mud was rutted. It was almost impossible to walk without tripping up and the carts and ponies slipped and became wheel jammed as they made their way along.

He saw Elizabeth arguing at the front door and smiled when he saw her. He didn't know why he smiled, he just felt like doing so.

"This weather has come early to our part of the world, ladies," he said, addressing Mistress Gregory and the maid.

"That may well be Reverend Prideaux, but it isn't getting the baby fed is it?"

"Baby? I'm sorry I don't understand. Are you having trouble feeding the children, Mistress Gregory?"

"Not the others, perhaps I will with this one." She patted her belly, which John now realised was large and round.

"A baby is due!" said John.

"Any day now according to Agnes, but she said that this child will cause me trouble my entire life," announced Elizabeth.

"That was a comforting thing to tell you." exclaimed John.

"Well she's mostly right about these things. But this stupid little maid won't let me in to see the two Annes."

"I have been told not to let anyone in today. It's not just Mistress Gregory. Mistress Anne is too poorly at the moment to receive visitors."

Mistress Gregory seemed unconvinced, when suddenly Anne Gunter flung open the windows above them and screamed and screamed. Everyone looked shocked, but before they had time to react, Mistress Gunter had appeared behind her daughter and was covering her bare shoulders with a blanket. John realised that Anne was naked and turned away momentarily while she was covered up.

"What's happening, Mistress Gunter?" asked John.

"I wanted to come in and speak to you about something private. Mistress Gunter!"

As John and the maid looked at her in amazement, Mistress Gunter answered, "We are having a few problems with Anne. She isn't very good today."

At that moment Anne spat at Mistress Gregory and hit her directly in the face.

"You filthy cow witch Gregory. You have done this to me. I am bewitched because of you!" Anne threw a vase of flowers which smashed on the ground in front of the woman.

Mistress Gregory looked shocked and sat down on the ground. She didn't look very well. Anne continued screaming and tearing at her hair. Every so often the blanket left her shoulders as her mother tried to put it back on. The maid ran upstairs on John's instruction and helped Mistress Gunter pull her daughter back in from the window. Anne went in once and then escaped her captors and leaned out of the window again, bare breasted and hair wild about her head and body. Her eyes were black and wide and she said in a voice which did not belong to a young woman, "You will have this devil child of Brian Gunter's.   It will make your life hell and you will suffer every day of your life after its birth. Your birth will be painful and the child ugly. Your life is ruined Elizabeth Gregory. You are a fornicator and are going to hell."

These words were screamed, spat and hurled at the woman until Mistress Gunter and Sarah Rose managed to get her in the house and the window slammed shut. Elizabeth went completely white and John noticed a pool of liquid spilling away from her legs.

"Mistress Gregory is the baby coming?" asked John, who was used to childbirth, there having been eight children born after him back home on Dartmoor. Dartmoor, where the biggest drama of his life had been a horse bolting with him. He was paying a high price for fame and fortune.

"I think so, Reverend, I think so. I need help. Please help me." The robust complaints were no more. Elizabeth Gregory was a frightened woman.

John went over to her and tried to lift her up, but the task was too much for him.

"We need to get you into the house Mistress Gregory. It looks as though the baby will be arriving shortly."

"Yes, it's coming. My devil child," she answered breathing shortly.

"I shouldn't take any notice of that. Mistress Anne is ill and doesn't know what she is saying."

"Is she? Is she ill? She's a witch, I know that. And this child is Brian Gunter's," she added.

John decided to make no further comment, for if he was to acknowledge what the woman was telling him, he would have to take it further.

"Well we still need to get you into the house," he said.

John opened the front door and stepped into the hallway, calling for someone to help him. Eventually a maid came down the stairs and asked what he wanted. On discovering his requirements she ran back upstairs to inform her mistress and two minutes later was running down them again.

By now, Mistress Gregory had her colour back and was making grunting and panting noises. "This child isn't far off, Reverend," she said.

The maid was speaking to John, "The mistress says that she's not having that woman in her house and she must have her bastard elsewhere." The message was delivered triumphantly.

"But Mistress Gregory is having the child right now!" he shouted.

He turned round and Mistress Gregory, currently between contractions had raised herself to her feet and was staggering towards the gate which separated The Rectory garden from the churchyard.

"I will have my devil child in the church," she panted, "God will protect us both."

John couldn't find a decent argument against this reasoning and helped her through the gateway, stopping only for another almighty contraction. He looked up because he could hear banging on the upstairs window and saw Anne, wildly smashing it with her hands and shouting words he didn't want to hear.

Blood was now flowing from Mistress Gregory and it was only with the timely assistance of Gilbert Bradshawe that they managed to get her in through the church door and lying down by the font upon some shawls he found hanging by the door.

"We need some help for this," said the vicar.

"We do, but I don't want to leave the woman on her own. She has had a shock which has brought on her pains."

Gilbert got up and ran to the Gregory farm on the other side of the church and soon brought back two maids from the dairy, who knelt down beside the screaming woman and began to help her.

"Fetch some water and cloths and get out," one instructed the two men. They were happy to oblige and went outside into the church yard.

"I will tell her husband," said Gilbert. "He wasn't back when I went in there just now."

John was almost going to stop him and confess the information he had been so recently party to, but decided against it. If it was the ravings of a sick woman, he would cause unnecessary harm.

"I will stay here in case I am needed. Tell someone to bring the water and cloths. And something to wrap the new child in." he added.

As Gilbert left the church, he heard loud screaming which sounded more like a wounded wolf than a woman in labour. It seemed to John that darkness was falling and snow began to fall heavily. There were rumbles of thunder and lightning flashed. For a moment, John believed he saw a dark shape run across the churchyard from the direction of the Rectory towards the Gregory farm. It almost made his heart stop, the whole experience was unreal and for a short time John wondered if he had been hit by lightning and was actually dead and watching the scene as a ghost. It was unnerving and John was torn between going back into the sanctuary of the church and running over to the Gregory farm to see what was taking Gilbert so long.

His indecision was over when Gilbert ran back, clutching some wool blankets and a large kettle, which John rightly presumed contained hot water. Another young woman followed him while carrying a large jug. They both went into the door, but Gilbert was turned back as soon as his load was deposited.

The two men remained there considering their options, when Brian Gunter appeared out of the dark and stood in front of them, hands on his hips.

"What is going on in there? My daughter is screaming and shouting that Elizabeth Gregory is visiting her and cursing her to the devil."

"That isn't possible, because Mistress Gregory is in the church giving birth to her latest child."

"She's a witch though isn't she? She can go anywhere she wants. Cursing my daughter and my house." He leant forward into Gilbert Bradshawe's face, "and whatever that witch says, that bastard devil child is not mine." He spat on the floor and walked away.

The men looked at each other and Gilbert said, "What was that about?"

"Mistress Gunter shouted at Mistress Gregory saying that the child was her father's. No, she didn't say it was her father's, she said the child was Brian Gunter's."

"As though Anne wasn't Anne?"

"Exactly."

"Witchcraft," he said, "she was bewitched."

"I thought you weren't a believer in witchcraft?" said John.

"What makes you say that? A religious man is a fool if he doesn't believe in witches. I've seen much to convince me of their existence."

"So have I, Bradshawe. But I am not so sure that there are witches in North Moreton. I have seen women who profess to be witches, but I am not convinced."

"Come to my house Prideaux, I shall tell you some stories that may make you change your mind."

As they walked towards his cottage, Susan Holland ran after them and said, "Come with me John. I need you to take a look at Anne. She is getting worse."

The men turned on their heels, but Susan said, "Don't come Vicar. My father won't allow you in the house."

"What have I done to offend your father?"

"I think you know perfectly well, Master Bradshawe."

John followed Susan and Gilbert went home.

Susan took him directly into Anne's room which, like the rest of the house, was dimly lit and smelt of burning hair. Anne lay on top of her bed dressed in her Sunday dress. Her eyes were open and her mouth smiled, but it was as though there was no one home.

"Anne? How are you?" asked John.

She didn't answer or look in his direction. He didn't repeat the question.

Susan said, "She has calmed down a little now John, but before she was screaming about Elizabeth Gregory. She thought that she was in the room with her, taunting her. She screamed and writhed and her belly swelled. It was frightening to watch."

"Mistress Gregory has given birth to a child in the church just now. Her labour was brought on by your sister shouting at her earlier."

"Witches can travel during the labour and torment a vulnerable girl," said Susan sagely.

"Can they? I have never heard of that."

"It's true. It happens a lot."

Anne stirred, moving side to side on the bed. John leant down towards her.

Her eyes opened suddenly, making him step back. They were dark pools of nothingness, which did not see him. Her body arched slowly, cracking as it did so. The top of her head touched the sheets and her stomach pointed to the ceiling. Her legs, splayed apart made her dress ride up revealing petticoats... The further she arched her back the more her body cracked and the strain on her clothes began to cause the lacing on her bodice to come undone.

Susan reached out and touched her sister on the stomach. "It's rigid," she said. "Like wood."

"Has she done this before? Acted like this?" asked John.

"She has been acting worse and worse as time has gone on. Everyone is sure she is bewitched. The doctors say so. The apothecaries say so."

"Do you have any idea who is bewitching her?"

"Mother says it is Elizabeth Gregory."

"Why though?"

"Bad blood over a long period of time," answered Susan.

Anne's hands bent to either side of her head which began to turn sideways, working against all the laws of physics. The cracking sounds increased and Susan put her hands to her ears.

"Do you think her bones are breaking?" she asked.

"I hope not," answered John, who was feeling more than a little queasy.

Now her lacing was almost undone and her nipples exposed.

Anne screamed and fell down flat on the bed and as she did her clothing closed again around her chest. Her eyes closed firmly shut as did her mouth and she stopped moving. The whole process had taken less than two minutes.

"She's not moving," said John.

"She goes like that sometimes, she always ends up alright."

"She doesn't look very well to me," said John.

Anne's lips were turning a blue grey colour and her skin was quickly following suit. Green foam was coming from her mouth and dribbling on the cream sheet, discolouring it. There was a strange smell, which John could not identify.

"We should do something," he said, alarmed at the state of Anne, but not wanting to touch her because of her loose clothing.

"Yes we should," said Susan. She went out of the room and bellowed. "Mother! Anne is bad again. You need to come quickly."

Mistress Gunter came into the room and ran over to the bed. She lifted Anne into a sitting position and leaning her forward, slapped her hard on the back. Pins shot from her lips and Mistress Gunter put her fingers inside her daughter's mouth and removed more. She took a flask from the drawer in the bedside table and poured it into her mouth. She laid her back down and rearranged her clothing. With a minute her colour was returning and although she still looked bad, there seemed to be more life there.

"Help me Susan," she said. "And please leave us, Reverend Prideaux. Go downstairs and fetch her father."

John found Brian outside, staring at the sky. "There will be more snow tonight priest. Snow covers tracks."

"Yes indeed. But if you could go and visit your daughter, that would be excellent. Mistress Gunter wants you there. I am afraid I just witnessed another of her episodes and it was frightening sir. I think that we should bring in someone from Oxford, someone with experience of witchcraft."

"You are a firm believer, Master Prideaux?"

"I saw many things back home that could not be explained any other way, Master Gunter."

"You are from Dartmoor aren't you?"

"Yes sir, I am."

"Get lots of witches there, do you?" asked Brian.

"We get some. Not lots. There is talk of many things happening on the moor. Sometimes it can be a very mysterious place in the fog, or the rain, or the snow. Desolate, boggy and lonely. It's easy to get lost on

Dartmoor and many have lost their lives there. I miss it a lot actually."

"Sounds horrible," said Brian and went out of the room.

John was unsure whether or not to follow him and instead moved himself to the kitchen, to watch the scurrying of maids. He helped himself to wine and cheese while he waited. Even from there he could hear shouting and banging and crashing and assumed that Anne was again in her fits.

After an hour, no one from the family had returned down stairs and John having finished the cheese and wine, decided to put his cloak around his shoulders and go for a walk. It was almost midnight and he could see the snow falling against the kitchen window. He wasn't sleepy and thought he ought to stay away while the family were still tending to Anne. Maybe Gilbert Bradshawe was still up and he could have a few drinks with him.

He went out into the garden, now covered in snow. Winter had come early this year, it was only November. John wondered if it was God's way of ensuring that the last drops of plague would be killed off completely. He liked to think that was the reason.

He walked across the grass, his boots crunching on the snow and his mind went back to Stowford and how he would crunch up the snowy lane with his family when they went to Harford church. Funny how these thoughts of home would sweep over him from time to time and he wished he was there. But when he visited, after a couple of days of watching his parents work the farm and his brother Thomas talk about next year's crops, he thought he could die of boredom.

The snow fell heavily and he pulled his cloak tighter around him, glad of its warmth. He walked to the church door to make sure that everything had been finished. No sign of lights or people or new babies or devil children for that matter. He turned his feet in the direction of the green and walked on to Gilbert Bradshawe's house. A quick look through the window showed that he was sitting by the fire with a drink in his hand. John knocked on the glass and Gilbert turned and beckoned him in.

John went to the door, stamped his snowy boots on the step and went into the warm cottage.

CHAPTER TWENTY ONE

The men talked until the early hours about Oxford and God, the Gunters and witches. They talked about whether the death of Bradshawe's family was predetermined by God or not.

"I have heard some at Oxford debate whether we are in control of our own destiny and that every thought we have is creative."

"You mean that the only life we have is the one we think of?"

"Yes and as most of us do it without awareness, we have a crazy, depressing life ending in death."

"I think I would need that explaining to me in detail. It sounds interesting."

"I also know that it is in this way that an accomplished witch can control the minds and lives of others."

"Do we think that Elizabeth Gregory is a witch?" asked Gilbert.

"If she is, I don't think she has mastered her thoughts. She doesn't seem in control of her own life let alone be able to affect anyone else's."

The men laughed at their cleverness. When the knock came at the door at 5 o'clock, they were snoring away gently in front of a low fire and feeling cold. His maid had not arrived for work and Gilbert had to answer the door himself.

"Oh sir, you must ring the passing bell, the doctor says. She won't last the day."

"Who won't?" asked Gilbert.

"Mistress Anne," said Sarah Rose.

"Oh my dear Lord, that is dreadful. We will be along soon, girl."

He came back into the room where John was stoking the fire.

"Did you hear that?" Gilbert asked.

"I did. It's bad news. Who rings the bell?"

"Mainly me, but others do too. During the plague, we took turns. Especially when it was someone we were close to." He tailed off, remembering his family.

"I know, my friend. I will go to the house and see if I can pray for her soul. I can't believe that she has deteriorated so much. It is very sad."

They split up in the churchyard and before John had reached the kitchen door of the Rectory, the bell tolled at the church. John walked straight in and made his way up the stairs. No one stopped him and he soon stood in the doorway watching the death scene play out. Anne lay motionless on her bed, arms by her sides over the cover. Her mother and sister were kneeling on either side of the bed and two maids stood against the wall, one holding a cloth and the other a jug and bowl. Brian came up behind John and clapped him on the shoulder.

"She's going to die it seems, Prideaux. Get in there and pray for her. Keep that Gregory witch and her devils away from my daughter."

John had a sudden urge to ask Brian how he felt about his new daughter who had been born the previous night, but guessed that now was not the best time. He walked into the room and was welcomed by the grateful face of Mistress Gunter.

"John, please pray for my child. I am told she will be with our Lord this day and I don't want her to be prevented from getting there by the devils sent by Elizabeth Gregory. Please save her soul."

John went over to the bed saying, "There is little evidence that Mistress Gregory has been responsible for any bewitching. I was present at her birthing yesterday and she didn't seem in any condition to send out demons."

"You are showing your naivety, Reverend," said Master Gunter. "The woman is a demon and would have had more power at that point. She would have had a great deal of power."

John decided to say no more and just deal with Anne. He moved Susan out of the way with a wave of his hand and leaned down into Anne's face. He began his prayers and the family and maids joined in where appropriate. Anne's face was grey and her lips blue. There was a low rattle in her chest, the only sign that the she was not yet passed. The bell sounded through the window even though it was closed. The fire crackled in the grate and there was sobbing from Mistress Gunter.

The peace was broken by shouting downstairs from men.

"My boys are here!" said Brian.

Harvey and William Gunter came thundering up the stairs and crashed their way into the bedroom.

"What is happening with our sister? We are told she is dying and the Gregorys are to blame!"

"Please! Please, keep your voices down!" said John. "We cannot disturb Anne's soul with this! It will not be able to travel so well."

"Shut up priest! Where is your husband, Susan? Where is Thomas? He could put a stop to this nonsense!" exclaimed Harvey, anxious to cause trouble wherever he could.

"He is in Oxford and has been sent for. Reverend Prideaux is standing in for him and praying for our sister. Reverend Bradshawe is tolling the bell."

"You aren't qualified for a job such as this, Prideaux. You are a priest in training surely?" said William.

"You have been away from home too long William," said Mistress Gunter. "Master Prideaux is more than qualified and has helped the family a good deal."

Anne had not moved during this drama and John returned to his praying. He would have said more to the girl had he not such a large audience. He wanted to tell her that he loved her and wanted her to live. The family waited for more than two hours until Anne appeared to have finally gone. They each kissed her and filed out of the room. The men supported the women in their grief.

"I should like to stay and perform final prayers, before the maids make her ready," said John.

Mistress Gunter nodded and left him alone with Anne.

Anne's face was paling to the familiar yellow and cream of the corpse. Her eyes were closed, but her mouth was beginning to open. She was already losing her beauty. John often thought that watching someone die was an excellent way to prove that a spirit is a separate entity to the body. As soon as it leaves, the body quickly becomes a shell.

He put his hand across her forehead and felt the warmth leave it.

"Anne, Anne. If only I could have told you to your face how much you mean to me."

He kissed her cheek and the tears he had streaming down his face, dropped slowly onto hers. They slid from down the contours of her face and onto the lace collar of her dress. The cover slipped down her breasts as he placed his elbows on the bed beside her. The pins, which must have been holding her clothes together, were lying on the material of her dress and on the pillow beside her head. The lace had come apart and her young nipples showed. John tried to straighten her clothing and returned the cover to its original modest positioning. He moved the pins to the table in a pile next to another pile of pins.

"I don't know if you can still hear me, if you are still in the room. I remember how you told me that you could float around the room when you were a child. Perhaps you are doing it now. So now I can tell you how lovely I thought you were when I first met you in that sheep pen, all those years ago. You seemed so much older than your years. Then all these times we have spoken and met since then, I have gradually grown to love you. I am slow to show my feelings and because I thought that we had so much time and I could further my career before I settled down, I never said anything. Now it's too late and I don't really know what to say or do. I'm good at debating the Bible and religion and how a man could save his soul. But I have forgotten over these years at Oxford how to converse with a friend. My family, my large family would have no trouble in talking and making me talk. I wish you could talk back to me. Be safe with Jesus, Anne. Be safe." He kissed her again, got up from his knees and walked towards the door.

He heard a rustling of skirts and hoped that the maids had not been listening to his speech.

"I am talking back, John."

He swung around and looked at the corpse on the bed, which did not move. The eyes were sinking into her face and the cheeks too. Her mouth opened so much that her bottom jaw rested against her chest. He walked back towards her, but slowly. He was sure that he had heard someone speaking, but no one was in the room. A tapping at the window made him turn sharply again, but it was only a branch. John walked over to the window and looked out. The snow still came down thick and fast and he saw William Gunter making his way through the snow towards the church. The bell still rang and John assumed he was going to tell him to stop. Surely Gilbert hadn't been ringing the bell himself for so many hours? He noticed that some villagers stood by the church, but looked up at the Rectory. It all seemed so unreal.

A bird, mesmerised by the falling snow, hit the window and fell to the ground. John jumped almost out of his skin.

"I am still here John. I am watching you. Shall I come back?"

"Do you want to come back?" he said to the corpse.

"I am up here John, like I told you. I have to decide a bit quick because my body is looking very grim. If I come back will you help me?"

"Help you?" asked John.

"Help me bring my father to justice."

"I will help you Anne. I want to help you."

He walked over to the corpse, now deteriorating more quickly than he had seen any corpse do. It's the bewitching, he thought. It's the evil rotting her flesh.

Mistress Gunter and Susan came back in.

"We must make her ready now Rector. We must wash and clean her body." Their eyes were red and faces puffy.

He waved them back in and they joined him at her bedside.

"She looks so dreadful!" exclaimed Susan.

Mistress Gunter put her handkerchief to her mouth and began to sob. The bell had stopped. John had not been aware of its peal, until it stopped. The silence in the room was broken only by sniffing and then suddenly Anne sat bolt upright, clutching the cover to her bosom with one hand. She was smiling broadly, all trace of corpse-like appearance gone.

"Hello all," she said, albeit rather hoarsely.

Mistress Gunter fell into a dead faint and Susan turned to John and asked, "What did you do?"

"I prayed Mistress Holland. I just prayed."

Susan tended to her mother sitting her in a chair, while Sarah handed her recently deceased mistress a drink of wine.

"Are you a ghost?" she asked.

"No I am not, Rose. Do I look like a ghost?"

"You looked like a dead woman, Mistress Anne. You look alive now. I don't understand how that could be." She took the glass back from Anne and bobbed a curtsey.

"Always tell the truth, Anne and you will be certain of sitting at the right hand of God."

She looked at him and said, "Alright."

Susan and Mistress Gunter looked from one to the other, feeling that they were missing something.

"I shall get up now mother. I need a wash and my clothes changing. I feel dirty." She got out of bed and walked to the window.

"Reverend Prideaux should leave now so that I can get washed. He doesn't need to pray over me anymore."

John bowed slightly and left the room. In the dining room waiting for any member of the Gunter family to return, he ate the food brought to him by Sarah Rose. He heard knocking at the door, and assumed it would be Gilbert or one of the North Moretoners. The man brought into see him was none of them.

It was Thomas Holland telling him that he could now stop with his wife for a few days and John was free to return to Oxford.

"There are so many duties you need to catch up with John. You could return tonight I think. I can take over here."

"I was hoping to stay with the family until Anne is well again. Also I may be able to find out what is causing the problem," said John.

"Anne? Mistress Anne, do you mean?"

"I do mean Mistress Anne," said John, cross with himself for making such an error.

"Well, whatever you mean. I can deal with this now. Go back to Exeter and catch up with your work. Students are waiting to speak to you and learn from you."

"I will go in the morning if that is fine with you. I can say goodbye to everyone."

"You will be back here soon, I am sure."

John smiled knowing that he would.

#

Anne felt much better the next morning and stood in front of her mirror, combing her long fair hair and admiring her pale features. She remembered leaving her body and watching John talk to it. But she didn't remember her body looking as bad as the family told her it had been. She remembered feeling out of control and separated from her body before she nearly died. And she remembered that someone must be doing this to her. She knew her own capabilities, her own skills. But this was something stronger than her. The lessons in the church from the other women had taught her about mind and its influence over her life. These latest dramas must be caused by one of those women. She didn't know who, but everyone else's opinion was that it was the fault of Mistress Gregory probably in cahoots with Agnes Pepwell. They were making her do things that she could not remember.

She continued brushing her hair which now shone after her bath earlier this morning. Sarah Rose had used some lemon and rose oil in the water.

She had been disappointed to learn that John had returned to Oxford.

"Master Holland sent him back Mistress," said Sarah Rose, now on friendlier terms.

"Did he now. Why did he do that?"

"Master Holland told him that his students needed him and that he must go. I don't think he wanted to leave you though, Mistress."

"Do you think so? I give him something to think about. I am colourful, aren't I?"

"You are, Mistress. And you have survived death, which makes you special in anyone's eyes."

She finished her hair and called Sarah Rose back to plait and dress it. She finally stood resplendent in dark blue with red trimmings.

"That should knock them dead," she said and swept out of the room.

She walked downstairs and into the dining room where her parents and brothers sat around the table.

"We have got to get this Gregory witch into the courts. She is bewitching Anne and must be stopped," announced Brian.

"How do you propose to prove that?" asked his wife.

"I will find a way,"

"You seem very keen on getting rid of her," said his wife.

He looked at her with contempt and turned away.

"I think we should get in touch with our lawyers about this," said William.

"We might be in with a chance of getting their land, if we can discredit them enough," pointed out Harvey.

"You are so sure that Elizabeth Gregory is the cause?" asked Anne.

"I am sure," said her mother. "The woman is a bitch and a whore and an evil witch."

Anne was surprised that she would say that, when they were members of the same group.

"Those are strong words, mother."

"But they are the truth Anne. I agree with William that we shall have to do something. Elizabeth is dangerous. The law will have to deal with her."

"But she only had a baby last night. I think I must have brought on her labour, with the way I was acting."

"If she is the one bewitching you, then it's all part of the same plot and she brought it on herself," said Harvey.

"I am not so sure that it is her that's doing it to me," said Anne.

"Take my word for it daughter. It is Mistress Gregory and I am going to make her disappear. And if I find out who else is doing this, then they will hang alongside her," said Mistress Gunter.

"Wasn't she once your friend, mother?"

"I don't remember that," came the reply.

Anne rescued her cloak from a hook and put it round her shoulders.

"Where are you going sister?" asked William.

"I need some air, William. I have been cooped up for weeks and feel the need to walk in the snow."

"You can't go out, you were dead yesterday!" said Mistress Gunter.

"I can go with you," said Harvey.

As the maid walked in with a tray at that same moment, Anne said, "Sarah Rose will come for a walk with me, won't you? That way if I have a funny turn, she can look after me. What about that?"

Harvey shrugged his shoulders, caring neither one way nor the other. He and William were away from their wives and families and this was a good excuse to play, while away from home. Babysitting his supposedly dying sister was not something he really cared to do. Sarah Rose on the other hand was very excited at the thought of going out with Mistress Gunter into the village during the day. She had never done that before and was bemused by the fact that her mistress had even asked her.

"Run and get your shawl, Sarah Rose and meet me by the front door."

Sarah Rose put the tray on the table and skipped out of the room.

"What's Anne up to?" asked William.

"I don't know yet, but don't worry. Sarah will report back to me. She is not a fan of my daughter."

#

Anne met Sarah Rose outside and as she pulled her cloak tightly around her asked, "Can you guarantee that everything that happens with me will be kept between us?"

"You mean today, Mistress?"

"I mean every day Sarah Rose. If you stay completely loyal to me and keep my secrets and do everything I ask of you, then you can be my maid. My lady's maid."

"Mistress Anne! Yes I will! Does that mean I have special duties? Better duties than the others?"

"Yes it does. You will look after me and although you will work in the rest of the house sometimes, there will be no more dirty work. And if I find out that you reported anything to my parents or brothers or the rest of the servants, you won't be my personal ladies maid for one more minute."

"I won't tell anyone anything Mistress. Will you tell the others that I'm your maid?"

"Yes Sarah Rose. Now come on, we are going to visit Mistress Gregory."

"To see the baby?"

"Yes, I want to see if it is a devil baby like they say." She pulled the hood over her head and led the way through the small gate which led to the road.

CHAPTER TWENTY TWO

Elizabeth Gregory was shocked to learn that Anne Gunter was sitting in her parlour ready for a visit. Anne had brought a maid with her, because she was apparently still wobbly on her feet. Elizabeth walked slowly into the room, still sore from her own recent dramas.

"I hear you almost died yesterday Anne. The passing bell was ringing long enough when I was trying to rest."

"And I hear that you had your latest child in the church. That must have been very disconcerting for you, is the child well?"

"The child is well, as am I Anne. Have you recovered from your death's door illness?"

"I appear to have done," she answered.

"Have they discovered what has been causing your delusions and fits?"

Anne hesitated before answering and said, "They tell me I am being bewitched."

"By whom?"

"By you."

Elizabeth sat down quickly on a wooden chair and put her hand to her mouth.

"Are you alright Mistress Gregory? I didn't mean to alarm you, I am only telling you what the gossip is, not what I believe necessarily."

"You don't believe you are being bewitched or you don't believe it is me?"

"I don't know anything. I am still very tired and confused after having been ill for so many weeks."

"You have made a remarkable recovery though."

"It's all to do with prayer. Reverend Prideaux prayed for my soul and I was revived. Quite miraculous."

"He must be a man of great power to revive you from death. You are looking very well, almost translucent."

"I must respond well to prayer," answered Anne.

"So it seems, Mistress Anne. Would you like some wine?"

"Please, it will work as a tonic. I think I need a few tonics. Yes I will take some sweets too!" She helped herself from the proffered bowl.

The two women sat down opposite each other, Sarah Rose had gone to the kitchen with the other maids, so they were alone.

"Why exactly have you come here?" asked Mistress Gregory.

"To see you and the baby. It can't have been fun having the baby in the church."

"It wasn't. It was embarrassing and painful and uncomfortable."

"Oh dear, I am sorry."

"You should be. It was your outburst that brought on my labour early."

"Me? What outburst?"

"Are you trying to tell me that you can't remember what happened?"

"I don't remember talking to you that day. But I don't remember anything of that day."

"I thought you had come round to apologise."

"I shall apologise to you Mistress Gregory, as soon as you let me know what you think I said to you."

Elizabeth relayed the conversation with added emotion and words. Anne didn't flinch. She remembered most of it anyway, but enjoyed causing trouble.

"Well, if it all happened like that, I am not surprised that you were upset. But, as you know I was very ill afterwards and cannot be held responsible for anything I said or did."

"Hmmm," said Elizabeth, not entirely believing the young woman.

Anne finished her sweets and wine and said, "May I see the baby?"

Elizabeth looked a little startled and said, "Of course you may. Follow me."

Elizabeth led her upstairs and soon they were looking into the wooden crib which rocked gently against the oak floor. Inside the white lace and wool blankets was a pink baby, fast asleep and sucking its thumb.

"Boy or girl?"

"You have a sister, Mistress Gunter."

Anne stared at her and said, "I shouldn't let my parents hear you say that. They will be less than pleased, especially my father."

"Threats don't work with me. But I have no intention of making the story public."

"Your husband won't be happy."

"My husband won't know. It's you that has been shouting the story about in your fits. It's not helping."

"No, I don't suppose it is. How did my father get you with child anyway?"

"It is not my job to teach you about getting a child."

"I know about that. I'm asking you how you managed to let my father get you pregnant. Are you his whore?"

"No more than your mother is Gilbert Bradshawe's whore."

"I can ruin you Mistress Gregory, so don't push the boundaries with me."

"I doubt she will be for long. Reverend Bradshawe is getting married before Christmas."

"Is he? Who is he marrying?"

This was something that Anne had not heard, but she recognised that she was out of date on numerous subjects.

"Elizabeth Brasier. She has been sniffing after him ever since his family died. She thought her marriage chances were pretty well gone, but has had more choice since this last plague. But her mother ensured that she caught herself a decent one."

"I see. This knowledge has not reached my family yet. I am sure that they will be interested. You have a fine daughter Mistress Gregory, I am sure that you and your husband are very proud. I must be going now, I am feeling a little tired."

Sarah Rose was called and the two women made their way back to the Rectory.

"Did you see the baby, Mistress?"

"Yes I did. It is a pretty little thing. I am not a fan of babies though. I don't think I shall ever be a mother."

"Really Mistress? I want to be a mother. I want six children as soon as I have a husband."

"I hope you don't intend to have one just yet, I shall need you as maid for a while. Do you have someone in mind?"

"I do have someone in mind, but his father wouldn't let him marry for a few years. They are trying to build up the farm and don't want a marriage. I don't mind though, Mistress. If I am going to be your very special ladies maid, I will enjoy that."

"You are my ladies maid, Sarah Rose. But as I said earlier, you must keep all my secrets whatever they may be."

"I will, Mistress."

As they went back into the house, Anne turned to Sarah Rose and said, "I think I may have overdone it today, I am going to bed. Please fetch me some food and drink and bring it to me in a couple of hours. I will have a nap."

Anne climbed the stairs slowly.

"Where have you been girl? I have been looking for you, there is work to do." Brian Gunter asked the maid.

"She's my maid now father. She has been looking after me. I need her to keep me well while the rest of you run about the place. And by the way, I have visited Elizabeth Gregory to see her new daughter. Funny though, the child doesn't have a likeness to either of them, although she does seem familiar to me somehow."

Surprisingly Brian didn't give an answer on either subject. He went out of the house.

#

John was back in Oxford and missing Anne.

He was also more than a little impressed with the way his praying had brought Anne back from the dead. That was pretty impressive. There was no one to tell either, because the only person who might have been interested was Thomas Holland and he had sent him away. If he talked to anyone else at the college, he would have to talk about the bewitchment and he wasn't sure that was appropriate. So he caught up with his work and taught his students. John was already building up a good reputation as a teacher and some West Country men were sending their sons with specific instructions that they be taught by John. Some were his richer cousins from Devon.

John leaned back in his chair and stared at the fire. He was remembering visiting Modbury where one of the several large houses occupied by his Prideaux cousins sat in all its glory. Some other cousins lived north of Dartmoor. If John's branch of the family had descended from the eldest son instead of the second son, his family would have been living there instead.

He and the rest of the family would visit Modbury on route to the sea at Bigbury. It was a beautiful journey down and as long as they set off at first light, leaving the farm in the hands of servants, they could spend a good part of the day there. They would walk on the beach and explore the cliffs and rocks and best of all in John's mind, travel to the island.

The island was the place where they could imagine all sorts of pirate activity. The children would pretend that there was treasure buried there, or treasure washed ashore from Spanish ships. Once after a shipwreck, some Spanish horses swam ashore and the beautiful animals were taken away by locals. These were taken back from the peasants by the Bigburys and the Prideauxs and one ended up at Stowford with John's family. This horse was a real favourite of the children, who insisted that he was used only for riding and pulling the trap to church. He sired some beautiful foals around the town and made the Prideauxs some good money while he lived. He was with them for ten years before he was found dead one day in his paddock, his favourite mare standing guard over him. As no one knew his history they had no idea of his age, but John's father reckoned he must have been about 20 years old. They all helped in digging the large hole in which to bury him in the field next to the house. They prayed and sang and put up a cross upon which his elder brother Thomas had carved. 'King Philip'. It was one of King's sons that had run away with John that day.

John's mind came back to the present and he rubbed his face with both hands. There were tears in his eyes because for a moment he had been back with his family. He had also forgotten how much he had loved King. Perhaps he ought to think about getting himself a horse and stable it in town. Then he could talk to him as he had talked to the horses back home. Here, he must watch everything he did because of the eyes and ears ready to note down any slip and use it against a person once he began to climb the ladder. John was climbing the ladder and wanted to get to the top and for that reason could speak only what would cause no trouble. He had felt a closeness with Anne Gunter and for a time thought he could sometimes confide his real thoughts with her. But since her illness, he wasn't sure that was ever going to happen. Yes, he would see about buying a horse, he had heard that there were some Spanish horses for sale in London.

He was brought from his musings by the opening door. The heavy old door would never open properly, just stick on the stone slabs. A heavy push only ever brought it half open. The result was a head peeping round the edge.

"Hello John," said Thomas Holland.

"Hello Thomas. You are back in Oxford sooner than I expected. How is Anne?"

"Back as she was I am afraid, John. She has been taken to her brother's house in Stanton St John where they hope that Gregory and Pepwell can no longer reach her."

"That is bad news, do sit down and pour a drink and tell me what happened."

This Thomas Holland did, glad to be away from the female nattering and wailing that he had been party to for the past two weeks.

It seemed that Anne had relapsed substantially after her visit to Elizabeth Gregory. Her fits returned with a vengeance and she seemed to lose all touch with reality. The family called in another cunning man, who recommended that she be made to come into contact with her tormentors. He had added that at least one other witch was involved and through deduction it had been decided that these were Agnes Pepwell and her daughter Mary. They denied it, but were caught up in the increasing climate of self-righteous fervour in North Moreton and were accused alongside Elizabeth Gregory in the bewitchment.

"It's getting quite serious out there John. Particularly now that more than one woman is being accused it could get out of hand. It always ends up like this when people try to settle old debts."

John poked the fire and said, "What do you make of witchcraft, Thomas? I mean really, what do you think it is?"

"I could tell you the churches opinion on it, or the King's. Or I could tell you my beliefs."

"Tell me yours Thomas. I can't make too much sense of the church's teachings."

Thomas settled back in his chair.

"It's about mind control. Very clever witches control their own minds as well as that of their victims. The spells and chanting are all to accentuate the focus. That's the root of it all. Being able to keep the mind so focussed that the thoughts can do their work."

"And that is how it works for good or ill?" asked John.

"Yes. Witches believe that they can curse with thoughts."

"How?"

"It's only a matter of keeping the same thought going on and on with a lot of intention and power. It's very difficult to do."

"It's what the friars are supposed to do. I mean the monks who pray, not the ones who mess about with women and boys."

"I suppose good and evil aren't very far removed from each other. It's just a matter of intention."

"And being aware of your intention," answered Thomas.

"It would be interesting to see a witch in action wouldn't it? I mean if she couldn't see us and we couldn't be harmed, it would be interesting wouldn't it?"

"I should keep that to yourself, there are plenty at Oxford who would be ready to burn you just for saying that."

John coloured slightly, for it was true.

"When I was with Anne and we thought she had died, I heard her talking from another place in the room."

Thomas interjected straight away, "I've told you John. Be careful what you talk about, it will get you into trouble." He didn't ask him anymore and John thought it best not to say anything.

Thomas finished his wine and got up.

"So the girl will be spending Christmas with Harvey's family, which means Mistress Holland can come home and see to the children."

He shook his head at this last comment and even John realised that Susan rarely stayed at home to look after the children.

"Do you want me to go and check out the witches again?" asked John.

"In North Moreton? I wonder whether some of the witches went with her."

"Who has gone with her?"

"Her mother and her maid."

"You think they are witches?"

"Probably not, I am making bad jokes. I hope they haven't followed her. Leave North Moreton alone for a while."

John tried not to look disappointed. Thomas noted it and said, "I am sure they will all be glad of a visit at Stanton, it isn't a long trip."

"I do have a friend who is at the church there," mused John.

"Harvey lives opposite the church, in the manor," answered Thomas.

#

It was three weeks before John could get away, and so it was early January before he walked the six miles from his lodgings to the manor at Stanton.

John hadn't told them he was coming; he sent a note to his friend at the church informing him that he would drop in to wish him well. The walk was enjoyable. He set off early in the morning before the sun was up. He was in the village only an hour and a half later with heavy snow falling on him. The hood was up on his cloak and buttoned firmly around his chest. He walked with a tall staff which had been given to him by one of his West Country students. He bowed his head against the weather and marched into the village. Standing on the track between the church gate and the manor gate, he mentally debated which place to visit first. The clock struck ten and he thought he would call in to the church. George was highly unlikely to be there now, expecting John for lunch at twelve.

He would go in and pray so that he could face Anne and her family with confidence. The familiar click of a church door latch never failed to calm his mind and as he stamped the snow from his boots and shook his cloak. As he hung it up on a hook by the door, he heard footsteps near the north wall and shouted out, "Hello! I'm John Prideaux from Oxford."

There was no answer and John imagined that it was probably someone who shouldn't be in the church. He walked over, but saw no one. He placed his bag and gloves upon the Easter Sepulchre and heard the footsteps again. Heavy, booted steps and he shouted out.

"Hello! Who is there?"

The noise at the altar made him look over there. The cross was on fire and the flames were spreading to the cloth upon which it sat. The church was dark except for the flames and the mesmerised John could not make his mind work quickly enough and make sense of what was happening. There was a scurrying at his side and he turned round sharply to be met by the face of a demon.

Its red eyes and animal like stance held John in its gaze. It moved its head from side to side taking in what he was looking at. John was conscious of nothing other than the demon. He didn't think he was going to live or die, he was just totally aware of that moment in time. A very slow moment.

"Remember," it growled at him and vanished, leaving behind a strong smell and a grey fog.

John dropped to the floor as though the stare had been keeping him upright and now all his strength was gone. He breathed heavily and promptly threw up.

Looking at the cross he saw that there was no more fire and as he got up and staggered in the direction of the altar, saw that there was no sign of scorching. John leaned heavily against the table trying to pull his mind together.

What in hell had just happened?

He was disturbed by the sound of the door scraping open and two women entering. They were chattering away and carrying a small basket each. When they saw the priest they stopped and bobbed a curtsey in his direction. He nodded acknowledgement, picked up his things and left the church, swinging the cloak over his body as protection against the snow. He would visit the manor and see if he could learn anything new from the Gunters.

#

When he was shown into the dining room by the maid, he was met by Harvey, Harvey's wife, Mistress Gunter and Anne.

"Hello priest," said Harvey. "To what do we owe this honour?"

John was gratified to note that Anne seemed pleased to see him.

"I am visiting my friend, George Ryves and thought that I would come and pay my respects while I am here. Master Holland told me that Mistress Gunter and her mother had moved here for a while for Anne's health. You are looking well," he said to Anne.

"My sister is feeling much better since she moved in with us," said Harvey. "We are hopeful of her full recovery now."

"That, I am glad to hear."

"George is a friend of yours too? He is a friend of our family and we have done much business with him, to our mutual benefit," said Harvey.

"That is very good to hear. Our friends in Oxford send spider webs far and wide and bring us all together with only a few threads. It can only bring benefit to us all."

The Gunters looked at their visitor without speaking, for they did not understand him. John felt as though his mind was not connecting to his mouth.

"Will you stay with us for lunch, Reverend Prideaux?" asked Elizabeth Gunter.

"That is very kind of you, but I am lunching elsewhere, before my return journey this afternoon."

"You are not staying the night with George?" asked Harvey.

"No, I am needed back at the college by tomorrow."

"Why don't you two go for a walk? Sarah Rose can go with you in case you need anything," suggested Mistress Gunter.

"Perhaps we could walk round to the parsonage and see if your friend is there?" said Anne.

"I am supposed to meet him for lunch today, that was the arrangement," answered John.

Anne took his arm and said, "We shall call and see him. He may allow you to visit with us instead."

John acquiesced, as he often did with Anne and waited uncomfortably until she and her maid were ready. Mistress Gunter handed him a beaker of wine, which he drank while he waited. Her son and daughter in law sat at the table watching him without expression. He was glad when Anne returned, chattered incessantly with her maid. She winked at John and led the way out into the gardens through the large windows.

"You are looking much better Anne, have you been safe since you moved here?"

Sarah Rose giggled and Anne shot a glance at her which stopped the giggling immediately.

"You go off somewhere girl. Go and visit the boy from the blacksmiths, you were keen enough yesterday. Come back here in an hour."

The girl trotted off and Anne turned to John and said, "I can't trust anyone anymore, John. Come with me, we can go and sit on the church for a while and talk."

John paled and said, "I am not so sure I want to do that."

She turned and held his arm with her hand, "Have you seen it?"

"What?" he asked.

"You have seen it hasn't you? I've seen it and others have too. It's the devil."

"Nonsense Anne. Why would the devil come to Stanton St John?"

"Following us, that's why. He has been in North Moreton causing trouble and then he came here after us."

"How do you know he has come after you?"

"Because I have seen him and so have mother and Harvey. He is either here at the manor or at the church. So he must be after me."

"I still don't know why he would come after you."

"Because I'm special I expect," she laughed. "Come on, let's go into the church."

Two men walked past them and touched their hats and carried on up the lane.

"There aren't many people about in the village are there?" John said.

"Usually there are more people about. Perhaps it's because you are here. An important man from Oxford!"

"Very funny, Mistress Anne Gunter."

"Have you missed me John?"

"I have," he answered.

"Good," she said.

As they entered the churchyard, John shivered and Anne grabbed his arm. She led him in to the porch way and turned him to face her. He looked down at her and soon they were kissing passionately.

They were in the bliss of the first embrace, thinking of nothing but each other and so did not immediately notice the church door opening. The women with the baskets were leaving the church and laughed at the couple caught canoodling.

"You will have to marry her now sir," said one, as they scampered past.

John and Anne moved away from each other.

"You don't have to marry me John. But I don't mind if you think about it."

He rubbed her head and smiled. That was a very good sign.

Anne pulled him inside the church and told him to check that there was no one about. This he did and walked back towards her saying, "We appear to be alone Mistress Gunter, what shall we do?"

She moved towards him and put her arms around his shoulders. As they moved closer together, there was a loud crash at the altar. They both looked and saw the cross flaming.

"Satan is here. He has been waiting for us," said Anne.

"Why us?" asked John.

"Me anyway. The witches have conjured him up and sent him after me. I don't know what their end game is, but I have a feeling it's to do with my father."

"I suppose he has caused a bit of trouble in his life."

"Enough to bring a demon to me though? I only went to the meetings a few times."

"What meetings Anne?"

"The meetings in the church at North Moreton. Lots of the women go and try and learn about the meaning of life and death."

"In the church itself? That's blasphemous!"

"Gilbert Bradshawe knew about it and God didn't seem to be bothered about it. He certainly never stopped us," pointed out Anne.

"Perhaps it is him allowing these devils to plague you?"

"Well they seem to be plaguing you too. John Prideaux and you never attended any meetings."

She handed him a flask and beckoned him to drink. He hesitated, drank and handed it back for Anne.

"What's happening now?" he said, as the flaming cross rose into the air and moved silently towards them. They watched mesmerised as it stopped in front of Anne and fell against her dress. The cloth caught fire and the flames began to run up towards her face. John was as quick as a cat and pulled the gown from her body and threw it on the floor, stamping on it, in an effort to put out the flames.

"John! Aren't you being a little forward?" asked Anne.

He looked at her as she stood with her arms crossing her breasts and hanging on to her petticoat, endeavouring to hide her body from him. John looked down at the dress which was crumpled and dusty under his boots.

"Why did you do that John? Why did you rip my dress from me?"

"It was on fire!" he answered. But looking at the dress, it was quite obvious that it wasn't on fire. He picked the dress up and shook it.

"That's looks a mess, I shall have to pull my coat around me tightly when we go back home."

"I am so sorry Anne. I saw the flames from the cross and saw your dress alight. I can't understand what has happened."

She smiled at him and moved her hands to her sides. He could see the shape of her body underneath the petticoats and was finding it very difficult to control his body and his spirit against this temptation. His mind had been woozy since the drink and he felt as though he was someone else.

Anne moved towards him, holding out her arms and he raised his own arms to meet her. He touched her breasts and moved his arms around her body, bringing her towards him and he kissed her. She gave a sigh which reverberated around the church and he responded with one of his own. They kissed and glided in their embrace to the altar where they were soon lying on the floor in front of it.

Suddenly, there was a sharp crack and a flash of light which shone through the window onto the embracing couple. Johns stopped and noticed what he was doing. His hands were under her petticoats and he was positioning her body underneath his.

"Dear God, forgive me!" he shouted. "In your Holy Church!"

He lifted himself from her, pulled down her petticoats and smoothed them as she leaned towards him, with her weight on her hands.

"I don't know what possessed you John," she said, "Satan must have influenced you. Now fetch my dress and help me make myself decent enough to visit your friend and change your luncheon appointment."

He bowed slightly and fetched her clothes and then watched her get dressed. What had possessed him to act in the way he had? Lust or bewitchment, but which one? He needed another drink from the flask which Anne carried about, just to relax himself. He picked it up from the pew and swallowed a few drops. He immediately felt better.

He must pray as he had never prayed before, when he was back in Oxford. He wished he was there right now, in his rooms surrounded by his books and gifts from home. Anne was quickly dressed and standing in front of him. She bowed low in front of the altar and then turned and walked regally towards the church door. John hovered in front of the altar before he too walked outside. He tried to ignore the feeling that they were being watched from the pews by long dead worshippers.

As they stood on the snow covered grass outside, there was another flash of lightening which hit the church roof with an almighty crack. The sky went black for a second and John knew that the lightening had just missed them. Anne fell backwards and was soon on the ground in a fit, her limbs contorting horribly. Sarah Rose arrived at that very moment and John instructed her to fetch help without delay.

The two women who had passed them in the church earlier were standing on the grass, grinning.

CHAPTER TWENTY THREE

Getting Anne back to her brother's house was not an easy task. Up to now her fits had been in her own home, or so near to the house that it was relatively easy to get her out of the sight of prying eyes. The two women eventually left the churchyard, but soon returned with a gaggle of villagers. Stern warnings from Harvey Gunter and his man failed to disperse them. They remained unsympathetic witnesses to the young woman's sufferings.

Anne foamed and kicked as she lay on the ground. Her dress rose up and revealed her upper thighs, her breasts endeavoured to escape. John removed his cloak and covered her with it. Between them they tried to lift her, in order to remove her to the manor. They managed to get her to her feet, but she kicked and punched and screamed, so they couldn't hold on for long. In the end, they each held an arm and a leg and half carried, half dragged her to the manor.

Once there, maids were instructed to take her to her room.

"Where is that damn fool maid of hers?" shouted Harvey above the screaming.

"I am here sir," said Sarah Rose. "I have been here all the time."

"Help get my sister up the stairs and then look after her until these fits stop. Did you see any of the witches at the church?"

John stopped and said falteringly, "No! No witches or devils or any such thing."

"Something has set her off," said Harvey.

"I don't know what it was," said John.

Anne was quieter now, but dead weight and it took six people to get her upstairs and into her bedroom. Sarah Rose told the other maids to leave as soon as Anne was on the bed. She undressed her mistress and wiped the vomit from her body. This was the first time that she had cleaned Anne after she had peed herself and Sarah Rose grimaced while she did it. Within ten minutes, Anne was clothed in a clean nightgown and lay unconscious in her bed. Sarah Rose put the dirty clothes into a reed basket and went out of the room. As she closed the door, she bumped into Harvey Gunter. He put his hand between her legs and grabbed her crotch, hard.

"Sir! Stop that. What are you doing?"

"What is going on with my sister? You know more than you are telling us. Are you one of those witches?"

"No sir! No, I am not a witch! You should not say that. And please take your hand away, I do not like it."

"You are a maid. I can do what I like." He wriggled his fingers and began forcing them upwards, ignoring the resistance of her clothes. If he pushed any harder, the material would rip.

"You like that, don't you?"

"Oh yes sir. There is nothing I like more than having a man's dirty fingers shoved up my minge while I am trying to go about my work. I like to tell Mistress Anne and Mistress Gunter about it." Her surprising frankness caused him to stop and take a step back. Sarah took advantage and shot past him and down the stairs. Harvey walked away in the direction of his room and was rewarded by the sight of his wife looking at him with utter contempt.

He hung his head, turned around and followed Sarah Rose down the stairs. In the room below he found John Prideaux drinking wine with Robert Vilvaine and a couple of his friends. They stood up as Harvey entered, anxious to hear the latest news.

"She is asleep at the moment," he informed them. "We will learn more when she wakes. But it seems that the witches of North Moreton have a further reach than we originally thought."

He sat down and reached for a drink. John remained quiet, for he did not trust that he would be able to keep silent about the church episode.

"Are you travelling back tonight, priest?" Vilvaine asked him.

"I shall set off within an hour, I must call at my friend's house first and then I have duties to perform at college tonight."

I think that would be for the best," said Harvey. "Anne was fine until you got here."

John put down his glass and was about to say something, when shouts from upstairs stopped everyone. Sarah Rose ran from the kitchen and the men followed her. Anne was standing on the landing in her nightgown, arms outstretched and her ankles pointing at right angles to her legs. John put his hand to his mouth and Sarah Rose screamed.

"I heard you talking to my sister in law in the garden, Master Vilvaine. It appears she may be interested in having sex with you, so long as my brother does not find out," said Anne.

"What the hell are you talking about?" asked Vilvaine. His manner gave away the fact she was on target. Harvey's wife began to cry as she listened to Anne speak.

Anne's head cracked loudly to one side, until her ear was almost on her shoulder. Her eyes rolled back into her head. Her nightgown began to slip down her shoulders, revealing her breasts for the third time today. John walked forward with his cloak outstretched. He put it round her shoulders as she raised her head to the straight. When her eyes rolled back to normal and she stood on the soles of her feet as opposed to the inside of her ankles, she seemed almost creepier.

"There are no witches here and there is no way this is a normal sickness, so what the hell does this mean?" asked Harvey.

"It means the witches can find me even when I have moved away from home," said Anne. She handed back the cloak to John and walked with a kind of dignity into her room.

\#

Over the next few months Anne remained in her fits and her father trailed learned friends from Oxford and London in and out of her room at North Moreton. Academics and politicians, often joined by the mutual membership of a certain brotherhood watched the young girl writhe and perform upon her bed. Her clothes rode up and down her legs and her breasts were regularly revealed. Brian allowed anyone who entered to feel her breasts and place their hands under her skirts in order to touch her bottom and check for pins or evidence of witchcraft.

"How does allowing your daughter to be abused in such a disgusting way, prove that she is bewitched?" asked Anne's mother of Brian.

"Because these men are professional academics and can help us bring charges against the dreadful Gregory woman and the foul Pepwells," he said.

"And their conviction will assist you in obtaining the Gregory lands and keep the Pepwells quiet permanently."

"You are a cynical woman, Anne. You should keep your fat mouth shut. I intend that we will be much richer during the next year."

"How is that going to happen?"

"It isn't me who will get the Gregory lands, there is someone else I am helping and he is in a position to help me."

"What position?"

"He wants a country estate and will do whatever he needs to in order to acquire one. He is a friend of the Dunchs and needs to be near them. Some of our dealings in Oxford are gaining too much attention and so our little neck of the woods at North Moreton is an ideal place to hide out."

"You are a crook and a liar, my conniving husband. I have no idea what is really going on, but I am sick of my daughter being treated in this disgraceful way," snarled Anne.

He slapped her face hard and said, "Fuck off, bitch. Mind your own business." He walked away from her and out of the house. Anne rubbed her face and muttered, "You complete and utter bastard, Brian. I will beat you, you see if I don't."

John Prideaux, who had silently observed the exchange from a side landing, took note. He waited until this latest band of men had left Anne's rooms and went in. Anne lay still and was being attended to by Sarah Rose.

"I don't know how much more of this she will be able to stand," she said to John.

"No, neither do I. My thoughts swerve between bewitchment and illness," he confided.

Sarah Rose picked up a flagon of green juice and said, "Her father keeps giving her this stuff and it seems to make her unconscious or go off on one of her fits, sir. But then I am sure he gets Mistress Gregory to make it for him."

"What makes you say that?"

"I have seen him. He goes to visit her and that bastard daughter of her's and he comes out with a bottle of this every time. Mistress Anne gets me to follow him and that's what I have seen."

"It does not make sense when he calls her for being the witch who is attacking his daughter? Is he helping her? Why would he?"

"Because this whole thing is much more complicated then all you so called clever men can conceive. There are more twists and turns than…"

"Sarah Rose! I told you to keep your tongue still!" Anne had woken from her sleep and was propped up on her elbows.

Sarah Rose bobbed a curtsey and said, "I am sorry Mistress, but I thought you trusted the priest. I am worried about what is happening to you and I don't think you will be able to take much more."

"We do trust him, we do. My father has arranged a trial in Abingdon on the 1st March and the women will be arrested before then."

Mistress Gunter walked in on the group and sat at her daughter's bed.

"I have spoken to Master Hinton. He was here tonight and he knows what to do. A report is being prepared and everything is going to work out."

"I hope so mother. It is difficult to keep on doing this."

"I am sure, but you will be fine. It's taking longer than I planned."

"Are we sure that father will be ruined by this?"

"We are. The women are all playing their part and we will win."

"I am sorry," interjected John. "I don't know what you ladies are talking about. The women are playing their part?"

Mistress Gunter turned on him and said, "You are not a fool, Master Prideaux. You know which group we are talking about. The group of influential men who run the law and medicine and money. There is more than one member of this family who have already joined. They are bound by vows superior to their chosen profession, in order to maintain their brotherhood."

John did know which brotherhood to which they referred. He had been asked by Holland and Helme to join, but had refused. He hoped the King would never ask him, for then he could not refuse and would be bound for the rest of his life.

"But why do you want them brought down?" he asked.

"Not brought down, kept at arm's length. They are currently in Oxford and London as you are well aware and have intentions of bringing influence upon Abingdon. We women have our own influential groups. When we influence results, it is called witchcraft. When men influence results, it is called commerce."

John could not argue this point for it was one he agreed with.

"How is feigning bewitchment helping that?" he asked.

"Feigning? I am not feigning John. I have been bewitched, by potion and by spell." Anne turned to her mother and said, "Should I tell him mother?"

"You can daughter. But if he tells, I shall have him bewitched myself."

John had no doubt that she would.

"You can trust me," he promised. "I swear it."

Anne nodded. Sarah Rose was cleaning her dress and changing her garments while she spoke. No one passed comment on her near nakedness while she was attended to. It seemed far less titillating than her skirts riding up and her top riding down.

John thought that Anne was an exceptionally beautiful young woman.

"My husband is an abusive pig, Master Prideaux. You may have observed that for yourself."

"He certainly is a difficult man, Mistress Gunter. I don't feel that it is appropriate that I comment further."

"Because you are afraid of your position at Oxford? Master Holland and my husband and Master Helme all have an influence over what happens to you and where your career goes. Being a good academic or holy man on its own is not enough," pointed out Mistress Gunter.

"And being lucky makes no difference whatsoever," added Anne.

"And it's not God's doing," said Sarah Rose.

"How are you saying that it works?" asked John, intrigued.

"Simple. The whole world is our imagination, a dream world. It's just that most people think that everything they see is real and exists from its own side," said Anne.

"And once you accept that everything is just imagination and that we are inventing our lives as we go along, you are free," added Mistress Gunter.

"Because if everything is you, then how can anyone else make a difference?" said Sarah Rose.

"Dream world?" said John.

"You dream when you are asleep, don't you John?" asked Anne.

"Yes, of course I do."

"And when you wake, you think you are in the real world."

"Yes, Mistress Gunter."

"That's the thing. You are still asleep, thinking you are now awake. Once you start to consciously imagine your life ahead, you are free."

"And where does God and Satan come into your ideas?" he added petulantly.

He was surprised to see the women laugh at this question which he was sure could never be answered satisfactorily.

"We can be God or the Devil. There is no judgement with knowledge of this power. Start to read your scriptures from that angle, priest. You will discover that the Bible is merely an instruction book about states of mind development and not a history book." Mistress Gunter was in full flow with her lecture.

"That borders on blasphemy," said John.

"Don't be ridiculous, John. You cannot scare us. You are only affecting your own life, not ours. Look at Deuteronomy. I kill and I make alive. I wound and I heal."

"What do you mean?"

Your imagination, which is God, can do good or ill. It has no compassion. It is we who experience the results of our thoughts and beliefs and the accompanying emotions. God doesn't care. It's all a dream."

"Anne, I shall have to think about this," answered John.

"While you are thinking about it, make sure that you don't upset our plans," said Mistress Gunter.

"I don't know what your plans are," he retorted.

"We are double-double crossing my husband. He is using this bewitchment to further his connections in Oxford and London so he can make more money. He thinks he is using Elizabeth Gregory because he will tell about the baby."

"But Elizabeth Gregory is fooling him, while making sure that I am bewitched safely."

"But the trial!" said John.

"Trial! They won't be found guilty. Agnes is too clever, Mary too slow and Elizabeth knows exactly what she is doing."

"And what happens after the trial?"

"Just you wait and see," said Anne.

CHAPTER TWENTY FOUR

After the March trial, everything changed.

Brian Gunter had spent several weeks prior to the Abingdon trial attempting to have the Pepwells and Elizabeth Gregory   convicted of witchcraft. Agnes fled in terror when she heard that they were to be arrested. In the event, Elizabeth was arrested first and was closely followed by Mary Pepwell. The arresting officers were terrified during the procedure and were sure they would be cursed for evermore. Elizabeth certainly told them they would be. The women were held at Reading Gaol in less than salubrious circumstances for several weeks. It had taken many promises and bribes to keep them from telling the truth about everything.

"It's the long game that matters Elizabeth, the long game," said Mistress Gunter.

"Well that's all very well Mistress High and Mighty, but you aren't the one sitting in gaol," answered Elizabeth.

"You want him to pay for the deaths of your kin, don't you? How else are you going to make sure that happens?"

The whole idea was too complicated. Elizabeth Gregory did want Brian to pay for his crime against her family, but wasn't so sure that this was the best way to go about it.

"If they convict me, I'm going to be spending weeks in this gaol and it is disgusting and dangerous. And that is if they don't hang me, or burn me or worse."

"It won't take weeks and when everything is done and dusted you will have paid him back for what he did."

"Enough to warrant what I'm going to go through? Seems that you won't be going through anything," complained Elizabeth.

"My daughter will and I will be protecting her and advising her. I have to keep her safe and make sure I have planned for every possible twist and turn."

"I hope you have, Mistress Anne Gunter."

"I obey orders where things like this are involved. We both have orders from above. If their brotherhood gets any more powerful, we shall all be in trouble," said Mistress Gunter.

"And we have to stop them coming to Abingdon," agreed Elizabeth.

"We are to have one more meeting before the trial," said Mistress Gunter.

"Send a message to Master Hinton and those two doctors, make sure they know their part," said Elizabeth.

"They already know, stop worrying."

"Have they given a trial date yet?"

"1st March," said Anne.

"Another week in this stink hole. Make sure I get some clean clothes and get me a bath before then. And for her," she said, pointing to the pile of filthy rags in the corner of her cell.

"I will, though I doubt there will be any clean clothes at her cottage."

"Well get her some of your precious daughter's cast offs then."

"I like that blue dress she wears," the pile of rags informed them.

"I will see what I can do, Mary," said Mistress Gunter.

"Come back soon," said Elizabeth in an unusually quiet voice.

"I doubt I shall have time to travel all this way out Elizabeth. It's too far. I expect the next time we meet it will be at the trial. But you will be going back home after that."

"Is my baby alright?"

"Fine, you will be seeing it again soon."

Even with their joint venture, Anne could not bring herself to speak well of the child.

The women's group arranged with Master Hinton that he should speak out against Anne's bewitchment, His testimony and the advance warning to the judges of a report to be published by the doctors three days later stating that Anne's symptoms were faked, was enough to release the accused women.

The two judges sitting, unusually allowed the trial to go on for several hours, instead of the 30 minutes they would generally give. They appeared to have no problem acquitting the women, citing that they believed Anne was suffering from illness and not witchcraft. What was evident was, that this case had been attracting attention nationally, not just the relatively small circles the Gunters moved in locally. There was no doubt that the judges had been previously briefed of the interesting subject matter of the trial and at least half of the attendees wanted to see the downfall of Brian Gunter. He had made a lot of enemies during his lifetime. The people he had done favours for, were maintaining a low profile, hoping he would end up in gaol.

The most talked about event was when Anne was carried into the court on a chair. On her father's instructions she fell into her usual fits, showing the whites of her eyes and falling unconscious upon the floor. She remained there while the court argued legal points. Elizabeth stared at her antics, unmoved. She would like to announce that she had supplied the potion to Brian that he gave to his daughter, which made her act in this ridiculous way. Brian thought he was winding Elizabeth around his finger and helping him become more famous. If convicted, he intended to get her out of gaol later on. How, he had no idea. He believed that Elizabeth loved him so much that she would do anything for him. Agnes was doing it for the money he was giving her, although she was yet to be found. Mary, would do as she was told.

When the verdict was announced, Brian was incandescent with rage and swore he would pursue the matter as far as he could, perhaps even with the King. Mistress Gunter cared far less and laughed out loud when the news was brought to her at the Rectory. She had refused to attend the trial, but enjoyed seeing her husband so apoplectic. Brian was a nasty violent man, but it seemed that these distractions with Anne and her bewitchment were keeping his wife safe from his fists and temper for now. She wanted it to remain that way. She also had a women's meeting to attend…

Now the witches and Anne were free to come home, fits or no fits.

Mistress Gunter went into the kitchen and straight to the larder. She found the flagons at the back and brought them all out one by one. Placing them on the small trolley, she wheeled them out of the back door and towards the yard. She emptied their green contents down the drain. Brian was not to start this off again. It didn't fit into her plan.

As fate would have it, all the women arrived back in North Moreton on the same day. Anne and Brian trotted in grandly in the carriage. Brian was all bluster and show, while Anne had her arms crossed in front of her body, tightly holding onto a shawl as she shuffled into the house. Brian cared if the neighbours were viewing him from the village or the churchyard. He wanted them to think he was in control. Anne wanted exactly the opposite.

Elizabeth Gregory arrived home during the afternoon in a rather less salubrious cart than the Gunters. She came home alone, her husband having left her at court following yesterday's trial. She was acquitted and that was all Walter needed to know. Apart from the gossips, he wouldn't have minded if his wife never came home. Elizabeth had stayed with a friend overnight, feeling too tired to return. She was going to have a proper talk with Mistress Gunter and find out what the next move was to be. Elizabeth felt a good deal older than she should do.

Mary Pepwell walked home from Abingdon overnight. It should only take her three hours at the very most, but tonight she walked very slowly, savouring the freedom. They had been in that horrible gaol for weeks and Mary could still smell the shit and piss on her clothes. Mistress Gunter had brought her one of Anne's dresses. Not a best one, but a nice one nevertheless. Mary was going to wear this dress until it fell off her back. She danced and skipped along the bank of the River Thames as much as she could. Moving water held energy giving spirits. She walked into the quiet, dark village in the early hours. It meant she could sneak back into her cottage unnoticed.

Agnes Pepwell had still not been found since running away before the trial. It was generally believed that she was staying with friends. The women who knew, knew differently. The villagers of the two Moretons gossiped incessantly about their opinions on the case, but there were no further conclusions.

Anne spoke to her mother in the bedroom soon after they returned.

"What's next mother?" she asked.

"We have to wait a while, Anne."

"I thought we were going to get Brian sorted out once and for all."

"We will, but there is a little further to go yet."

"Please tell me that I don't have to be bewitched, I want to put all that behind me. It's so undignified."

"Undignified it may be, but necessary it is. And to be honest the fits are not all fake, are they? I am worried that you are becoming addicted to the potions. But we have our equinox meeting in a couple of weeks. We will be able to call up help and begin the final stage then. You have a very important role to play."

#

The day before the meeting saw John Prideaux arrive at the house. He accompanied Thomas and Susan Holland. Anne was quite nervous to see John, as she hadn't seen him since the trial and was unsure about the reception she would have. She was, however, not disappointed.

"Anne. Mistress Anne, I should say. How are you feeling now?"

"Ill and tired, John. That's how I feel. I'm not sure how much more of this drama I can take."

John sat down next to Anne on the garden bench. They both looked at the church from their part of the garden, noting the garden gate where Gilbert Bradshawe looked back at them. He walked to the gate and leaned over it.

"Is the meeting being held here tomorrow night, Anne? There has been some word that it will be held in the woods as it is quarter day." Gilbert seemed unmoved by the idea.

"It will be in the church, Master Bradshawe. Surely my mother has informed you of our plans when she saw you this morning?"

"I only saw her briefly when she called with some flowers for the church," he answered nervously.

"Oh! She was gone from the house for so long!" answered Anne and was happy to see his face redden as she spoke.

"Perhaps she was visiting a friend," said Gilbert.

"Yes, that's why I thought it was you." Anne laughed and John looking at her knew that she could cause trouble anywhere she wanted.

"It was not with me, Mistress Gunter. I shall see both of you here at church tonight. Will you be attending Reverend Prideaux?"

John had not thought that he would and answered stutteringly, "I-I don't think so, Master Bradshawe. I am not sure that my presence would be appreciated."

"Nonsense, John. You are coming and you will have Thomas and Gilbert for company. You should have your eyes opened tonight I expect," laughed Anne.

Neither John nor Gilbert were very sure they wanted their eyes opening. Recent events at Abingdon and during the past year almost anywhere in the neighbourhood had left them wishing for a quiet and uneventful life. It seemed unlikely that they were going to get one yet.

Gilbert walked back towards the church and John turned to Anne.

"What is this meeting tonight Anne?" he asked.

"You will find it very interesting, John. I think you will learn a lot." Anne stretched her arms above her head and yawned. The movement caused her shawl to slip from her shoulders and her breasts attempt an escape over her neckline. John looked without thinking.

"Enjoying yourself, John?"

He looked embarrassed.

"I have wanted to talk to you about the day at Stratford," he said.

"You mean you want to relive it?" she asked.

"No, I mean yes. I mean it should not have happened," he said.

"Why? Because of what we did or because of what else happened?"

"Afterwards too. You became ill again, I feel bad about that."

"Don't feel bad. It's all working out. Now come in and have some food and a rest before tonight. You will need all your strength," she told him.

\#

It was still light when the women began arriving at the church. They chatted away to each other as they walked from every direction and each of them carried a large bag. John watched the procession from his room at the

Gunter house and considered staying where he was. Women scared him and lots of women scared him in exact relation to multiples of women compared to one. Perhaps this is why he was so comfortable with the company of the male college at Oxford. He pondered this thought as he recognised Elizabeth Gregory, Mary Pepwell and some of the women who attended the trial. Mistress Gunter and Anne walked with this group and they appeared comfortable together.

"Are you ready John?"

John turned round to see his colleague Thomas Holland leaning round his bedroom door.

"I suppose so Thomas, although I am not entirely convinced that it is a good idea to attend. Are you happy about it?"

"I think it is only a meeting. It might be an idea to clear the air after the trial and whatnot."

"I suppose so. It just all seems to be not quite right, what with the church being involved and the women taking control of everything."

"I don't think it is so much that they are taking control, John. They are having one of their regular meetings and have asked us to attend. That's all. Well that is what my wife and her mother tell me."

"And Anne?"

"She doesn't really say much. Probably frightened that she is going to go off into one of those fits again."

"Yes, I suppose."

"Have this," said Thomas, handing him a large glass of wine. "It will take the edge off the ordeal to follow."

"Thanks Thomas, I could do with a drink." John took a large swallow. "I have never properly asked you Thomas. Do you think she is bewitched or just ill?"

"The courts have ruled that she is ill and those women are not witches. So we must take their word for it. I personally think that Anne has been seeking attention and probably would be far happier if she was married off and pregnant. That way I can get on with my career at Exeter."

"That is a bit mean. I am not so sure that a woman's problems can be cured by pregnancy." John was thinking of his sisters.

"Well it certainly hasn't calmed my wife down any. I dread to think what she would be like if she was still single," acknowledged Thomas.

They laughed at his joke, John not being liberated enough to make further comment in defence of the female sex. It would have done him no good anyway. He finished the wine and placed the glass on the dresser. He had a fleeting thought that he may be in trouble for not putting it in the correct place. The men walked down the stairs and were overtaken in the hallway by Sarah Rose.

"I haven't seen you about for a while," said John.

"You haven't been here much, have you?" Then, remembering her position added, "Mistress Anne has needed me to look after her constantly these past difficult months."

"Yes, yes of course," he agreed. "We all hope that the troubles are behind her."

"I doubt that very much Reverend," she retorted and ran out of the front door.

"Very full of herself, isn't she?" said Thomas.

"Perhaps she needs to be pregnant too," answered John.

They walked across the garden and through the side gate onwards the church. There were a few latecomers scurrying across the church yard, who kept their heads down and their baskets tight to their bodies.

"Everyone has a basket," said John.

"We don't," noted Thomas.

"No."

They went through the church door and were taken aback to see that the church was crammed full of women. Gilbert Bradshawe stood near the altar and John was suddenly taken back to that first day he had entered this building, so long ago. Gilbert beckoned the men over and they did as they were bid. The women were talking amongst themselves and it was impossible to hear anything they were saying. There was just a low hum.

"I don't recognise half of these women," Thomas said to Gilbert.

"No, this is one of the regional meetings. Women come from all over the county to these. They take turns at each one of the local gatherings."

"So, not always at the church?" asked Thomas.

"As far as I am aware, we are the only church who will allow them to meet as a group."

What does the Bishop think of that?" asked John.

"He doesn't know. I'm hoping he won't find out."

Thomas pulled a face at John. Surely Gilbert didn't intend to keep this a secret? He would be in so much trouble if he were to be found out. At this point there was a rhythmic knocking beside the men. Mistress Gunter and Mistress Gregory stood side by side as two sisters, with no recent dramatic history.

Anne said, "Now ladies, you all know why we are here. Please settle down and listen to what we have to tell you."

The ladies present acquiesced and the men sat down following a firm waving of the hand in their direction from Elizabeth Gregory.

"We have distinguished guests here tonight ladies. They will act as witnesses and have promised that they will never speak of what they see and hear at this meeting."

John said nothing, though he could not remember having agreed to any such thing. He would have to see whether the events of the evening would affect his vows or loyalties in any way.

"After the trial, we have allowed everyone time to gather their thoughts and their strengths. Our job is only half done and we must see it through to the end."

"So you still intend to make sure that your husband is going to pay for his crimes against women?" asked a yet unidentified woman.

"Yes, that is so. I took a vow and will not break it."

"We ask that you all come together in the usual way and further our cause. Mistress Anne is still weak, but we can rejuvenate her here. Please come forward Anne." It seemed that Elizabeth Gregory was in charge as much as Mistress Gunter.

Anne came forward and smiled brightly at John. She took him by the arm and led him to the altar table which John noticed was clear of all paraphernalia except for what appeared to be a cushioned tapestry.

"Sit there," she instructed him.

John did as he was told, but looked over to Thomas and Gilbert for support. They smiled and sat down on a pew alongside Elizabeth Gregory and Susan Holland. They looked very drunk or perhaps drugged. Mistress Gunter stood in front of John and beckoned Anne to sit next to him.

"Are all the doors locked and bolted?" she shouted.

"Yes Mistress," answered Sarah Rose who was standing behind Mistress Gunter and awaiting any instructions from Mistress Anne.

"And there are no strangers here with us? Check your neighbour and make sure you know who each person is," instructed Mistress Gunter.

The women looked to their left and right to confirm identity. Alice Kirfoote stood up and checked around the rear of the church.

"Everywhere looks secure," she shouted.

"Proceed. You all know your roles," said Mistress Gunter.

"I don't," said John. "I don't know my role. I don't know what is going on and would like to leave."

John Prideaux did not like this atmosphere and was feeling out of control. There were too many people here and they all appeared to know what was coming next. Locked doors? Check your neighbour? He tried to get up, but his legs did not appear to be working.

Anne smiled at him.

John opened his mouth to speak, but his face didn't appear to be working either.

"It was the wine I gave you I am afraid, John. Gilbert and me too. We are all part of a very important experiment. A bit sneaky, but necessary for tonight," said Thomas.

Necessary? Why? Anne stood up and moved in front of him. The congregation had an excellent view of the proceedings and every pair of eyes were firmly fixed in the direction of the altar.

"I told you that I would do anything to experience proper bewitchment. Tonight is my chance," Thomas added.

They were all to be rewarded by watching a memorable episode unravel.

Anne began to sway in front of John and although under the spell which had been forced upon him, John waited for her to fall into one of her fits.

But she didn't.

Anne moved rhythmically to a slow drumbeat that the women had started up. She turned and danced, her arms above her head and her hips gradually flicking towards his face. And then the movements and the drumbeats became more insistent. Anne began to remove her clothes in a practised and incredibly seductive manner. John was transfixed and soon gave up glancing at Thomas and Gilbert who remained sitting, apparently unconcerned about the process they watched.

Soon Anne wore only a shift, similar to that which he had seen her in in the church by her brother's house. Her long hair was loose and swished around her body. John was still sitting, feet on the floor and hands propping him up from the altar table. As Anne danced towards him, her maid walked in front of her and began to lift John's robes and remove his breeches.

John felt anxious, but also discovered that he was becoming increasingly aroused as the dance progressed. Sarah Rose removed the shift that Anne wore so that she was stark naked, swaying and dancing in front of him. The entire congregation cheered and clapped. The drumming stopped and the women stood and began singing a haunting melody. John was now so aroused that he no longer felt embarrassed or self-conscious.

"He has settled into the job in hand now," said Thomas.

"Anne is good at this isn't she?" said Gilbert. Thomas nodded in agreement.

John Prideaux heard these exclamations, but was still unable to make a comment. Anne bent down in front of him, very slowly. She took two steps backwards and sat on his lap. He was finding it difficult to control himself now and as if sensing it, Anne stood up again. Her mother walked over to them and was accompanied by Elizabeth Gregory.

"We must make sure this is done properly now. Everything depends upon it," said Mistress Gunter.

"Anne, move astride his lap, forwards now, legs either side of the priest's legs. That's it, he is ready for you. Now lower yourself gently onto him," instructed Elizabeth.

"This is difficult mother, I can't dance and be seductive and aim without help," complained Anne.

"Oh for goodness sake, child. Do I have to do everything for you?"

Mistress Gunter placed her hand between her daughter's legs and held her lips apart, while Mistress Gregory held onto John as Anne lowered herself slowly onto him.

"Oh!" she said. "This is nice."

"You have to move more than that Anne. He will never fire off, if you just sit there waiting," instructed Thomas Holland.

John Prideaux was now torn between questioning his colleague and tutor's actions and enjoying the event being thrust upon him. Perhaps it was him doing the thrusting. But he still felt as though he had no control of his muscles and although he so desperately wanted to thrust, he felt he could not. Anne would have to do all the work, something she appeared to have no problem in doing.

"Would you like me to move a little more John? Like I did before? Would you like me to slide up and down?" Anne whispered in his ear.

"Mmmmm," was the only assent he could make, but it appeared to have a satisfactory effect as Anne did as she promised.

"This is no good," shouted Gilbert. "We have no proof that penetration is taking place!"

"Then come and see Gilbert. Both of you come and check we are fulfilling our part of the bargain."

The men moved nearer, Thomas standing behind John and Gilbert kneeling by his legs, for ease of view. Thomas removed the remaining items of John's clothing, to satisfy his experience.

"Raise yourself up Anne, I cannot see whether he is inside you or not."

Anne did so, finding that she must hold on to John's shoulders in order to keep her balance. Her breasts were now fully in John's face and she swung her long hair over her back so that his experience was the better. Thomas leaned over and helped her rearrange her hair. He smiled at his sister in law and moved his hands across her breasts as he did so.

"Ensure that he is in the correct place. We have been tricked by that before," he instructed Gilbert.

Gilbert moved his hand to Anne's body and felt around until he was sure the staff was in the correct department. He placed his face as near as he could to double check.

"I cannot stand like this any longer Master Bradshawe, my legs are aching. And I don't know how much longer John will be able to keep his staff erect, that potion won't last forever."

"Get on with it girl!" shouted one of the women.

"I'm moving nearer," said another. "I don't want to miss any of this."

There was a shuffling of feet and an untidy rush as the women began to cram the altar area.

"Now move, before the man dies of a stroke," said Gilbert.

Anne gently lowered herself again and put her hands against John's face, drawing it towards hers. She kissed him, quietly at first and then with more fervour. As she did, she squeezed her pelvis harder and harder.

"You are free," Anne whispered to her lover.

John found himself freed as soon as she said the words and immediately joined in the sport. There was a fleeting moment where he thought about stopping the whole procedure. But really, why?

He rose with her, groaned with her and sweated with her. He lifted her onto the altar and fell upon her, giving her exactly what she appeared to need. He managed to ignore Gilbert and Thomas flitting from side to side, checking out the mechanics of the process. He was only vaguely aware of the women clapping and shouting as though they were watching a fight. Anne was so noisy. John made his usual sounds, but Anne screamed and shouted John's name until they finished the task. This was greeted with applause from the congregation and shouts of 'Well done!' from the men.

The young couple were still naked upon the altar table, John half sitting and Anne laying back, her legs spread apart. John was quite sure that he would be going directly to hell after this. The women laughed and cackled and to John's eyes seemed to be changing shape. Amongst their number he noticed someone, no, something, large and dark. It stepped forward, holding out its hands which dripped blood. The blood caught fire and the fire ran across the floor. John watched it come towards him and guessed Satan was claiming his soul for his own. John screamed with terror and regret.

CHAPTER TWENTY FIVE

John woke alone in the dark church. He was laying on a pew and as he looked down, noticed that he was thankfully, fully dressed. He rubbed his aching head and as he got up, noticed his aching body.

"What happened to me?" he said, in the general direction of the altar. God, for now, did not answer.

John walked to the chancel and over to the altar table. It was all as it should be. Everywhere was clean and tidy and in its correct place. He ran his hand over the rails and sent his mind back to the sight of Anne and her breasts and her...

"There you are Reverend! We were wondering where you got to. Don't tell me you have been in here all morning?" This was from the mouth of Mistress Gunter.

He turned around quickly and hoped he hadn't gone red in the face. He certainly felt as though he had.

"I am not sure what happened after the - err meeting last night. I must have passed out. The potion I was given I imagine."

"Potion? What potion? I certainly don't remember you being at our meeting. Thomas told me that you were unwell and then when one of the maids brought a tray of supper to your room, you would not answer the door. We were most disturbed when you were not in your room this morning."

John could not think of an answer to this statement, choosing to accept it as a mutual agreement that they would not speak of last night. But John wanted to, needed to, speak of last night. He must ask Gilbert or Thomas.

"Do go back to the house, John and have some breakfast. I believe that Brian and Anne are still eating."

"Yes, I shall go there immediately, I am hungry. I didn't realise," said John. He bowed slightly and walked out through the south door.

This was madness. He would be brave and see what transpired in the dining room at Gunters. Back at The Rectory, it appeared to be a normal day.

"Ah Prideaux, just in time for breakfast. Sit yourself down man," said Brian.

Anne smiled at him. It was no more than any young woman of his acquaintance would do.

"Are you well?" he asked her and immediately wished he hadn't.

"I am feeling a little under the weather today, Master Prideaux. I shall rest a while and then take a walk."

"Would you like me to accompany you?" he asked.

"No, indeed not. That would not be appropriate, Sarah Rose shall come with me," she answered in a curt tone.

"Had your wings clipped there!" said Brian.

Any further conversation along this line was curtailed by the arrival of a maid.

"There is a gentleman to see you sir."

"Who is it?" asked Brian.

"He says he is the Bishop of Salisbury, but he doesn't look like a Bishop."

Both Brian and John gave each other a quizzical look and John got up from his seat.

"No need for you to come, Prideaux. Go and fetch Holland, Alice, he can come in with me."

Brian and the maid left, so Anne and John were left alone in the room. He looked at Anne, but she seemed uninterested in his attention.

"Anne, what was last night all about?"

"Last night? You mean our meeting?"

"Yes the meeting."

It was a normal women's meeting John. You should have come there, why didn't you?"

"But I did!"

"I didn't see you. Were you hiding in the vestry?"

"No I wasn't hiding in the vestry! Don't you remember what happened between us with everyone watching and cheering us on?"

Anne blushed and said, "I think you may have been having a man's dream John. I attended the usual boring meeting and you apparently got drunk and wandered off somewhere. I don't think Thomas is very pleased with you." She got up from her chair, collected her things and left the room.

John remained in his seat and considered that perhaps he had dreamt the whole experience. It would certainly make more sense than it really having happened. But it had felt so real. Perhaps he should walk through the village and see if any of the women he met there would acknowledge him. Patting his mouth with a cloth, he left the dining room. Creeping quietly along the hallway he stopped outside the library door and listened. From the few moments he was able to remain there before Sarah Rose ran down the stairs, he learned that the Bishop wanted Anne to accompany him and stay with him and his household at Salisbury, this very day.

John nodded at Sarah Rose and asked, "Do you remember what happened in the church last night?"

"Of course I do Reverend, but I'm not telling you anything."

"I am confused. I am being given the impression that I dreamt the whole thing up."

"Perhaps you did, or perhaps you were bewitched. Perhaps everyone was bewitched? Perhaps everything was a dream like they told you before. Who can say?" She continued on her way to the kitchens.

John went out through the front door and stood on the driveway for a minute. Should he continue down the drive and onto the street or go through the gate to the church? As he turned to look he noticed the skirts of Elizabeth Gregory entering the church. That was a sign if there ever was one.

Continuing his recent skill of listening at doors, he went into the porch and stood quietly by the locked door. He recognised the voices of Elizabeth Gregory and Mistress Gunter.

"How did you handle it this morning?" said Elizabeth.

"I acted as though nothing had happened. Like we decided."

"Does he remember?"

"I am not sure. But if no one acknowledges it, we will be alright whether he remembers or not."

"The most exciting thing for me, is that it works!" said Elizabeth.

"Oh yes. It works!"

"What if there is a baby, Anne?"

"I hope there is a baby. We were told there would be a baby and that baby is going to be our pupil."

"And then our master. What about Bradshawe and Holland? Are they going to keep quiet?"

"They don't remember most of it, they are not proper initiates. And we all know that they will do anything we say, in order to gain advancement."

"Because the men won't let them in their ridiculous and powerless little team."

"Not so powerless, but they will be once the child grows."

"How long will that take?

"Not as long as you might think."

John didn't know whether to throw up, force his way into the church or go back to Oxford.

He quickly decided on the latter and went back to the house. There, he met Brian talking to a very well dressed man.

"John come and meet Henry Cotton, the Bishop of Salisbury. He is going to take Anne to his house and look after her there. He hopes to cure her of her problems. What do you think of that?"

"Hello sir, I am very pleased to meet you. I think that it is an excellent idea, I am sure he can help keep her safe."

"Safe? From the witches?" asked Brian.

"The judges have already ruled that the women are not witches and so I think it better that we do not repeat any accusations," said the Bishop.

"Especially in public!" laughed Brian.

John took his leave of the Bishop and went upstairs. He intended to leave this house and North Moreton as soon as possible. He didn't intend to return.

He may have thought that before.

#

When Sarah Rose told Anne what was being decided downstairs, there was plenty of emotion.

"Will I be coming with you?" asked Sarah Rose.

"I have no idea. We must speak to mother before they take me away," answered Anne.

"She is at the church with Ma Gregory. If we are quick, we shall catch them before your father finds them there."

Aware that the men were probably still in the hall, the women decided to climb out of the bedroom window and out across the tree branch outside. Anne had done this many times as a girl and she chuckled to herself. They jumped down the tree and ran across to the church. The church door was being closed by her mother by the time Anne arrived there.

"Father is sending me to the Bishop of Salisbury for goodness sake mother! What are we to do?"

"Henry? Henry Cotton? That is interesting. The wheel moves quicker than I thought, our little tricks are working."

"You know Henry Cotton?" asked Anne.

"No, I know his housekeeper," answered her mother.

"I think John remembers about last night, mother. You said he wouldn't remember. You said Thomas and Gilbert would not remember either."

"I expect they may remember something, but it is so outrageous that they will never be able to tell anyone and be believed. Worse things happen at their other secret society meetings. They rape girls there."

"And what happened to you wasn't rape," said Elizabeth. "You have been after that man for years. You were very impressive last night Anne. We all enjoyed the performance."

"As you well know, I wasn't myself."

The women looked at each other and raised their eyebrows.

"You must go with the Bishop and out of your father's way. I will keep in touch with you and guide your next steps."

"If you say so mother. I am worried about going there. What about my medicines?"

"Sarah Rose will attend you there and be one of our main links."

"I need those medicines mother. I can't go for very long without them now. It's ironic that they all think that I am ill and really it's because I need the medicine. You won't ever stop it will you mother? I would die if I couldn't have it anymore."

"Don't work yourself up into a state Anne. You will have your medicines. I will make sure of that. Now back to the house, I shall follow you in a minute."

Sarah Rose took Anne's arm and said, "I will always look after you Mistress Anne, no matter what."

"Is she going to be alright taking the potions with that baby coming?" asked Elizabeth.

"We will just change the mix. She will do as we say."

#

Brian ordered Anne to maintain her fits when in the presence of the Bishop and his staff and servants.

"We must make them see that you are still afflicted by the witches, Anne. There is so much attention around the country that I can name my own price on business deals. We have made a lot of money since all of this started."

"Yes father. I will do. Do you have my potions?"

Brian handed over several flasks and Anne put them in her skirts.

"If I run out father, I shall send Sarah Rose for more supplies."

"I will make sure I keep a good stock. Just don't take too much, we don't want too many problems and I need you to continue this bewitchment as long as possible while I am making money."

Sarah Rose and Mistress Gunter collected clothes, provisions and possessions to fill the two chests that were loaded onto the back of the Bishop's carriage. There was a long journey ahead of the group and so Henry Cotton insisted they move as quickly as they could. Anne scarcely had time to think before the carriage was rolling southwards. They were to stop at Highclere overnight, where the Bishop was to visit the Bishop of Winchester on some personal business.

As the party arrived at the Highclere later that day, Anne expected to go straight to her room with her maid. She was most surprised to be told that she would be accompanying Henry Cotton to a meeting with Thomas Bilson, the Bishop of Winchester.

"He is not usually staying here at Highclere, but has asked to meet you specially," Henry informed her.

"Why does he want to see me?"

"He has heard all about you Anne, and your fits and problems."

Sarah Rose accompanied her mistress to their room and dressed her in readiness for the meeting. They chose a demure blue dress which was beautifully made from expensive material.

"You look lovely, Anne."

"Please refer to me correctly when we are not on coven business."

"Yes Mistress. What are you going to do about the fits?"

"I am not sure. Father wants me to keep having them and mother wants me to keep this baby safe. I don't feel as though the two mix very well."

"No. Perhaps if you just have a small fit, Mistress. That should keep them happy. We won't know about the baby for a few weeks yet."

"I will take my potion from mother and some of the one from father. I can't do without those."

"No of course not, Mistress. If you stop taking the potions, the other trouble may start up again."

"Yes, I know," said Anne as she smoothed her dress. "The funny thing is, the only regret I have about all of this, is hurting John."

"I think he enjoyed himself. He didn't appear to be upset. And it wasn't the first time was it Mistress?"

"He did enjoy himself and no, it wasn't the first time."

The women giggled.

The knock on the door which made them both jump was from a maid who informed them that Anne was expected downstairs without delay. Anne took a few deep breaths and followed the maid down the stairs and into the room she was led into. There stood the Bishop of Salisbury, the Bishop of Winchester and John Prideaux.

"John! Reverend Prideaux I mean. What are you doing here?"

"I arrived here earlier on today. I did not know that you were coming here too."

"Oh. I am going to stay with the Bishop. That Bishop, the Salisbury one, not the other one."

"Reverend Prideaux knows all about that. I think he agrees with us that you may well get better more quickly away from North Moreton and its people," said Henry Cotton.

"I do agree Mistress Gunter. Perhaps your fits will end once you are supervised by His Lordship."

"Perhaps, Master Prideaux. But I don't know if there is a guarantee of that. The witches spell that was cast was a strong one and reaches me wherever I go."

"You are surely not saying that you are still bewitched, Mistress Gunter?" asked the Winchester Bishop.

"I don't know about that sir. I do know that even since the trial I have had several bewitching episodes. I had one recently. My family and friends looked after me during that." Anne was rewarded with the sight of the scarlet face of her recent lover.

"I was hoping that you would honour us with a fit tonight, Mistress Gunter," said Thomas Bilson.

"I cannot fit on demand sir. I must wait until the curse reaches me."

"And that is the trigger for the fit? And where do the pins come from? Forgive the questions, but I am very interested."

"The witches cause them to happen. I have no control over when they decide to do it."

"But why? Why do they do it?"

"Sir, if I could answer that, I would be able to stop the problem." Anne was beginning to look tearful.

"Master Prideaux, do I have to listen to this? I am so exhausted and I am at my most vulnerable then."

John was not quite sure what to do. Anne was obviously capable of being bewitched, but so was he. If not, what was all that palaver last night?

"I think it only fair that we do not pester Mistress Gunter. Master Cotton is going to look after her from now on," he said.

"Thank you. I am hoping that the fits and the bewitchments stop when I stay in Salisbury. I am hoping that the witches do not know I have left North Moreton and will not try and affect me."

"Hmmm," said Thomas Bilson. "I still don't understand why a witch would want to make a young woman go into spectacular fits both in court and out. For what purpose?"

The two Bishops looked at each other. They considered themselves intelligent men and felt that a scientific approach was necessary. John Prideaux didn't know what on earth to think or do. He had hoped to have this sleepover at Highclere and then travel to Salisbury and back to Oxford. He had been given several missions.

The meal passed without any dramas and Henry Cotton asked John to join their carriage to Salisbury in the morning.

"You can see the Magna Carta, we have a copy in the vaults of the cathedral," he told him.

"We had better not mention that to any of the King's supporters," he answered.

"No, perhaps not."

#

When the group arrived at the Bishop's lodgings in Salisbury, they separated immediately. They had discussed little other than pleasantries during the journey, none wanting to start a conversation which may prove uncomfortable. Last night's dinner had been awkward enough, but luckily there had been no fits or bewitchments or inappropriate public sex.

Anne and her maid were collected by a housekeeper, who introduced herself by saying, "Hello Mistress Gunter. I am a senior member of the Salisbury ladies and am instructed to assist you in whatever way is appropriate."

"Thank you. I trust that the appropriate way is one I agree with."

"Don't be rude Mistress. During your stay, I shall be treating you with deference in front of the ordinaries. At all other times, you will treat me with the respect I deserve. If you do not, there will be consequences."

Anne nodded. Her training was excellent and she knew the rules.

Her rooms were small but well furnished. Anne suspected that she would have more freedom here and the ability to be herself for the first time ever.

"I work for Doctor Haydock, but persuaded him to let me look after you. Joan Spratt will also attend you. I am Joan Greene and know everything about you. Everything. I ensured that Master Prideaux came here and will ensure that he stays for another day. We must repeat the mating in order to guarantee a child."

"Again? I was told that it was a one-time occurrence! There were enough checks put in place last time."

"It wasn't the first time you two mated though, was it? You didn't conceive that first time and we can't take a risk. This is an important act you are doing on behalf of us all. I will take care of the arrangements, but you must be ready tonight." Joan Greene handed over a flask to Sarah Rose. "Make sure she drinks this when you return to your rooms after dinner."

"Yes Mistress," she answered and took the flask. She looked to Anne for confirmation.

Anne nodded and they went into their rooms.

"I can't go through this again, Sarah Rose."

"You can if you take the potion, Mistress. Five minutes after a drink and you will be ready for any party!"

"That's true. I was just hoping that I would be safe for a while. The after effects are getting worse. Oh Lord, you don't think it will have to be in public again?"

"I don't know, Mistress. But I don't think a meeting has been called. I have heard nothing."

"You are a new member Sarah Rose; I doubt they will tell you everything."

Sarah Rose hung her head. She had been proud to sit amongst the elite women and did not appreciate her mistress belittling her in this way. It was understood that they were all equal, no mistress no servant.

"Well it looks as though you will have to do as you are told Mistress, doesn't it?"

Anne sat down on the bed and vowed to do nothing she did not want to do.

\#

John answered the knock on his door and saw a small maid standing there.

"Evening sir. I need to bring some towels and drinks for your room."

"Oh, come in. Put them over there," he pointed to a table.

"This wine is with the compliments of Bishop Cotton. I wouldn't drink any of it until after dinner sir. There will be plenty of wine there and this bottle tends to have a soporific effect."

"I shall take your advice..."

"Joan."

"I shall take your advice, Joan."

#

Dinner was over quickly. The Bishop was tired and wanted to go to bed early. His servants had the meal cleared away quicker than they had ever done. John felt strange to be left in the dining room so early in the evening.

"I should drink that wine now sir. And here is a very early copy of Chaucer's Tales. Have a read of that before you go to sleep," said Joan Greene.

John went to his room and did as he had been advised. It was an hour later when he answered a second knock at the door. Joan Greene was standing there again and asked him to accompany her.

"Did you drink the wine?" she asked.

"I did. I drank it all. It was full of loveliness."

"Well done sir. It sounds as though you enjoyed it."

John willingly followed the maid and was soon standing inside Anne's room. Another woman handed him a beaker, full almost to the brim and John took a long drink.

"This tastes nice," he said.

John looked into the dimly lit room and noticed there were several women in there. The two maids of Cotton's household and Sarah Rose had been joined by three others he knew not. Sitting in front of a mirror was Anne. She stood up and he noticed that she was dressed with a fitted red cloak. The cloak was not fastened and as she moved towards him, gave him a splendid view of her young body. Her eyes seemed glazed and were almost black.

"Hellooo," he found himself saying to her.

"I see you have taken your medicine John. Me too. You had better get on with this before mine wears off. I find I have to take more recently. It doesn't have such an effect on me."

"Weeellll, my medicine is working very well. Shall I take off my clothes? Or will one of you lovely ladies do it for me?" John was aware of what he was saying, but finding that he didn't care too much about the words.

"You may remove your own clothes, Reverend. As long as we can witness the mating, we are happy. It is best done while you are both disrobed," said Joan Greene.

"Disrobed. That is what I shall do then, ladies. Another drinkie please?" John was hopping around the room as he endeavoured to remove his boots.

"No more drinkies, Master Prideaux. How much did you give him?" asked the second Joan of the first.

"One beaker, but he had that wine before. It won't be too much; it was the only way to get him calm and willing."

"I'm willing," he said as he stood naked in front of the group with a very obvious demonstration of his readiness for the mating.

"I need another dose," said Anne. "If I am to accommodate that again."

"No more dosing. You will accommodate it," said one of the women as yet unidentified. She helped Anne out of the cloak and the two young people stood opposite each other. John walked towards Anne with the intention of kissing her.

"I am not kissing him," she said.

"You don't have to," answered Joan Spratt.

"There was apparently some difficulty in keeping track of it all the other night. We have a different approach. Come here girl."

Anne shivered suddenly and walked over to the woman.

"I need more potion," she said quietly. "I haven't had enough."

Ignored by the women, she was pushed towards the bed.

"Bend over the bed and put your hands on the covers. Spread your legs, Anne. Ladies, move round to this side and all make sure you have the best view. Everyone happy?"

"I am not particularly happy," said Anne.

"Mistress Anne? Do you want me to do anything?" asked Sarah Rose.

"Potion. Get me more potion."

Sarah Rose handed her a flask and Anne took a drink. She waited a moment and then shook her hair.

"Well get on with it, John."

John had been grinning like a fool, hands on hips and muscles on alert. The woman standing behind Anne beckoned him over. She grabbed hold of him and smeared oil on him and also around the rear of Anne.

"Stand firm Anne," she said. "John, make sure your aim is good."

John moved in and Anne moaned.

The women moved closer and began to hum a monotone note. The rhythm changed as the couple moved. The nearer they came to the end, the room began to glow red. Smoke filled the air and light exploded towards the ceiling. An image of a face began in the mirror and grew as it invaded the room.

"Master!" shouted the women.

John finished his task shouting Anne's name and opened his eyes, to be surrounded by and enveloped in, a red hot mist and the face of a demon looking straight at him.

"Father," it growled.

John collapsed on the floor.

\#

At breakfast the next morning, Anne was asked if she had heard all the commotion last night.

"I was tossing and turning in my bed all night," said Bishop Cotton.

"What was the problem sir?" asked John.

"Bashing and crashing around, all from the direction of your room, Mistress Gunter. I came to your door and heard much moaning and groaning. I thought you must be in your fits again. But your maid told me that you were merely having a bad dream."

"Yes, she told me. I wasn't really aware of it, I was asleep."

"Hmmm. I actually thought that you had a man in there. There were certainly a lot of voices."

"Apparently I speak a lot during these nightmares. Some assume that it is part of my bewitchments."

"I see," said Cotton. "What is your opinion Prideaux? I know you have been a witness to the fits before today?"

"I have sir. But I heard nothing last night. I went to bed early and must have slept right through." John remembered going to his room and starting on the wine he had been given. There followed nightmares, where he was sure he had seen Satan and he had woken up feeling sore, with a terrible headache.

"I feel as though I may be sickening for something and am not looking forward to the trip to London today."

"Then stay one more night," offered Cotton.

"Is your business in London very important Master Prideaux?" asked Anne.

"Yes it is. There are many plots against the King and one in particular. I have met with this person before and want to find out exactly what his intentions are. It seems the Catholics are planning something big."

"You must go then if it is to defend our King," said the Bishop.

The meal was eaten in silence before the Bishop excused himself as he had business to do.

"Anne, I need to talk to you."

"What about?"

"Lately I have been having dreams about you."

"What kind of dreams?"

"Very vivid ones. And about lots of women too who are members of the secret coven your mother was talking about."

"Sounds as though you are hallucinating."

"I only seem to hallucinate when I am around you. I also thought I saw Satan."

Anne looked at him, silent for a moment and then said, "Perhaps you did see him John. Just lately I am wondering if he is nearer to us than usual. You and me, I mean. We have been crossing paths for so long. When you were dreaming about me, what were we doing?"

"I don't think that I should say. It seems so wrong. I am either going mad or I need to pray more. Or get married."

"Who would you want to marry? Would you marry me? Or do you still have eyes for the stupid martyr girl?"

"That is not a very nice thing to say. Would you marry me? If I asked you?"

"In a different world I would say yes. But both of us are under the control of so many people. If we could go to a big house in the country, perhaps in your West Country and you preached in the local church and we had a lovely son of our own. That would be nice, but it seems so unlikely doesn't it? You are destined for great things. I am destined for an early grave I should think."

"Don't say that Anne. You are right about it not working if we married. Can you imagine your father allowing it? I want only the best for you."

Joan Greene interrupted their musings and said, "You must come with me Mistress Gunter. Reverend Prideaux, your bag is ready for you to leave on your journey."

The young people looked at each other and gave a half smile. It felt like an ending.

CHAPTER TWENTY SIX.

John Prideaux didn't see Anne again for nearly three months.

He spent some time back at Oxford after his Salisbury visit and kept himself busy, teaching and praying. There had been several invitations to the home of Thomas Holland and he had made excuses for every invite by return note. After a few weeks the notes stopped arriving. He found that he was hiding in his lodgings in order to avoid any contact that was not directly connected to the education of the young men under his wing. It seemed better that way.

One evening in June, he had been praying in St Michaels at the North Gate. He was sure that no one else was present, the vicar having mentioned that he was going home early tonight. John had been plagued by guilt of his assignations with Anne, remembering more and more as time passed. He was still unsure whether he had dreamed it or done it. But seriously? Could it be true?

Outside, it was getting dark. Inside it was almost dark and the church, lit sparsely with only a few candles and lamps, meant there were shadows everywhere. He was rarely spooked by dark churches, but recent events meant that he could not easily ascribe his feelings to fantasy and imagination. He shivered, but carried on praying. He realised that he was repeating the family prayer.

The candles behind him blew out and an icy wind crept along the aisle and swirled around him. Freezing rain it felt like. John recognised it from another time. He stopped praying, but remained leaning forward, head in hands. The swirling frosty air moved towards the altar. John watched with mounting horror as the mist collected to form a tall figure. It was a man and when it began to speak it was clear it was an unworldly man.

"Father," it said.

"You want to speak to your father or the Father?" asked John, really wishing that this was not happening.

"Father," repeated the shape and raised its hand in John's direction.

"I don't know your father," he answered.

"My father."

It moved towards him and as it did it formed into a handsome young boy of about 5 years old. He reminded John of the little boys back in Devon. John moved towards the boy and as he did, it turned into exploding firecrackers. John jumped back in shock.

There was orange smoke and fire and a strong choking smell. Arms reached out from the melee and tried to touch John's robes. John squealed and backed away from the grabbing fingers.

"Who are you?" he shouted.

"I am your baby boy. Your flesh and blood. Your son."

"No. No. That cannot be. What are trying to do to me?"

"We can change this country. We can take it over between us, priest. This country is moving into hard times. Dangerous times. I have such plans."

"I don't know what you mean. Hard times are upon us all the time. I fail to see how they could be worse." John was saying things he didn't feel, but what else could he do?

"I don't like these Scottish Kings. Elizabeth was wrong to give him the throne."

"King James is related to her. He has a right to be King. His son will rule after him and their line will maintain peace," said John loyally.

"You are his loyal little friend, aren't you? Let us see who rules after whom, shall we? It won't go as you think. And there will be plenty of trouble for our King very soon. Trouble that will make these firecrackers seem like nothing at all."

The firecrackers doubled and trebled in number around the church and the smoke thickened.

"You are my father, priest. Ask the young witch from Moreton about the baby she is carrying. It has long been in the planning and we have succeeded. I will be born into flesh and I will change the world."

John did not know how to answer the misty demon for he had never been taught how to.

"What is going on here sir? Is there a fire, sir?" The voice was owned by a servant of the house on the opposite corner of the lane.

"I am not sure. It was as though one of the lamps had something in it and exploded. It quite gave me a turn!"

"So long as you are unharmed, sir. Shall I clean up do you think?"

"I will help you. It is late and we do not wish to disturb anyone else."

John's hands were shaking as he reached for a broom and swept the broken glass in the direction of the servants shovel."

"It's odd, sir. This is not the first time something like this has happened."

"A fire you mean?"

"Similar to a fire. Small explosions and fireworks like tonight. We often hear it from across the street and when I came in to investigate, I was very surprised to find you here. Is it you who does it?"

"No indeed not. I have been here before, often in fact. But no, I have no idea what caused this trouble." John was feeling better and getting in control of his emotions. He could speak with the authority of his position.

"Yes sir. I will clean up this mess. You get along back to the college before you are missed."

John stood up and looked at the man.

"Thank you. I will," he answered.

There was only one week left of college and John decided that he would leave as early as he could and return to Stowford. Walks across the moors and games with his nephews and nieces would soon clear his head.

Surely Anne could not be pregnant with his child? A devil child? He could not decide whether to contact Anne or leave well alone. She must know by now whether she was with child?   They would have contacted him. And, if those experiences were not dreams, it meant that they were real.

Stowford. He must go to Stowford and pray in his little Harford church.

#

Brian Gunter was not happy when Anne left his house. He liked control, needed it. It seemed the whole country was interested and excited about the witches and his young daughter's fits. He had enjoyed bringing the middle aged and sex starved acquaintances of his to view Anne in her erotic movements. For deals and advancements he had allowed a touch or a stroke. On top of her clothing for some small favour and a lingering feel of her breasts or between her legs for more. Contracts had been exchanged and a considerable amount of land and money had been added to the Gunter estates.

There were clergy, lawyers, doctors and gentry involved in his schemes. It helped that they were all part of the same society, but the touching and observing of a well-bred young woman had been a surprising attraction to these men. Perhaps it was because they must either have a consenting affair with a woman of their own class or pay for a common woman or servant. It was rare to have easy access to a half-naked unconscious woman, complete with an audience and then to safely discuss the process in polite society.

Now, Anne had been stolen by the Bishop and Brian considered that it may be for his own ends. He suspected that Cotton was allowing similar audience participation at Salisbury. He had sent notes with his wife when she visited their daughter, but she returned with news of Anne's health and comfort. It seemed that the Bishop was recommending that Master Gunter did not visit. But Brian had heard that the King was to visit Oxford and decided that he would confront him and insist that he investigate the witches. His wife wanted him to leave well alone, but he never took his wife's advice.

He was going to go to Salisbury to fetch his daughter.

#

Anne enjoyed her new life in Salisbury. She was tended by the two Joans under the roof of Bishop Cotton and their care continued when she was moved to the country house of a friend of his. Anne kept up the fits for a while, but gradually found that her potion dosage had to be steadily increased to have any effect. This alteration in tolerance resulted in an overwhelming tiredness and lethargy and she felt less inclined to feign a fit. The real fits had stopped many months prior. Well before the trial. It was lovely not to have men paw at her under instruction from her father. Or have her mother parade her around for the delectation of the women. She hadn't minded the sex with John, even in front of everyone. That had made it more exciting, especially as John appeared to have little recollection of it. Her mother told her that he would never remember and as soon as this part of the process was finished, they could see about getting him to marry her. That was the main reason she agreed to go along with it. Not the baby. It wasn't really their baby anyway. She wasn't going to be able to keep it and she didn't want to keep it. This baby was meant for other things and she would never be attached to it.

She wanted some more potion. Anne always wanted more potion.

The Bishop had assigned a young man to look after her. His name was Ashley and he was the most beautiful man that Anne had ever seen.

"Who is that young man?" she had asked Joan.

"That is Ashley Prideaux. He is the son of a Cornish gentleman and is staying nearby. He helps the Bishop with some of his business. Ashley will inherit a lot of land when his father dies and he is looking for a wife."

"He has travelled across the country to Salisbury to find a wife? How do you know that?"

"We know that he is looking. He doesn't know he is looking. What do you think of him?"

"I think he is very handsome," she answered. "Is he kin of the Reverend?"

"Yes he is. But this one will suit you better I think."

Anne turned to look at the maid.

"Have you planned this?"

"Perhaps I have put it in the mind of the Bishop."

"Am I to be introduced to him?"

"Tonight I believe. At dinner."

"Send Sarah Rose to me."

"Yes Mistress."

Sarah Rose had been given many other duties while they had been at Salisbury and was not at her mistress's side as often as they both wanted. There was an intention to keep her from all North Moreton influence.

Joan left Anne alone and the young Ashley Prideaux looked across the garden to her. He smiled and winked.

Anne giggled. When she was speaking to Sarah Rose later that afternoon she said, "I felt childish Sarah Rose. It's hard to describe. It felt as though everything I do from now on must include his opinion of me."

"Mistress Anne, it sounds as though you are in love again."

"How can I be? I have only just met him."

"I expect you want saving,"

"Yes, I expect I do. I know I can catch him. That will be easy enough. But there are a lot of problems to overcome yet."

"Like this special baby."

"Yes." Anne tapped the brush against her mouth.

#

Dinner that evening was enjoyed immensely by Anne. Ashley was exactly as she wanted him to be. He smiled shyly but had great self-confidence. He told entertaining stories but wanted to listen to others. He was tall with dark wavy hair that he often moved from his face and put behind his ear. Anne could not keep her eyes off him. But when he looked at her, she found it difficult to maintain eye contact.

"Ashley has heard about your problems Anne and he has said that he will help."

"Oh!" said Anne. She had forgotten about the fits and pins and witch trials and demon babies, while she had been enjoying this dinner. Now she felt foolish and no longer an attractive woman.

"You are famous Mistress Gunter. I am aware of your troubles and Bishop Cotton has asked me to assist you. I hope you will be able to trust me as a friend and tell me everything that has happened to you. From the beginning."

"Oh," repeated Anne. She wanted to be his friend, naturally. But there was no way on this earth that she was going to tell him most of what had happened. Or what she was.

"Not now though? I become tired at this time of night."

"No my Lady," he laughed. "Not now. Tomorrow, when you feel well."

"I am not a Lady, but am grateful for your consideration," she answered.

Ashley smiled and glanced at the Bishop. When he ascertained that he wasn't paying attention, he turned back and winked again at Anne. She blushed.

Back in the room, Sarah Rose said, "He is handsome and you apparently are going to be spending lots of time with him."

"He is handsome and rich too. I learnt that he is to inherit large estates in Cornwall somewhere. I would like to live in a large house by the sea with servants and plenty of money."

"How do you intend to do that Mistress?" Sarah Rose asked this as she removed her mistress's clothes.

Anne held her hand against her stomach. "Is it beginning to show do you think? I know my breasts are bigger. It's disgusting."

"We can't let the Bishop or your new man, know anything about this. You are going to have to eat less. Lose weight, don't gain it."

"So I should vomit more? I can eat and vomit when I am back in my rooms and that way it doesn't look noticeable. Perhaps I should vomit now." Anne dedicated to anything she set her mind to, went over to her pot and put her fingers down her throat. Within minutes most of her dinner was in the pot. Sarah Rose passed her a drink of wine.

"Thank you. Now get rid of the evidence."

As Sarah Rose picked up the pot, Anne murmured, "It would be better if this baby ended up in the pot too."

Her maid said, "There are ways, Mistress. But if the women find out, we will both be in serious trouble."

"Rue and pennywort. I know. Have you seen any?"

"Yes Mistress. Don't you think we ought to see which way the wind blows with this Ashley first?"

"Whether I can catch his heart you mean?"

"Perhaps. But we must make sure that nothing is mentioned anywhere. Those women and their coven know about everything. They seem to have contacts everywhere too."

"I think Cornwall may be safe."

"It is far enough away. And people seem to leave Cornwall, not travel there. We must watch our backs."

"Yes of course. And we must find a way to protect ourselves."

"I shall pray that something will turn up."

"And I shall expect it to," answered Anne as she climbed into bed.

#

Ashley Prideaux appeared to know what he was about and when he met Anne the following morning for a walk in the gardens, he handed her a lidded basket, ribbonned and covered in flower heads.

"A gift for you, Anne. I want us to be firm friends."

Anne accepted the basket and placed it on the low wall they were standing next to.

"What is it? Apart from a very pretty basket," she laughed nervously.

"Perhaps a picnic!" he answered with his lovely laughing voice. "Open it and see! You are like my sister Johanna, always asking questions!"

Anne giggled again, a habit she had recently acquired and gently opened the lid. Inside was a rose coloured blanket which first moved, then squeaked. She lifted the blanket and said "Oh Ashley! Oh my goodness, this is the most perfect gift I have ever had in my life!"

Sarah Rose scurried forward, eager to see. Under the blanket was a tiny bundle of brown and white hair. It was a spaniel puppy. Anne lifted it out of the basket and held it to her face.

"She smells just like a puppy! My parents would never let me have a puppy and I always, always wanted one. Does she have a name? Can I choose my own name? I shall call her Bella. I will never know why you chose to give me exactly what I wanted and I shall never forget that you did." Anne reached over to her new friend and kissed him on both cheeks. "Thank you Ashley, thank you."

Ashley Prideaux had hoped that Anne would be pleased enough with the gift, to open up to him a little. He was shocked at her reaction. And surprisingly pleased. Anne was glowing and beautiful. Some of the effect may have been due to the dose she had insisted on drinking just before they left the house, but Ashley wouldn't know that.

"For my nerves," she said to Sarah Rose when demanding the dose.

But the rest of the emotion was genuine and not guile.

This little puppy had removed any nerves, any self-consciousness or any intention of continuing her given role as a badly done to or bewitched girl. She would collect this young man, marry him and travel to Cornwall with him and Bella and Sarah Rose.

"I'm am glad that you like the puppy Anne, now perhaps we can be friends and you will trust me."

"I do trust you Ashley, what do you want to talk about?"

"Your fits and the witches and what it is really all about. I know about witches, we do have them in Cornwall. Your witches were found innocent, so why are you still suffering?"

"It is too complicated to explain quickly. I need a long time to tell you, do you have a long time to listen?"

"I do, let us go and sit in the garden. There is a seat there under the roses and the clematis and it will be pleasant to get out of the sun."

Anne passed the basket to Sarah Rose and cuddled the puppy.

"Fetch some milk for the puppy and bring it to me over there."

Sarah Rose scampered off and the young couple sat on the seat.

They sat and talked like this often during the next two days. They returned to the house only for meals and sleep. Anne told Ashley about the potions and her father's actions and instructions. She did not tell him about her mother and the women or the sex and the impending baby. She was playing her own game now. She had seen a way out of her ridiculous life and would follow this path to the end. Anne had a vision and would stick to it.

Ashley Prideaux listened to the terrible troubles of the chaste young girl and as he did, he fell in love. Perhaps this beautiful young woman was exactly the sort of woman he could be with for the rest of his days. A beautiful woman, who would run his house and warm his bed. He would report favourably to the Bishop and recommend that she be removed from her parent's influence.

And perhaps into his own.

As they talked and laughed and played with the new puppy, they were suddenly disturbed by the Bishop and some guests who had entered the gardens. There was a great deal of shouting and waving of hands. The couple looked up and Anne said with great disappointment.

"My father, my father is here. What does he want?" She snuggled her puppy to her face and the puppy snuggled back.

"Anne! Anne! You are coming with me to Oxford. We are to see the King there!"

"Sir! Anne is to stay here until she is fully recovered from her recent ordeals!" protested Ashley.

The Bishop agreed and said, "Anne is doing so well, Master Gunter. My advice is to leave her under our care in Salisbury for a while longer."

"I thank you for your advice, but Anne is my daughter and she will do as I say."

"I want to stay here father. Please let me, I have never felt so well."

To everyone's surprise Brian raised his hand and slapped his daughter hard across the face. She dropped to the floor and the puppy fell from her arms and ran yelping across the garden. Sarah Rose chased Bella and picked her up, as Ashley reached for Anne.

"Take your hands from my daughter, sir and what the hell is that little rat you have been holding? Is this another witch's trick?"

"No father, Ashley gave me a puppy of my own," she croaked.

"You are coming back with me to Oxford this very moment and that rat is not welcome."

Brian snatched the puppy from Sarah Rose and held it over the stream. "I will drown the little demon." He let go, but before little Bella hit the water; Ashley had reached across and caught her. He fell into the water, but held the puppy aloft.

"Father, why are you doing this? I hate you, you have no idea how much I hate you!"

The group surrounding him in the garden looked at him in disgust, but Brian, used to unpopularity, brushed them all aside.

Within an hour, Anne was in a coach with her bags strapped to the back and Sarah Rose jammed between her and her father. There was no talking and the three miserable faces accompanied each other in silence all the way to Oxford. Ashley had taken Anne's puppy back into his own custody and swore that he would look after her and keep her safe until Anne returned.

"Write to me at Master Holland's residence," she urged, as he saw her to the coach.

"I promise Anne. I will come and visit you."

"Don't, not until I tell you it is safe. Father has a lot of friends at Oxford and they will be enemies of yours."

No more was said. Brian shoved her roughly onto the coach and she watched until Ashley and his waving was out of sight. For the six hour journey back to Oxford, Anne plotted and schemed about how she would make her father pay and pay for this. Once and for all.

It seemed that the King and Queen were to be in Oxford tomorrow and Brian wanted to tell them about Anne and her witches.

"We will be rich Anne, if you catch his eye. Make sure you do as I instruct, or there will be no dowry for you."

Anne went into deeper thought on hearing this. Would Ashley marry her without a dowry?

#

Brian was so audacious that he walked directly up to King James and Queen Anne while they walked around Exeter College grounds, accompanied by their two sons and several courtiers. He left the company of Thomas Holland and William Helme who were standing with him against the hall walls and asked King James outright to intervene in his case. He told him of the fits and the witches and the trial. King James was well aware of Anne Gunter it seemed and he had a great deal of interest in the truth of the story.

"Send your daughter to our quarters and we shall examine her until we get to the bottom of this."

"I shall be happy to work with you, Highness," said Brian bowing low, now confident of his further progress.

"I said send her, Gunter. That is all. You need not stay, she has her own maid?"

"Yes Highness."

"Then send the maid. She will attend to her. No need for you to bother."

Brian, as always, did not want to let this chance slip away and went too far, "Highness, I insist on accompanying my own daughter, as her chaperone, as her protector."

Queen Anne stared at the man coldly. Her hair piled high and her silver dress reflecting the morning sunshine gave her extra majesty.

"The King has spoken. Anne will be under my care and no harm will come to her," she said.

"Do as I have bid you, Gunter and let me hear no more about it," growled the King.

Brian knew that there was nothing further to say. He bowed and retreated. He heard the Queen say to her husband, "There is a Reverend Prideaux who knows Mistress Gunter. You met him when he was consulted along with Dr Holland about the new Bible translation. I think you should involve him."

"Is he a Catholic?"

"No."

"Then we shall have him too."

Brian Gunter went directly to his son in law's residence and demanded that John Prideaux be brought to him.

"He no longer attends us here. I have not seen him all summer. I believe he has returned to the West Country. He should be back for the college term, but I have not seen him yet. I cannot help you with this Brian."

Brian was purple with rage and threw his glass across the room. Before Thomas could stop him, Brian was raging and smashing glass. He held his arms above his head and bellowed. The bellow was incomplete, when he clutched his chest and fell to the floor. By the time the servants had him lying on a bed and the doctor sent for, Brian had used all his current strength. It would be months before he found it again.

\#

John returned to his Stowford home absolutely drained.

He was chewing some of the leaves he had been given by Thomas as a pick me up on the journey. He needed this lift twice a day now. Sometimes he took powder and sometimes potion. It made him feel so much better, but the times between the lift in spirits were becoming increasingly difficult to bear. He was suffering memory losses more often and hoped that this holiday would recharge him. Perhaps his mother, his ever vigilant mother, would spot what his problems were and help him.

Agnes noticed the state her son was in before he walked through the door. His white face, the dark rings under his eyes and the shaking.

"What are you taking, John?"

"Nothing, mother. Just some remedies the doctors have given me."

"You are not taking anymore," she answered and took away everything medicinal he had brought with him. She sent him to work on the farm with his elder brother Thomas and ensured that he teach the children archery. She spoke to the Rector at Harford and had John preach to his local audience. No one else knew of his addictions, only that he was suffering exhaustion from overwork.

"He should never have gone to England," some said.

"He can't handle doing a proper job, if he gets worn out lording it in Oxford," said others.

Within a month, John was almost back to his old self. He told his family nothing of his escapades with the Gunter family. It seemed better that way. His mother would worry and his father and brothers would want to come back with him and sort out Brian once and for all. John walked on the moors for hours on end and sat among the rocks and meditated. He came to realise that he had been further away from his God these past few months than he ever had in his life. That was why he had been feeling so cold and lonely. He decided that he was going back to Oxford where his destiny lay, but he would have nothing to do with the Gunter family and would study and straighten his life out.

That is what he would do.

CHAPTER TWENTY SEVEN

While Brian was laying sick at the Holland quarters at the college, John Prideaux had returned to his own lodgings. He was feeling calm and in control of his feelings and most importantly for him, he felt close to his God. He was wrapped around with comfort and ready to put the past behind him.

He unpacked his belongings and went to the college chapel. He had considered going to St. Michaels, but remembered his last visit. He had avoided the college chapel for weeks prior to his trip home in the hopes that he would not see Thomas Holland, but now it didn't seem to make much difference. They could all move on with their lives and forget everything that had happened to date.

But it was Holland's servant, who ran after John as he walked into the chapel shouting,

"Reverend Prideaux, you are wanted at the Rector's lodgings."

"I am about my prayers."

"Yes sir. I was told that you must come to Master Holland's rooms as soon as I found you."

"And what if you say that you cannot find me?"

"Then he will be in lots of trouble," said Susan Holland.

John looked at her, hesitated for only a moment and followed Susan out of the chapel and over to the

Hollands. Led to the bedroom Brian was laid up in, John found himself becoming dizzy and tense. His bags were hardly unpacked and here he was back in the ring.

"Prideaux come in, I need your help."

John was shocked to see Gunter looking so pale. He had blue lips and had aged several years since their last meeting.

"What help?"

"Anne is to be kidnapped by the King, I want you to remove her from Oxford and hide her somewhere. I shall tell the King that you have been instructed to keep her safe."

"That is something I shall not be doing Master Gunter. Crossing King James will not have a good ending. I will not jeopardise my near or far future for you, or anyone. I shall help you if you require while you are ill, but nothing else."

Brian looked deflated and a little bluer.

"I am worried for Anne and for me. If we don't keep control of her, we may lose everything."

"I doubt that very much. You are unlikely to allow that to happen. I suggest you rest and follow your doctor's instructions and get well."

Brian did not answer. He closed his eyes and pulled up his sheets. John walked out of the room and ran downstairs. There he was met by Susan, Thomas and a man who John did not know.

"What has happened to your father? He seemed very ill just now."

"He has got himself all stressed out about Anne. Everything is about Anne and she has no care about it at all. She was always the selfish one and the rest of the family must pay for it."

"Now calm down wife, it is not good to talk about private matters amongst strangers."

"I assume that you mean me," said the stranger. "I have come to find you Reverend Prideaux. His Highness King James has asked that you attend him this evening while he examines Mistress Anne Gunter for signs of witchcraft."

"Are you sure he wants just me?"

"He has asked for you alone Prideaux and you are to accompany me to St. John's College, where Anne Gunter has been brought."

"Aaaah! I understand what Master Gunter was talking about now."

"I doubt he was pleased. Come with me Reverend Prideaux."

They walked to Turl Street, went through the turnstile gate and across the full ditch and the muddy tracks. There had been plenty of rain recently and John idly thought that the black mud would be draining back into the college, as usual. They walked briskly up the track until they reached St John's College. It was here in the hall that the King and his courtiers were waiting.

"What does Laud think of this?" asked John.

"It doesn't matter what Laud thinks, only what the King thinks. I am sure you are aware it is only ever about what the King thinks."

John recognised Richard Neile among the men. The others he did not know and there were no women present. They approached the King as he beckoned them over and he said,

"Prideaux thank you for coming. I know you are aware of the Anne Gunter case and have witnessed her fits. Do you believe that she is bewitched?"

John knelt in front of James knowing that the answers to the following questions were very important.

"Highness, I have seen Mistress Gunter in her fits and I have also witnessed events which I cannot explain."

"Events?"

"Yes. I have seen witches use their powers to alter the minds of people and make them do things they would not otherwise have done. Or perhaps make them think that they have done things that they haven't actually done."

"You speak in riddles Prideaux. I brought you here to assist, not confuse."

"I am sorry. I did not mean to do that. But I do believe that there are witches both good and evil."

"What about the Bible and the Christian teachings? Do you reject those?"

"No Highness! On the contrary. The Bible acknowledges the potential existence of dark and light. What matters is what we choose to follow and what we choose to ignore."

"We shall have these discussions at a later date Prideaux. Tonight I must attend the theatre after this examination and so we must get on. I am to see Matthew Gwinne's play and I gather it is dreadful. But the Queen insists. Bring in the girl," he said to a young man sitting next to him.

It was the first time that John had noticed the handsome young boy. He could not really describe him as a man. He appeared to have the King's attention and John wondered if the stories he had heard were true. As it was, the boy skipped off and soon returned with a terrified looking Anne Gunter and her maid. She bobbed a curtsey at the King and smiled with great warmth at John.

She prostrated herself in front of James and Sarah Rose did the same.

"Tell me about these witches, Anne Gunter. Bring her a chair. The maid can stand over by the wall."

"I have been troubled by the witches in my village since I was a girl, Highness. They have sent their creatures to use me and I have been suffering for many years."

"But I know that the trial at Abingdon found the women innocent and you merely suffering from hysteria."

"I am still suffering from them today," confessed Anne.

"Do you feel their power upon you now, Mistress Gunter?" asked the pretty young man.

"I do sir. Someone must have sent a message that I am back in Oxford. I was safe in Salisbury."

"I would be obliged if you could find time to show us your fits," instructed the King. It was an instruction not to be ignored.

"I am unable to have a fit by my will Highness, but I know I am being bewitched as we speak here tonight."

"Are you to enter your fits?" asked the young man.

John was frightened for Anne. These men were powerful and could decide the rest of her life tonight. Anne put her hand in her pocket and then cupped the hand round her nose and sniffed hard.

"What are you doing?" asked the King.

"I am feeling ill, Highness."

Ann stood up and began to sway in the dance reminiscent of her display at North Moreton church. She turned and danced and began to undo her hair until it fell about her body. The men in the room were mesmerised with the performance, while Sarah Rose looked bored. Anne soon moved with more abandon and began to unlace her gown. As she danced, the bodice moved in unison and showed half her breasts, first the right and then the left. John wanted to intervene, but held back. He silently prayed that Anne would not sit astride the

King's lap and undo his breeches. She wouldn't, would she?

Suddenly she froze. Arms above her head and standing upon her toes. She stood like that for two full minutes. The men said nothing at first, but soon began murmuring to each other and the King told his young friend to go and check upon the girl.

"Jamey, I mean Highness. She is definitely standing only on her toes and maintaining her balance that way. How can she be doing that?"

There followed a loud crack and her ankles both turned to the outside and her body weight rested on her ankle bones, the feet pointing straight out. Everyone jumped at the noise and Sarah Rose squealed. Anne's eyelids opened and closer inspection by the group showed that her eyes were black.

"She isn't dead is she, Thomas?" asked the King.

His friend Thomas put his hand in front of her mouth. "There is air coming out, she can't be very dead."

They all laughed but stopped abruptly when Anne screamed. She held her arms in crucifix formation and projectile vomited pins in the direction of the King. He held his hands up to save himself but appeared unconcerned. Anne returned her feet to the normal position and span around while her dress fell to the floor. She was not naked, much to the pleasure of John, for she wore a tight shift which accentuated her figure.

"Her belly is swollen. Is she with child, Prideaux?" asked King James.

"I do not know Highness. I would doubt it though. She is an honest young woman."

"Bewitchment can make a woman show lewd and unseemly behaviour. She is of marrying age and should have a husband servicing her regularly in order to put an end to this nonsense," said Richard Neile.

John was about to speak in her defence when Anne dropped to the floor with a loud thump. He went over to her and watched her shake and quiver while foam came from her mouth. The audience surrounded her on the floor and watched her arms bend this way and that. She showed her breasts as she did this and her shift began to ride up her legs.

"Pull up her shift, Neile," instructed the King.

"Highness?" questioned John. The raised hand stopped him from speaking further and he watched helplessly as his friend's shift was raised up enough to reveal her naked body.

"She looks pregnant," said Neile. "Girl! Is your mistress with child? Has she been with a man? Or men?"

Sarah Rose was adamant and said, "No sir! My mistress does not do anything like that. She is true to God."

John did not interject, but was becoming dizzy and sick.

Sarah Rose ignored the King and covered Anne's body again. "She needs to rest now," she said.

"Yes of course," said the King and he stood up. "Have her taken back to her quarters. I shall refer the matter to Bancroft. Neile, I want you and Harsnett to examine the woman properly and then I shall see her again in a month. Do not let her family attend to her at all, for any reason. Prideaux, you may assist Neile and Harsnett and their servants. Come Thomas, attend to me and then we shall all go and see this play. The Queen expects me."

They all swept out of the hall and left John and Sarah Rose to look after Anne.

"What was all that about? What did she take? There are no signs of the witches anywhere."

"She can fit now just by taking the powder. While we have been in Salisbury, she hasn't been taking it much. She hasn't needed to stay in her fits and stick to her story. Her father hasn't been around and she has felt safe."

"I am glad about that. What about the pins?"

"I don't understand about the pins. But she has found a potential suitor who could take her away from this place. She thought that he could, but now she is in the custody of the King, her life is back to being difficult."

"A suitor?" Was he jealous?

"Yes. I believe he is a kinsman of yours. He is a Prideaux from Cornwall. Ashley Prideaux his name is."

"I do not know him, but there are one or two branches of the family that I am unfamiliar with. Does he return her love?"

"I think so. He brought her a puppy."

Anne was beginning to stir. Sarah Rose fetched Anne's dress and helped the semi-conscious woman into it.

"Where are the servants? They take their time. This fellow, is he a decent man?"

"He seems to be, Master Prideaux, he is a rich man and Anne has told him much of what has happened to her."

"What about this baby?"

"She is being forced into that by her mother and the rest of the women. The baby is to be under their control and is going to change the world, they say. They chose Anne because she has unusual gifts and they said there have been signs that the country will go through great changes when this boy is of age. They want to influence what is going to happen. They say a King will be murdered."

"Hush girl, do not speak of things like this when we are in earshot of courtiers. Who has told you these stories?"

"I am forced to listen and partake in events I have no interest in. I would like to come to your church and make a confession as soon as I can, Reverend. My soul is not at ease."

John was taken aback by this request, but nodded and said, "Come whenever you wish, Sarah Rose."

Before they had any further discussion, they were joined by five servants of the King who deftly lifted the still comatose Anne onto a stretcher and took her away to her rooms. John, left standing by himself pondered on what he had just seen.

"What kind of test is this, my God?" he asked out loud.

"Perhaps He is testing your faith, John."

It was Richard Neile.

"I have been involved in this case for a few years now Neile. It does not become any clearer to me."

"I am pleased to have your assistance in this case and others similar. It should help me in my next role. I am to be made Dean of Westminster on 5th November, all things being well."

"I hadn't heard that," said John.

"Keep it under your hat. It isn't common knowledge yet. I had to agree to make a conclusion of this Gunter case. The country is becoming too excited about the witch problem and the King does not like that. Mark you, he doesn't like the father either."

"Not many do I am afraid."

"Holland is married to one of the daughters?"

"Yes. They seem to roll along well enough."

"Gunter has certainly made enough money out of these Oxford connections. I hope you don't give him any tips."

"Tips? What sort of tips could I give him? Unless you mean about the Bible."

"I mean financial. King James has noted how many of these new building contracts he is involved in. He has managed to acquire some land at the walls. He can only have heard of that from you or Holland or Helme and the college are bound to want to buy it from him."

"I do not involve myself in those kinds of dealings. I know we are moving into a modern world, but I am not particularly interested in how to make lots of money."

"This case is a definite leg up, Prideaux. You and I have travelled our own road to this city and we both want to climb higher. That is why I understand your determination to avoid alliances with men like Gunter. But your association with the King will help you. I suggest you follow my lead and assist us to come to the proper conclusions. I do not intend to remain as Dean. I am moving up."

"I am willing to help. I also want to climb up higher in the college and the church. Make my family proud."

"Excellent. We shall make a bargain to travel this bit of the road together. I shall be in touch."

With that, Neile left John alone.

#

By Monday 3rd October, Anne had been regularly examined by Neile and his men. She had initially been put in the care of Richard Bancroft, the Archbishop of Canterbury, who in turn sent her to his chaplain Samuel Harsnett at his rectory in Shenfield. Harsnett was another sceptic and a member of the closed circle which also included Holland, Neile, Helme and Bancroft.

Brian Gunter was desperate to become a member of this clique and had pestered Thomas about it for years. But even Thomas would not, could not, be persuaded on this matter. Thomas was discovering that working with the men and the women was the best way for him to keep safe. Play both sides. He considered that Brian Gunter was unreliable cannon.

Once the King had removed Anne from Oxford, Gunter was not allowed to see her and had no idea that she was at Shenfield. Her mother did not try and visit. None of her women were installed as servants wherever Anne was living. She had lost track of her daughter once she left Oxford. She was desperate to discover her whereabouts, knowing that the child would be arriving soon. Six months only it may be, but this child would be born early. All favours were being called in, in an effort to find her daughter and the demon child.

Anne had had only one fit since living at Shenfield, but her growing belly was preventing her taking her potions quite so often and she was tired all the time. Sarah Rose attended her and said, "We must do something about this child, Mistress Anne. We must tell."

"Harsnett and the others must know. They are doctors and learned men, not fools. But they say nothing."

"I cannot let your clothes out any more than I have already. I shall have to ask for some cloth. Perhaps if they are suspicious, we can say that you are becoming fat from lack of exercise."

"That won't be necessary. I feel as though the child will be born soon. When it is, we shall do it quietly and you get rid of it."

"How? You don't mean kill it?"

"No, we shall give it to some family who cannot have a child."

"I don't think it will be as easy as that."

There was a knock at their door and a maid said, "Mistress, you have a visitor downstairs. It is the Reverend Prideaux."

"Oh how wonderful! So well timed. We shall be straight down."

She was as good as her word and skipped into the room as John stood up. She beckoned Sarah Rose to the other side of the room.

"I am so glad you are here John. Why has it taken you so long to call?"

"I went to Salisbury and then have had my own work to attend to. I hear you are much better and have had no fits for three weeks."

"That is true. I have had no fits and have only taken my potions once. That is why there have been no fits. But I have more troubles than that I am afraid and I need your help."

"I shall always help you in any way I can. But first I wanted to bring you some news from your Ashley."

"You have seen him? Oh, what did he say?" She grabbed his arm.

"He sent you this," and gave her a small portrait of a spaniel puppy. "He said to tell you that he is looking after Bella and that she is growing well. I saw the little thing and she is very sweet. He also says that he will wait for you and that he has told his sister Johanna about you and she is looking forward to meeting you."

Anne broke down and sobbed.

"He won't be waiting for me when he knows about this," she said and opened her cloak to reveal her enlarged stomach.

"Are you really having a child, Anne? You have grown so large since we last met."

"I am huge and I hate it. I am as fat as butter and it's terrible. Look how I...Aaaah!"

She screamed and bent forward in pain, as a mixture of blood and water began to stain the front of her dress and spill onto the floor.

"The baby is coming, Mistress. We have to get you up the stairs before the servants see you."

"Get her to her room. I shall mop up and follow you. I will see what I can do." He grabbed a throw from a sofa and wiped up the mess. He took another cloth, wrapped it around the throw and followed the women upstairs. A maid crossing the hall noticed him.

"Confession," he said. "I am to take her confession."

The maid bobbed and scurried away. It was none of her business what these people got up to. John ran up the stairs and realised that he did not know which room

Anne was in. The only light was from lamps halfway up the stairs and at either side of the top of the stairs. This meant that the long corridors bearing right and left were in darkness. He called out softly, but there was no answer. He picked up one of the lamps and stood for a moment turning this way and that, hoping for some navigational inspiration, which sadly did not come.

What did come however was the familiar mass of mist currently hovering at the far right end of the corridor. This mist glowing and shimmering, gave off only a dim light, but it was enough to allow John to see it. He hoped and hoped that the shimmering mist would not float towards him. But he hoped in vain because it moved carefully and intentionally in his direction. It's arms were thrust forward and it's undressed body floated behind.

"Why are you doing this to me?" he asked.

There was no answer. The mist moved at speed towards him and John tried to turn left and run along the corridor away from the horror. But his legs were frozen to the ground and he helplessly held his lamp out on front of him awaiting his fate. The demon mist stopped and moved its head from one side to the other as if analysing its prey. It had now taken the shape of a tall but cadaverous man. It possessed putrefying yellow and spiky teeth in the style of a half rotted corpse. The eyes were black holes and any hair it possessed stuck directly up, sparse and white. It smelt of rotting rats.

John decided that he would no longer be frightened, the emotion being wearing and useless. The mist appeared to guess his thoughts and it said, "Father, I shall talk to you tonight from a flesh and blood body." This was said so slowly and carefully that John felt the adrenalin race through his system and wobble his legs and unsettle his stomach.

"No," said John. "We cannot allow that. You are not to take human form."

The mist moved backwards and pulled one of its arms in front of its body in protection. "I come tonight and the girl will die and you will die."

"Then who will look after you?"

"I shall look after myself when they take me to London where I shall grow and flourish. This ridiculous King will take an interest in me as I am the child of the known witch. Once he does, I cannot be stopped."

"Why are you telling me this? Telling me gives away your power."

It laughed a terrible laugh and then shot past him and vanished into a room. John was left in the poor pool of light casting from his lamp. He walked in a measured determined fashion in the direction of that same room. Before he could knock, the door opened and he was dragged in by an annoyed looking Sarah Rose.

"Where have you been? Her time is almost here."

He looked across to the bed and saw Anne with her skirts around her waist and the crowning head of a child appearing between her legs. She was sweating and red-faced and emitting low grunts.

"Shut the fucking door, John," said Sarah Rose. "We have to help her and decide what to do."

"Did you see the demon?" asked John.

"Demon? What fucking demon? Don't go all stupid on us now. We must deliver this…" Before she could finish her sentence, the baby slipped out onto the bedcover dragging the cord and placenta behind it. It was happening too quickly. Out of the tail of his eye, John saw his demon appear from the corner of the room and move towards the child.

"We must stop him," hissed John.

Anne was semi-conscious and the blood seeped quickly from between her legs. The baby grunted and held out its arms towards the spirit. John leapt between the two and picked up the child and held it close. The placenta followed the child and slapped against John's legs, staining and ruining his cloak. The demon shot forward and John held up his rosary crucifix in its face. It moved back a short distance.

Sarah Rose ran around the end of the bed and taking out her own crucifix, held it to the demon's face. She muttered some words, which John thought were Hebrew, although he could not make out exactly what she said. The demon went back to its corner and Sarah Rose took out a knife and cut the child's cord and deftly tied it off. She took hold of the placenta and threw it at the demon, covering it in blood. John was astonished to see it scream and disintegrate.

"Has it gone?" he whispered.

"For now. It will return."

"It wants the child, we must hide it."

"It doesn't want the child, you fool," snarled Anne. "It is the child."

John's mind was not helping him understand the position they were in. He felt freezing cold as he looked down at the small white child crowned with a mass of black hair as it stared back at him. He knew that this child could only have been inside Anne for about five months and he had been surprised to see it born as if full term. Yet now, it looked like a two year old.

"This is not right," he said.

"Really? You think?" answered Anne. "Now do something about this bleeding, Sarah Rose. I could die and I don't want to."

Sarah Rose moved to her and spread Anne's legs again. She put two of her fingers inside Anne and fished around for a few moments. John squirmed and Anne moaned while Sarah Rose brought out another piece of placenta.

"Push again Anne, whether you want to or not."

This, Anne did and after two minutes of panting and straining there lay another placenta, more shrivelled than the first with a tiny dead baby attached to it.

"Fuck. That was them making sure. At least this one is dead," hissed Anne.

"Should you speak of your child this way?" asked John, his priestly training rising in him again.

"It is not my child, nor yours. It is a devil child and loves neither of us. It loves itself and we must kill it before my mother and her cronies find out about it."

"No!" said John. He looked down at the live child, who now appeared to be almost four years old.

It grinned at him and said, "Food! I hungry!" John grimaced and holding the child at arm's length he placed it on the chair. In front of their eyes the child's hair began to grow longer and the body matured.

"Don't let it go," said Sarah Rose. "If it breaks free, we are all lost."

John, shaken and nervous, asked Anne, "Are you alright?"

The bleeding had stopped and Anne slowly raised herself up and swung her legs carefully out of the bed. She began to undress and instructed Sarah Rose to wash her and hide the soiled clothes.

"I shall tell the maids that your monthly bleeding has come and it has been heavy. I can wash everything myself and fetch you more bedding. Here, take this potion, you will feel better soon."

"This child! What are we to do with this...?"

"Young man you mean, priest?"

And Sarah Rose was correct. The child was almost 14 years old and uncomfortably naked in front of them.

"We must dress him and remove him to a place of safety," said John, still fearful of the demon and of being caught.

"You must kill him, John. You are his father and as such you are the only one who can. His mother gave him life and you must take it away."

"You are telling me to kill a child? My child? I cannot and will not!"

The demon returned as if called by John and swirled around the room. It grinned and mocked him and frightened the women. John was enraged. This had gone on quite long enough and he would stop it. He picked up his crucifix and held it up and was about to quote suitable scripture to vanquish the demon, when he changed his mind. He heard his mother's voice telling him to pray. Say the prayer.

Prayer, what prayer?

But of course, the family prayer. He quoted with spirit and determination.

"O God, That knows us to bee set in the midst of so many and great dangers, that for Mans frailenesse we cannot always stand uprightly, guard to us the health of Body and Soul, that all those things which we suffer for sinne, by thy holy wee may well passé and overcome, through Jesus Christ our Lord."

The demon mist stopped swirling and mocking and floated in one spot, as if hypnotised. It looked with sadness as John prayed and suddenly fell to the floor like a dropped cloak. John finished the prayer and began to shake from the effort.

Anne and Sarah Rose held their hands up at the space behind him and he turned to look where they pointed. The young man, now mature and with long hair about his shoulders, smiled sweetly and dropped in the same manner as the demon. They both vanished and there was nothing left in the bedroom other than one terrified Reverend and two shaken and bloodied young women.

"Wrap the placenta and the dead child, Sarah Rose. Wrap it tight and box it. We shall give that to mother and tell her the plan didn't work."

CHAPTER TWENTY EIGHT

John returned to Oxford the next day and was very glad of it. He left a note for Harsnett, apologising for visiting on the evening he was not at home and thanking him for his hospitality in his absence. He told him that he had met with Anne and found her much improved under his and Neile's care. He felt sure that the problem would soon be resolved. Anne stayed in bed the next day and the servants accepted that she was suffering from a particularly severe woman's problem and cleaned up and supplied new bedding for Sarah Rose. The remaining evidence had been securely sealed in a box so that it would retain much of its freshness for Mistress Gunter and her coven to examine. They did not know when the next meeting would take place, but would be ready for it. Anne was now determined that she would partake no longer in any of the ceremonies and formulated a plan to satisfy her mother and herself.

"So Ashley does love me," she confided in Sarah Rose.

"So it seems. We must pursue that and get you away to Cornwall with the King's blessing. And me too. I am not stopping here with any of this lot."

"It seems you and John are the only people I can trust and for that you will always be by my side. We shall catch you a fine West Country husband. Perhaps I shall raise you to the level of my companion and that way you can make a better match."

"You will never regret that, Anne."

"I know. We have travelled a complicated road since our first meeting. Now hide the box in my chest. It is well sealed so that there will be smell?"

"Yes. How are you feeling now? Are you sad?"

"About the demon child? No I am not. As soon as I am healed below, I shall exercise and practice my dancing until I am firm and tight again."

"When I examined you earlier, all was almost as it should be."

The women hugged.

The next day Dr Neile returned and once he had read John's letter and sent a reply, he called for Anne.

"We are to travel to Hinchingbrooke on Saturday. King James will be there for the hunting and wants to examine you. Has all been well? I note Prideaux visited you."

"I was a little under the weather and so spent virtually no time with him. But it has passed now and I am feeling much better. I feel that I may speak freely to the King about my troubles. Do you advise that to be wise?"

Dr Neile looked at is charge and smiled. "Yes, always be honest with the King, he will treat you with sympathy. What is your truth?"

"I must confess only to the King and throw myself on his mercy."

#

Anne wore her finest clothes at Hinchingbrooke. Sir Oliver Cromwell, who had recently taken over from his father, was an excellent host and appeared to spare no expense in entertaining the Royal party of whom there appeared to be many. Sarah Rose told her that she had never seen her looking so chaste and so beautiful. Anne, recently potioned, agreed wholeheartedly.

Dinner on Saturday night was an extravagant event and Anne listened to her King talk of Sir Oliver's ancestor Thomas who had been executed. He felt that they had an affinity, he said, as his mother had been executed too. Everyone drank and ate great quantities. She idly wondered how easy Sir Oliver found all of this hospitality to pay for. She was pointed out on several occasions as being the famed bewitched woman, witch or beautiful temptress. She was glad that the King appeared to prefer the company of his young male companion and that he deterred any man who showed her more than polite interest.

Sunday evening was different however. The group had been hunting for most of the day and drinking too. Anne had spent the day in intense anxiety, dreading what might happen. It was for this reason that she took more potion than was probably good for her. The group of men were loud and jovial and ate and drank even more. The atmosphere was gladiatorial by the time Anne was invited to stand in the middle of the tables and tell them how she was progressing.

"I am well, Highness and happy. Master Harsnett and Dr Neile have looked after me very well."

"And do you still suffer from your fits?"

"I have had only one since we last met your Highness."

"And do you attribute this to being hidden from your witch tormentors?"

"No, I do not. I attribute it to being away from my family."

"How so?"

The Royal party did not interrupt, recognising that this change of tone from King James meant they must treat this examination seriously.

Anne knelt down in front of James and said, "I wish to confess to you."

"Aaaah... Confessions are good for the soul. Pray continue."

"With your Highness's permission, I wish to confess that I have done all that I have done, under my father's instruction. The stories of bewitchment have been largely untrue. I was under threat of assault and imprisonment if I did not follow his demands."

"Why would he force you to do this? What is his benefit?"

"There has been a long running dispute between my father and the Gregory family and some of their friends. It goes back to a football match in 1598, where my father was involved in the deaths of two of the Gregory men. There have also been financial disputes and my father wished to make them pay. When he forced me to do as I did, he discovered that he was attracting a great deal of attention and as a result a great deal of business."

"And all this was enough to persuade you?"

Anne prostrated herself fully, feeling that this would be a suitable time so to do.

"No. He beat me and assaulted me and gave me potions which affected my mentality. Most of the time I have not been in my proper senses and since I have been sent away under your wise advice and suspicion of fraud, I have become well. I shall forever be in your debt for saving my soul. If however, you wish to punish me for my sins, then I shall accept that gratefully and with good grace. I bless and thank and pray for you every moment of every day for the help you have given me. I only ask that my punishment does not involve my being sent back to my father's control. Any other punishment I shall accept."

There was much muttering among the men until the King raised a hand, signalling silence.

"I am happy that you have chosen to confess as you have, Mistress Gunter. Your words make a great deal of sense and explain the way you have behaved. Upon investigation of your father and his dealings, I find that there are many who judge him to be a crook and a liar. Dr Neile, I appreciate your work here and ask that you continue for another month in order that we ensure Mistress Gunter is properly well. I also want warrants issuing for the arrest of Brian Gunter and we shall decide what is to be done. Now, Mistress Gunter I ask that you dance for us and prove that you are not still affected."

Anne stood and bowed. She knew the examination was now going her way and was wondering how she should dance. Should she be provocative or demure? She decided on a little of both, but would dance full of energy, proving that a fit could no longer be encouraged.

Sarah Rose was hiding at the back of the room and ran forward with two bands of ribbons. These Anne held aloft and as soon as the King beckoned the musicians to play, she danced as she had practiced all her life. There were no breasts on show and the only time her skirts lifted was when she spun or leapt. There was much clapping and shouting as she gave her all to the performance. The only person there who knew what Anne had been through less than a week ago, merely prayed for success. The dance ended with Anne throwing herself at the feet of the King and breathing heavily as she endeavoured to get her breath back.

"We can see that your afflictions are improving, Mistress Anne. Your figure is now in the form of a chaste young woman. I am pleased. I shall send for you in the morning before we hunt again and I shall give you my decisions."

Anne got to her knees and thanked the King and kissed his hands with warm gratitude. She was dismissed. As they left the room, Sarah Rose said, "almost there."

"Almost there," Anne agreed.

#

King James was much more subdued in the morning, apparently having been drinking all night and gaining only a little sleep. He was joined by Dr Neile and a couple of his personal advisors.

"Is there anything further you wish to confess to me, Anne? I hear from Bancroft that you made a friend of his servant, Ashley Prideaux?"

"I did, Highness. He was very kind to me and helped me see that I should consider other possibilities. He thought that I should come to my King and tell him the truth. He told me that my soul would be cleansed by your Highness as Head of our Church. He told me that the potions I was being given could be harmful to me and the cause of some of my fits. I know that because of your wise and kind advice and sending me to the right people, I have finally seen my life as it really is. I did not know that before. I was only obeying my father, as is my duty."

"What about this Ashley? Do you love him?"

"I do, but we can never be together."

"Why is that?"

"Because I cannot marry without a dowry and my father will not give me anything now that I have told you the truth of his actions. He told me that would be so and that he would throw me onto the streets to earn money where I can."

Dr Neile sighed. "Your father is not a godly man I am afraid."

Anne dropped her gaze to the hands on her lap. She had never looked so sweet, so broken.

"We cannot have this, Anne. I shall promise you a dowry if you marry this young man. I have asked my advisors and they tell me that he is a loyal supporter of mine and has a true faith in God. I approve of your marriage and give my permission for it to take place."

Anne thanked him profusely, knowing that the King's approval was the same as an instruction to marry. She hoped that Ashley would not be too cross, but she could quite legitimately say that the marriage was to be on King James's order.

"I shall want to see Mistress Anne in a couple of weeks when I have time, Neile. Please see to it that she is available. Keep her at your house until I dismiss her to her husband."

Dr Neile bowed and took Anne from the room.

"What happens now?" she asked.

"We must contact this Ashley fellow and tell him that he must be married. You did well here Anne. I don't doubt that your father did as you said, but I wonder if it is as simple as that. Not to worry, I don't care either way. This whole episode has done me no harm at all. I will send you back with your maid, while I return to London and deal with more of our Catholic problem."

Anne smiled at him and murmured her thanks. She scurried back to her room, joined by Sarah Rose on the way.

"I heard," said she. "This is excellent news. Don't forget your promises to me."

"I won't forget," said Anne.

#

John Prideaux went straight back to his rooms at Exeter College after his trip to Shenfield. He felt as though he could take no more shocks without going mad. He was dropped off outside the turnstile in the walls by the college. Everyone was busy with their own business and there was no acknowledgement of his arrival. He stopped and looked at the walls and the tower and the gates and had a vivid vision. One day he would make this college a most beautiful and advanced educational establishment. And he would be in charge. He had seen a part of life that most others hadn't and he felt as though this adventure would not be the last.

John Prideaux was not only a changed man, but a better one.

He had only just closed the door to his rooms when a note was passed underneath. It asked him to join Thomas Holland at St Michael at the North Gate within half an hour. This was an unusual meeting place and John thought that he would go. It took him a little longer than half an hour to finish his unpacking, run down the stairs and out of the side gate of the college to walk briskly down to the church. He felt a shiver as he lifted the latch, remembering his last visit there. But of course that little problem was solved. Dead and gone he hoped.

Thomas was praying at the altar and continued until John came to kneel next to him.

"You are returned John, I am glad of that."

"Why so, Thomas? We haven't spoken for a little while now and I cannot say that I have missed you."

Thomas got up, crossed himself and beckoned John to a pew.

"How is Anne?"

"Anne?" he answered carefully.

"I have it on good authority that she is in the care of Harsnett and Neile. I know they are current favourites of the King and that they are supervising her return to health."

"I know nothing of these things," John answered.

"I see. You would be wise to keep me on side, John. I am one of the few you can trust in this changing world."

"My recent experience of you is the opposite of that, Thomas. I repeat, I do not have the ear of the King and know nothing of Anne. I would not tell you if I did."

"You know that there is much in this world that most do not understand. Our group have much power as it is the only one which aligns itself with the women. You have seen things you cannot unsee and will have to take sides somewhere. Being alone is not healthy."

John said, "I shall deal with you where I have to Thomas, but I remain loyal to my King, my God and my family. You do not feature in any of those."

"You put yourself in danger John."

"I do not Thomas. I have the power of prayer on my side. I don't need you."

John bobbed to the altar and strode out of the church feeling stronger than he ever had.

#

Another note arrived a week later. This time it was hand delivered by a messenger from the King. When John read it he smiled. The King was graciously thanking him for his assistance and friendship to Mistress Anne Gunter and informing him that she was under the King's charge and would remain so. She was to be married to one of John's kinsman as soon as was practical and Brian Gunter would be brought before the Star Chamber to answer the charges that were to be brought against him. The King also asked John to repeat the contents of the letter to no one under pain of severe punishment, but he was given permission to visit Anne at Shenfield whenever he thought he could. This was good news.

As it turned out he was not able to visit until the end of October. He had been absent from college for so long recently that it took him three weeks to catch up with his students, his lectures and the business of college. He spoke to Thomas when he needed to and avoided him at all other times. He felt that Thomas was missing his company and his counsel. But there it was.

The trip was pre-empted by an evening visit from Sarah Rose on the 29th October.

"Please come back with me to North Moreton, Reverend Prideaux. The Gunters have discovered that Anne is there and her mother has written and insisting that unless she knows what happened to the child, she will tell all."

"Have you given her the box?"

"No. But I have it with me here and wanted you to help me give it to her. I am afraid that if I go to North Moreton alone, they will kill me or worse."

"I was going to say that I don't know what could be worse, but of course I do."

"Then you will help me? This should be an end to it and we can be safe again."

John went back into his rooms and put on his cloak, "I shall be glad when I can just get on with my job here at college. I shall be told to leave if this keeps up."

"You won't, John. You will achieve great things before you have finished. It's written in the stars. Think of the influential friends and contacts you've made since this began. The great and the good are now in your circle. Think of that before you start moaning."

John grunted and followed Sarah Rose out of the door.

"I have arranged for a cart to take us. He's waiting outside the turnstile and we must hurry for he is to return to Oxford before dawn. So get a move on!"

#

Two hours later, at eight o'clock, they presented themselves at the front door of The Rectory in North Moreton. The door was answered by a maid who neither of them recognised.

"Is your mistress at home?" asked John.

"No sir, she is at the church at one of her meetings. They are getting ready for a big event tomorrow night, or the night after. I don't know what it is, but it seems to mean a lot. You are a priest aren't you? I'm not so sure that the Lord will approve of the goings on over there."

"Are you Irish?" asked John.

"That I am Father and that's why I don't approve. I only came to work here to try and support my mother, but I don't know that I shall be staying."

John smiled and Sarah Rose giggled at the frank confessions of a maid to two strangers calling late at night. They continued around to the church, Sarah Rose clutching the oak box under her cloak.

"Almost there," she whispered.

They walked into the church, lit by lamps. There were several women there who he recognised. There was Mistress Gregory and Mistress Gunter huddled in a corner together. It felt strange being back here after all this time and all that had passed, but here they were. They walked over to the two women and Sarah Rose announced their presence.

If they had hit the women over the head, they could not have been more surprised. Mistress Gunter grabbed Sarah Rose by the arm and hissed, "How is my daughter? Where is the child?"

"Here," said Sarah Rose and handed her the box.

"What do you mean? Have you killed it?"

"No I haven't. It died at birth, but we kept it for you to do with as you wish."

"Wait here," Mistress Gunter ordered.

She and Mistress Gregory took the box into the vestry and prised it open using some tools they found there. They did not seem concerned by what they saw. John followed them in and asked to see inside. He was feeling guilty and wanted to bless the little dead child he knew was in there.

But what he saw did not warrant blessing. It looked like a tiny doll and a dried piece of leather. No smell, no stickiness, nothing. He stepped back.

"Off you go then priest and you girl, can fuck off and tell my daughter to do the same. Tell her she is no longer welcome in our village or our home. She has let us down and that will not be forgotten. I never want to see her again. After all I have done for her, she repays me with cruelty."

John escorted Sarah Rose out of the church to the sound of the women hissing at them.

"Back to Oxford," said Sarah Rose.

"What about Shenfield? How will you get there?"

"I am staying with a cousin in Oxford tonight and am catching a cart there tomorrow. All sorted. Not to worry about me. It's all done now."

John wasn't so sure.

Back at the church, Mistress Gunter and Mistress Gregory took the box back into the church, holding it aloft.

"We have him here ladies. He will be back in two days. We have all that we need."

The hissing stopped and the chanting began.

#

Back at Shenfield, Anne was talking to Samuel Harsnett and Richard Neile over lunch.

"I don't think I can take any more examinations, sir. I will sign the documents about my father and the things he made me do. I will go to your Star Chamber if that is what you want, but please do not let me endure anymore poking and prodding. I just want to marry my Ashley and go to Cornwall and have children and a good life. I will follow God and do good works. Ashley is rich and will inherit lands and I will be in a position to do much charity."

Richard Neile looked again at the letter in his hand. He and Samuel Harsnett listened intently to the pleading. The King was at Ware taking advantage yet again of the hospitality of the Fanshawes, hunting and placing orders for their excellent peaches and grapes. The Fanshawes, like the Cromwells had spent goodly amounts on their King.

The King had sent instructions with a rider to have Anne sent to Ware for a further examination. The two men knew that it would be to parade her in front of yet another party where they could discuss her problems and laugh at her. They wanted to please the King as much as the next social climber, but had come to think of Anne as a sister and sympathised with her plight. She was so happy and well and Cornwall would be an excellent place for her to escape to.

"Let us put him off, Richard."

"I will do what I can."

Neile went into his study and wrote a letter saying that they were busy doing examinations and could not transport Anne in anything suitable to arrive at Ware by that night. He wrote that Anne was willing to swear of her father's involvement to the courts. He would explain in more detail to Cecil tomorrow. Harsnett went over to the church to pray. Neile gave the rider his answer and went back into the dining room to find Anne and Sarah Rose together.

"You are safe, Anne. I have sent him away."

"Thank you Richard, I shall not forget what you have done for me." She had tears in her eyes.

He smiled and left them together.

"What did my mother say?"

"That both of us can fuck off and that she will never forgive you."

"And the box?"

"She took it with Mistress Gregory and that was that. Perhaps they will start on someone else now."

"But now it is all done Sarah Rose. We will go to Cornwall and you will be my companion and will marry a nice rich man and we can be friends proper."

"Yes."

They held hands.

CHAPTER TWENTY NINE

John Prideaux was praying in the chapel at Exeter College. It was the summer of 1608 and John was preparing to go to Stowford for the holidays.

The proceedings at the Star Chamber had been wearing, but interesting. His evidence of Anne's symptoms had been listened to with great interest. He told a censored version of how he had seen her in her fits, while in the company of other academics. The court heard evidence from everyone involved with the Gunters and the bewitchment over the past two years, whether they are villagers, doctors, academics or clergymen.

It was deemed in the end, that Brian was responsible for forcing his daughter to fake her bewitchment for his own advancement. The proceedings had taken over two years to complete and Brian had already been in prison since November 1605, when Dr Neile had begun to prepare the case against him. Brian had finally been released back to his home at North Moreton only a week ago. It was widely believed that because of the secret meetings and the secret societies, where land and leases exchanged hands, he was never likely to serve very long. Fleet Prison had been no picnic for Brian, but it did not alter his belligerent nature.

Anne was married and had already given birth to her first child, a son they called Ashley John Prideaux. The family lived happily in a large house near Fowey. John had promised to visit during his trip home. Their wedding in 1607 had been a wonderful event and John had been happy to see Sarah Rose dressed in fine clothes and courted by a handsome young man.

"We must find you a wife, John," teased Anne. She was carrying her puppy Bella, dressed in a white silk dress similar to her mistress's.

"I don't need a wife. I need to catch up on my studies, Anne. They have been sadly neglected these past few years."

"I doubt that. I am going to miss you but will write to you often. You must write to me with news of Oxford and everything that happens to you. I hadn't realised just how quiet Cornwall is."

"There will be plenty to do. You have Sarah Rose and Bella and Ashley. Soon you will make new friends."

"And have new adventures!"

"Not like the last lot, I hope."

She laughed and kissed his cheek.

"Always write to me," she instructed. And of course he had. They could not lose touch. They had been through too much together.

King James had examined her no more. A few days following the letters from Neile and Harsnett, King James was contending with Guy Fawkes and his attempts to blow up Parliament. He happily honoured his promise to give Anne money upon her marriage, along with some fine cloth and jewels and land. These were for Anne alone and not passed to her husband. He respected her desire to be independent.

John finished his prayers and stood up. Thomas Holland stood behind him, arms crossed in front.

"I hope that we are finally putting the past behind us John."

"I told you before Thomas. It will be a long while before we can be friends again, but we will be good colleagues. I am concentrating on my work and studies. I expect to take over from you when you finally go."

"Do you now. There's ambition for you. I expect you will take over from me, but I shall be around for a little while yet. Are you ready to let us know what has happened to Anne? Where is she?"

"I have no idea Thomas. She was in the care of the King as I told you. Ask him to his face and see what he says."

"Hmmm. Not likely to happen. Have you been back to North Moreton at all?"

"I have not been there for years and if I am able, I shall never visit there again."

They walked out of the chapel together.

"I wish I didn't have to visit either, John. That lot will be the death of me."

I hope you enjoyed that. I am already pulling the characters together in my head for the next instalment...

A A Prideaux

AUTHOR'S EPILOGUE

I began researching my family history many years ago. During that research I came across John Prideaux, a Stowford blood ancestor who ultimately became the Bishop of Worcester. He was involved in so many significant events during his busy life that he was easy to find in many articles, books and archives. Apart from the biography list, there is no central point where his life and achievements are described in any detail. I eventually managed to collect together all the references, facts and figures that I found. Initially, I wanted to write a factual and historical book, but found it to be dry and unemotional. I wish I could write about history in the style of one of my heroes. A. L. Rowse, but sadly I cannot. So my plans changed and I decided to put my spin on the life John may have had between the known facts, in an effort to bring him to life. I have so much research on JPx (as I refer to him in my notes) that I now intend to write a series of books about him and hopefully each one will not take the eight years it has taken to bring this one together. I have enough research for two or three further books and so that could take me…. a while.

I researched the history of Oxford, Exeter College, North Moreton and all of the characters featured in the story. I tried to ensure that each person could have been in the right place at the right time. And I think generally that they were. I am sure you will tell me if I am wrong. I really don't mind if you do.

I visited Worcester Cathedral, Bredon, Harford, Stowford, Salisbury and Oxford while I was tracking him down. I stayed at the home of the Gunter family at The Rectory at North Moreton and visited the church and ate at the Bear Inn and walked the lanes and tracks there. I was allowed in the Worcester Cathedral Library to go through John's own books and walked in his footsteps in his childhood village, church and school. I can only guess what he was really like, but I have been following him for so long that he became my friend along the way and gave me glimpses of his personality. His framed picture looks at me from four rooms in this house alone and his eyes follow me everywhere. I feel so many times that his ghost is tailing me. I feel it now. I believe he approves of my personification of him, but perhaps I am delusional.

I have checked and checked the facts of his life and his contemporaries, but there may be errors and for that I apologise. What I don't apologise for, is my linking those facts together and putting my interpretation on what propelled him from one fact to another. I can't prove that he did this or that and equally you cannot prove that he didn't.

Most of the people involved in this story actually lived and were contemporaries of his. Many of the places still exist, although they have been modernised and added to many times. His likeness can be viewed in several places and after I collected all the information together, his personality and style shone out. The bullet points of his life are available online, but that is not the same as marrying it all together. I hope I make you understand how he matured and I hope you get to like him.

I have a copy of his Will and that is very interesting reading. He wrote several books and pamphlets and owned lots more. Many of his owned books are at Worcester Cathedral Library and John has written in many of them. He seemed to be trying to find his peace with God. He wrote 'Euchologia' for his daughters, giving them instructions on how to live a good life through prayer and join him in Heaven. His scribblings though, did give a clue to his worries about whether he would end up there.

He enjoyed a lifetime of debating the Bible teachings and had been involved in the translation of the King James Bible along with his fellow worthy contemporaries. Following his involvement with the Gunters, he became tutor to Prince Henry and Prince Charles because King James valued his loyalty and knowledge. JPx continued during his long and successful involvement with Exeter College with the friendship and ear of Charles I.

It was King Charles who made him Bishop of Worcester during the Civil War. The bishopric was taken from him when Worcester fell. JPx was almost a broken man once he was stripped of his roles and livings and was incredibly lucky to escape with his life. Many of his contemporaries did not.

It was written somewhere following his death and then widely copied, that after his downfall, he was poverty stricken. His Will however, does not show that. He had lost much following the arrest of Charles, his livings, his positions, his titles and many of his friends. But he still managed to leave several valuable items to his family. Further checking shows that these possessions such as King Henry's staffe, his large collection of rare books and silver plate, were sold off by his grandchildren. These have been scattered around the world.

This book is called 'The Bishop and the Witch' and although JPx was not a bishop during this time, each book in the series will be called 'The Bishop and….'

While writing I have tried to keep facts as accurate as possible, but sometimes found anomalies which are difficult to overcome. As an example, I searched for the day of the week for 30th October 1605 on an established website to be informed that it was a Sunday. But the letter in the archives of the papers of Robert Cecil record, that the letter from Richard Neile about not being able to send Anne for examination on that day, was apparently a Wednesday. Now I know that this could have been recorded incorrectly and so I tried to establish facts elsewhere. Instead I chose not to mention the day, merely the date. You see why it has taken me eight years? Don't get me started on the twirling gate...

Several people mention JPx in their books and research and I shall try and list all the ones I know of in the Bibliography at the end of this book.

Below is a list the facts known which I joined together for the fictional/factual tale you have already read. Perhaps you have turned directly to this page and for that I shall punish you by giving you few dramatic details.

- John Prideaux did walk the 170 miles from Stowford to Oxford in the clothes he kept in his closets until the end of his life, so that he could never forget his beginnings. The dates I gave are approximate, but I don't think I can be far out.
- The prayer was a Prideaux prayer handed down through his family and used as a means of warding off illness, bad luck and perhaps, demons. I mention it in many of the Prideaux stories. JPx talked about the prayer regularly and taught it to his daughters in his latter years.
- He signed himself as John Worcester once he became Bishop.
- The first born son of his parent's was called John, but he died almost immediately. It was said that the son born praying would become a great man. This child was our Bishop John.

- The Gunters were living in North Moreton in 1596 and John's walk would have taken him within a couple of miles of their village. Anne was a young girl at the time.
- Brian Gunter was known to assault Anne; it was reported in Star Chamber records.
- The football match of 1598 took place and the two Gregory men were killed by Brian Gunter. The story is written in many records both parish and courts of the time. There was a great deal of ill feeling between the families.
- Anne Gunter had terrible fits and body movements as described throughout this story. She also constantly vomited or found pins. Her body swelled and her head turned and her ankles twisted. Not all of the fits could be put down to fakery.
- Elizabeth Gregory gave birth around the time of Anne's fits and complained that Anne's spirit was harassing her during childbirth.
- Once released from prison, Brian Gunter continued to live in his usual stroppy and vindictive manner until 1628 when he died in Oxford. He is buried there; he survived his wife by 11 years. She died at North Moreton and was buried in the church.

- There is no record of Anne either returning or contacting her family after 1606 and she is not mentioned in any wills or documents that I have found. She did tell the King that she had fallen for a servant of Bancroft named Ashley and the King agreed to give her a dowry.

- Anne Gunter eventually confessed all to King James during an examination.

- Gilbert Bradshawe suffered several assaults in the years following the trial. These attacks were from Brian and his family and included Susan Holland who became prone to violence once her husband was dead. Apparently the Gunters wanted him out of the church. Gilbert took his case to the Star Chamber in 1620.

- Thomas Holland, the Regius Professor of Divinity and Rector of Exeter College lived (1539 – 1612.) was 40 years older than his wife Susan Gunter, but they managed to have 6 children. John Prideaux succeeded him as Rector upon his death and as Regius Professor in 1615. He was one of the translators of the Bible.

- Dr Richard Neile (1562 – 1640) was chaplain to Robert Cecil and became Dean of Westminster on 5th November 1605, the day Parliament was to reconvene. He could have been blown up had the treasonous plot been successful, but he wasn't. He became Bishop of Rochester, Lichfield and Coventry, Lincoln, Durham and Winchester. He often sat at the Star Chamber, the Gunter trial being one of the cases.

- Samuel Harsnett (1561-1631) was another man with a heady career. He was chaplain to the Archbishop Bancroft. He later became Bishop of Norwich and Bishop of Chichester. At the time of this story he was a resident at Chigwell, where he later established a school and he also had the living at Shenfield.

- Richard Bancroft (1544 – 1610) was a great favourite of King James and became Archbishop of Canterbury in 1604 and oversaw the translation of the King James Bible. He was with Queen Elizabeth when she died, but he didn't kill her... He was also Bishop of London. Although a Cambridge man he became Chancellor of the University of Oxford from 1608 until his death.

- William Laud (1573 – 1645) was John Prideaux's nemesis for much of their parallel careers. He was a homosexual, a fact which matters not a jot these days, quite rightly, but back then he needed to hide his feelings. He was chaplain to Richard Neile and became Dean of Gloucester and Bishop of St Davids. He later became Bishop of London and Archbishop of Canterbury during

Charles 1 reign, but he made many enemies. Once he established a religious point of view he would force it through with little regard for other opinions. In 1640 he was accused of treason, but at his trial there were only a few who could agree a treasonable charge. Personal vendettas came into play and Laud was sentenced to death, although on no specific charge. In spite of a Royal pardon he was beheaded and died with dignity at 72 years old. Although John Prideaux had argued with him for much of his life, it seems likely that he would miss him once he was gone.

- William Helme was tutor to John in his early Oxford years. He was a fellow of the college until 1615 when he left to become a vicar until his death in 1639.

- The map of Oxford drawn by John Speed and reproduced in this book was drawn in 1605 and shows the layout of Oxford and the colleges and streets at the time of this story.

- Turl Street which runs along the western perimeter of Exeter College was so named as it led from the turnstile in the north wall. The turnstile also known as the 'twirl' or 'twirling gate' was to keep cows and other animals out of the city.

- John Prideaux assisted with the translation of The King James Bible.
- The story of Dr Rowland Taylor is a true one. He was one of the martyrs during Queen Mary's reign. Miss Goodwin eventually became John's first wife and mother of his children. He wrote about her in books and letters to his daughters near the end of his life.
- John Prideaux surveyed the college during his tenure and oversaw many changes. Excellent details and maps can be found here.
- On the NW corner of the college fronting Turl Street between the chapel and the more modern looking building on the corner with Broad Street is known as Prideaux buildings and the front is all that remains of the house he built.
- On either side of the wall to which parts of the college abutted, were ditches and small ponds full of black mud which often flooded into the college.
- Elizabeth Gregory, Mary and Anne Pepwell were the three North Moreton women accused of witchcraft. They were found innocent of bewitchment at their trial in 1604.
- He buried his wife and children either at St Michael at the North Gate or at Exeter College Chapel. His son Mathias was the first buried at

Exeter following its foundation and the inscription reads 'Are you trying to make out what the little child is saying? Read, you will die as did Mathias Prideaux, the Rector's son, who was the first one to be buried in this chapel after its foundation.

- There were poems written about each child as he/she died young and are still available here.
- From his nine born children, only two daughters survived John.
- John Cleveland wrote a long poem about JPx upon his death. It can be read in John Cleveland's Poems.
- The likeness of John Prideaux can be found online.
- The Bear Inn at North Moreton.

Lots more can be found at www.aaprideaux.com

JOHN PRIDEAUX – BIOGRAPHICAL INFORMATION

- Born in Stowford, Devon on 17th September 1578
- Died at Bredon, Worcestershire on 29th July 1650 (aged 72 years) of a fever
- Buried at Bredon, Worcestershire on 16th August1650
- Married in 1612, Anne Goodwin, the daughter of William Goodwin. She died in 1627 and was buried at. St. Michael's, Oxford
- **Children by Anne**:
- 1615 William, later a Colonel in the King's army. Killed at Marston Moor, 1644
- Mary baptised on 10th February. 1617, buried on. 9th December. 1624
- 1618 Anne, baptised on 3rd March 1618 at St. Michael's, Oxford, buried. 29th September. 1624
- 1619 Sarah, baptised on 15th December 1619, St. Michael's, Oxford, married. William Hodges. Died 17th April 1652, buried in. Ripple, Worcs.
- 1621 Elizabeth baptised. 25th March 1621 at St. Michael's, Oxford, and married Henry Sutton died 2nd February 1659/60, buried. Bredon, Worcs.

- 1622 Matthias baptised. 1st September 1622, Exeter College Chapel, buried. 14th September 1624/5
- 1622 John, baptised on 1st September 1622, Exeter College Chapel, buried on 1st August 1636
- 1624 Robert, baptised on 14th May 1624, Exeter College Chapel, died of poisoning. Buried. 17thFebruary 1627
- 1625 Mathias Captain in King's Army. Author of *"All Sortes of Histories...."* Died in London of Smallpox in 1646.
- Married in 1628, Mary (Marie) Rendell, daughter of Sir Thomas Reynell of Ogwell, nr. Newton Abbott
- **No children by Mary**
- Several poems were written for the children after they died and some can be read here.
- John walked the 170 miles to Oxford under the sponsorship of Lady Fowell in 1596
- Pupil at Exeter College under Mr. William Helme, B.D. 1596
- He matriculated from Exeter College Oxford on 14 October 1596
- B.A. 31st January 1599
- Elected Fellow of Exeter College 30th June 1601
- M.A. 30th June 1603
- Took Holy Orders

- Gave evidence at the Star Chamber in regard to the Gunter Witch case in 1606
- Chaplain and tutor to Prince Henry the son of King James and later to King James and King Charles I
- Fellow of Chelsea College 1609
- B.D. 6th May 1611
- Elected Rector of Exeter College 4th April 1612
- D.D. 30th May 1612;
- Vicar of Bampton 17th July 1614
- Regius professor of divinity at Oxford 1615
- Vice-Chancellor Oxford University, July 1619 to July 1621. July 1624 to 1626, and from 7 October. 1641 to 7 February. 1624/5
- Canon of Christ Church 16th March 1616
- Vicar of Chalgrove 1620
- Canon at Salisbury Cathedral, 17th June 1620
- Rector of Ewelme 1629
- Rector, St. Martin's, Bladon, Oxfordshire 1st April 1625 to 1641
- Plaque erected at Harford Church 20th July 1639
- Member of Lords' committee 1 March 1640-1 to meet in the Jerusalem chamber and discuss plans of church reform under the lead of Williams
- Bishop of Worcester, appointed 22nd November 1641, consecrated at Westminster 19th December 1641. He was a loyalist, and the

surrender of Worcester to the Parliamentary forces in 1646 ended his episcopate. He is listed as being Bishop until his death in 1650

- He spent his last years with his daughter and son-in-law who was the Rector of Bredon.
- He was a prolific writer, mainly in Latin, his principal works in English being The Doctrine of the Sabbath (London, 1634), and Sacred Eloquence (1659); he also wrote on devotional subjects. He had many pamphlets and books published, most which are in print now.
- Many of the great and the good attended his funeral.

BIBLIOGRAPHY

The words and pictures in following books, pamphlets and links have not been copied, or quoted, but I thought it would be helpful to researchers to have an idea where to look for more information on Cornwall, Devon, the Prideaux family and the Gunter family. I have many books which may also help in research, but have not listed them all here.

- An Obscure Place by Louise Ryan.
- A West Country Clan by R M Prideaux
- A Devon Family. The Story of the Aclands by Anne Acland
- Survey of Cornwall 1602 by Richard Carew
- Sir Bevill Grenville and his times by John Stucley
- Highways and Byways in Devon and Cornwall by Joseph Pennell and Hugh Thomson
- Devon Its Moorlands, Streams and Coasts by Lady Rosalind Northcote
- Survey of the County of Devon by Tristram Risdon
- The Cornish Witch-finder by William Henry Paynter
- Catholic and Reformed by Anthony Milton

- The Hammer of Witches (Malleus Maleficarum) by Christopher S Mackay
- The Bewitching of Anne Gunter by James Sharpe
- Cecil Papers
- Oxford History
- North Moreton History
- A selection of poems about the children of John Prideaux. (Sadly, after their deaths)
- John Cleveland's poem written as a Eulogy for John Prideaux.
- History of Exeter College
- Dictionary of National Biography
- The Doctrine of Practical Praying by John Prideaux
- North Moreton church registers
- Public Record Office
- Victorian County History of Berkshire vol iii
- A British Library search brings up at least 50 books referencing John Prideaux
- A guide to Harford Parish Church
- The Heraldry of Worcestershire
- An Historical Account of the Lives and Deaths of the Most Eminent and Evangelical Authors and Preachers by the Rev. Erasmus Middleton

- Lives of Individuals by R A Davenport
- A History of North Moreton by Gerald Howat
- Laudian and Royalist polemic in 17thC England by Anthony Milton
- Personal papers, books and documents of A A Prideaux.

A SELECTION OF PUBLICATIONS

Of

PAGANUS PUBLISHING

Shudder by A A Prideaux.

Who or what is Shudder?

The Old Mill was the place in Mill Town where most people worked. Years passed and the mill closed, but something remained inside. The townspeople had ignored the missing children and the frightening stories of devils and ghosts for as long as they could remember. It was easier to carry on and accept the money the Snooty family provided in return for working at the mill. Everyone allowed the Council members to run their lives and control their ideas without question. Questions were always ignored and the questioner punished. When Lydia Prix returned to the town after her marriage failed, she had no choice but to face the demons of the past and ultimately face the truth. The town would never be the same again.

If you go down to the woods today, you may end up being frightened of more than you think...

The Specials by A A Prideaux is a murder mystery set in 2012.

An old man is found dead in his home and DCI Revie and DS Jackson face the task of discovering who murdered him. At first, it appears that there is no reason the quiet widower should have been killed. But the investigation soon reveals that the gentle old man had been a long term and particularly deviant paedophile. As the story unfolds throughout the year and the body count rises, the police discover more people who have been living an apparently normal life while successfully hiding their past. The lives of all the people involved can never be the same again.

The Specials reaches its dramatic conclusion in Snowdonia.

A Ghost Story by A A Prideaux.

John Prideaux (1505-1568) lived in Stowford and had a wife and two children. He had lots of friends and great connections and lived in one of the largest houses in Stowford.

One evening in 1547, he and his family and friends were at their usual Tuesday night dinner. They took weekly turns as to which house the dinner and entertainment were held. This night was the turn of the Prideaux family at Stowford Manor. They ate their meal and as they settled down, John told the gathering a ghost story. He told them of a stranger he once befriended and the mysterious path the meeting led him along. Present at the dinner were Parson William Hele, Robert and Sybil Fox, Thomas and Joan Rogers and John and Ann Prideaux. Before the evening ended, the friends are on a mysterious quest of their own, leading to a remarkable conclusion at St Petrocs church on snowy Dartmoor.

A Christmas Story by A A Prideaux is about Clifford Prideaux (1902-1963).The story begins in a modest home in early Edwardian Leeds, where the Prideaux family await a surprise event on Christmas Day 1902. The story takes the reader from 1902 through to 1993 in a short story and gives a flavour of what Christmas meant to Clifford and his family. A Christmas Story tells of the times prior to the Great War for those with no money and no property. What the family did have, was their love for each other and that love cannot be exaggerated.

A A Prideaux has written about each of her Prideaux ancestors from 1040 to the present day. Clifford Prideaux and her mother were responsible for setting the fire in her soul that turned into a Prideaux obsession. A Christmas Story is one of her fictionalised tales which draw on known facts. In this case, the story is written with personal experience of the author. This Clifford Prideaux (1902-1963) story takes us to Leeds and a tiny stone cottage full of love and warmth. These stories bring the Prideauxs to life, giving them personalities and allowing the reader to know them as people, not just names.

"A Christmas Story is about my grandma and grandad. Christmas was always a special time for Grandad Clifford. It's magic ran through his veins from the first day. Clifford was a kind man, but also a mystical one. Even after his death, he has visited his family on many occasions. I think of him as a hermit character, cloaked and walking with a long staff. He appeared in his role of Clifford for only 60 years before he returned to being the hermit."

A A Prideaux.

𝕿𝖍𝖆𝖓𝖐 𝖞𝖔𝖚. 𝕯𝖔 𝖈𝖆𝖑𝖑 𝖆𝖌𝖆𝖎𝖓 .